CREATED BY

ROBERT SCOTT M. CHRIS
KIRKMAN GIMPLE BURNHAM

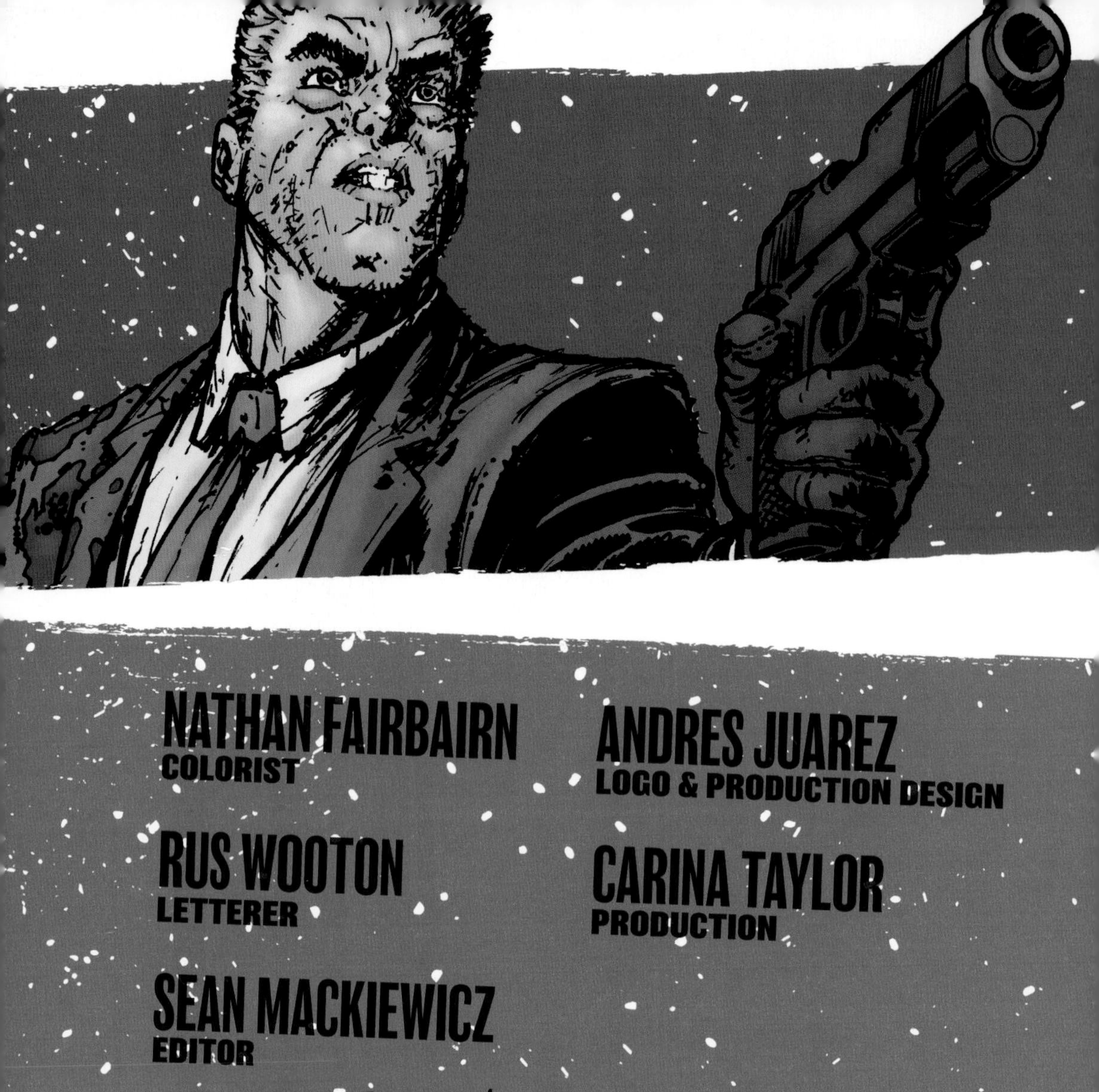

NATHAN FAIRBAIRN
COLORIST

ANDRES JUAREZ
LOGO & PRODUCTION DESIGN

RUS WOOTON
LETTERER

CARINA TAYLOR
PRODUCTION

SEAN MACKIEWICZ
EDITOR

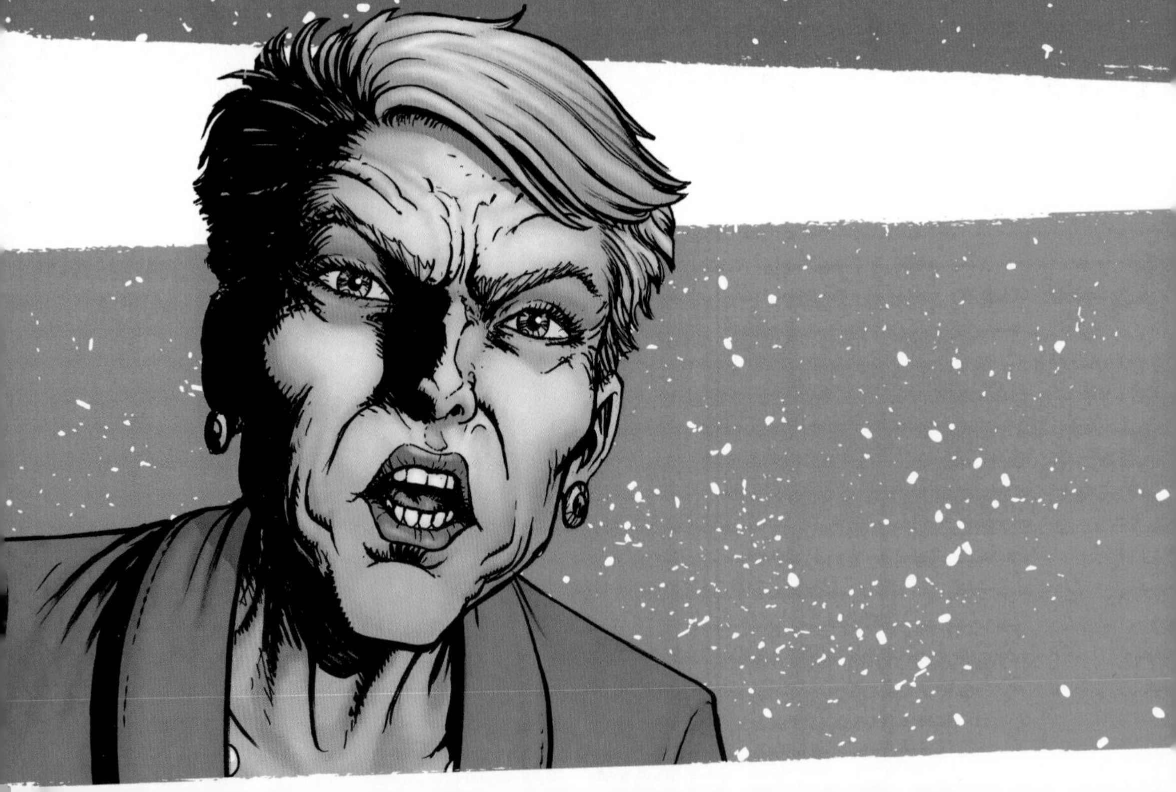

ROBERT KIRKMAN
WRITER, CREATOR

SCOTT M. GIMPLE
CO-PLOT, CREATOR

CHRIS BURNHAM
ARTIST, CREATOR

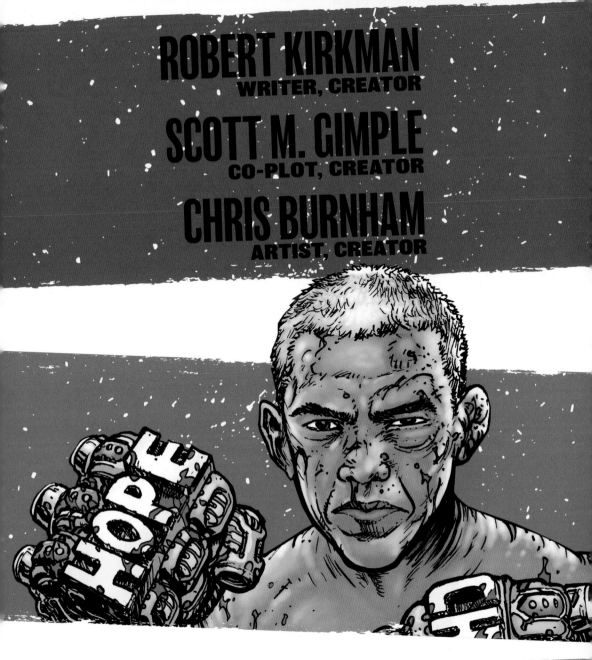

SKYBOUND LLC.

ROBERT KIRKMAN Chairman
DAVID ALPERT CEO
SEAN MACKIEWICZ SVP, Editor-in-Chief
SHAWN KIRKHAM SVP, Business Development
BRIAN HUNTINGTON VP, Online Content
SHAUNA WYNNE Sr. Director, Corporate Communications
ANDRES JUAREZ Art Director
ARUNE SINGH Director of Brand, Editorial
ALEX ANTONE Senior Editor
JON MOISAN Editor
ARIELLE BASICH Associate Editor
CARINA TAYLOR Graphic Designer
JOHNNY O'DELL Social Media Manager
DAN PETERSEN Sr. Director, Operations & Events

FOREIGN RIGHTS & LICENSING INQUIRIES:
contact@skybound.com

WWW.SKYBOUND.COM

TODD MCFARLANE President
JIM VALENTINO Vice President
MARC SILVESTRI Chief Executive Officer
ERIK LARSEN Chief Financial Officer
ROBERT KIRKMAN Chief Operating Officer
ERIC STEPHENSON Publisher / Chief Creative Officer
NICOLE LAPALME Controller
LEANNA CAUNTER Accounting Analyst
SUE KORPELA Accounting & HR Manager
MARLA EIZIK Talent Liaison
JEFF BOISON Director of Sales & Publishing Planning
DIRK WOOD Director of International Sales & Licensing
ALEX COX Director of Direct Market Sales
CHLOE RAMOS Book Market & Library Sales Manager

IMAGE COMICS, INC.

EMILIO BAUTISTA Digital Sales Coordinator
JON SCHLAFFMAN Specialty Sales Coordinator
KAT SALAZAR Director of PR & Marketing
DREW FITZGERALD Marketing Content Associate
HEATHER DOORNINK Production Director
DREW GILL Art Director
HILARY DILORETO Print Manager
TRICIA RAMOS Traffic Manager
MELISSA GIFFORD Content Manager
ERIKA SCHNATZ Senior Production Artist
RYAN BREWER Production Artist
DEANNA PHELPS Production Artist

WWW.IMAGECOMICS.COM

VOLUME
TWO

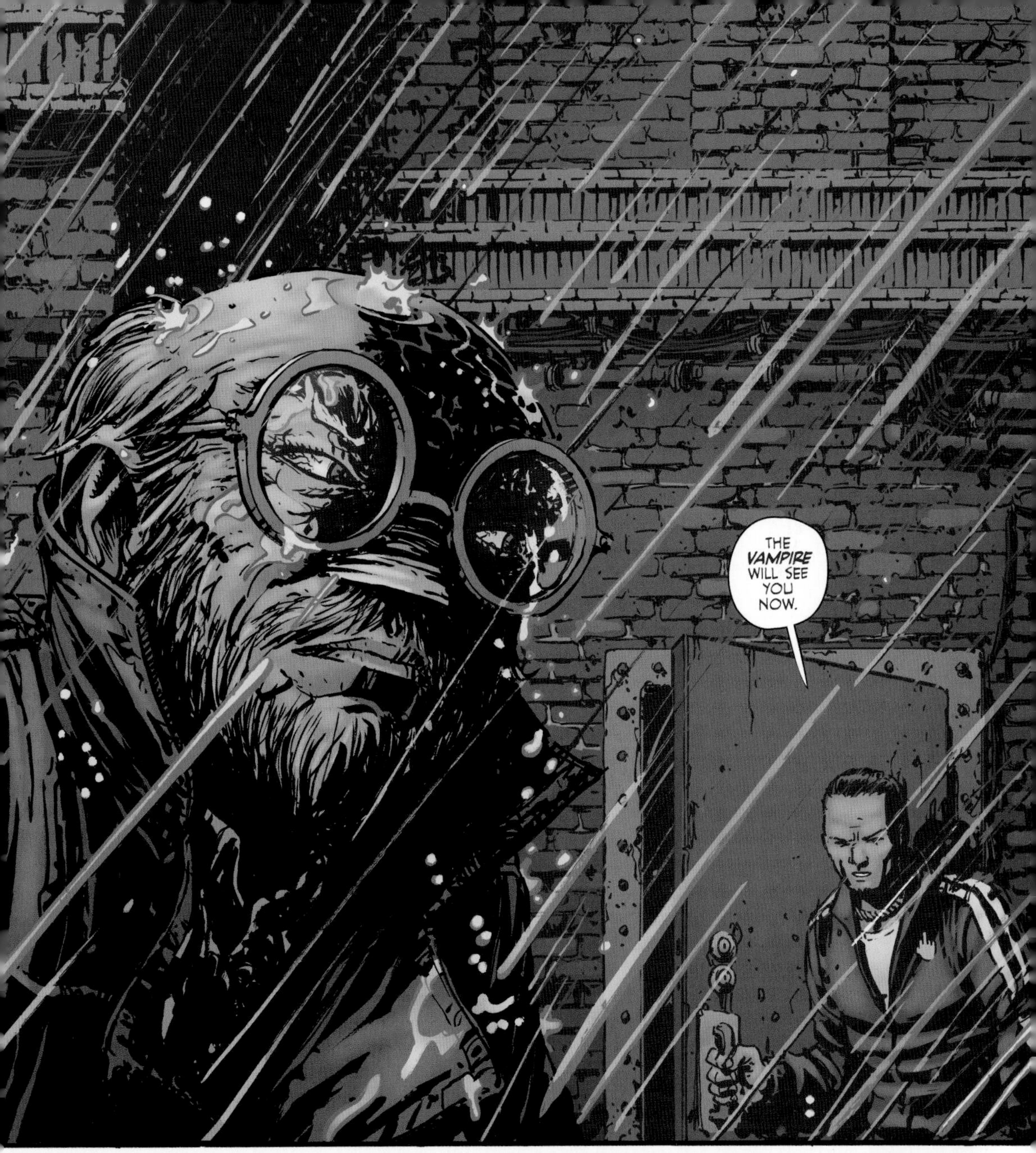
THE VAMPIRE WILL SEE YOU NOW.

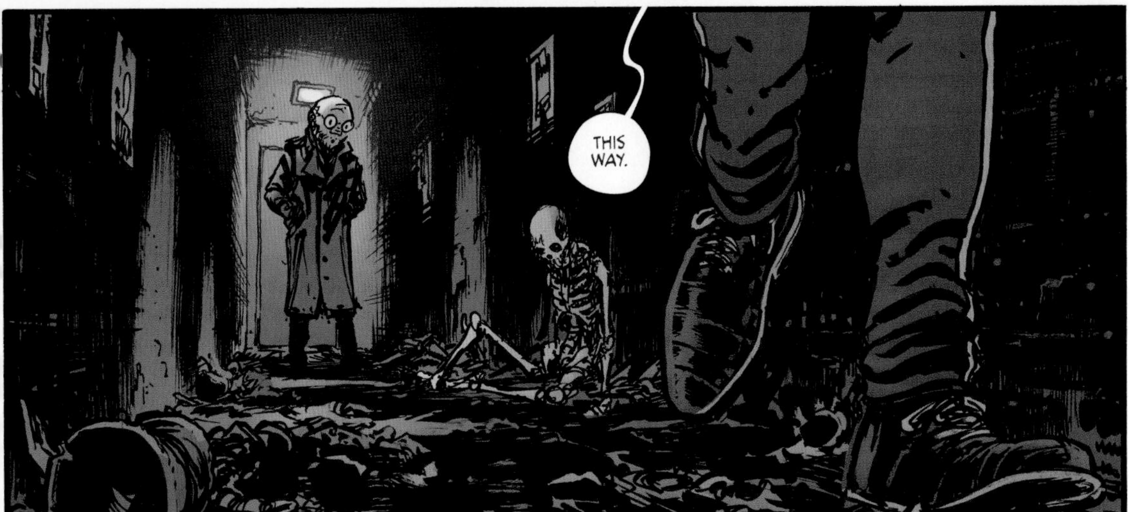
THIS WAY.

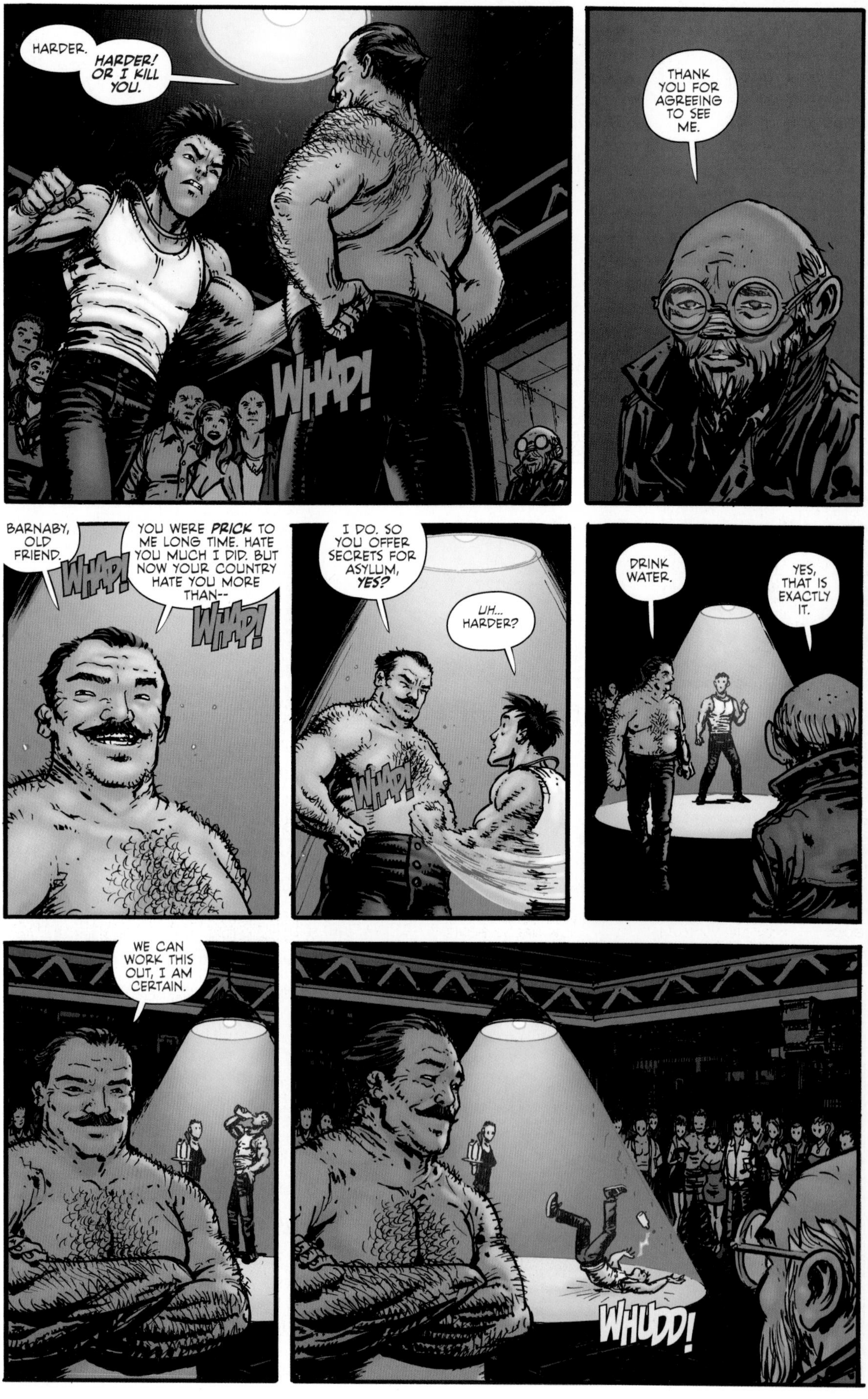
HARDER. HARDER! OR I KILL YOU.
WHAP!
THANK YOU FOR AGREEING TO SEE ME.
BARNABY, OLD FRIEND.
WHAP!
YOU WERE PRICK TO ME LONG TIME. HATE YOU MUCH I DID. BUT NOW YOUR COUNTRY HATE YOU MORE THAN--
WHAP!
I DO. SO YOU OFFER SECRETS FOR ASYLUM, YES?
UH... HARDER?
WHAP!
DRINK WATER.
YES, THAT IS EXACTLY IT.
WE CAN WORK THIS OUT, I AM CERTAIN.
WHUDD!

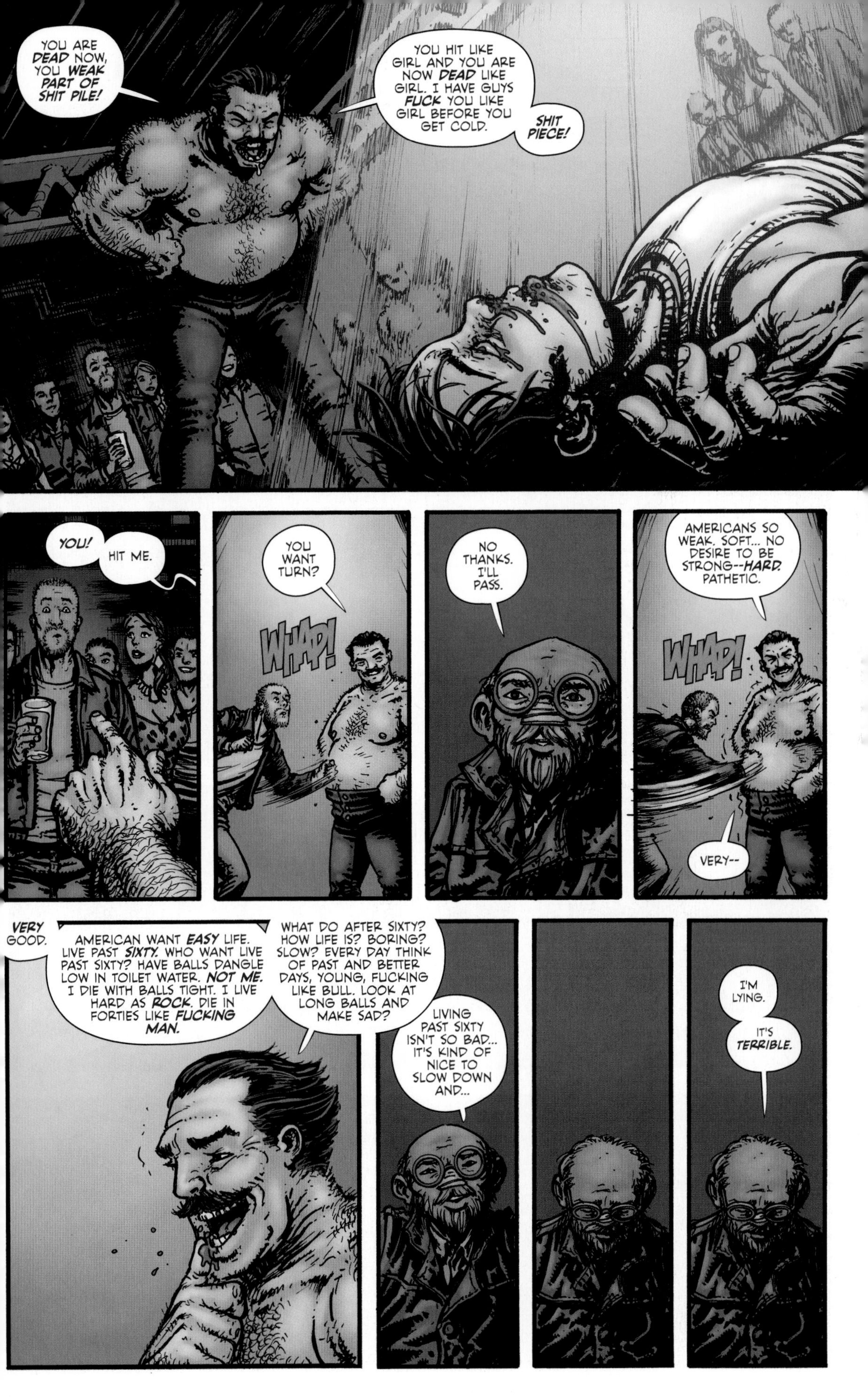

YOU ARE DEAD NOW, YOU WEAK PART OF SHIT PILE!
YOU HIT LIKE GIRL AND YOU ARE NOW DEAD LIKE GIRL. I HAVE GUYS FUCK YOU LIKE GIRL BEFORE YOU GET COLD.
SHIT PIECE!
YOU!
HIT ME.
YOU WANT TURN?
WHAP!
NO THANKS. I'LL PASS.
AMERICANS SO WEAK. SOFT... NO DESIRE TO BE STRONG--HARD. PATHETIC.
WHAP!
VERY--
VERY GOOD.
AMERICAN WANT EASY LIFE. LIVE PAST SIXTY. WHO WANT LIVE PAST SIXTY? HAVE BALLS DANGLE LOW IN TOILET WATER. NOT ME. I DIE WITH BALLS TIGHT. I LIVE HARD AS ROCK. DIE IN FORTIES LIKE FUCKING MAN.
WHAT DO AFTER SIXTY? HOW LIFE IS? BORING? SLOW? EVERY DAY THINK OF PAST AND BETTER DAYS, YOUNG, FUCKING LIKE BULL. LOOK AT LONG BALLS AND MAKE SAD?
LIVING PAST SIXTY ISN'T SO BAD... IT'S KIND OF NICE TO SLOW DOWN AND...
I'M LYING.
IT'S TERRIBLE.

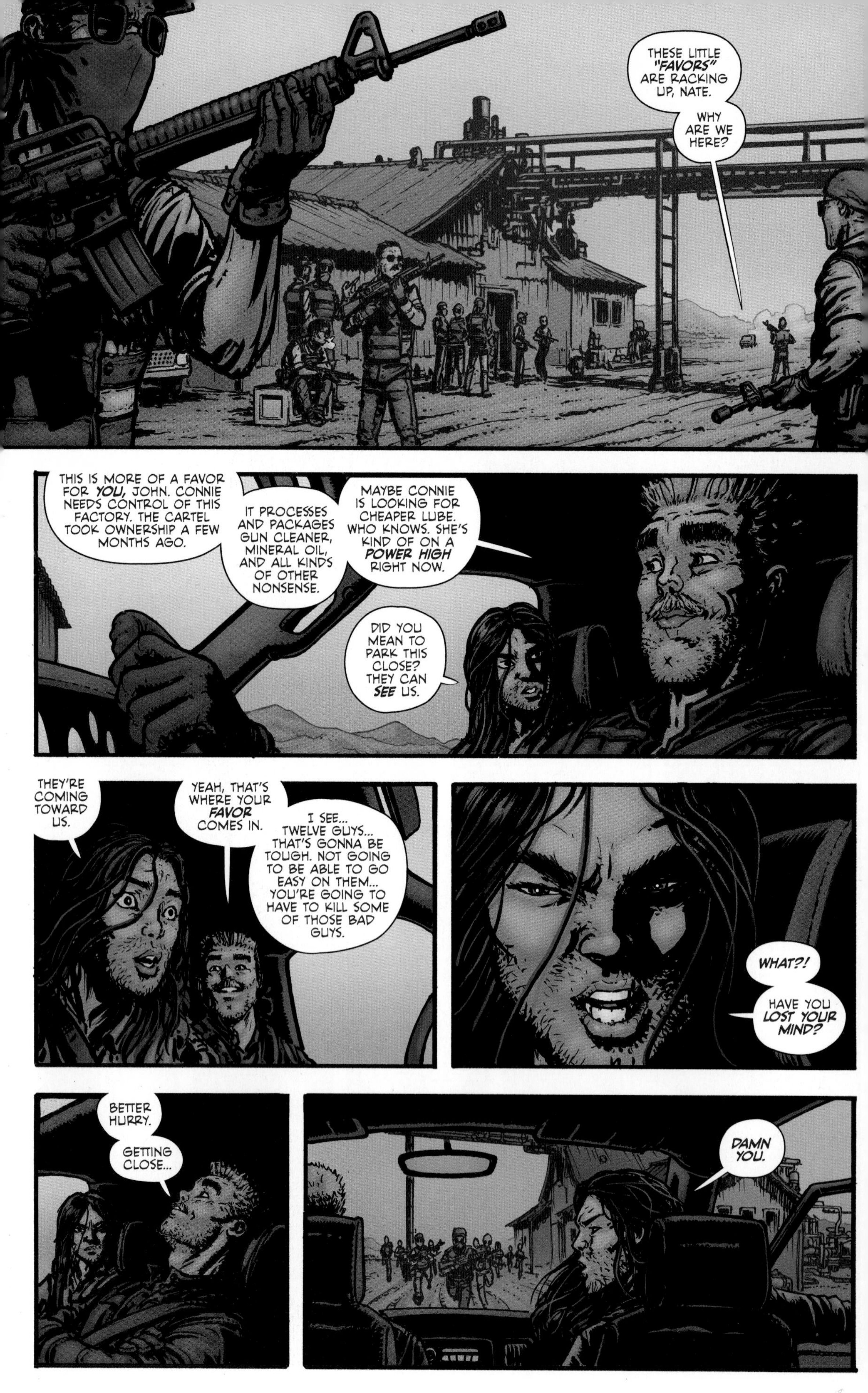
THESE LITTLE "FAVORS" ARE RACKING UP, NATE.
WHY ARE WE HERE?
THIS IS MORE OF A FAVOR FOR YOU, JOHN. CONNIE NEEDS CONTROL OF THIS FACTORY. THE CARTEL TOOK OWNERSHIP A FEW MONTHS AGO.
IT PROCESSES AND PACKAGES GUN CLEANER, MINERAL OIL, AND ALL KINDS OF OTHER NONSENSE.
MAYBE CONNIE IS LOOKING FOR CHEAPER LUBE. WHO KNOWS. SHE'S KIND OF ON A POWER HIGH RIGHT NOW.
DID YOU MEAN TO PARK THIS CLOSE? THEY CAN SEE US.
THEY'RE COMING TOWARD US.
YEAH, THAT'S WHERE YOUR FAVOR COMES IN.
I SEE... TWELVE GUYS... THAT'S GONNA BE TOUGH. NOT GOING TO BE ABLE TO GO EASY ON THEM... YOU'RE GOING TO HAVE TO KILL SOME OF THOSE BAD GUYS.
WHAT?!
HAVE YOU LOST YOUR MIND?
BETTER HURRY.
GETTING CLOSE...
DAMN YOU.

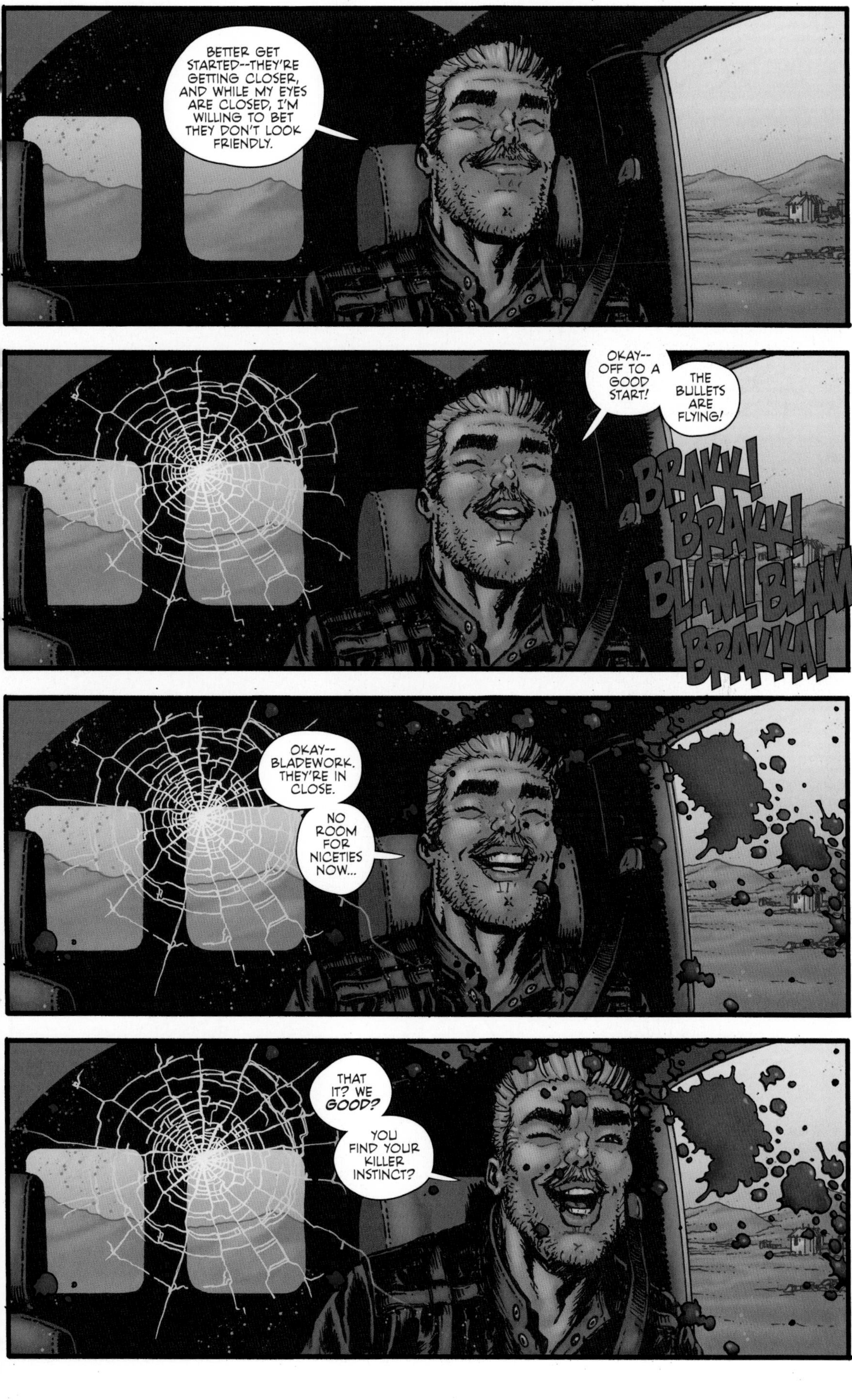
BETTER GET STARTED--THEY'RE GETTING CLOSER, AND WHILE MY EYES ARE CLOSED, I'M WILLING TO BET THEY DON'T LOOK FRIENDLY.
OKAY-- OFF TO A GOOD START!
THE BULLETS ARE FLYING!
BRAKK! BRAKK! BLAM! BLAM! BRAKKA!
OKAY-- BLADEWORK. THEY'RE IN CLOSE.
NO ROOM FOR NICETIES NOW...
THAT IT? WE GOOD?
YOU FIND YOUR KILLER INSTINCT?

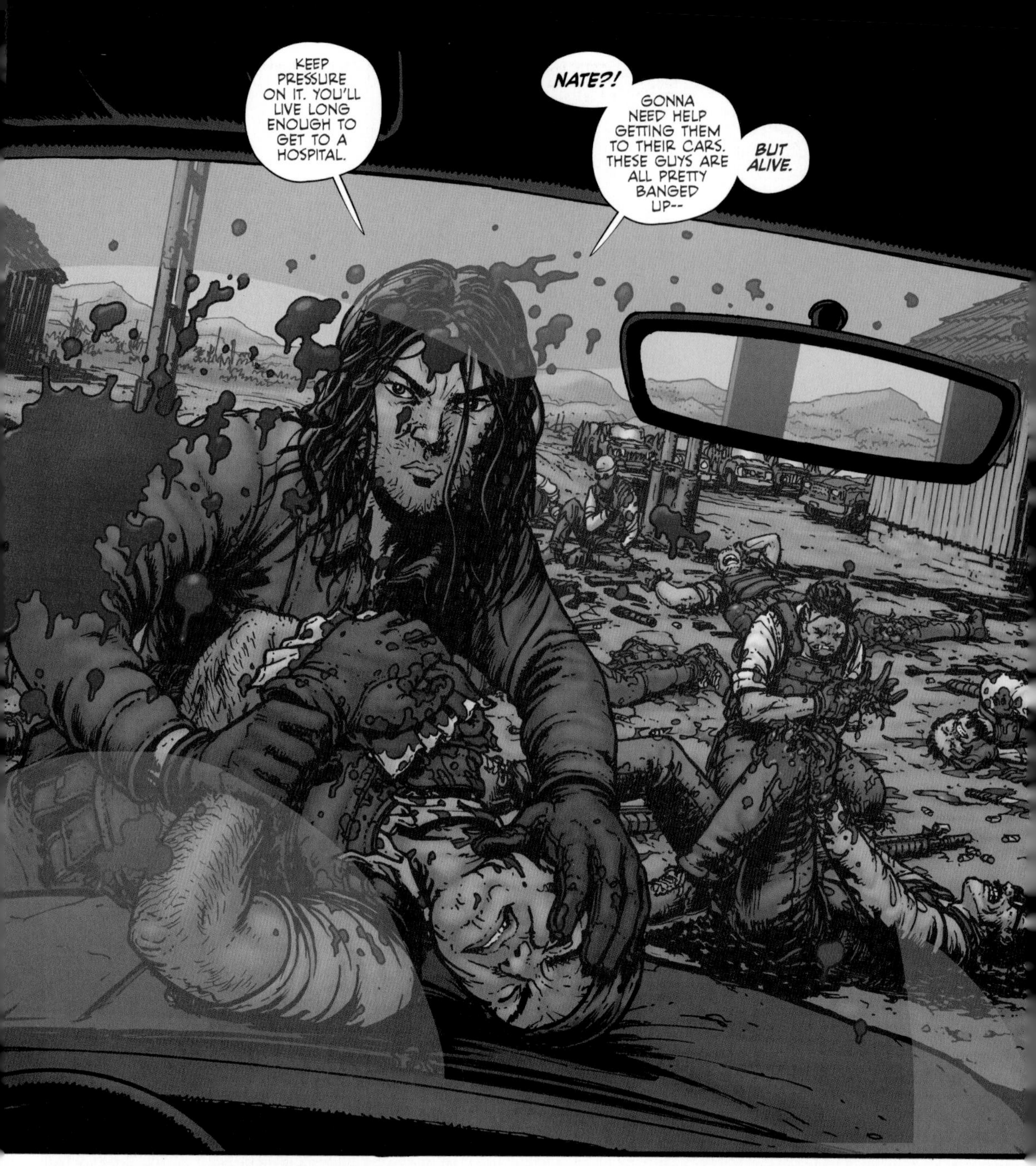
KEEP PRESSURE ON IT. YOU'LL LIVE LONG ENOUGH TO GET TO A HOSPITAL.
NATE?!
GONNA NEED HELP GETTING THEM TO THEIR CARS. THESE GUYS ARE ALL PRETTY BANGED UP--
BUT ALIVE.

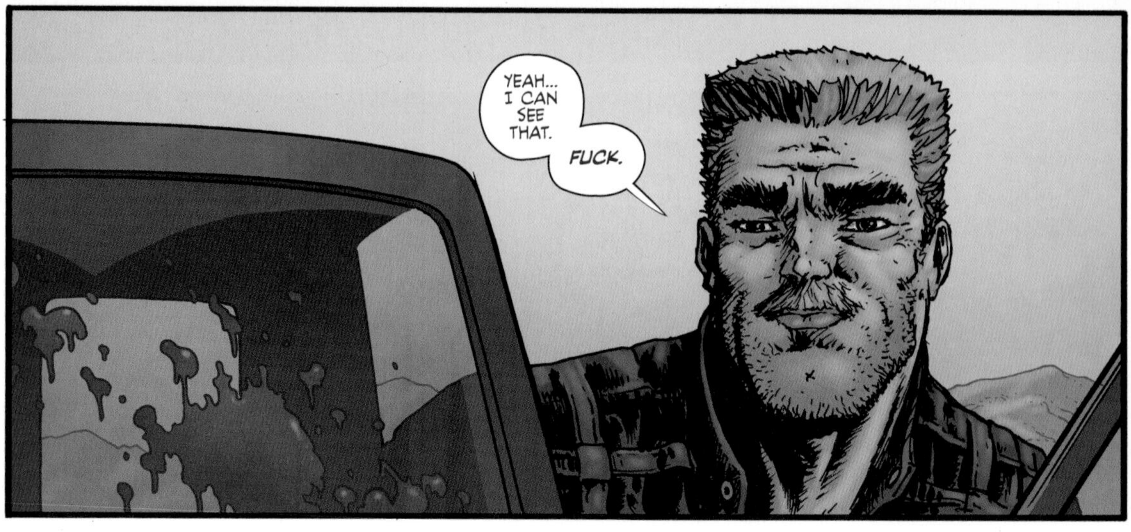
YEAH... I CAN SEE THAT.
FUCK.

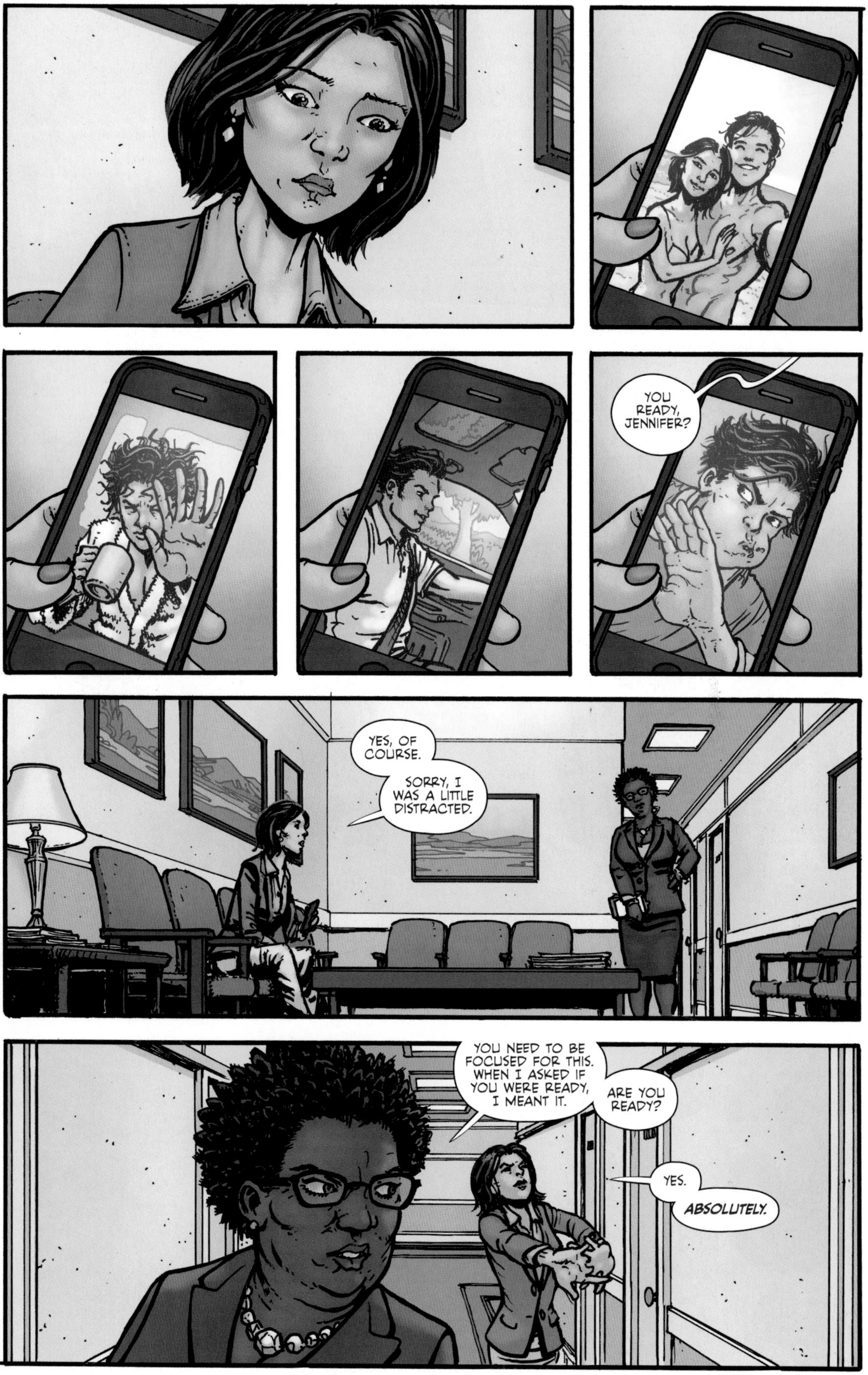
YOU READY, JENNIFER?
YES, OF COURSE.
SORRY, I WAS A LITTLE DISTRACTED.
YOU NEED TO BE FOCUSED FOR THIS. WHEN I ASKED IF YOU WERE READY, I MEANT IT.
ARE YOU READY?
YES.
ABSOLUTELY.

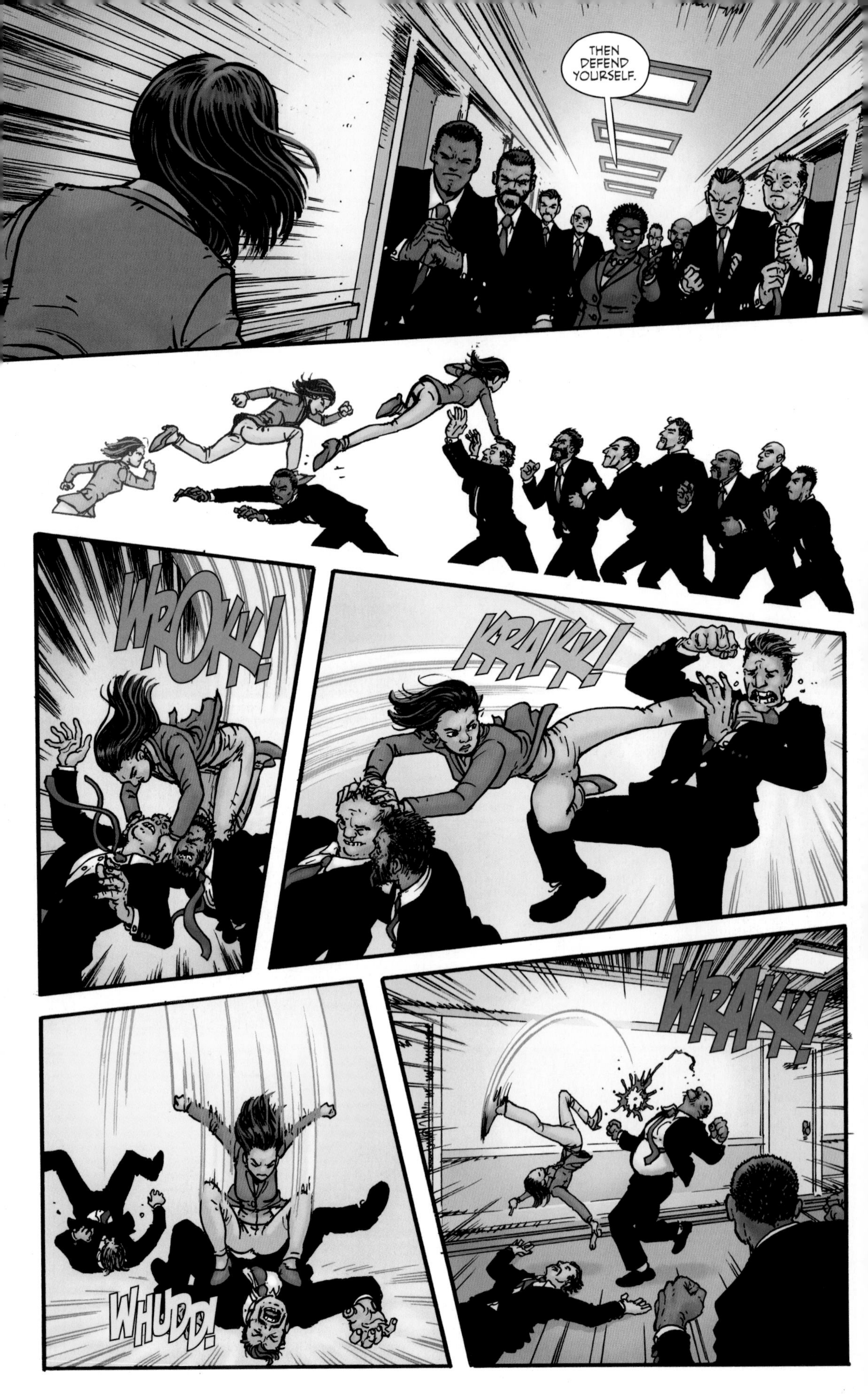
THEN DEFEND YOURSELF.
WROKK!
KRAKK!
WHUDD!
WRAKK!

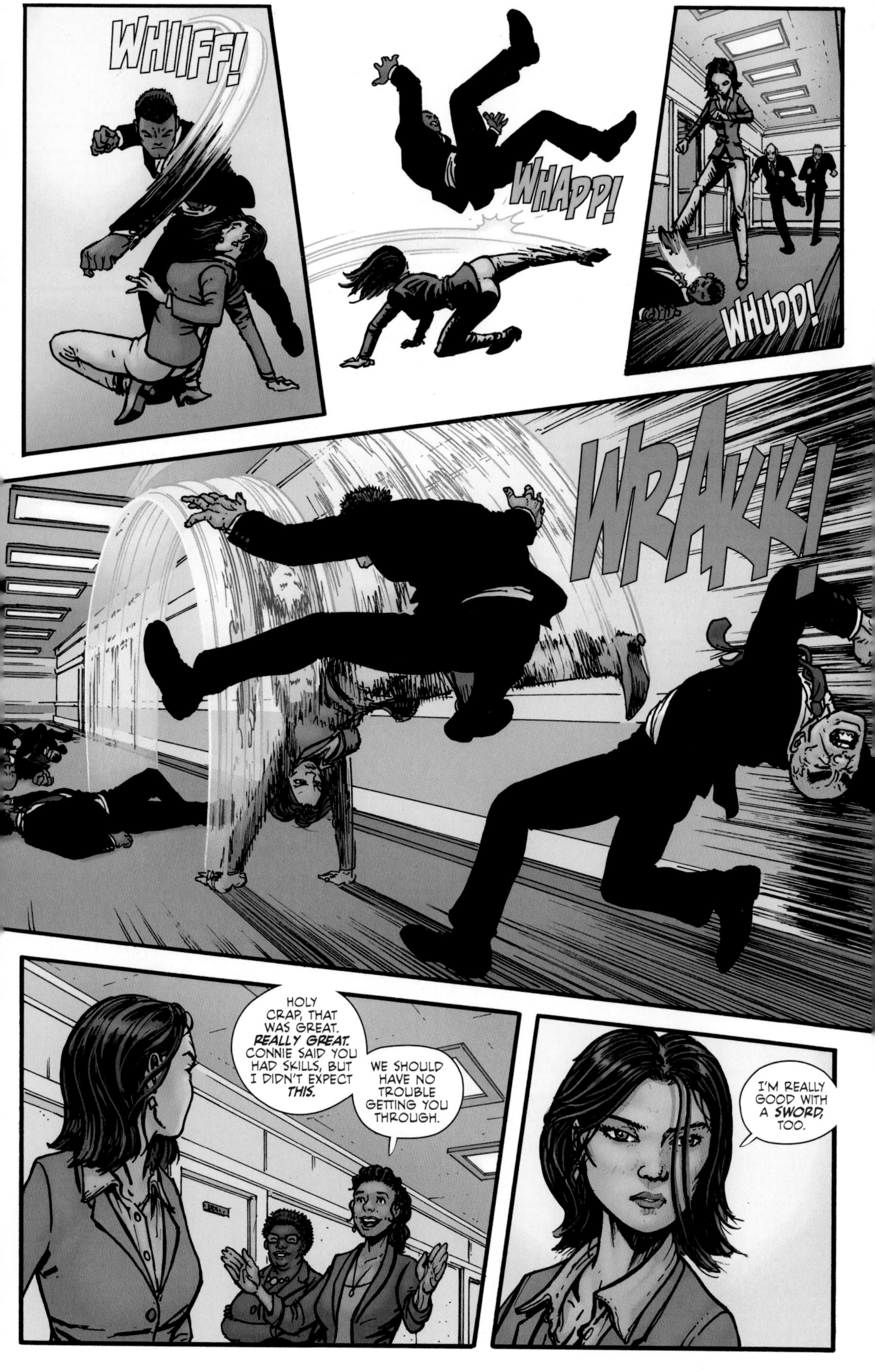
WHIIFF!
WHAPP!
WHUDD!
WRAKK!
HOLY CRAP, THAT WAS GREAT. REALLY GREAT. CONNIE SAID YOU HAD SKILLS, BUT I DIDN'T EXPECT THIS.
WE SHOULD HAVE NO TROUBLE GETTING YOU THROUGH.
I'M REALLY GOOD WITH A SWORD, TOO.

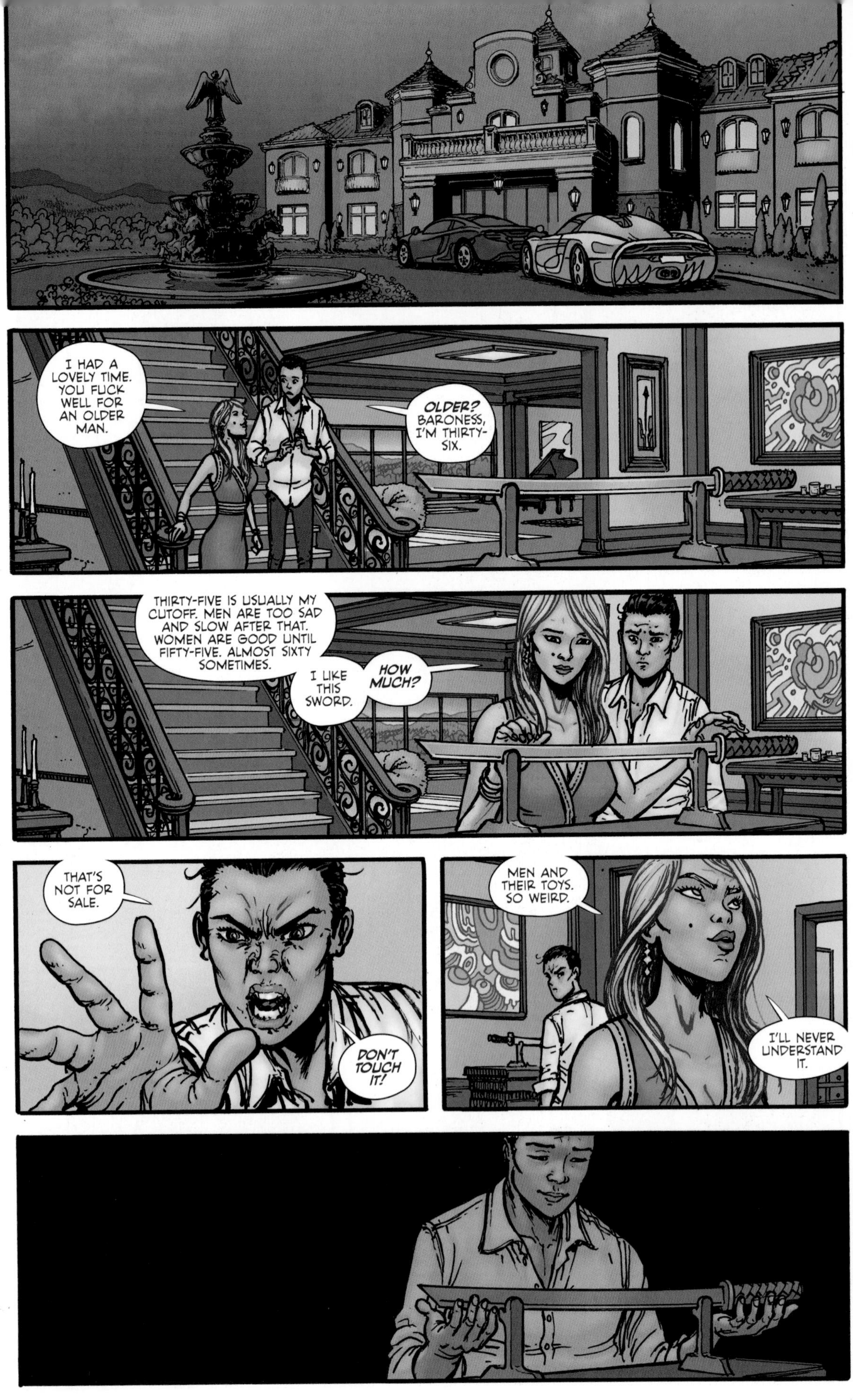
I HAD A LOVELY TIME. YOU FUCK WELL FOR AN OLDER MAN.
OLDER? BARONESS, I'M THIRTY-SIX.
THIRTY-FIVE IS USUALLY MY CUTOFF. MEN ARE TOO SAD AND SLOW AFTER THAT. WOMEN ARE GOOD UNTIL FIFTY-FIVE. ALMOST SIXTY SOMETIMES.
I LIKE THIS SWORD.
HOW MUCH?
THAT'S NOT FOR SALE.
DON'T TOUCH IT!
MEN AND THEIR TOYS. SO WEIRD.
I'LL NEVER UNDERSTAND IT.

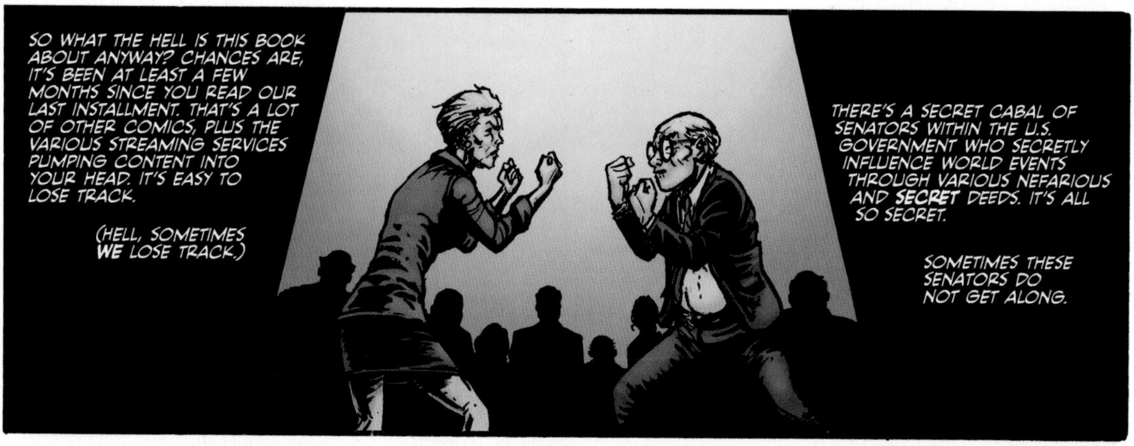
SO WHAT THE HELL IS THIS BOOK ABOUT ANYWAY? CHANCES ARE, IT'S BEEN AT LEAST A FEW MONTHS SINCE YOU READ OUR LAST INSTALLMENT. THAT'S A LOT OF OTHER COMICS, PLUS THE VARIOUS STREAMING SERVICES PUMPING CONTENT INTO YOUR HEAD. IT'S EASY TO LOSE TRACK.
(HELL, SOMETIMES **WE** LOSE TRACK.)
THERE'S A SECRET CABAL OF SENATORS WITHIN THE U.S. GOVERNMENT WHO SECRETLY INFLUENCE WORLD EVENTS THROUGH VARIOUS NEFARIOUS AND **SECRET** DEEDS. IT'S ALL SO SECRET.
SOMETIMES THESE SENATORS DO NOT GET ALONG.

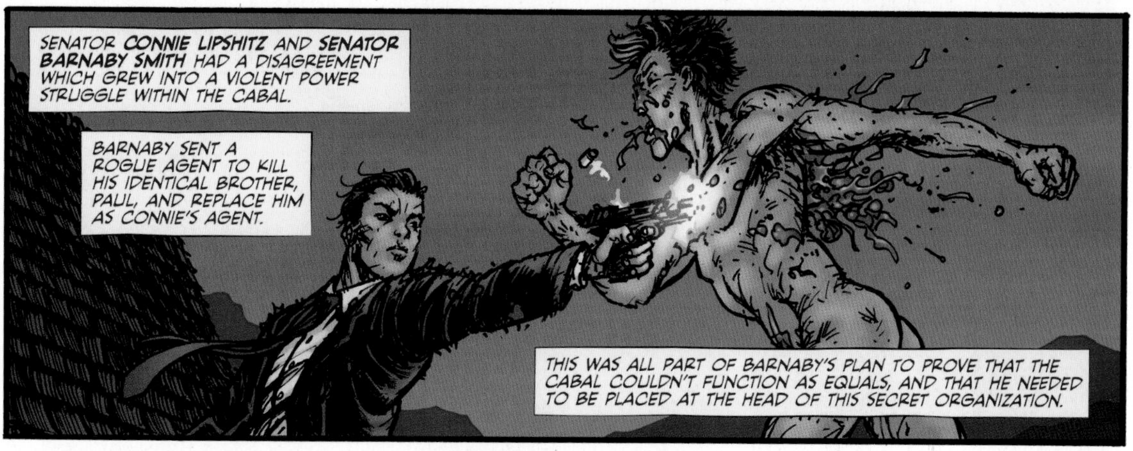
SENATOR **CONNIE LIPSHITZ** AND **SENATOR BARNABY SMITH** HAD A DISAGREEMENT WHICH GREW INTO A VIOLENT POWER STRUGGLE WITHIN THE CABAL.
BARNABY SENT A ROGUE AGENT TO KILL HIS IDENTICAL BROTHER, PAUL, AND REPLACE HIM AS CONNIE'S AGENT.
THIS WAS ALL PART OF BARNABY'S PLAN TO PROVE THAT THE CABAL COULDN'T FUNCTION AS EQUALS, AND THAT HE NEEDED TO BE PLACED AT THE HEAD OF THIS SECRET ORGANIZATION.

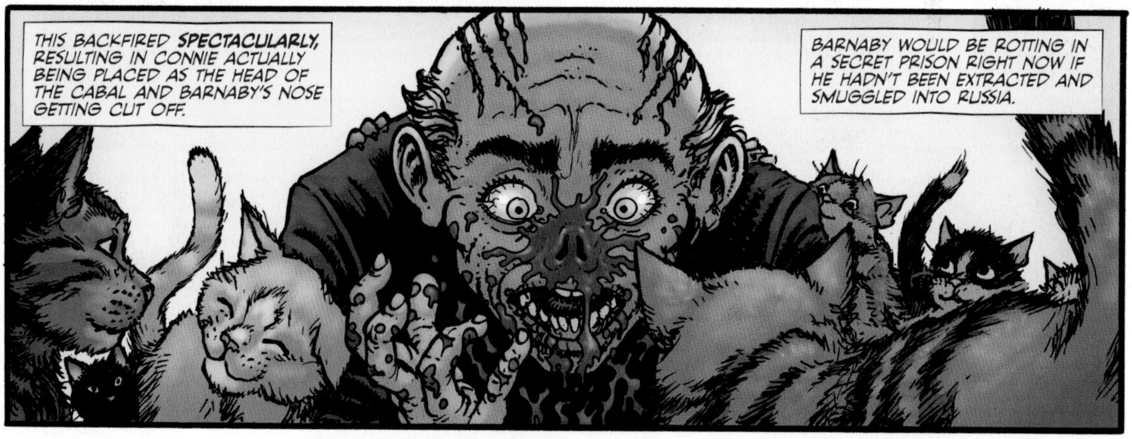
THIS BACKFIRED **SPECTACULARLY**, RESULTING IN CONNIE ACTUALLY BEING PLACED AS THE HEAD OF THE CABAL AND BARNABY'S NOSE GETTING CUT OFF.
BARNABY WOULD BE ROTTING IN A SECRET PRISON RIGHT NOW IF HE HADN'T BEEN EXTRACTED AND SMUGGLED INTO RUSSIA.

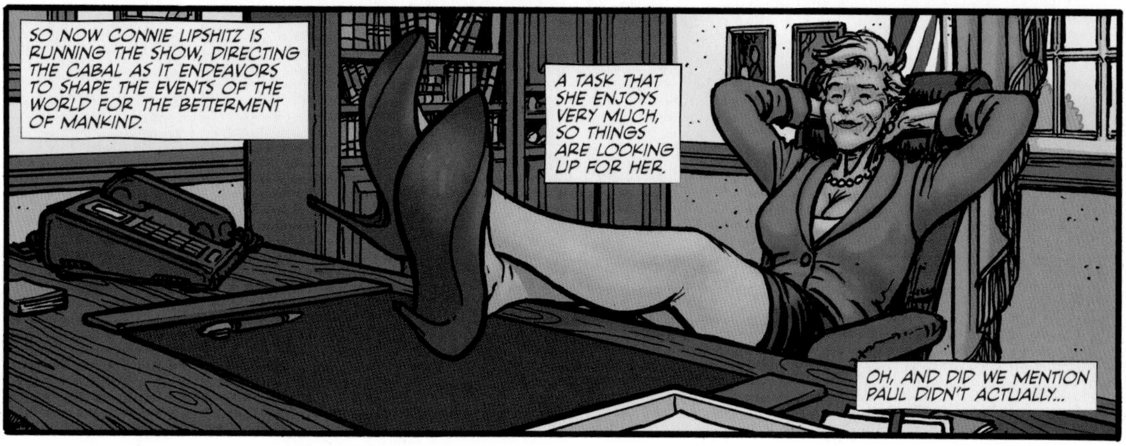
SO NOW CONNIE LIPSHITZ IS RUNNING THE SHOW, DIRECTING THE CABAL AS IT ENDEAVORS TO SHAPE THE EVENTS OF THE WORLD FOR THE BETTERMENT OF MANKIND.
A TASK THAT SHE ENJOYS VERY MUCH, SO THINGS ARE LOOKING UP FOR HER.
OH, AND DID WE MENTION PAUL DIDN'T ACTUALLY...

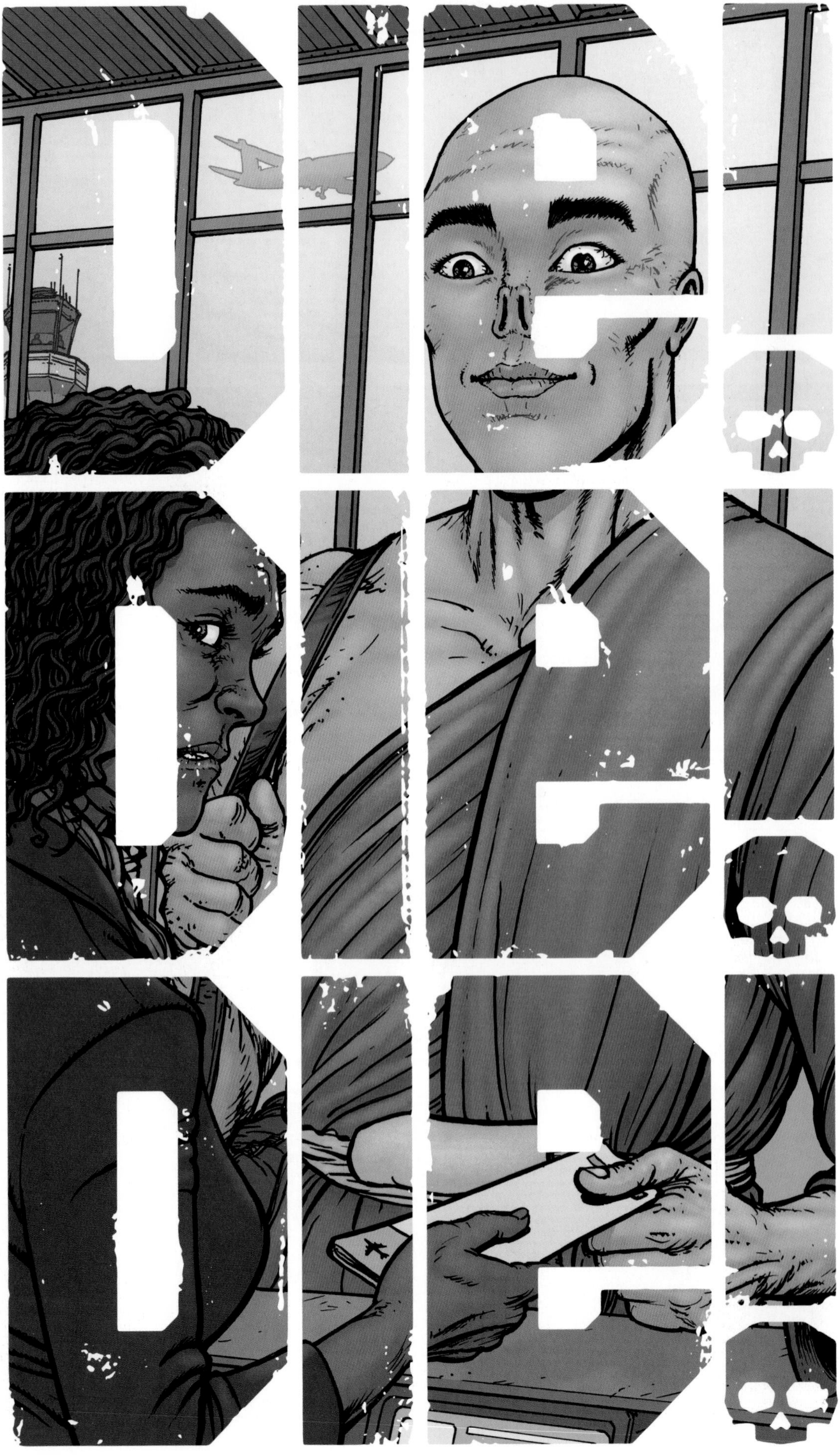
DIE!
DIE!
DIE!

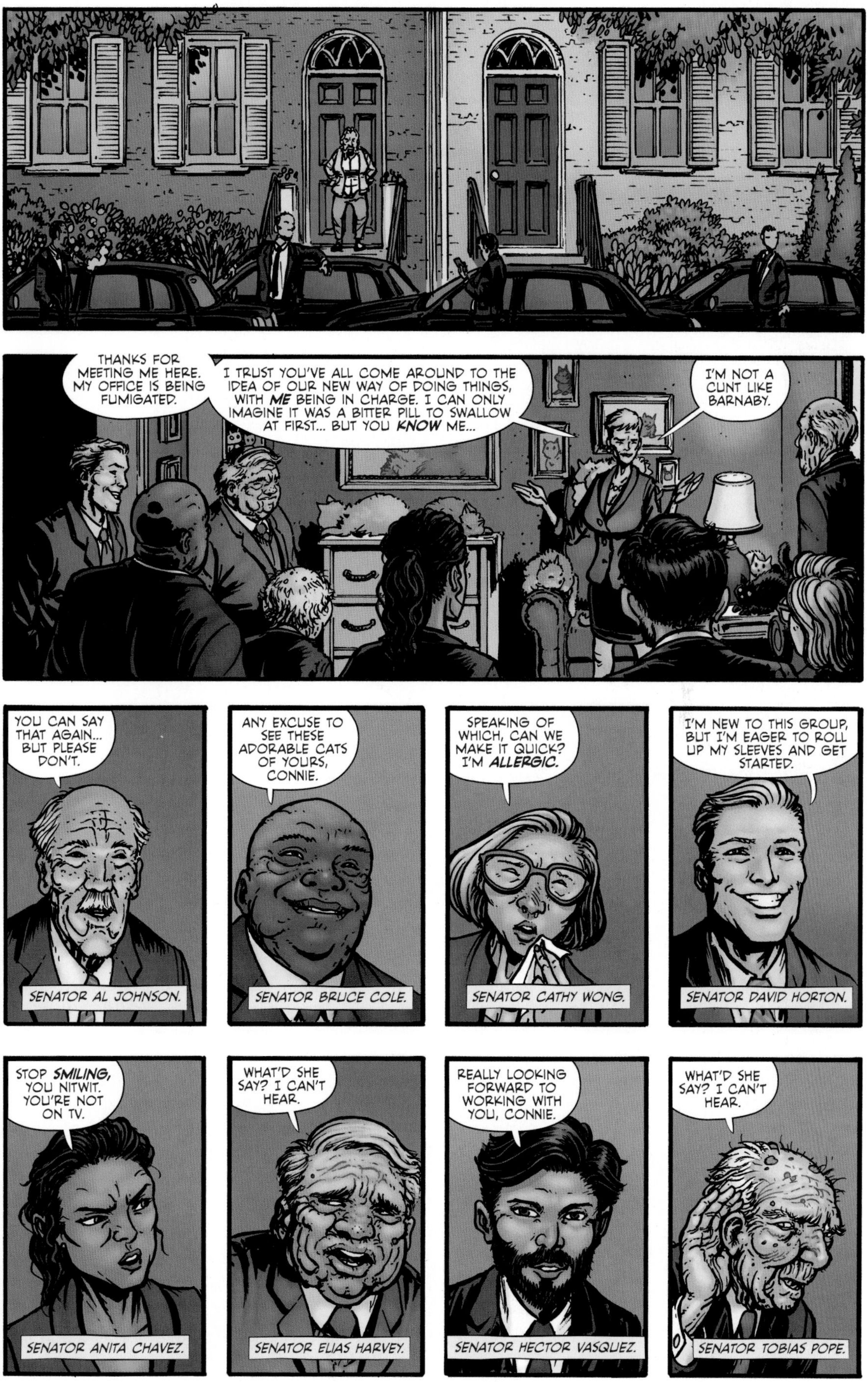
THANKS FOR MEETING ME HERE. MY OFFICE IS BEING FUMIGATED.
I TRUST YOU'VE ALL COME AROUND TO THE IDEA OF OUR NEW WAY OF DOING THINGS, WITH *ME* BEING IN CHARGE. I CAN ONLY IMAGINE IT WAS A BITTER PILL TO SWALLOW AT FIRST... BUT YOU *KNOW* ME...
I'M NOT A CUNT LIKE BARNABY.
YOU CAN SAY THAT AGAIN... BUT PLEASE DON'T.
SENATOR AL JOHNSON.
ANY EXCUSE TO SEE THESE ADORABLE CATS OF YOURS, CONNIE.
SENATOR BRUCE COLE.
SPEAKING OF WHICH, CAN WE MAKE IT QUICK? I'M *ALLERGIC.*
SENATOR CATHY WONG.
I'M NEW TO THIS GROUP, BUT I'M EAGER TO ROLL UP MY SLEEVES AND GET STARTED.
SENATOR DAVID HORTON.
STOP *SMILING,* YOU NITWIT. YOU'RE NOT ON TV.
SENATOR ANITA CHAVEZ.
WHAT'D SHE SAY? I CAN'T HEAR.
SENATOR ELIAS HARVEY.
REALLY LOOKING FORWARD TO WORKING WITH YOU, CONNIE.
SENATOR HECTOR VASQUEZ.
WHAT'D SHE SAY? I CAN'T HEAR.
SENATOR TOBIAS POPE.

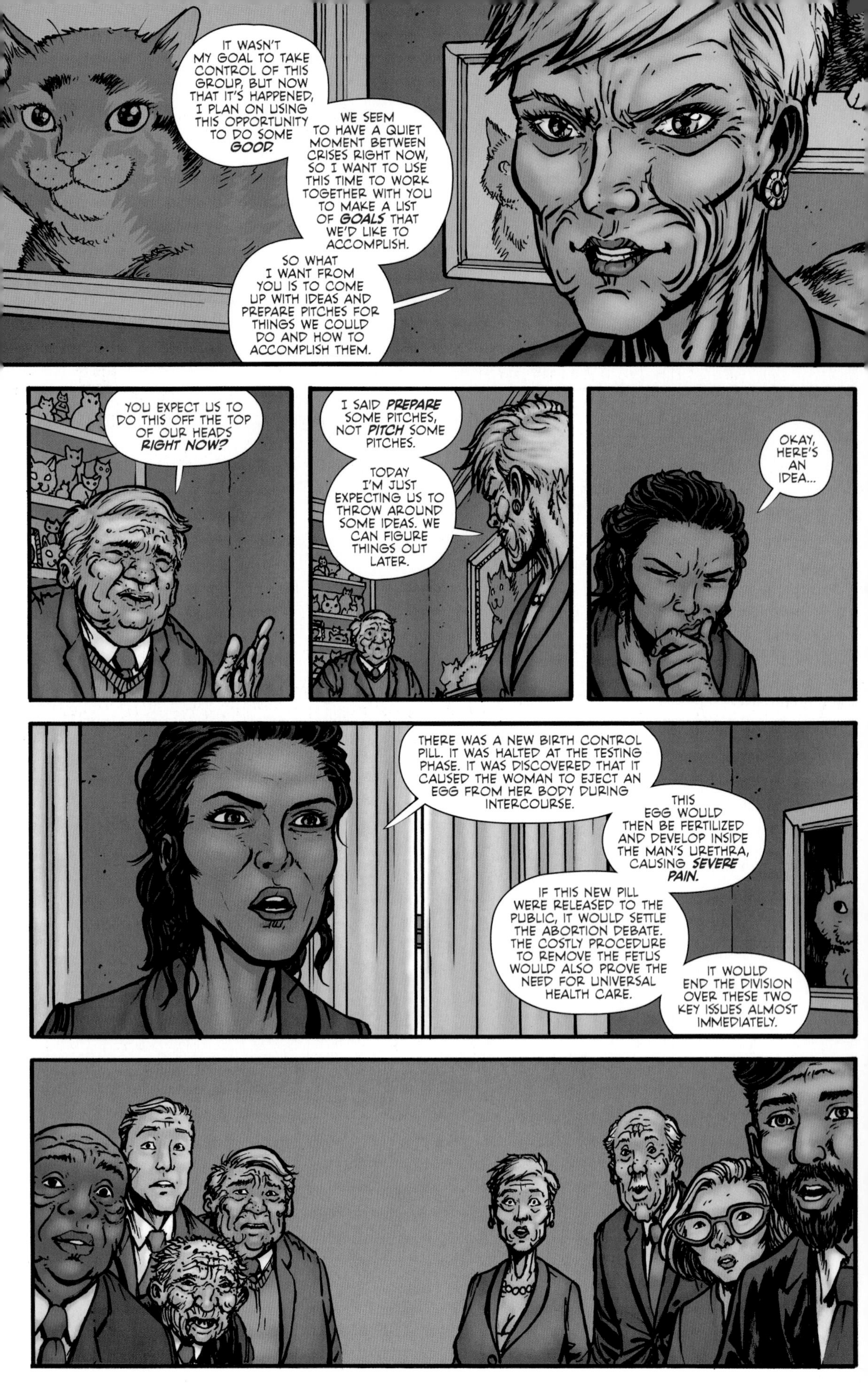
IT WASN'T MY GOAL TO TAKE CONTROL OF THIS GROUP, BUT NOW THAT IT'S HAPPENED, I PLAN ON USING THIS OPPORTUNITY TO DO SOME GOOD.
WE SEEM TO HAVE A QUIET MOMENT BETWEEN CRISES RIGHT NOW, SO I WANT TO USE THIS TIME TO WORK TOGETHER WITH YOU TO MAKE A LIST OF GOALS THAT WE'D LIKE TO ACCOMPLISH.
SO WHAT I WANT FROM YOU IS TO COME UP WITH IDEAS AND PREPARE PITCHES FOR THINGS WE COULD DO AND HOW TO ACCOMPLISH THEM.
YOU EXPECT US TO DO THIS OFF THE TOP OF OUR HEADS RIGHT NOW?
I SAID PREPARE SOME PITCHES, NOT PITCH SOME PITCHES.
TODAY I'M JUST EXPECTING US TO THROW AROUND SOME IDEAS. WE CAN FIGURE THINGS OUT LATER.
OKAY, HERE'S AN IDEA...
THERE WAS A NEW BIRTH CONTROL PILL. IT WAS HALTED AT THE TESTING PHASE. IT WAS DISCOVERED THAT IT CAUSED THE WOMAN TO EJECT AN EGG FROM HER BODY DURING INTERCOURSE.
THIS EGG WOULD THEN BE FERTILIZED AND DEVELOP INSIDE THE MAN'S URETHRA, CAUSING SEVERE PAIN.
IF THIS NEW PILL WERE RELEASED TO THE PUBLIC, IT WOULD SETTLE THE ABORTION DEBATE. THE COSTLY PROCEDURE TO REMOVE THE FETUS WOULD ALSO PROVE THE NEED FOR UNIVERSAL HEALTH CARE.
IT WOULD END THE DIVISION OVER THESE TWO KEY ISSUES ALMOST IMMEDIATELY.

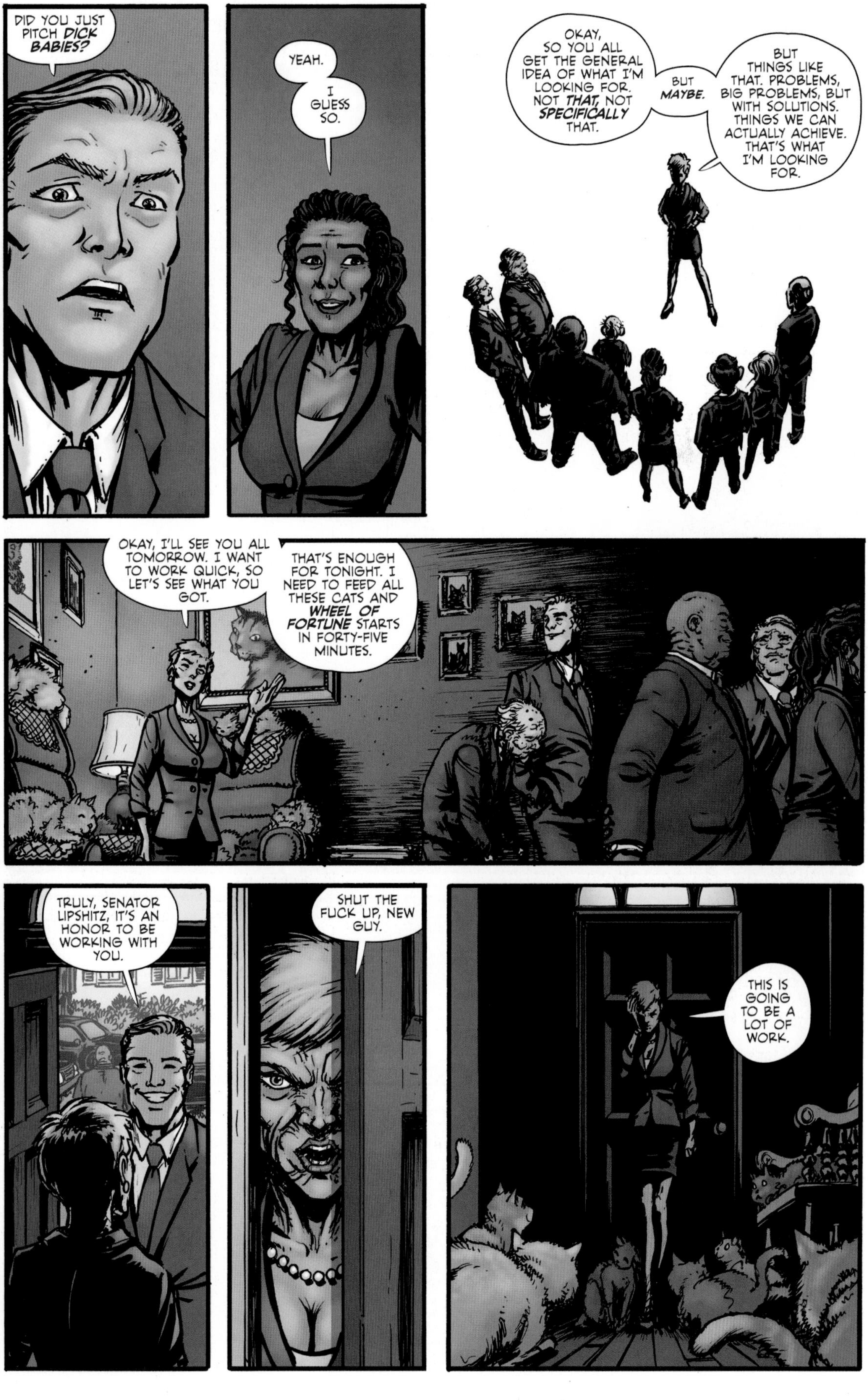
DID YOU JUST PITCH DICK BABIES?
YEAH.
I GUESS SO.
OKAY, SO YOU ALL GET THE GENERAL IDEA OF WHAT I'M LOOKING FOR. NOT THAT, NOT SPECIFICALLY THAT.
BUT MAYBE.
BUT THINGS LIKE THAT. PROBLEMS, BIG PROBLEMS, BUT WITH SOLUTIONS. THINGS WE CAN ACTUALLY ACHIEVE. THAT'S WHAT I'M LOOKING FOR.
OKAY, I'LL SEE YOU ALL TOMORROW. I WANT TO WORK QUICK, SO LET'S SEE WHAT YOU GOT.
THAT'S ENOUGH FOR TONIGHT. I NEED TO FEED ALL THESE CATS AND WHEEL OF FORTUNE STARTS IN FORTY-FIVE MINUTES.
TRULY, SENATOR LIPSHITZ, IT'S AN HONOR TO BE WORKING WITH YOU.
SHUT THE FUCK UP, NEW GUY.
THIS IS GOING TO BE A LOT OF WORK.

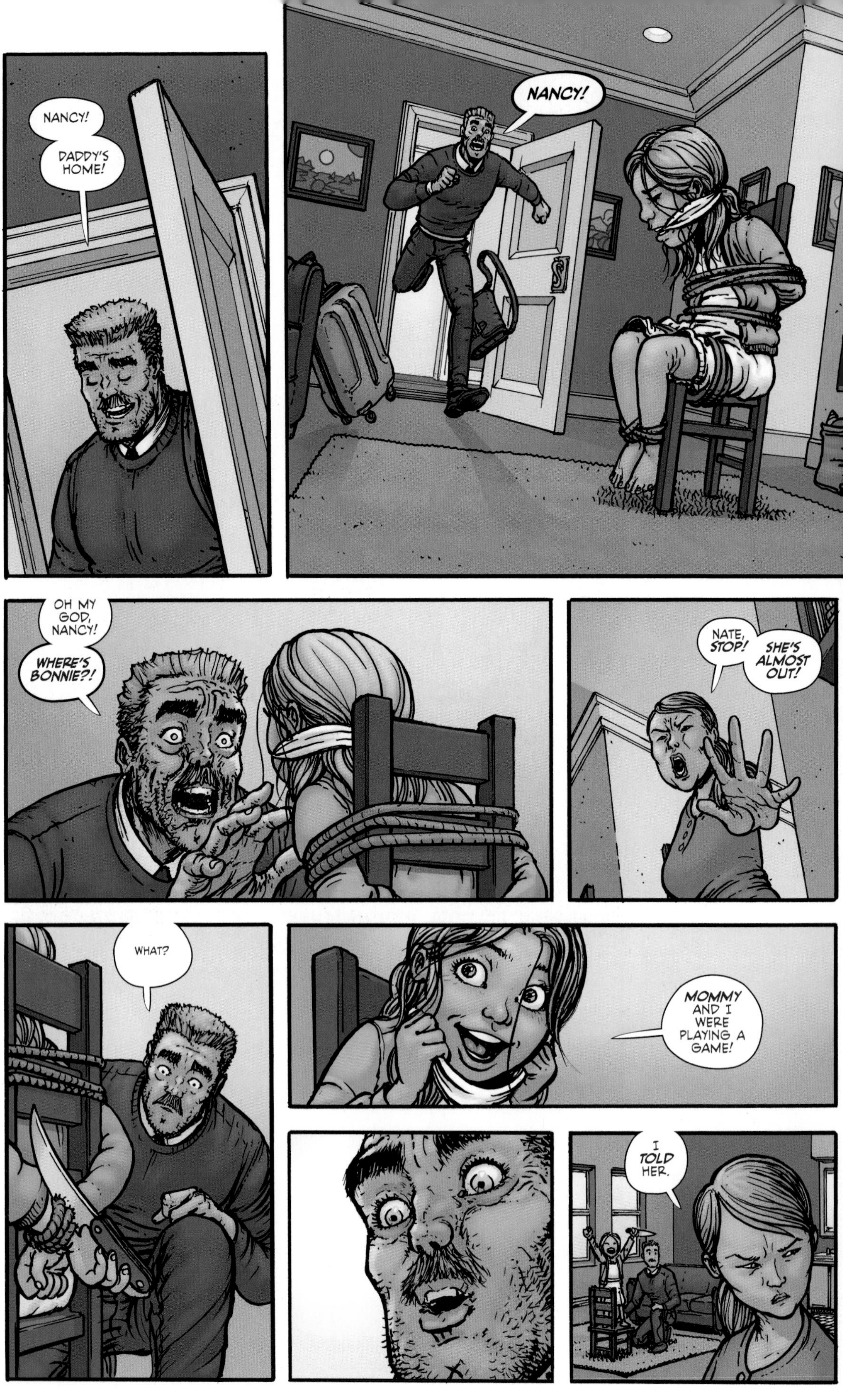
NANCY!
DADDY'S HOME!
NANCY!
OH MY GOD, NANCY!
WHERE'S BONNIE?!
NATE, STOP!
SHE'S ALMOST OUT!
WHAT?
MOMMY AND I WERE PLAYING A GAME!
I TOLD HER.

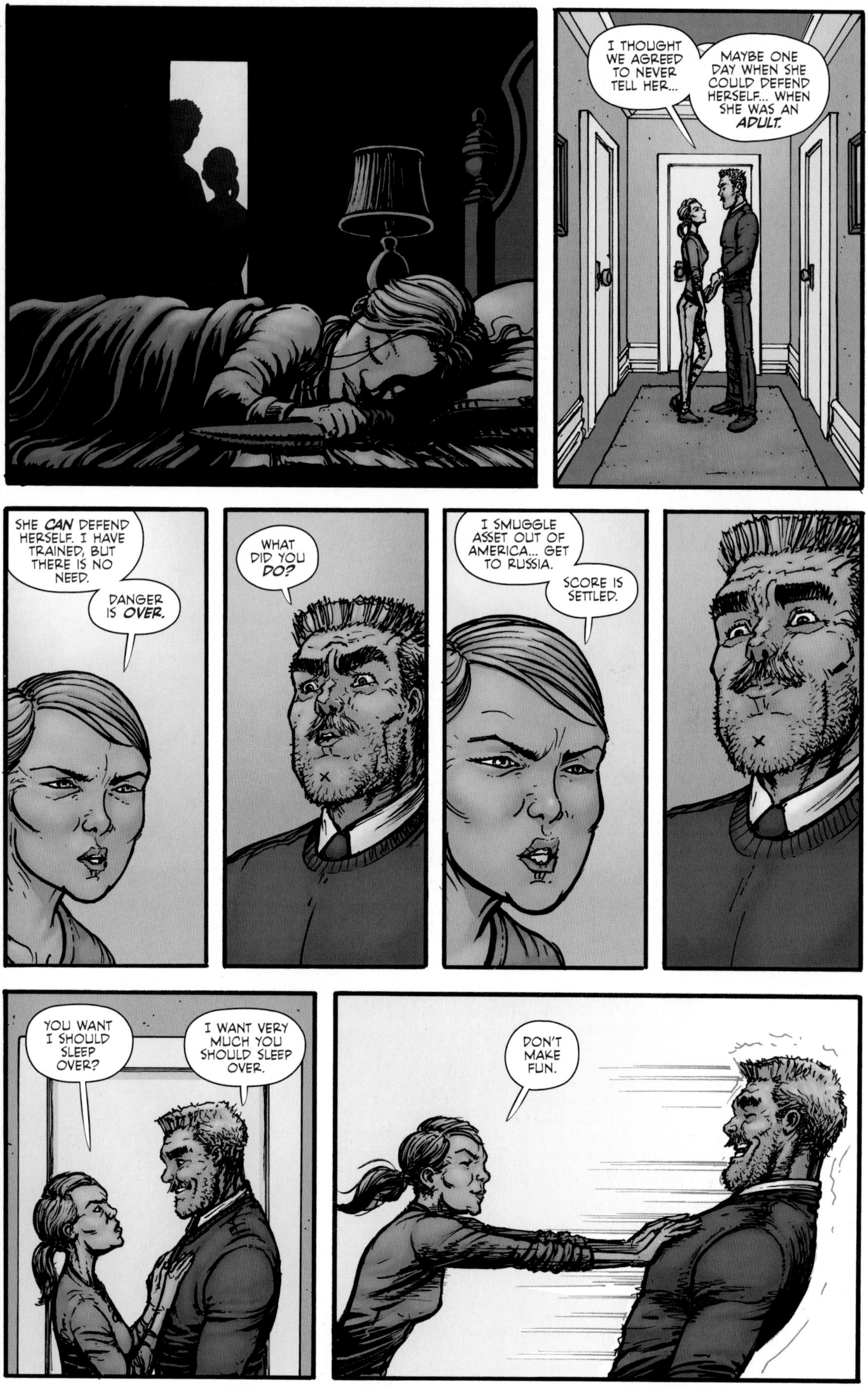
I THOUGHT WE AGREED TO NEVER TELL HER...
MAYBE ONE DAY WHEN SHE COULD DEFEND HERSELF... WHEN SHE WAS AN *ADULT.*
SHE *CAN* DEFEND HERSELF. I HAVE TRAINED, BUT THERE IS NO NEED.
DANGER IS *OVER.*
WHAT DID YOU *DO?*
I SMUGGLE ASSET OUT OF AMERICA... GET TO RUSSIA.
SCORE IS SETTLED.
YOU WANT I SHOULD SLEEP OVER?
I WANT VERY MUCH YOU SHOULD SLEEP OVER.
DON'T MAKE FUN.

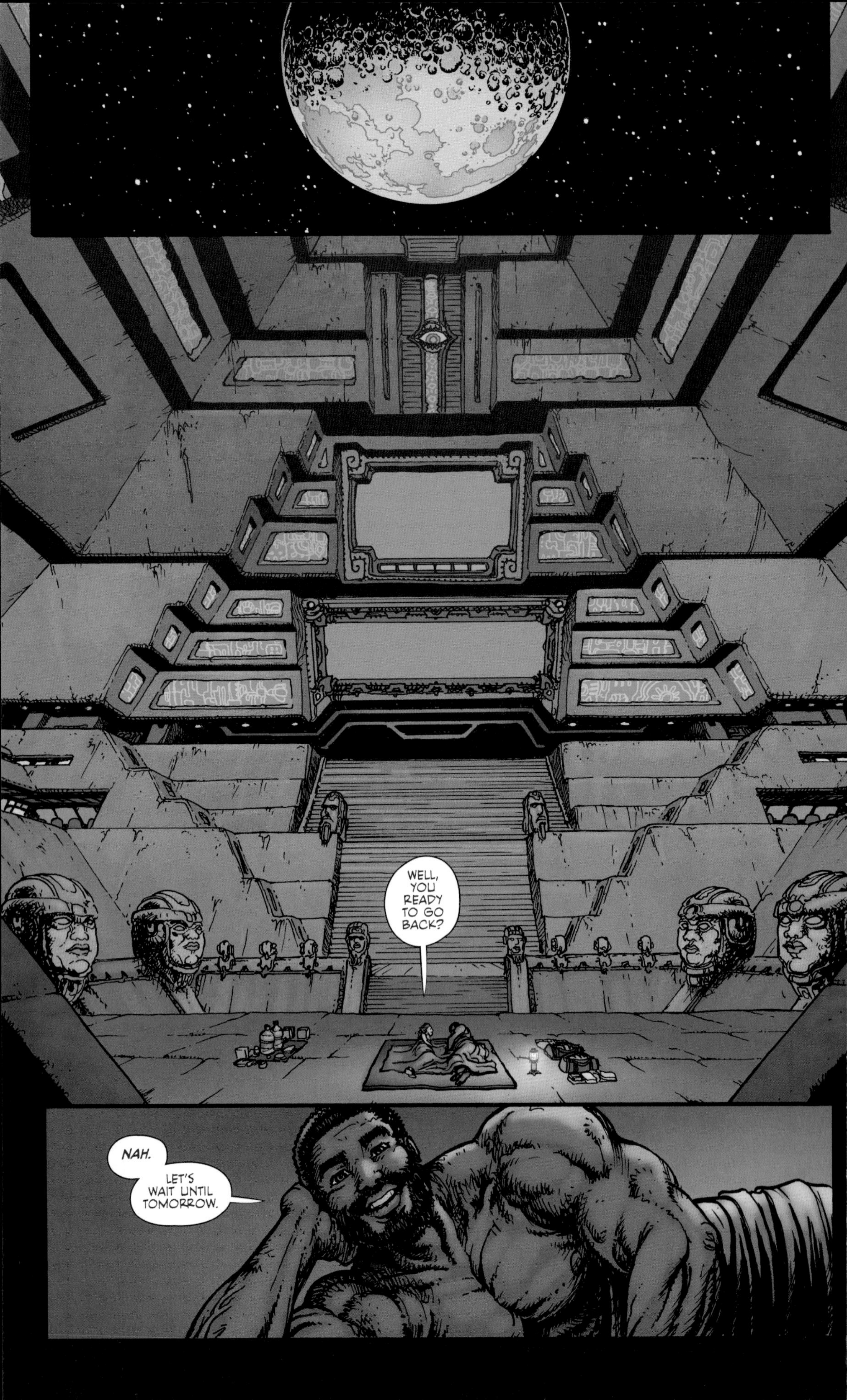
WELL, YOU READY TO GO BACK?
NAH.
LET'S WAIT UNTIL TOMORROW.

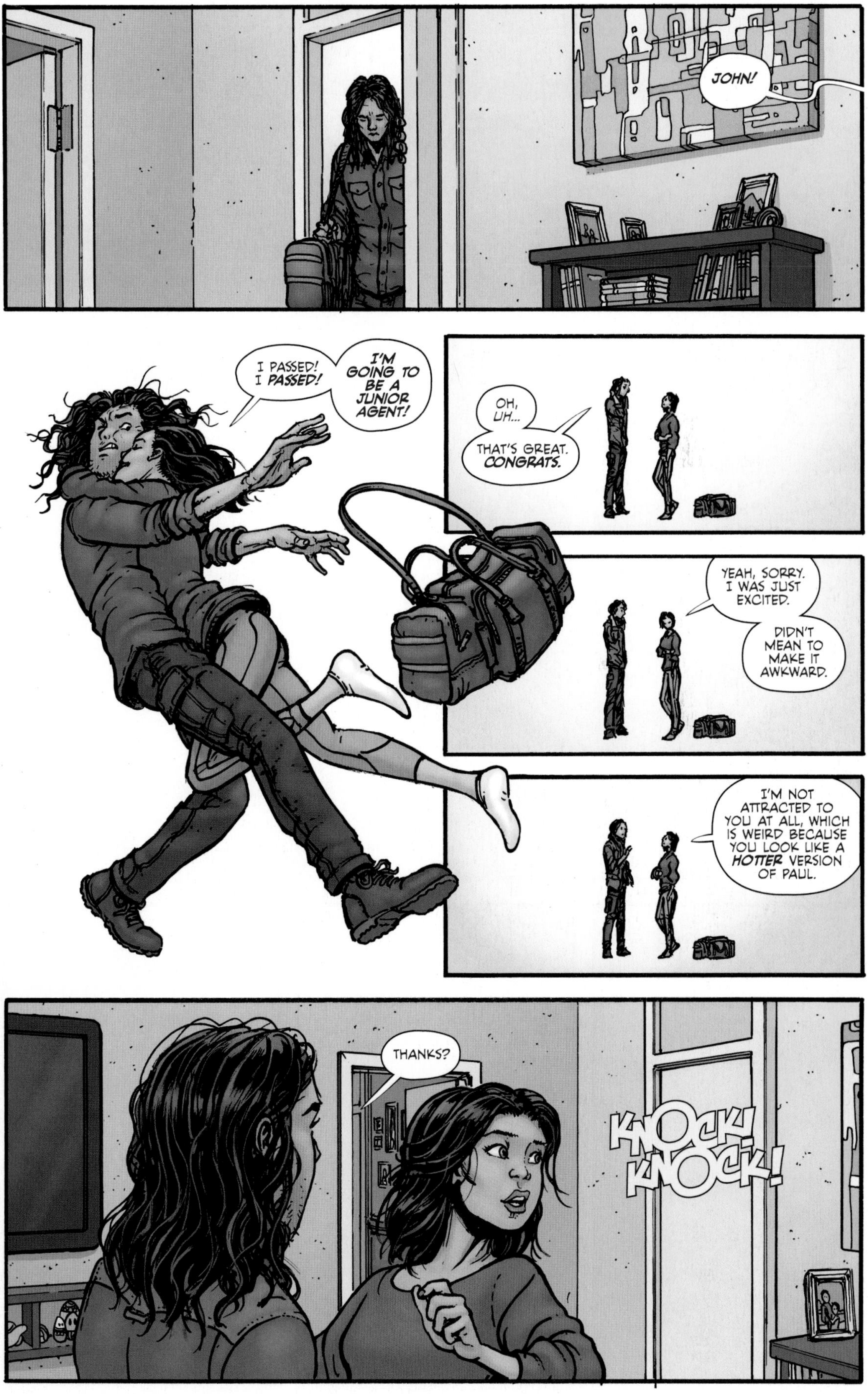
JOHN!
I PASSED! I PASSED!
I'M GOING TO BE A JUNIOR AGENT!
OH, UH...
THAT'S GREAT. CONGRATS.
YEAH, SORRY. I WAS JUST EXCITED.
DIDN'T MEAN TO MAKE IT AWKWARD.
I'M NOT ATTRACTED TO YOU AT ALL, WHICH IS WEIRD BECAUSE YOU LOOK LIKE A HOTTER VERSION OF PAUL.
THANKS?
KNOCK! KNOCK!

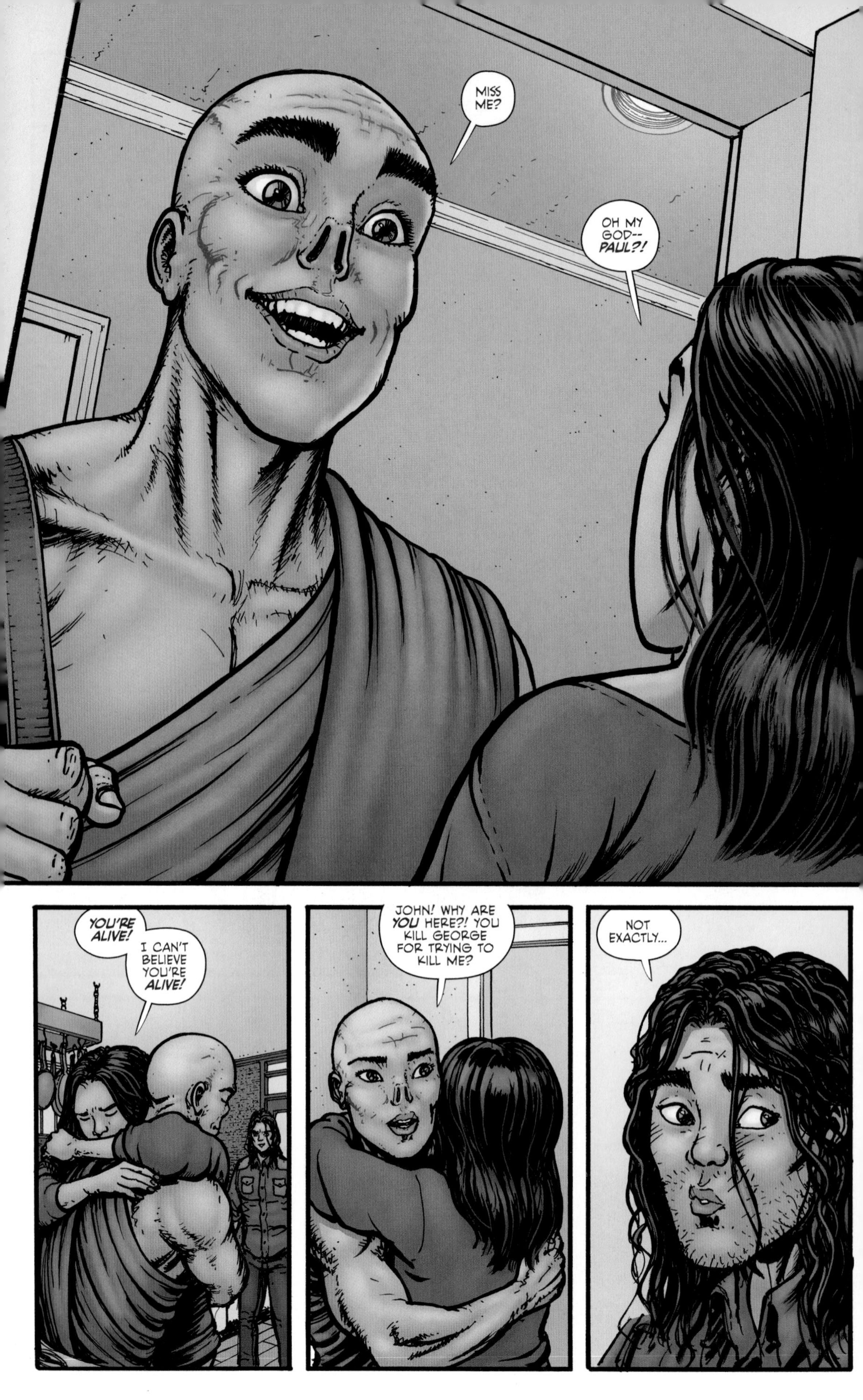
MISS ME?
OH MY GOD-- PAUL?!
YOU'RE ALIVE!
I CAN'T BELIEVE YOU'RE ALIVE!
JOHN! WHY ARE YOU HERE?! YOU KILL GEORGE FOR TRYING TO KILL ME?
NOT EXACTLY...

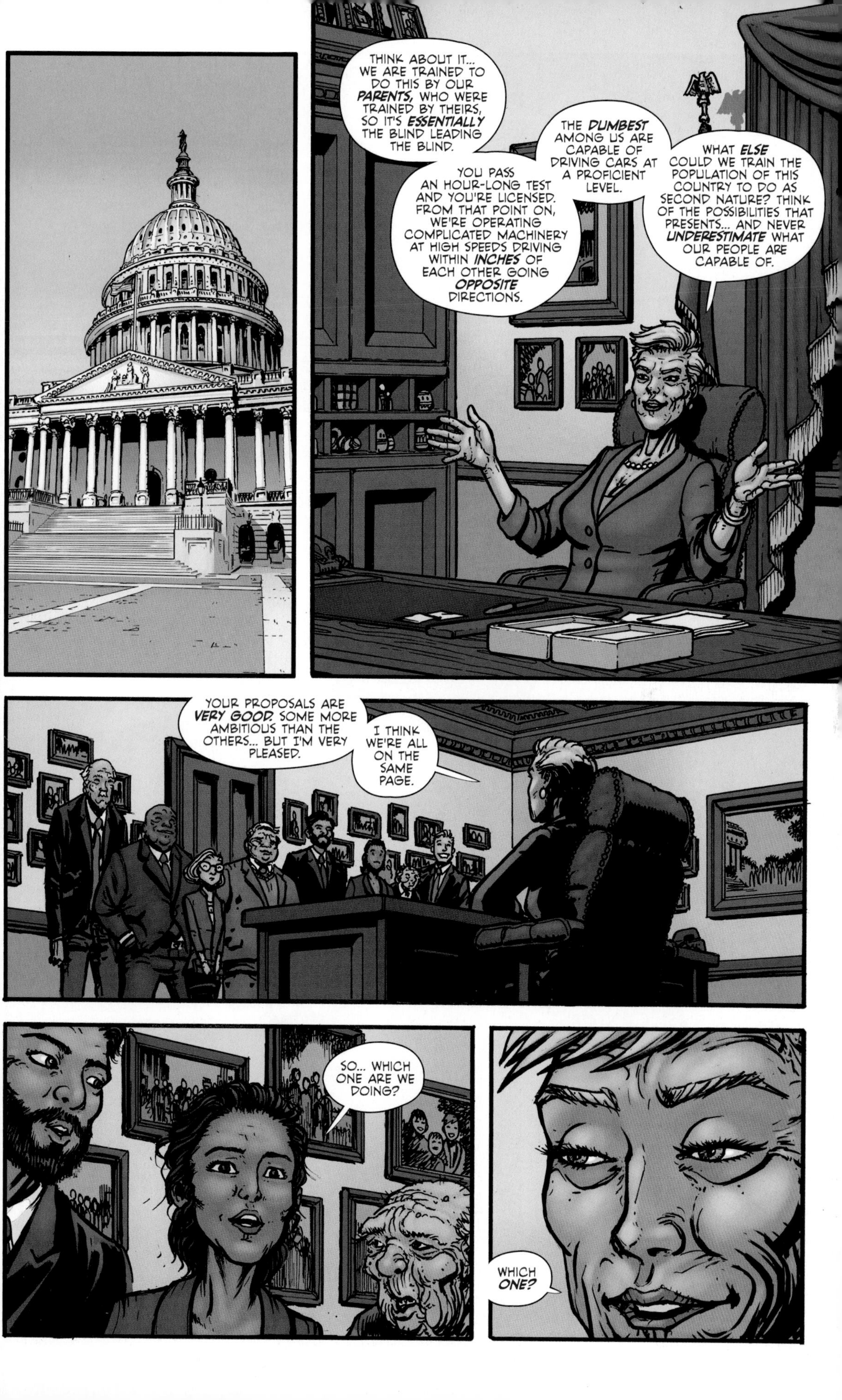
THINK ABOUT IT... WE ARE TRAINED TO DO THIS BY OUR PARENTS, WHO WERE TRAINED BY THEIRS, SO IT'S ESSENTIALLY THE BLIND LEADING THE BLIND.
THE DUMBEST AMONG US ARE CAPABLE OF DRIVING CARS AT A PROFICIENT LEVEL.
YOU PASS AN HOUR-LONG TEST AND YOU'RE LICENSED. FROM THAT POINT ON, WE'RE OPERATING COMPLICATED MACHINERY AT HIGH SPEEDS DRIVING WITHIN INCHES OF EACH OTHER GOING OPPOSITE DIRECTIONS.
WHAT ELSE COULD WE TRAIN THE POPULATION OF THIS COUNTRY TO DO AS SECOND NATURE? THINK OF THE POSSIBILITIES THAT PRESENTS... AND NEVER UNDERESTIMATE WHAT OUR PEOPLE ARE CAPABLE OF.
YOUR PROPOSALS ARE VERY GOOD. SOME MORE AMBITIOUS THAN THE OTHERS... BUT I'M VERY PLEASED.
I THINK WE'RE ALL ON THE SAME PAGE.
SO... WHICH ONE ARE WE DOING?
WHICH ONE?

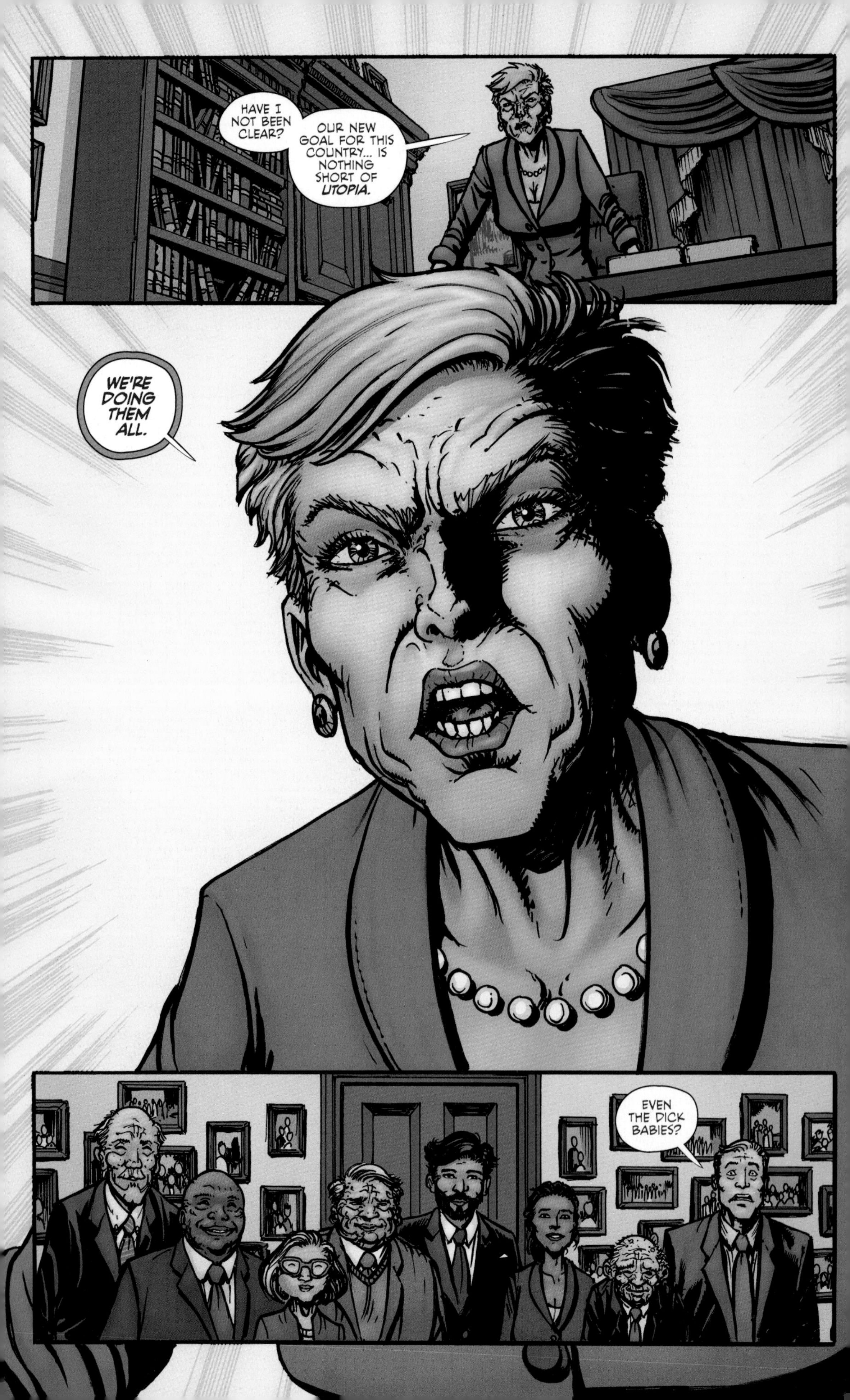
HAVE I NOT BEEN CLEAR?
OUR NEW GOAL FOR THIS COUNTRY... IS NOTHING SHORT OF *UTOPIA.*
WE'RE DOING THEM ALL.
EVEN THE DICK BABIES?

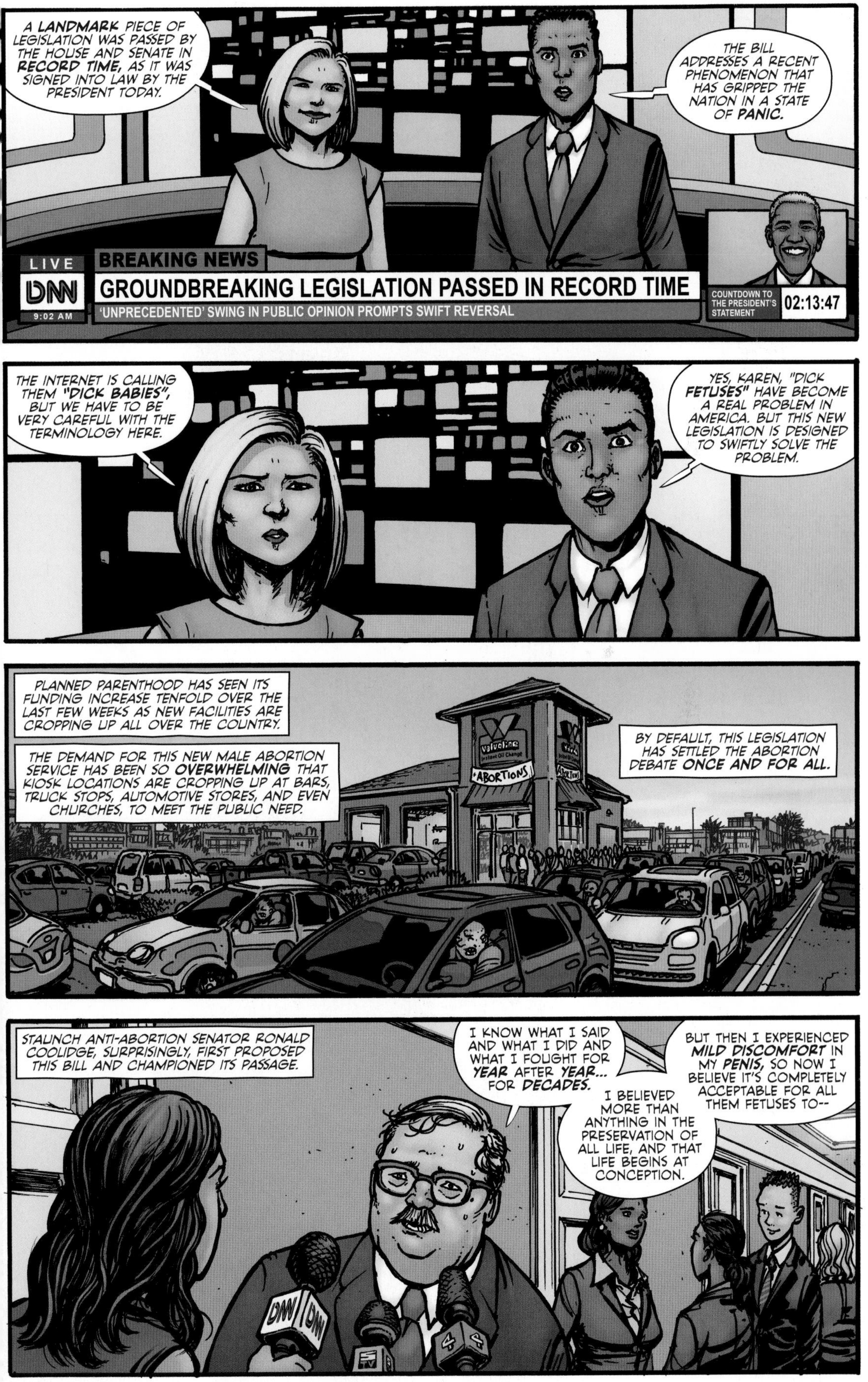
A LANDMARK PIECE OF LEGISLATION WAS PASSED BY THE HOUSE AND SENATE IN RECORD TIME, AS IT WAS SIGNED INTO LAW BY THE PRESIDENT TODAY.
THE BILL ADDRESSES A RECENT PHENOMENON THAT HAS GRIPPED THE NATION IN A STATE OF PANIC.
LIVE
DNN
9:02 AM
BREAKING NEWS
GROUNDBREAKING LEGISLATION PASSED IN RECORD TIME
'UNPRECEDENTED' SWING IN PUBLIC OPINION PROMPTS SWIFT REVERSAL
COUNTDOWN TO THE PRESIDENT'S STATEMENT
02:13:47
THE INTERNET IS CALLING THEM "DICK BABIES", BUT WE HAVE TO BE VERY CAREFUL WITH THE TERMINOLOGY HERE.
YES, KAREN, "DICK FETUSES" HAVE BECOME A REAL PROBLEM IN AMERICA. BUT THIS NEW LEGISLATION IS DESIGNED TO SWIFTLY SOLVE THE PROBLEM.
PLANNED PARENTHOOD HAS SEEN ITS FUNDING INCREASE TENFOLD OVER THE LAST FEW WEEKS AS NEW FACILITIES ARE CROPPING UP ALL OVER THE COUNTRY.
THE DEMAND FOR THIS NEW MALE ABORTION SERVICE HAS BEEN SO OVERWHELMING THAT KIOSK LOCATIONS ARE CROPPING UP AT BARS, TRUCK STOPS, AUTOMOTIVE STORES, AND EVEN CHURCHES, TO MEET THE PUBLIC NEED.
Valvoline
ABORTIONS
BY DEFAULT, THIS LEGISLATION HAS SETTLED THE ABORTION DEBATE ONCE AND FOR ALL.
STAUNCH ANTI-ABORTION SENATOR RONALD COOLIDGE, SURPRISINGLY, FIRST PROPOSED THIS BILL AND CHAMPIONED ITS PASSAGE.
I KNOW WHAT I SAID AND WHAT I DID AND WHAT I FOUGHT FOR YEAR AFTER YEAR... FOR DECADES.
I BELIEVED MORE THAN ANYTHING IN THE PRESERVATION OF ALL LIFE, AND THAT LIFE BEGINS AT CONCEPTION.
BUT THEN I EXPERIENCED MILD DISCOMFORT IN MY PENIS, SO NOW I BELIEVE IT'S COMPLETELY ACCEPTABLE FOR ALL THEM FETUSES TO--

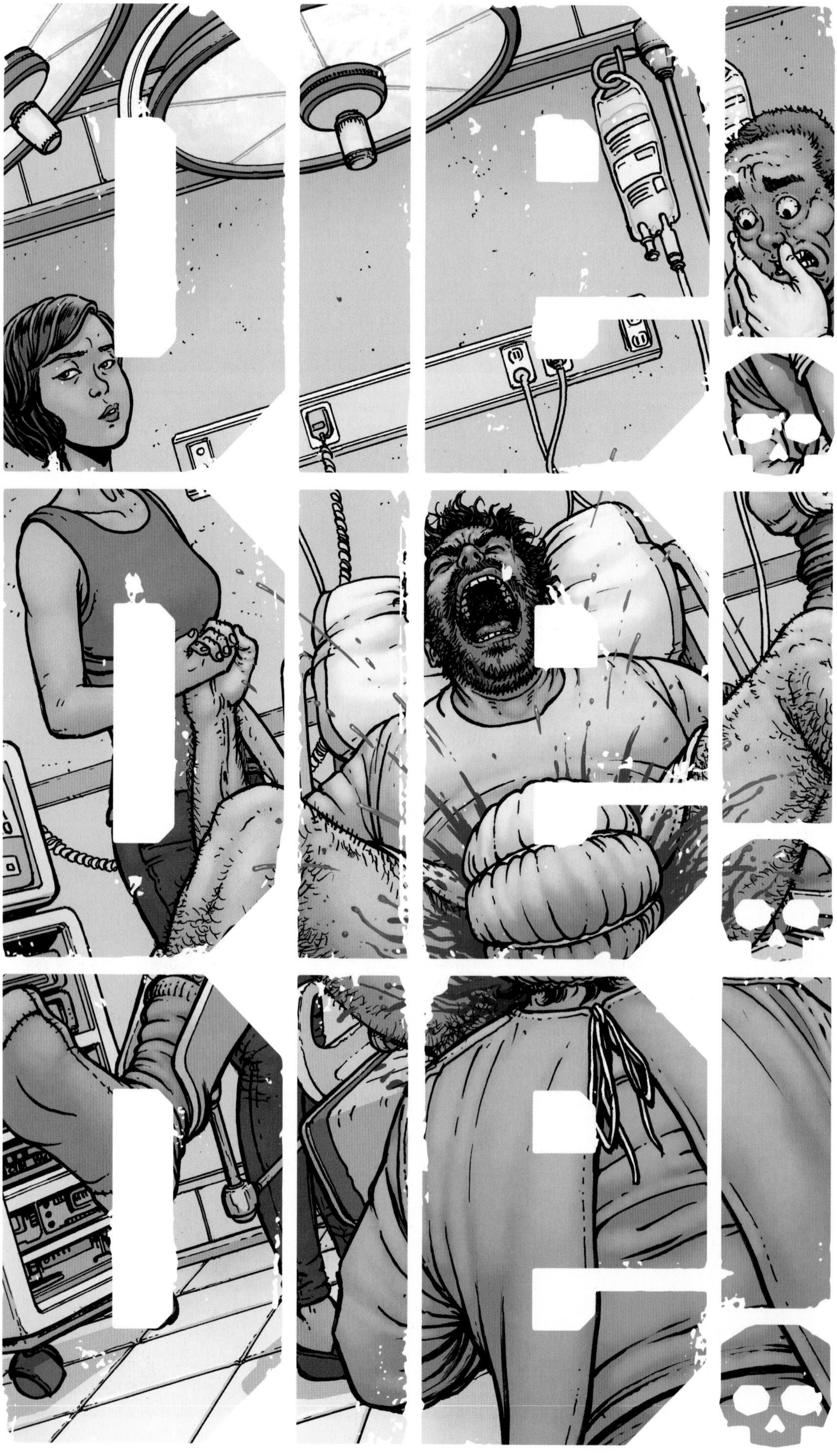
DIE!
DIE!
DIE!

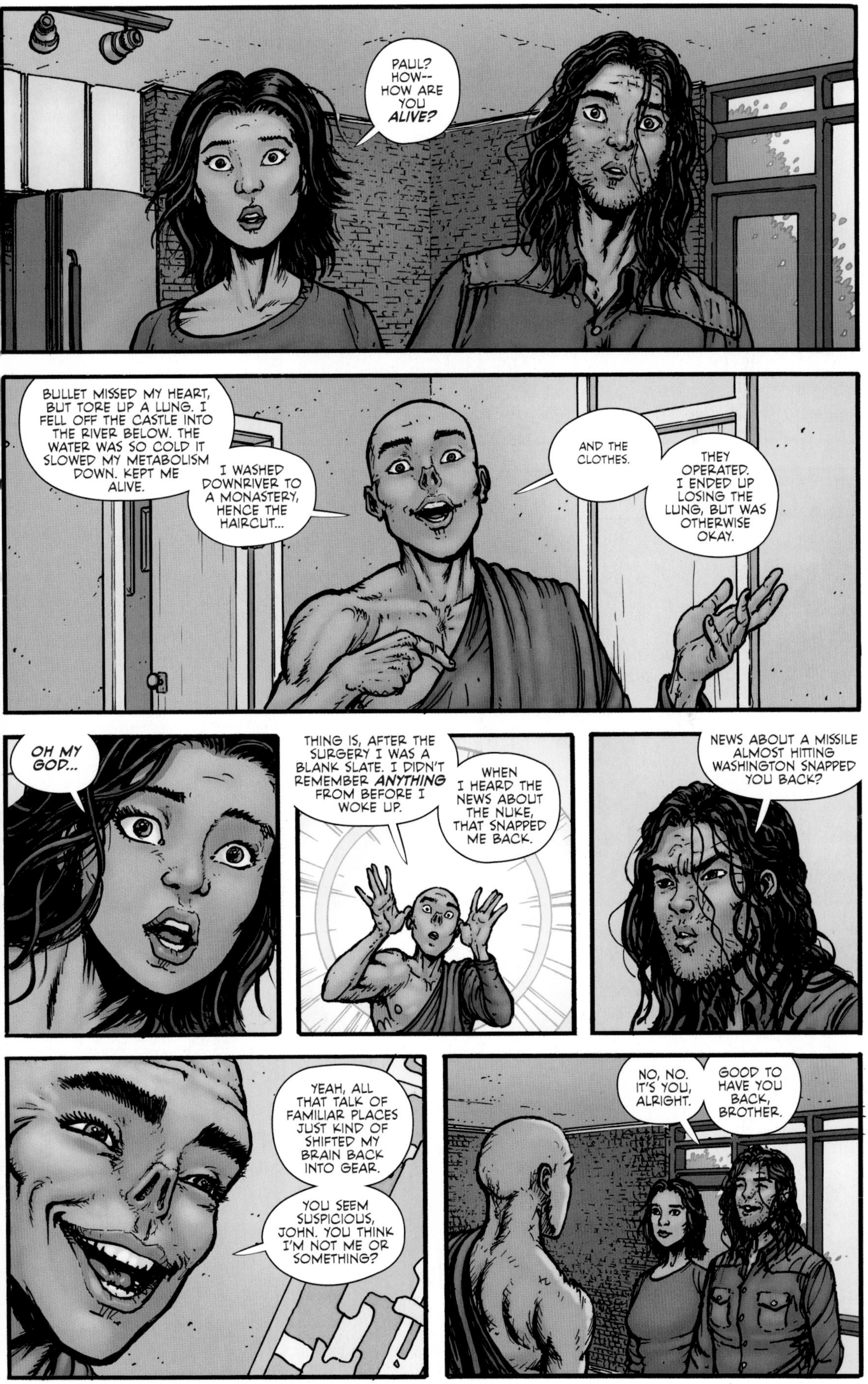
PAUL? HOW-- HOW ARE YOU *ALIVE?*
BULLET MISSED MY HEART, BUT TORE UP A LUNG. I FELL OFF THE CASTLE INTO THE RIVER BELOW. THE WATER WAS SO COLD IT SLOWED MY METABOLISM DOWN. KEPT ME ALIVE.
I WASHED DOWNRIVER TO A MONASTERY, HENCE THE HAIRCUT...
AND THE CLOTHES.
THEY OPERATED. I ENDED UP LOSING THE LUNG, BUT WAS OTHERWISE OKAY.
OH MY GOD...
THING IS, AFTER THE SURGERY I WAS A BLANK SLATE. I DIDN'T REMEMBER *ANYTHING* FROM BEFORE I WOKE UP.
WHEN I HEARD THE NEWS ABOUT THE NUKE, THAT SNAPPED ME BACK.
NEWS ABOUT A MISSILE ALMOST HITTING WASHINGTON SNAPPED YOU BACK?
YEAH, ALL THAT TALK OF FAMILIAR PLACES JUST KIND OF SHIFTED MY BRAIN BACK INTO GEAR.
YOU SEEM SUSPICIOUS, JOHN. YOU THINK I'M NOT ME OR SOMETHING?
NO, NO. IT'S YOU, ALRIGHT.
GOOD TO HAVE YOU BACK, BROTHER.

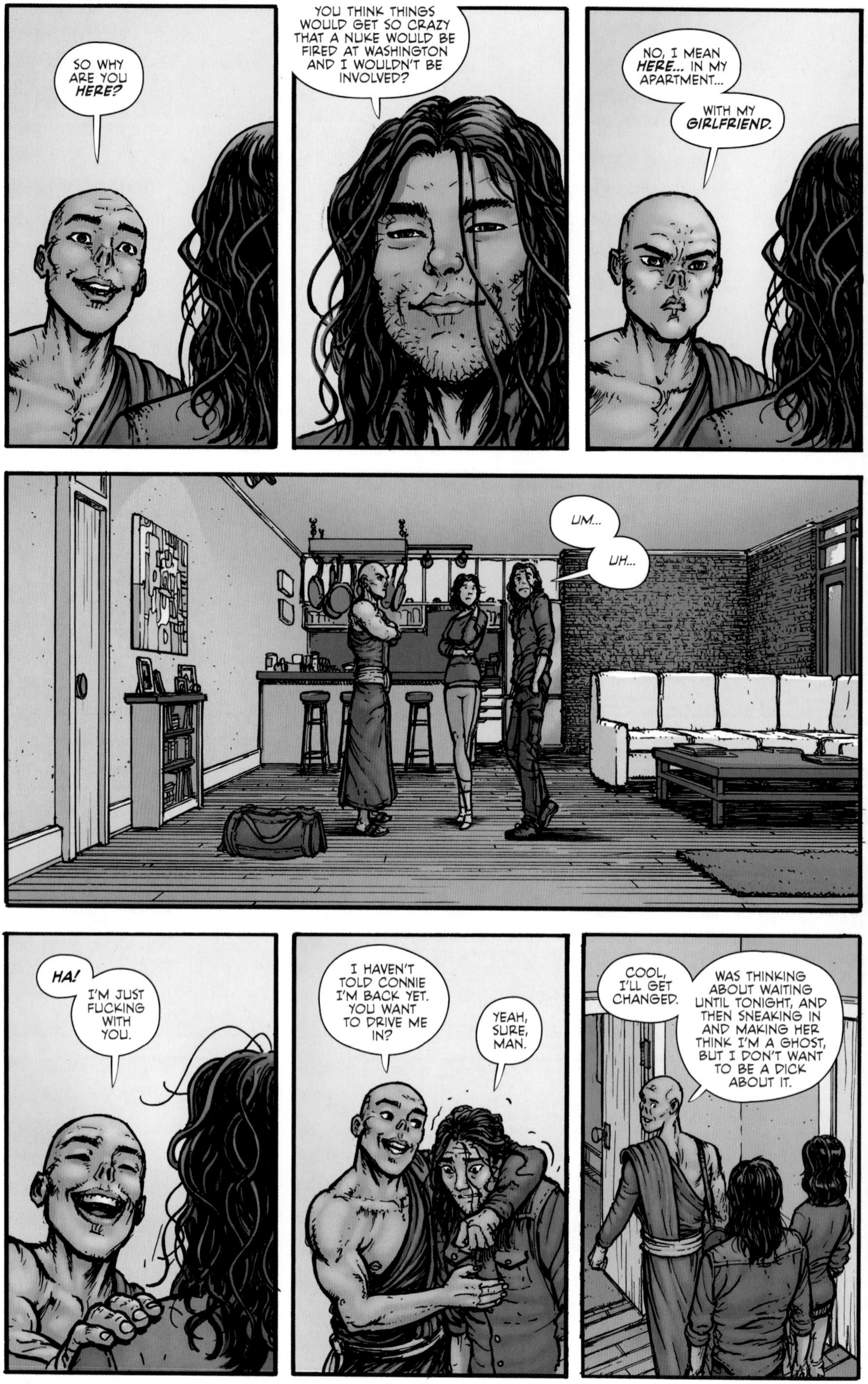
SO WHY ARE YOU HERE?
YOU THINK THINGS WOULD GET SO CRAZY THAT A NUKE WOULD BE FIRED AT WASHINGTON AND I WOULDN'T BE INVOLVED?
NO, I MEAN HERE... IN MY APARTMENT...
WITH MY GIRLFRIEND.
UM...
UH...
HA!
I'M JUST FUCKING WITH YOU.
I HAVEN'T TOLD CONNIE I'M BACK YET. YOU WANT TO DRIVE ME IN?
YEAH, SURE, MAN.
COOL, I'LL GET CHANGED.
WAS THINKING ABOUT WAITING UNTIL TONIGHT, AND THEN SNEAKING IN AND MAKING HER THINK I'M A GHOST, BUT I DON'T WANT TO BE A DICK ABOUT IT.

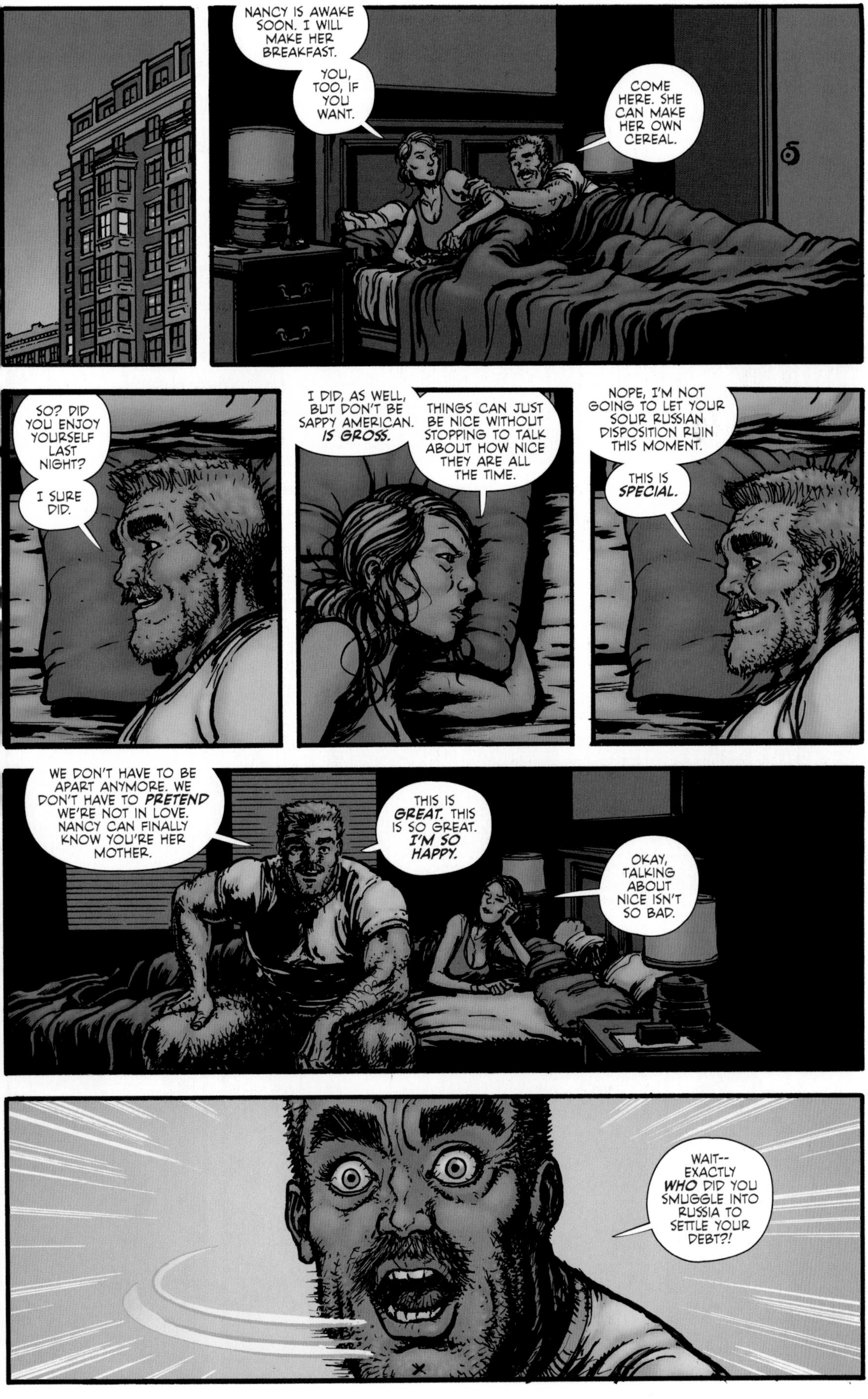
NANCY IS AWAKE SOON. I WILL MAKE HER BREAKFAST.
YOU, TOO, IF YOU WANT.
COME HERE. SHE CAN MAKE HER OWN CEREAL.
SO? DID YOU ENJOY YOURSELF LAST NIGHT?
I SURE DID.
I DID, AS WELL, BUT DON'T BE SAPPY AMERICAN. *IS GROSS.*
THINGS CAN JUST BE NICE WITHOUT STOPPING TO TALK ABOUT HOW NICE THEY ARE ALL THE TIME.
NOPE, I'M NOT GOING TO LET YOUR SOUR RUSSIAN DISPOSITION RUIN THIS MOMENT.
THIS IS *SPECIAL.*
WE DON'T HAVE TO BE APART ANYMORE. WE DON'T HAVE TO *PRETEND* WE'RE NOT IN LOVE. NANCY CAN FINALLY KNOW YOU'RE HER MOTHER.
THIS IS *GREAT.* THIS IS SO GREAT. *I'M SO HAPPY.*
OKAY, TALKING ABOUT NICE ISN'T SO BAD.
WAIT-- EXACTLY *WHO* DID YOU SMUGGLE INTO RUSSIA TO SETTLE YOUR DEBT?!

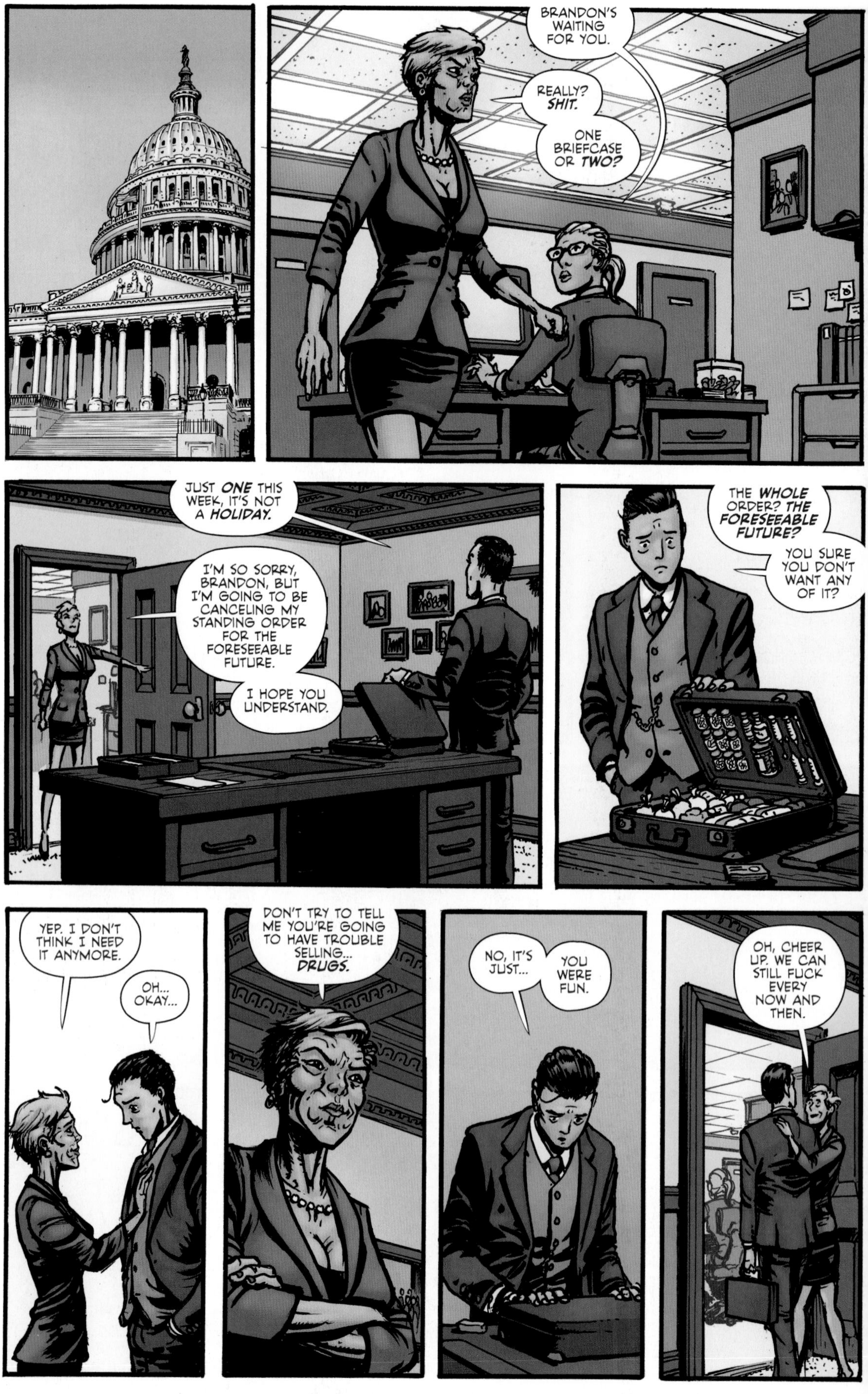
BRANDON'S WAITING FOR YOU.
REALLY? SHIT.
ONE BRIEFCASE OR TWO?
JUST ONE THIS WEEK, IT'S NOT A HOLIDAY.
I'M SO SORRY, BRANDON, BUT I'M GOING TO BE CANCELING MY STANDING ORDER FOR THE FORESEEABLE FUTURE.
I HOPE YOU UNDERSTAND.
THE WHOLE ORDER? THE FORESEEABLE FUTURE?
YOU SURE YOU DON'T WANT ANY OF IT?
YEP. I DON'T THINK I NEED IT ANYMORE.
OH... OKAY...
DON'T TRY TO TELL ME YOU'RE GOING TO HAVE TROUBLE SELLING... DRUGS.
NO, IT'S JUST...
YOU WERE FUN.
OH, CHEER UP. WE CAN STILL FUCK EVERY NOW AND THEN.

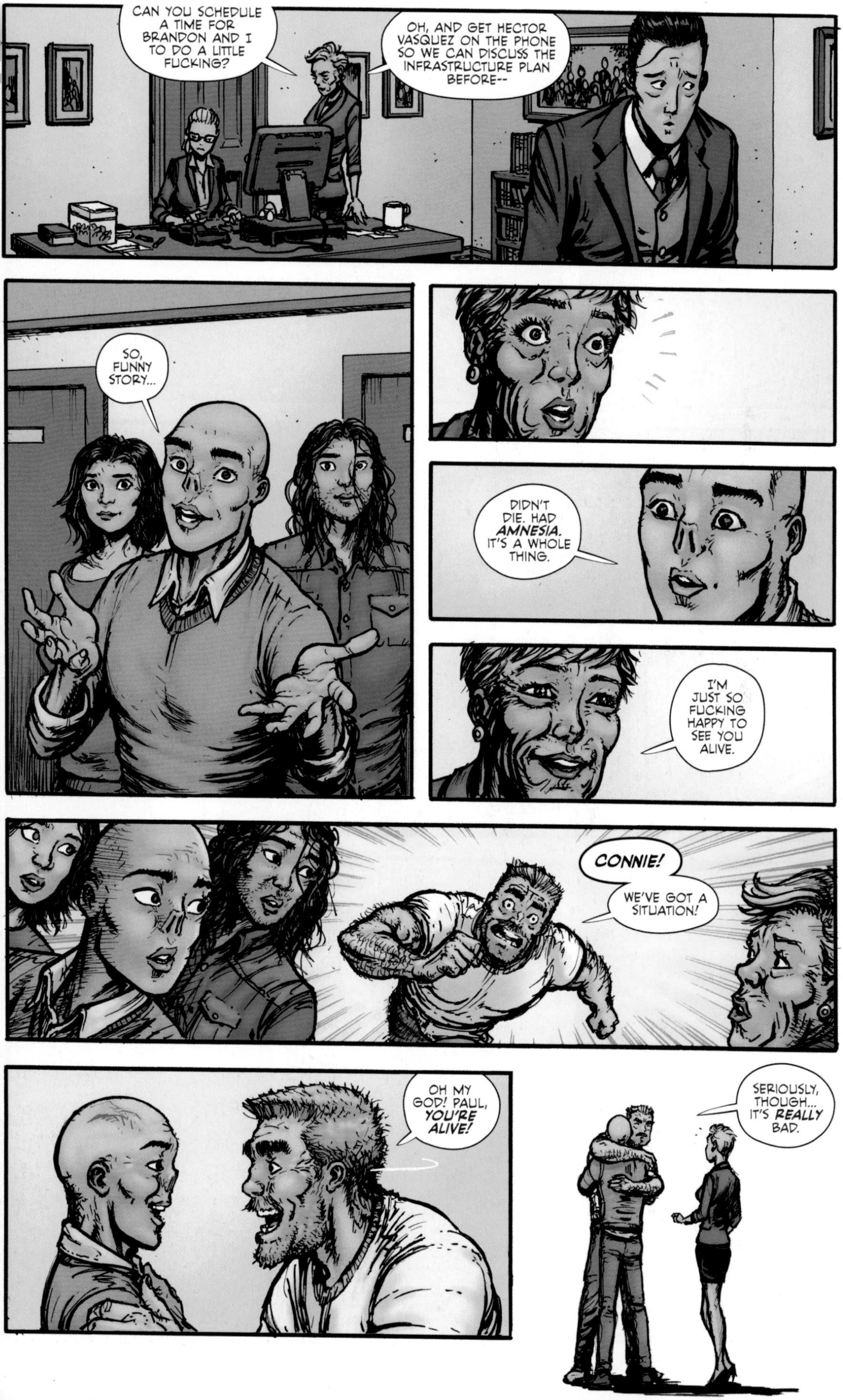
CAN YOU SCHEDULE A TIME FOR BRANDON AND I TO DO A LITTLE FUCKING?
OH, AND GET HECTOR VASQUEZ ON THE PHONE SO WE CAN DISCUSS THE INFRASTRUCTURE PLAN BEFORE--
SO, FUNNY STORY...
DIDN'T DIE. HAD AMNESIA. IT'S A WHOLE THING.
I'M JUST SO FUCKING HAPPY TO SEE YOU ALIVE.
CONNIE!
WE'VE GOT A SITUATION!
OH MY GOD! PAUL, YOU'RE ALIVE!
SERIOUSLY, THOUGH... IT'S REALLY BAD.

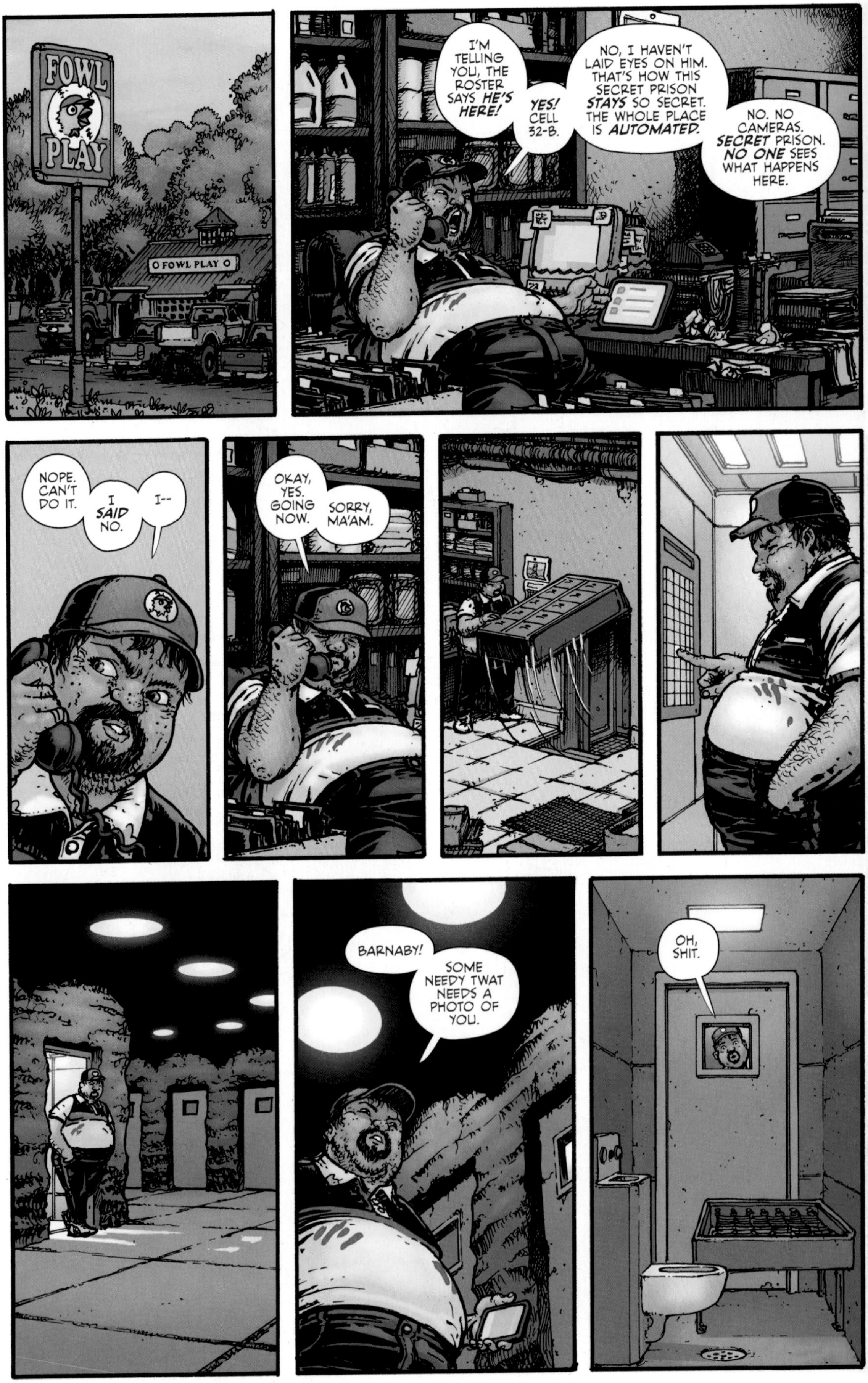
FOWL PLAY
FOWL PLAY
I'M TELLING YOU, THE ROSTER SAYS HE'S HERE!
YES! CELL 32-B.
NO, I HAVEN'T LAID EYES ON HIM. THAT'S HOW THIS SECRET PRISON STAYS SO SECRET. THE WHOLE PLACE IS AUTOMATED.
NO. NO CAMERAS. SECRET PRISON. NO ONE SEES WHAT HAPPENS HERE.
NOPE. CAN'T DO IT.
I SAID NO.
I--
OKAY, YES. GOING NOW.
SORRY, MA'AM.
BARNABY!
SOME NEEDY TWAT NEEDS A PHOTO OF YOU.
OH, SHIT.

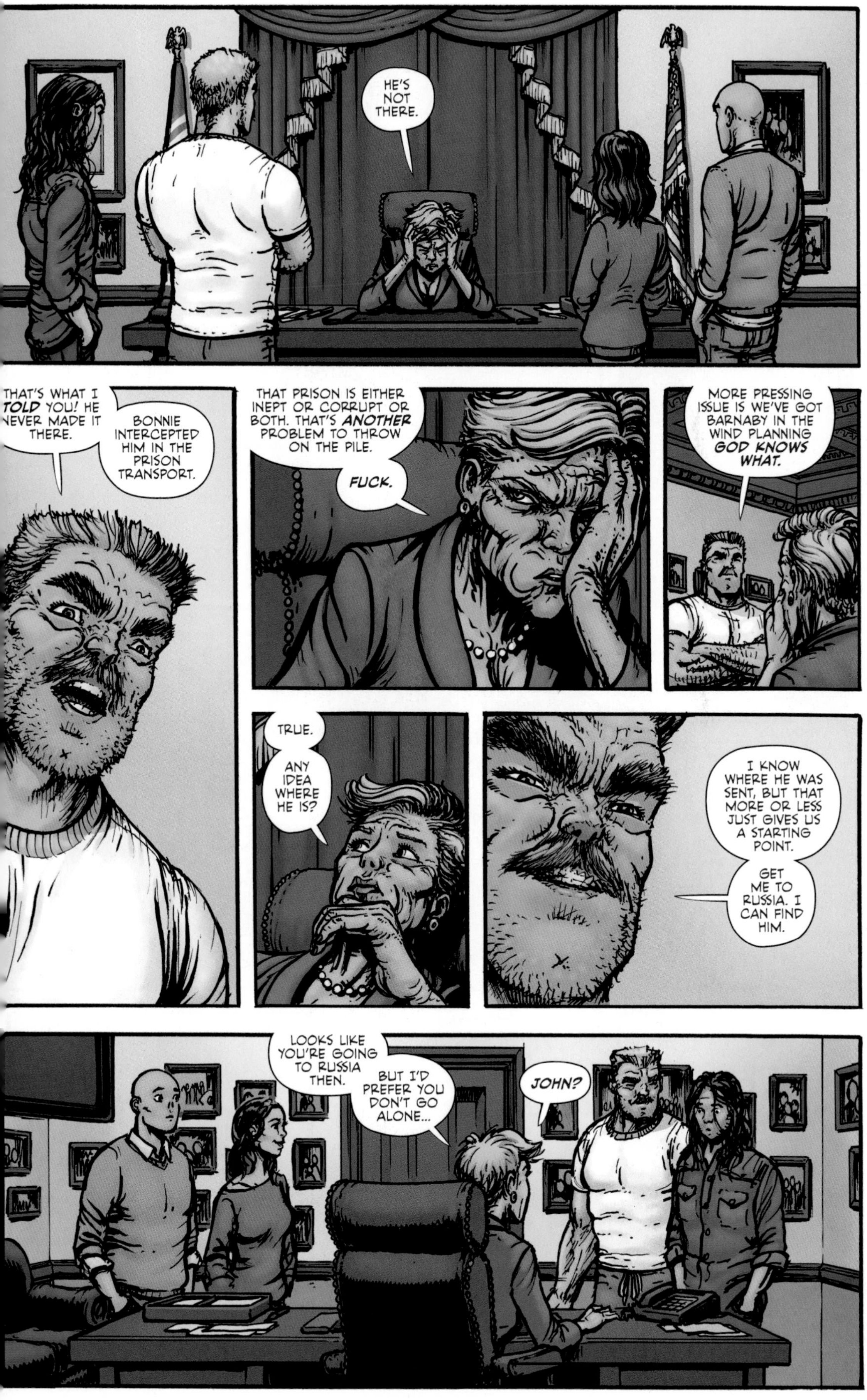
HE'S NOT THERE.
THAT'S WHAT I TOLD YOU! HE NEVER MADE IT THERE.
BONNIE INTERCEPTED HIM IN THE PRISON TRANSPORT.
THAT PRISON IS EITHER INEPT OR CORRUPT OR BOTH. THAT'S ANOTHER PROBLEM TO THROW ON THE PILE.
FUCK.
MORE PRESSING ISSUE IS WE'VE GOT BARNABY IN THE WIND PLANNING GOD KNOWS WHAT.
TRUE.
ANY IDEA WHERE HE IS?
I KNOW WHERE HE WAS SENT, BUT THAT MORE OR LESS JUST GIVES US A STARTING POINT.
GET ME TO RUSSIA. I CAN FIND HIM.
LOOKS LIKE YOU'RE GOING TO RUSSIA THEN.
BUT I'D PREFER YOU DON'T GO ALONE...
JOHN?

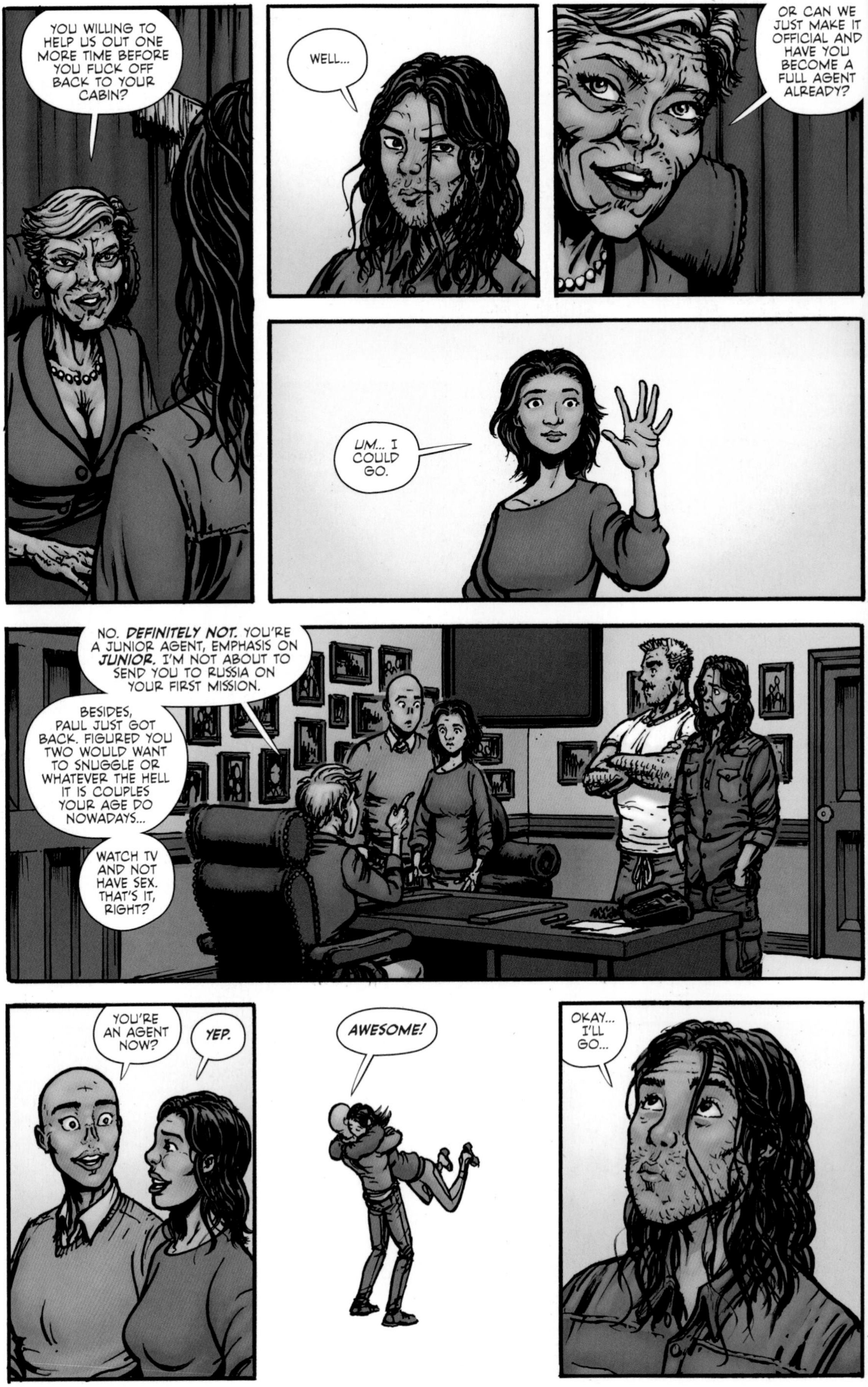
YOU WILLING TO HELP US OUT ONE MORE TIME BEFORE YOU FUCK OFF BACK TO YOUR CABIN?
WELL...
OR CAN WE JUST MAKE IT OFFICIAL AND HAVE YOU BECOME A FULL AGENT ALREADY?
UM... I COULD GO.
NO. ***DEFINITELY NOT.*** YOU'RE A JUNIOR AGENT, EMPHASIS ON ***JUNIOR.*** I'M NOT ABOUT TO SEND YOU TO RUSSIA ON YOUR FIRST MISSION.
BESIDES, PAUL JUST GOT BACK. FIGURED YOU TWO WOULD WANT TO SNUGGLE OR WHATEVER THE HELL IT IS COUPLES YOUR AGE DO NOWADAYS...
WATCH TV AND NOT HAVE SEX. THAT'S IT, RIGHT?
YOU'RE AN AGENT NOW?
YEP.
AWESOME!
OKAY... I'LL GO...

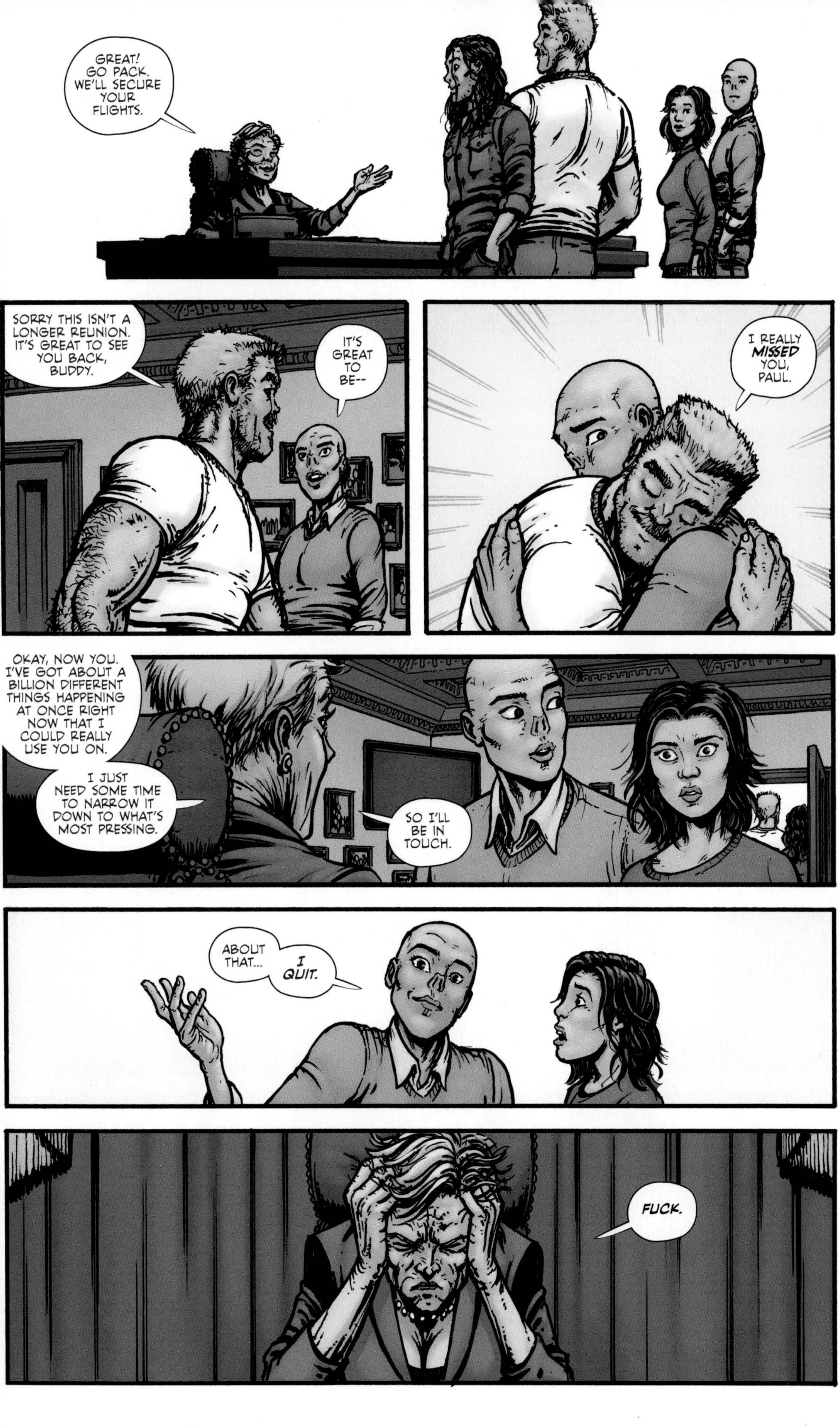
GREAT! GO PACK. WE'LL SECURE YOUR FLIGHTS.
SORRY THIS ISN'T A LONGER REUNION. IT'S GREAT TO SEE YOU BACK, BUDDY.
IT'S GREAT TO BE--
I REALLY MISSED YOU, PAUL.
OKAY, NOW YOU. I'VE GOT ABOUT A BILLION DIFFERENT THINGS HAPPENING AT ONCE RIGHT NOW THAT I COULD REALLY USE YOU ON.
I JUST NEED SOME TIME TO NARROW IT DOWN TO WHAT'S MOST PRESSING.
SO I'LL BE IN TOUCH.
ABOUT THAT...
I QUIT.
FUCK.

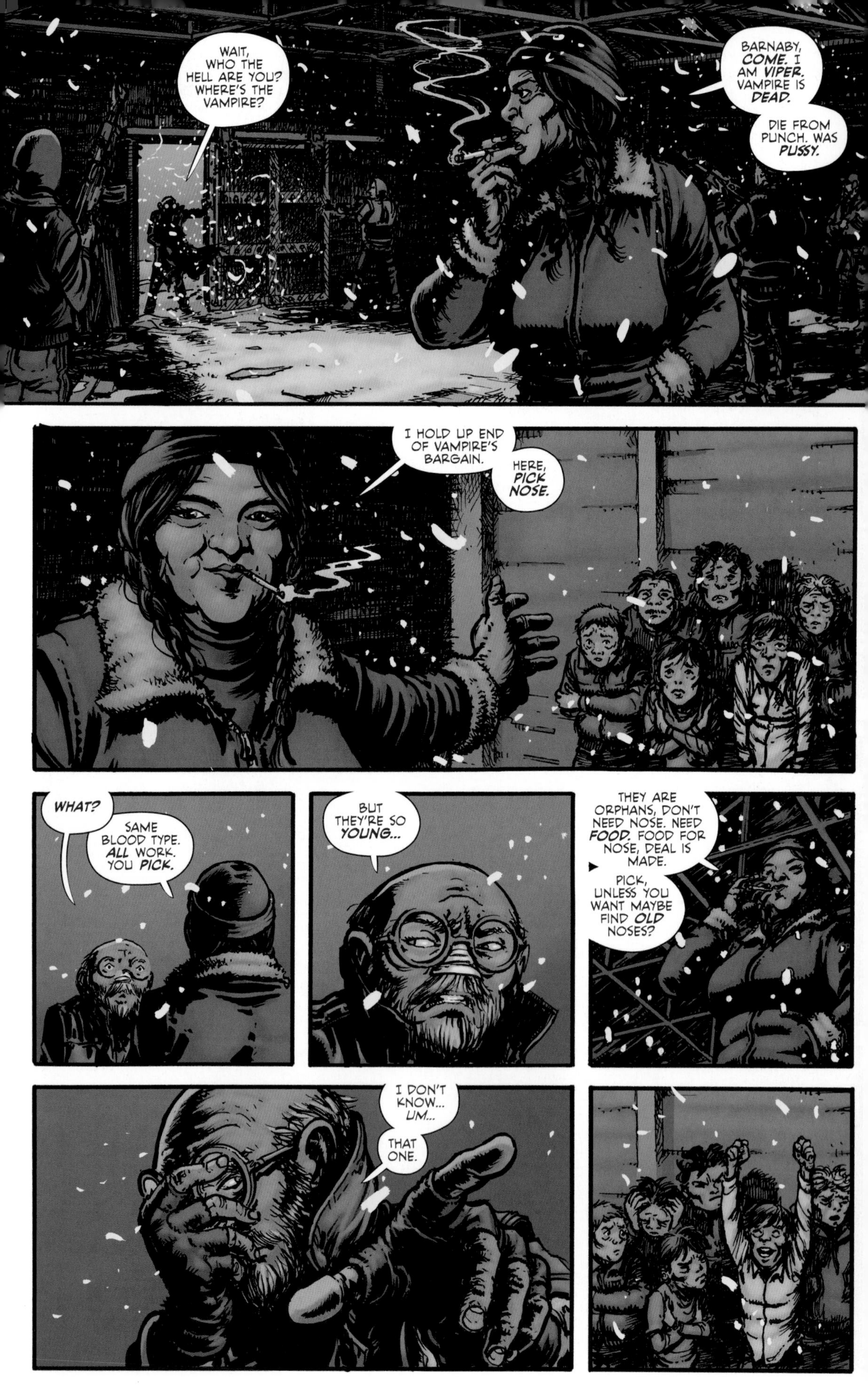
WAIT, WHO THE HELL ARE YOU? WHERE'S THE VAMPIRE?
BARNABY, COME. I AM VIPER. VAMPIRE IS DEAD.
DIE FROM PUNCH. WAS PUSSY.
I HOLD UP END OF VAMPIRE'S BARGAIN.
HERE, PICK NOSE.
WHAT?
SAME BLOOD TYPE. ALL WORK. YOU PICK.
BUT THEY'RE SO YOUNG...
THEY ARE ORPHANS, DON'T NEED NOSE. NEED FOOD. FOOD FOR NOSE, DEAL IS MADE.
PICK, UNLESS YOU WANT MAYBE FIND OLD NOSES?
I DON'T KNOW... UM...
THAT ONE.

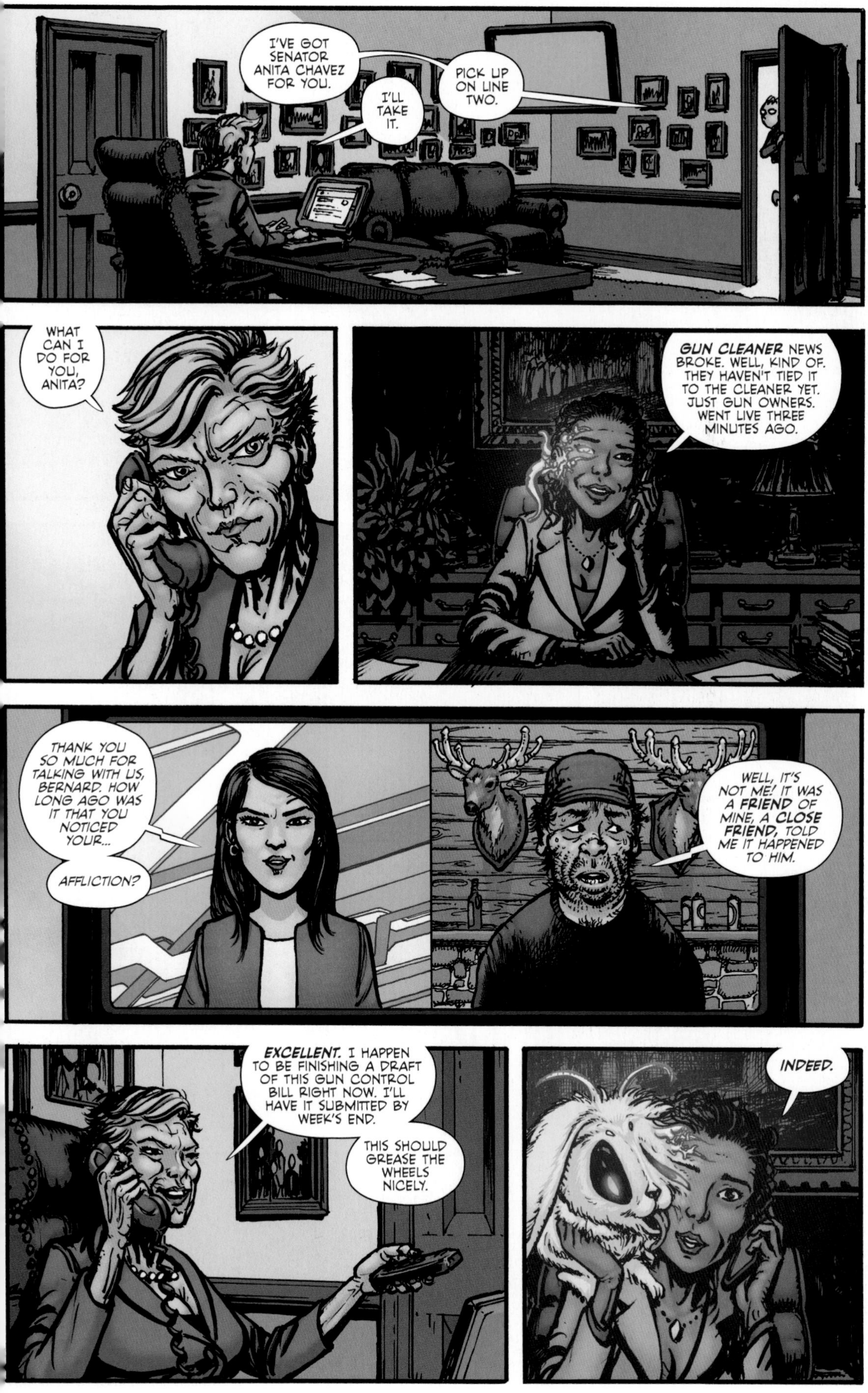
I'VE GOT SENATOR ANITA CHAVEZ FOR YOU.
PICK UP ON LINE TWO.
I'LL TAKE IT.
WHAT CAN I DO FOR YOU, ANITA?
GUN CLEANER NEWS BROKE. WELL, KIND OF. THEY HAVEN'T TIED IT TO THE CLEANER YET. JUST GUN OWNERS. WENT LIVE THREE MINUTES AGO.
THANK YOU SO MUCH FOR TALKING WITH US, BERNARD. HOW LONG AGO WAS IT THAT YOU NOTICED YOUR...
AFFLICTION?
WELL, IT'S NOT ME! IT WAS A FRIEND OF MINE, A CLOSE FRIEND, TOLD ME IT HAPPENED TO HIM.
EXCELLENT. I HAPPEN TO BE FINISHING A DRAFT OF THIS GUN CONTROL BILL RIGHT NOW. I'LL HAVE IT SUBMITTED BY WEEK'S END.
THIS SHOULD GREASE THE WHEELS NICELY.
INDEED.

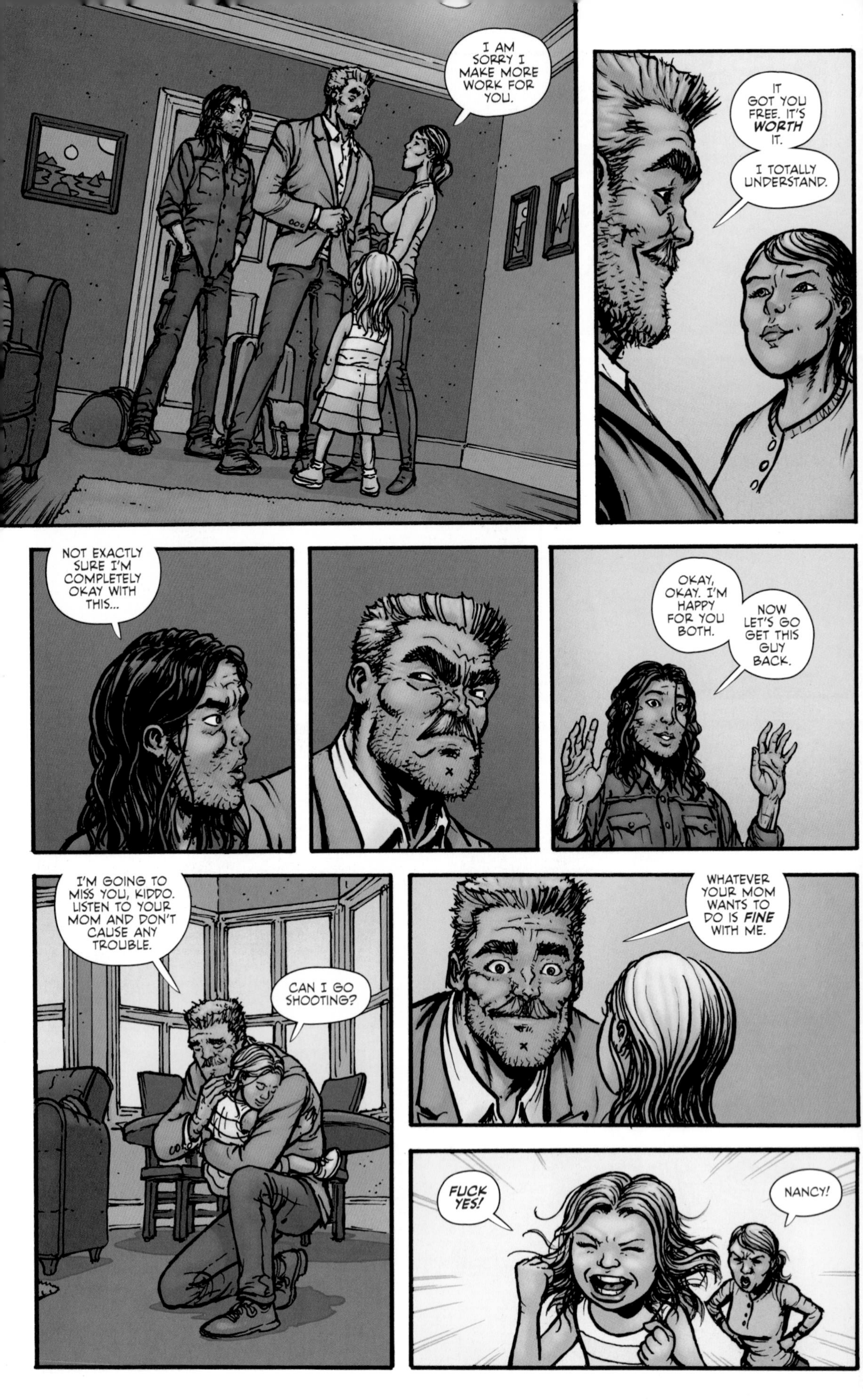
I AM SORRY I MAKE MORE WORK FOR YOU.
IT GOT YOU FREE. IT'S WORTH IT.
I TOTALLY UNDERSTAND.
NOT EXACTLY SURE I'M COMPLETELY OKAY WITH THIS...
OKAY, OKAY. I'M HAPPY FOR YOU BOTH.
NOW LET'S GO GET THIS GUY BACK.
I'M GOING TO MISS YOU, KIDDO. LISTEN TO YOUR MOM AND DON'T CAUSE ANY TROUBLE.
CAN I GO SHOOTING?
WHATEVER YOUR MOM WANTS TO DO IS FINE WITH ME.
FUCK YES!
NANCY!

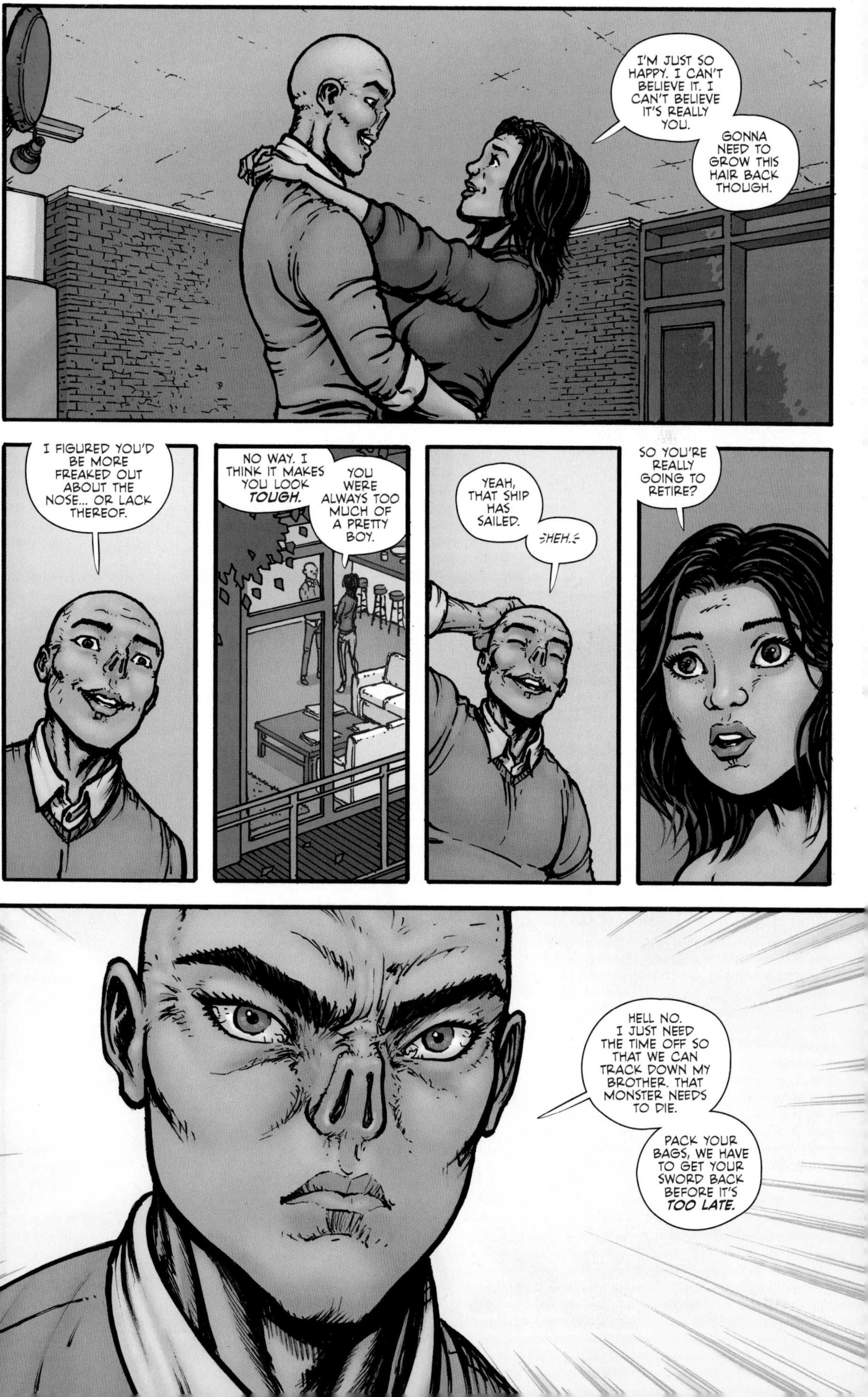
I'M JUST SO HAPPY. I CAN'T BELIEVE IT. I CAN'T BELIEVE IT'S REALLY YOU.
GONNA NEED TO GROW THIS HAIR BACK THOUGH.
I FIGURED YOU'D BE MORE FREAKED OUT ABOUT THE NOSE... OR LACK THEREOF.
NO WAY. I THINK IT MAKES YOU LOOK *TOUGH.*
YOU WERE ALWAYS TOO MUCH OF A PRETTY BOY.
YEAH, THAT SHIP HAS SAILED.
HEH.
SO YOU'RE REALLY GOING TO RETIRE?
HELL NO. I JUST NEED THE TIME OFF SO THAT WE CAN TRACK DOWN MY BROTHER. THAT MONSTER NEEDS TO DIE.
PACK YOUR BAGS, WE HAVE TO GET YOUR SWORD BACK BEFORE IT'S ***TOO LATE.***

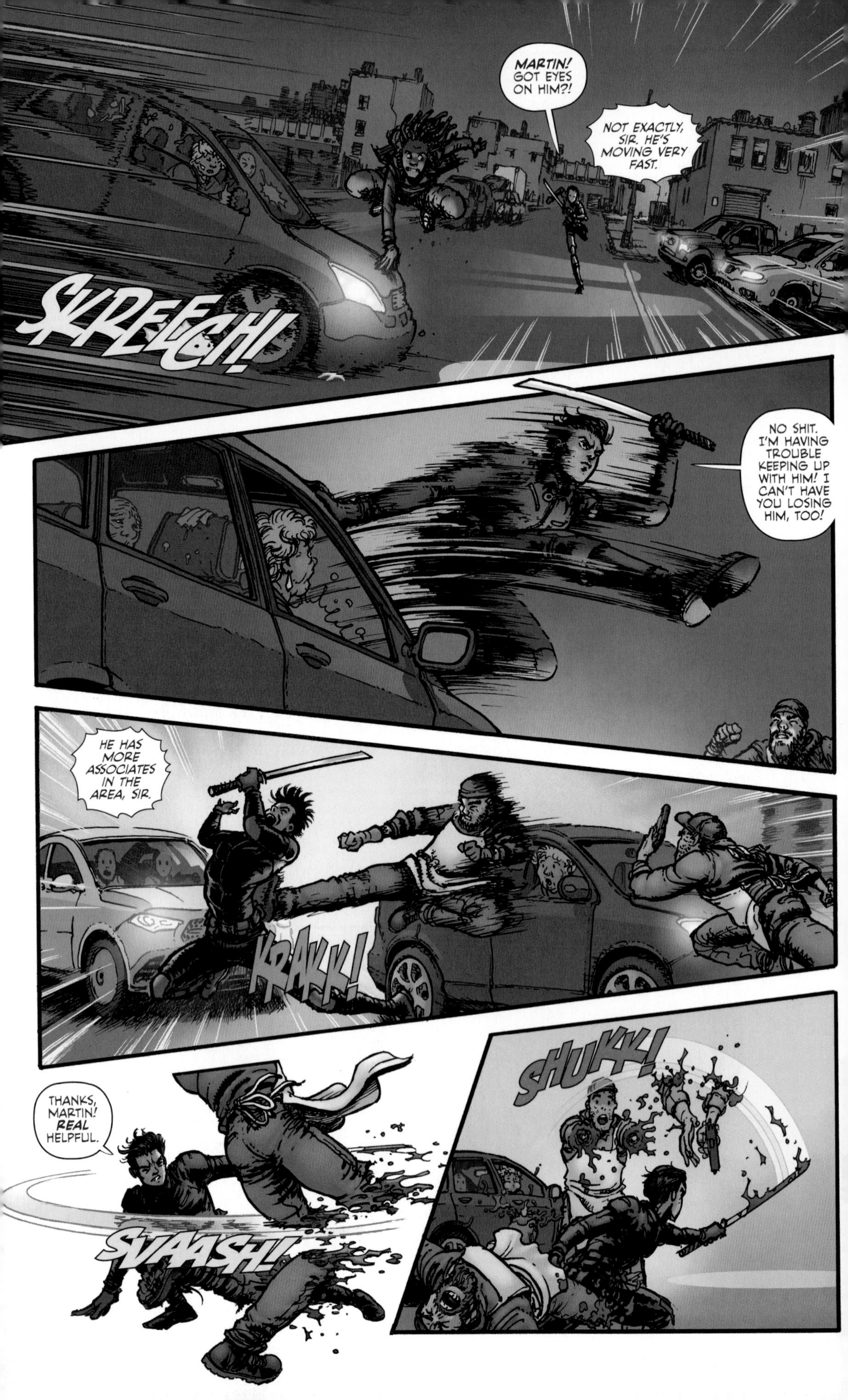
MARTIN! GOT EYES ON HIM?!
NOT EXACTLY, SIR. HE'S MOVING VERY FAST.
SKREECH!
NO SHIT. I'M HAVING TROUBLE KEEPING UP WITH HIM! I CAN'T HAVE YOU LOSING HIM, TOO!
HE HAS MORE ASSOCIATES IN THE AREA, SIR.
KRAKK!
THANKS, MARTIN! REAL HELPFUL.
SVAASH!
SHUKK!

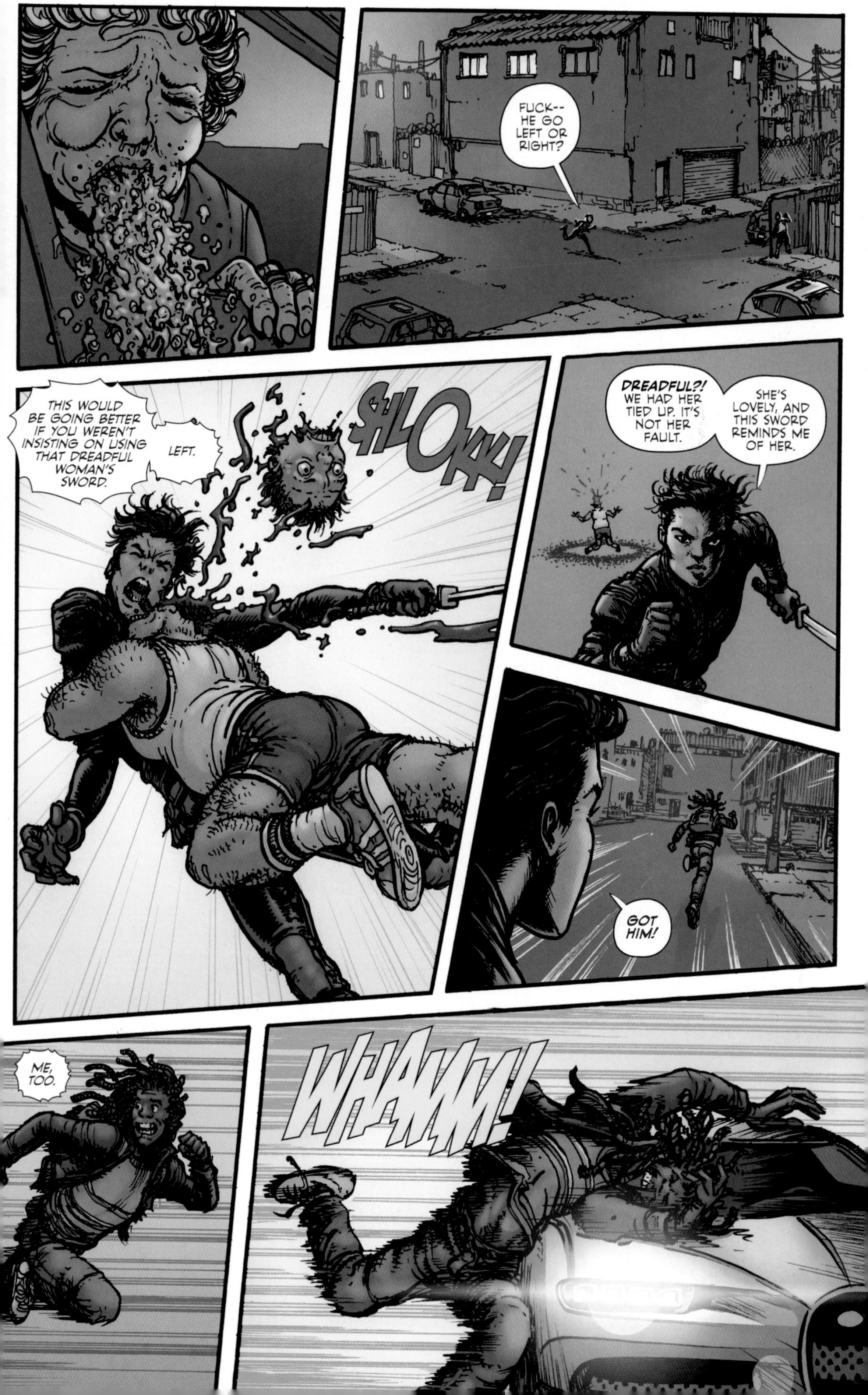
FUCK-- HE GO LEFT OR RIGHT?
THIS WOULD BE GOING BETTER IF YOU WEREN'T INSISTING ON USING THAT DREADFUL WOMAN'S SWORD.
LEFT.
SHLOKK!
DREADFUL?! WE HAD HER TIED UP. IT'S NOT HER FAULT.
SHE'S LOVELY, AND THIS SWORD REMINDS ME OF HER.
GOT HIM!
ME, TOO.
WHAMM!

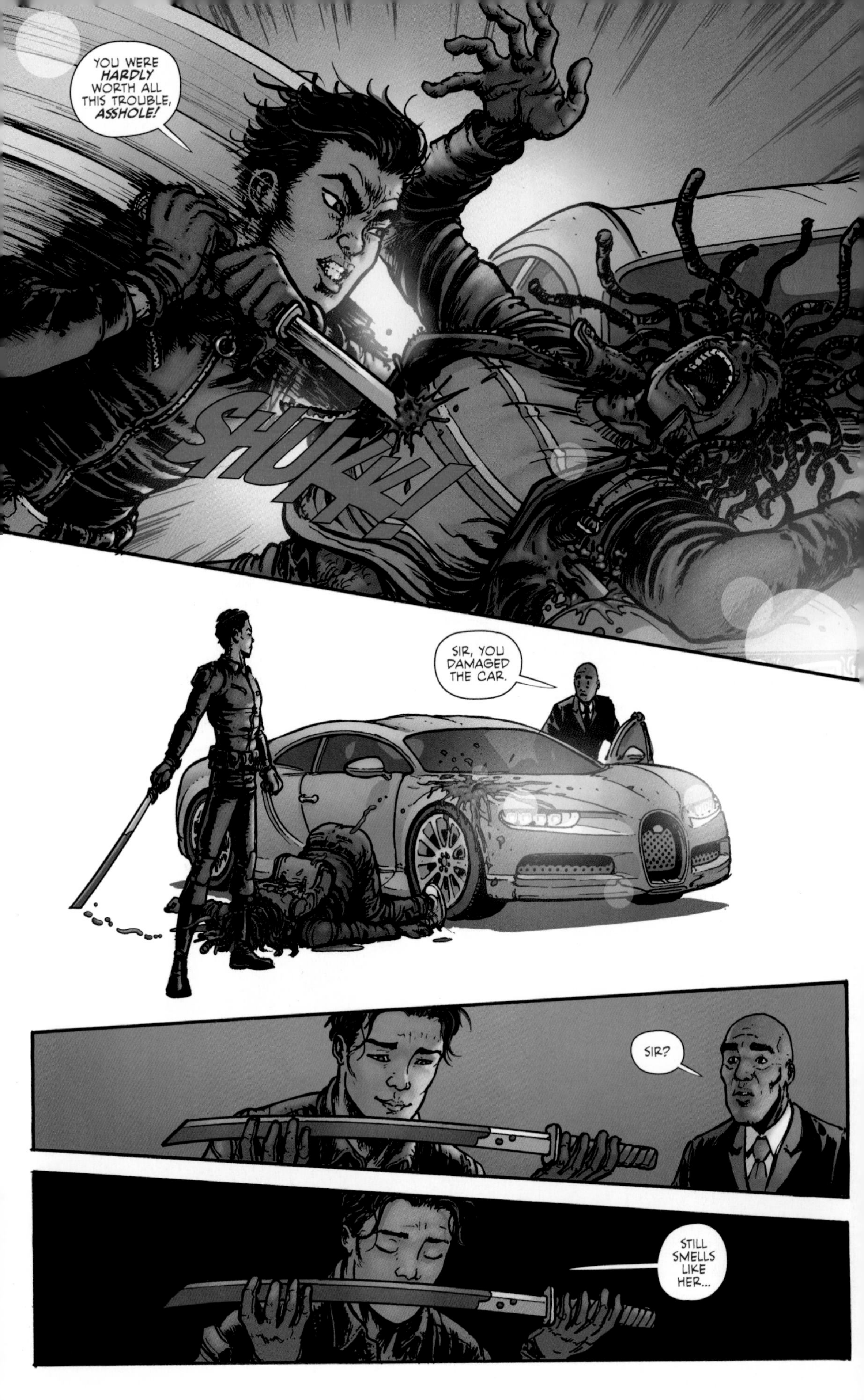
YOU WERE HARDLY WORTH ALL THIS TROUBLE, ASSHOLE!
SHUNK!
SIR, YOU DAMAGED THE CAR.
SIR?
STILL SMELLS LIKE HER...

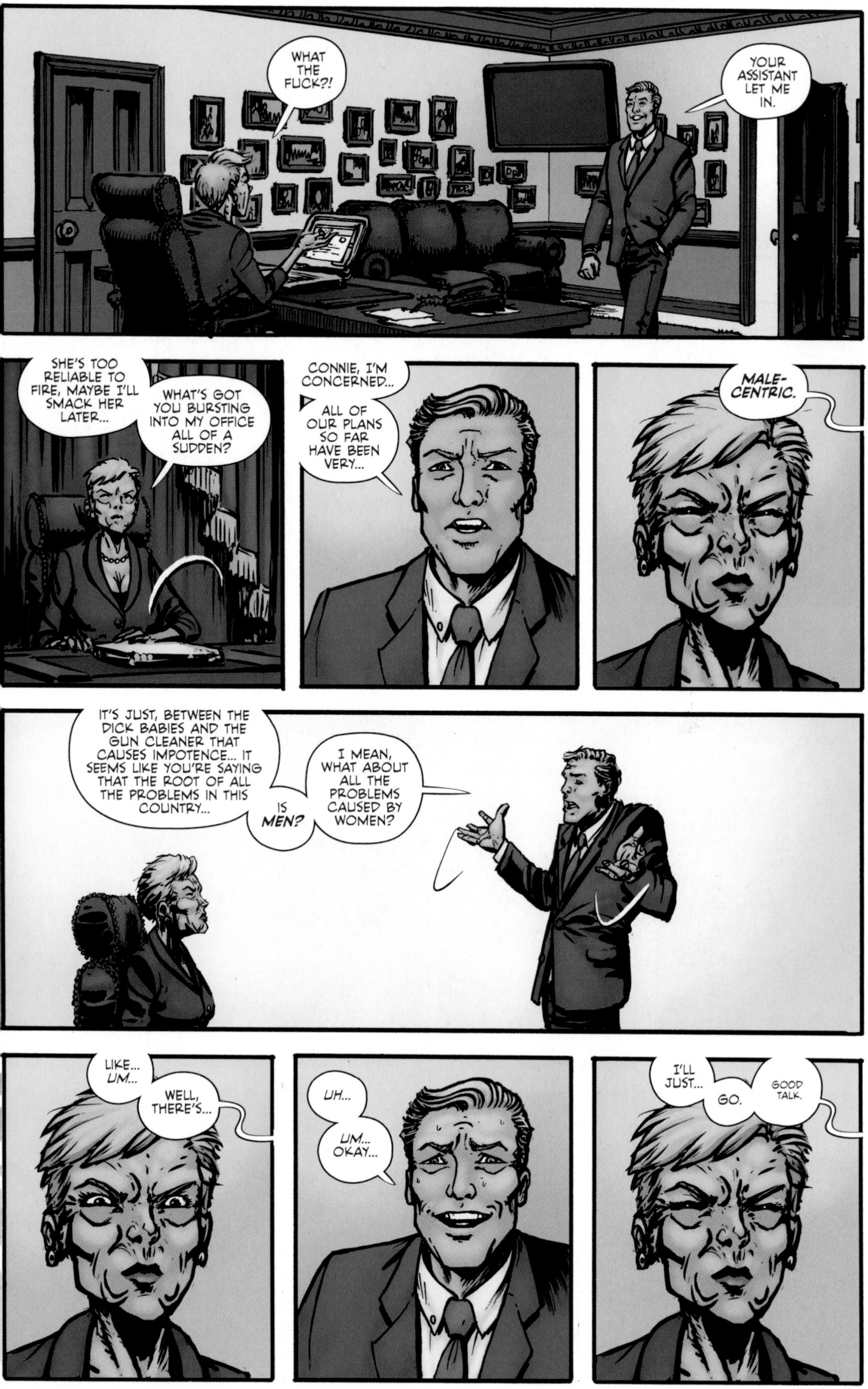
WHAT THE FUCK?!
YOUR ASSISTANT LET ME IN.
SHE'S TOO RELIABLE TO FIRE, MAYBE I'LL SMACK HER LATER...
WHAT'S GOT YOU BURSTING INTO MY OFFICE ALL OF A SUDDEN?
CONNIE, I'M CONCERNED...
ALL OF OUR PLANS SO FAR HAVE BEEN VERY...
MALE-CENTRIC.
IT'S JUST, BETWEEN THE DICK BABIES AND THE GUN CLEANER THAT CAUSES IMPOTENCE... IT SEEMS LIKE YOU'RE SAYING THAT THE ROOT OF ALL THE PROBLEMS IN THIS COUNTRY...
IS MEN?
I MEAN, WHAT ABOUT ALL THE PROBLEMS CAUSED BY WOMEN?
LIKE... UM...
WELL, THERE'S...
UH...
UM... OKAY...
I'LL JUST...
GO.
GOOD TALK.

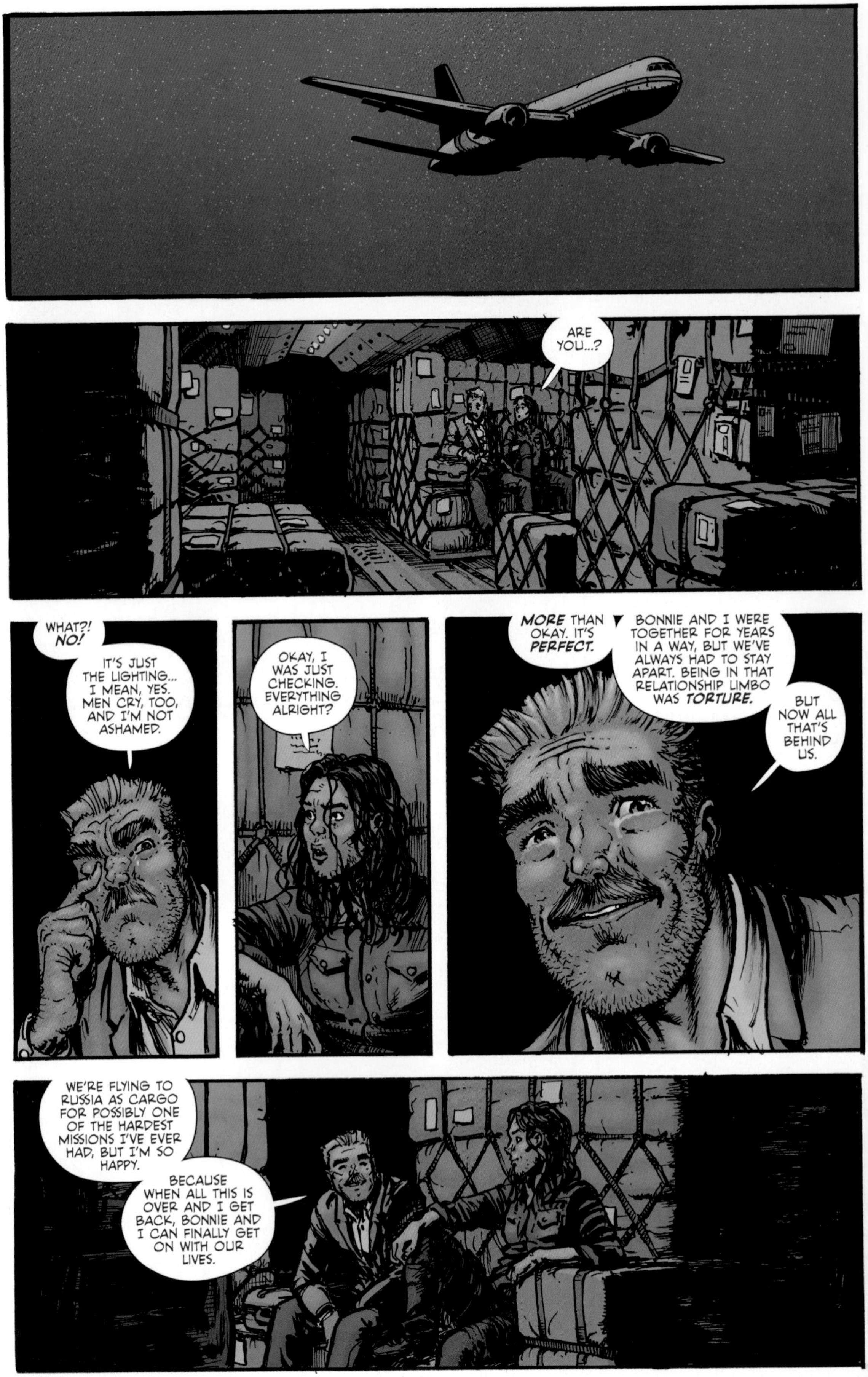
ARE YOU...?
WHAT?! NO!
IT'S JUST THE LIGHTING... I MEAN, YES. MEN CRY, TOO, AND I'M NOT ASHAMED.
OKAY, I WAS JUST CHECKING. EVERYTHING ALRIGHT?
MORE THAN OKAY. IT'S PERFECT.
BONNIE AND I WERE TOGETHER FOR YEARS IN A WAY, BUT WE'VE ALWAYS HAD TO STAY APART. BEING IN THAT RELATIONSHIP LIMBO WAS TORTURE.
BUT NOW ALL THAT'S BEHIND US.
WE'RE FLYING TO RUSSIA AS CARGO FOR POSSIBLY ONE OF THE HARDEST MISSIONS I'VE EVER HAD, BUT I'M SO HAPPY.
BECAUSE WHEN ALL THIS IS OVER AND I GET BACK, BONNIE AND I CAN FINALLY GET ON WITH OUR LIVES.

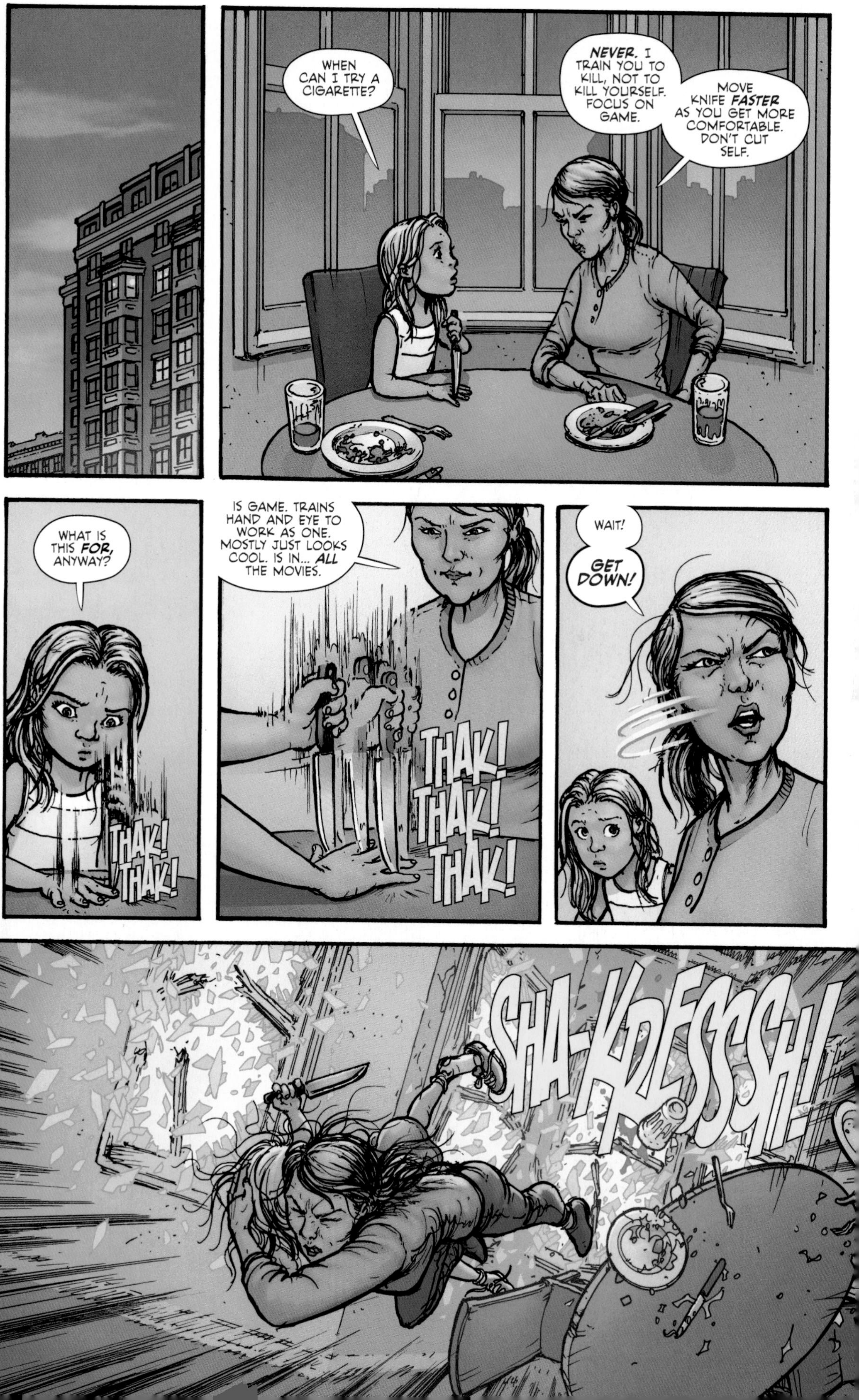

WHEN CAN I TRY A CIGARETTE?
NEVER. I TRAIN YOU TO KILL, NOT TO KILL YOURSELF. FOCUS ON GAME.
MOVE KNIFE FASTER AS YOU GET MORE COMFORTABLE. DON'T CUT SELF.
WHAT IS THIS FOR, ANYWAY?
THAK! THAK!
IS GAME. TRAINS HAND AND EYE TO WORK AS ONE. MOSTLY JUST LOOKS COOL. IS IN... ALL THE MOVIES.
THAK! THAK! THAK!
WAIT!
GET DOWN!
SHA-KRESSSH!

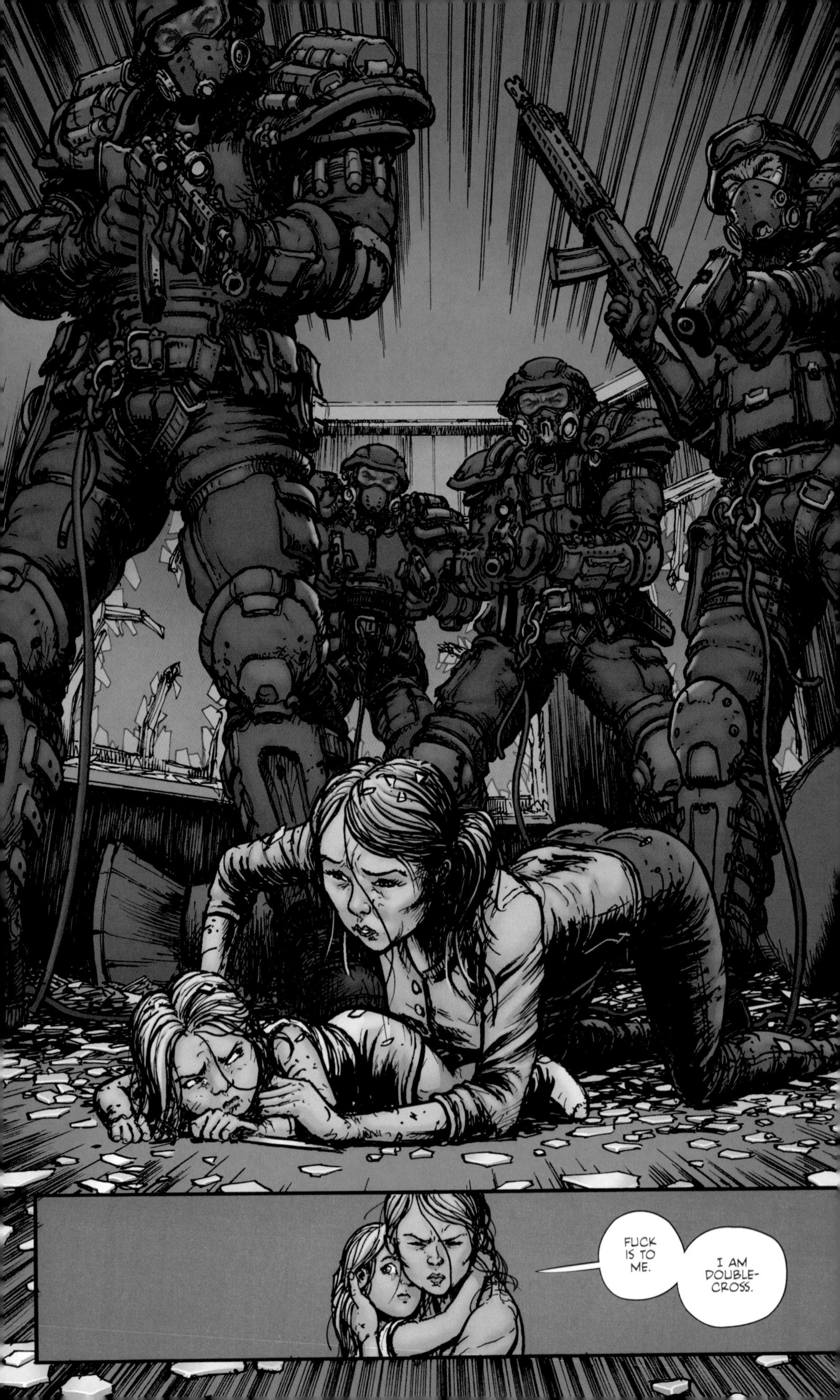
FUCK IS TO ME.
I AM DOUBLE-CROSS.

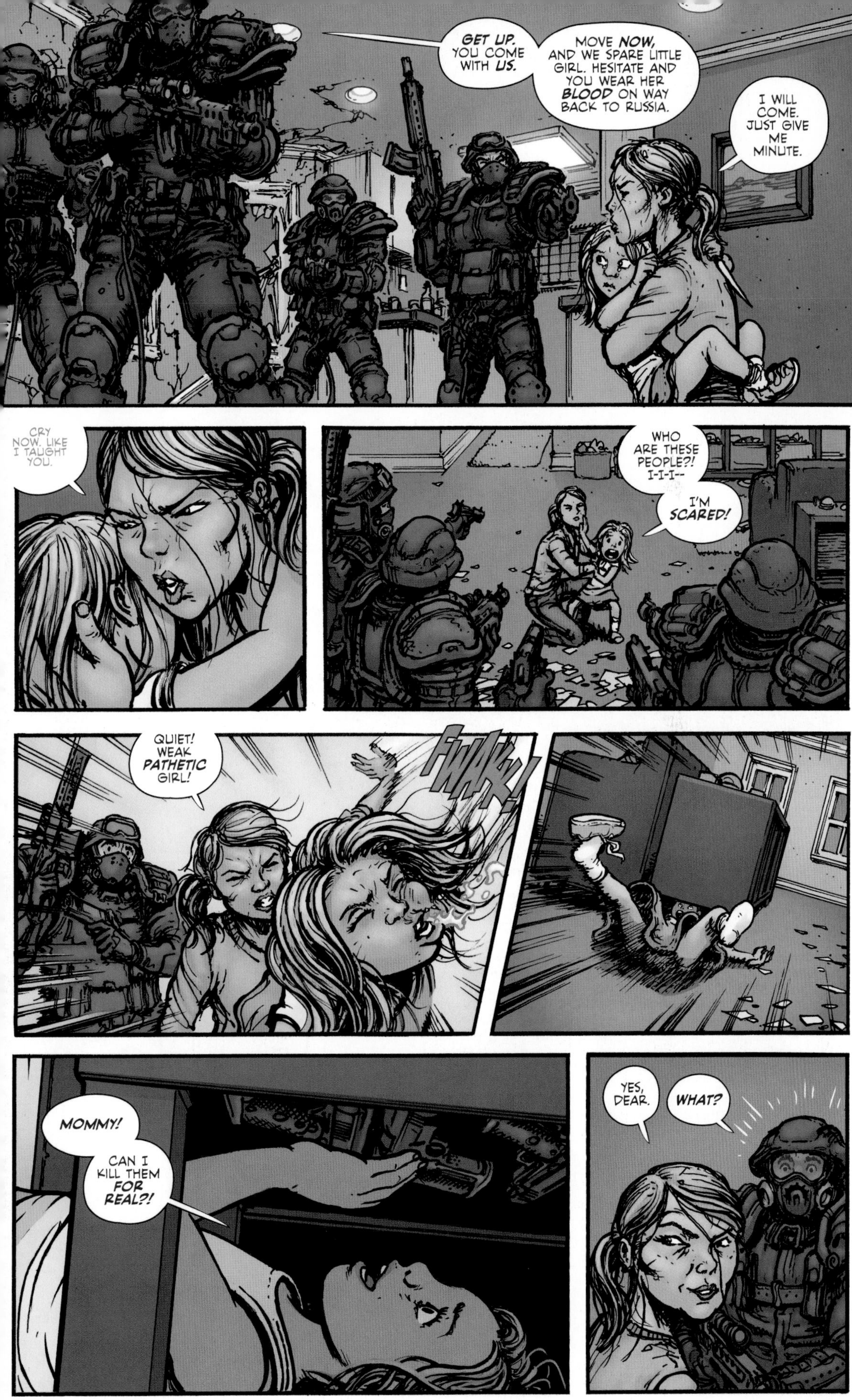
GET UP. YOU COME WITH US.
MOVE NOW, AND WE SPARE LITTLE GIRL. HESITATE AND YOU WEAR HER BLOOD ON WAY BACK TO RUSSIA.
I WILL COME. JUST GIVE ME MINUTE.
CRY NOW. LIKE I TAUGHT YOU.
WHO ARE THESE PEOPLE?! I-I-I--
I'M SCARED!
QUIET! WEAK PATHETIC GIRL!
FWAK!
MOMMY!
CAN I KILL THEM FOR REAL?!
YES, DEAR.
WHAT?

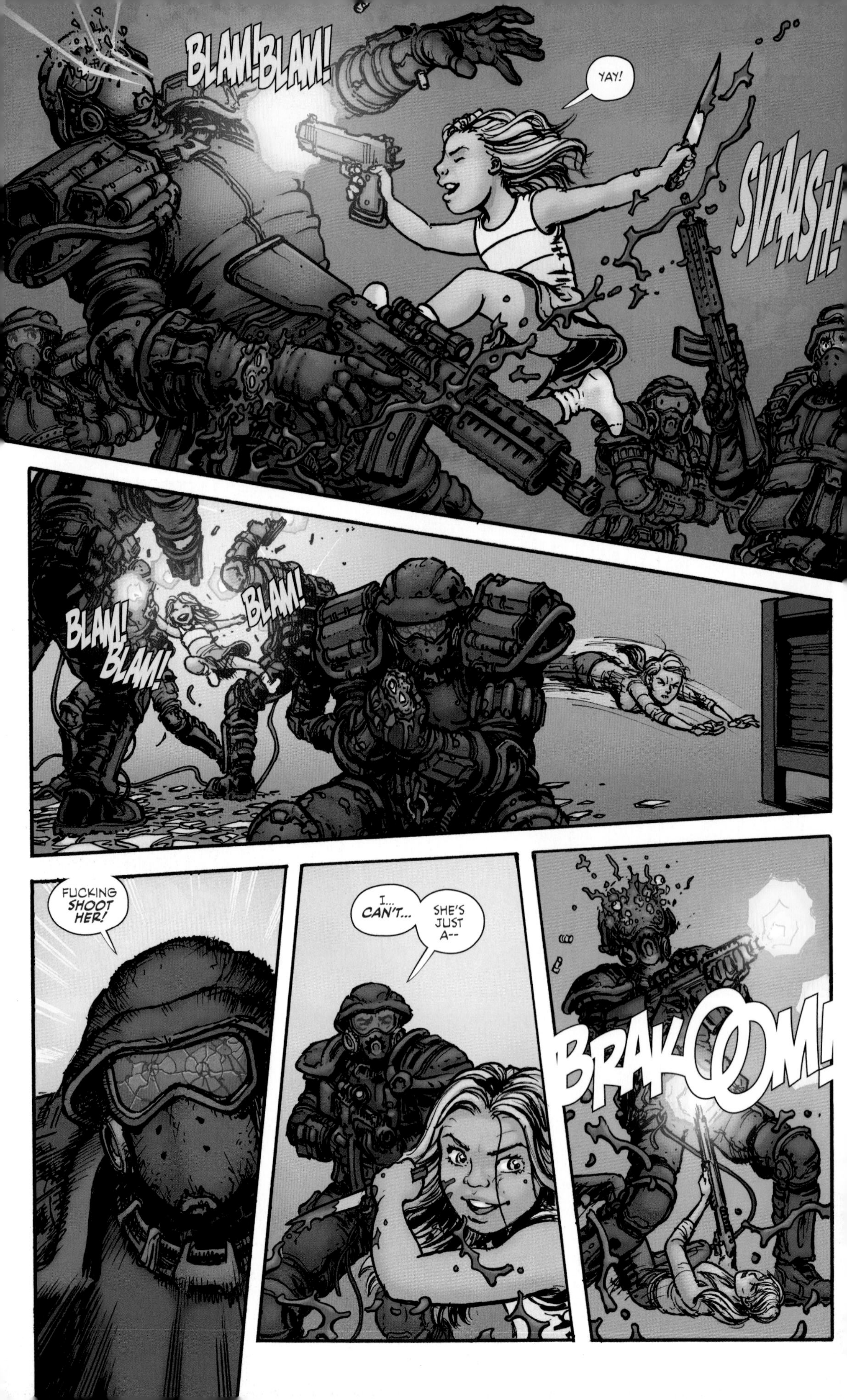

BLAM! BLAM!
YAY!
SVAASH!
BLAM!
BLAM!
BLAM!
FUCKING SHOOT HER!
I... CAN'T...
SHE'S JUST A--
BRAKOOM!

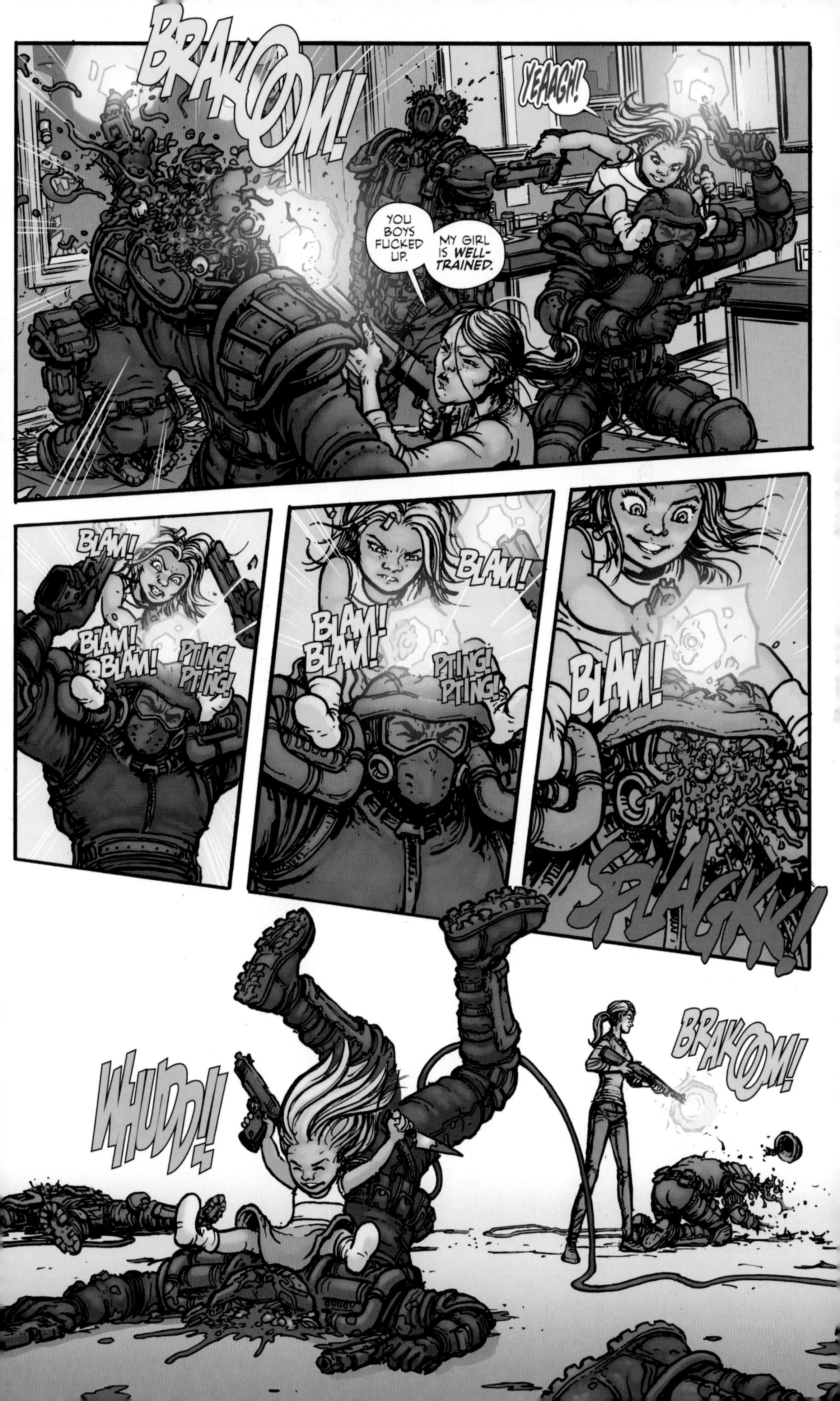
BRAKOOOM!
YEAAGH!
YOU BOYS FUCKED UP.
MY GIRL IS WELL-TRAINED.
BLAM!
BLAM! BLAM!
PTING! PTING!
BLAM!
BLAM! BLAM!
PTING! PTING!
BLAM!
SPLAGKK!
WHUDD!!
BRAKOOM!

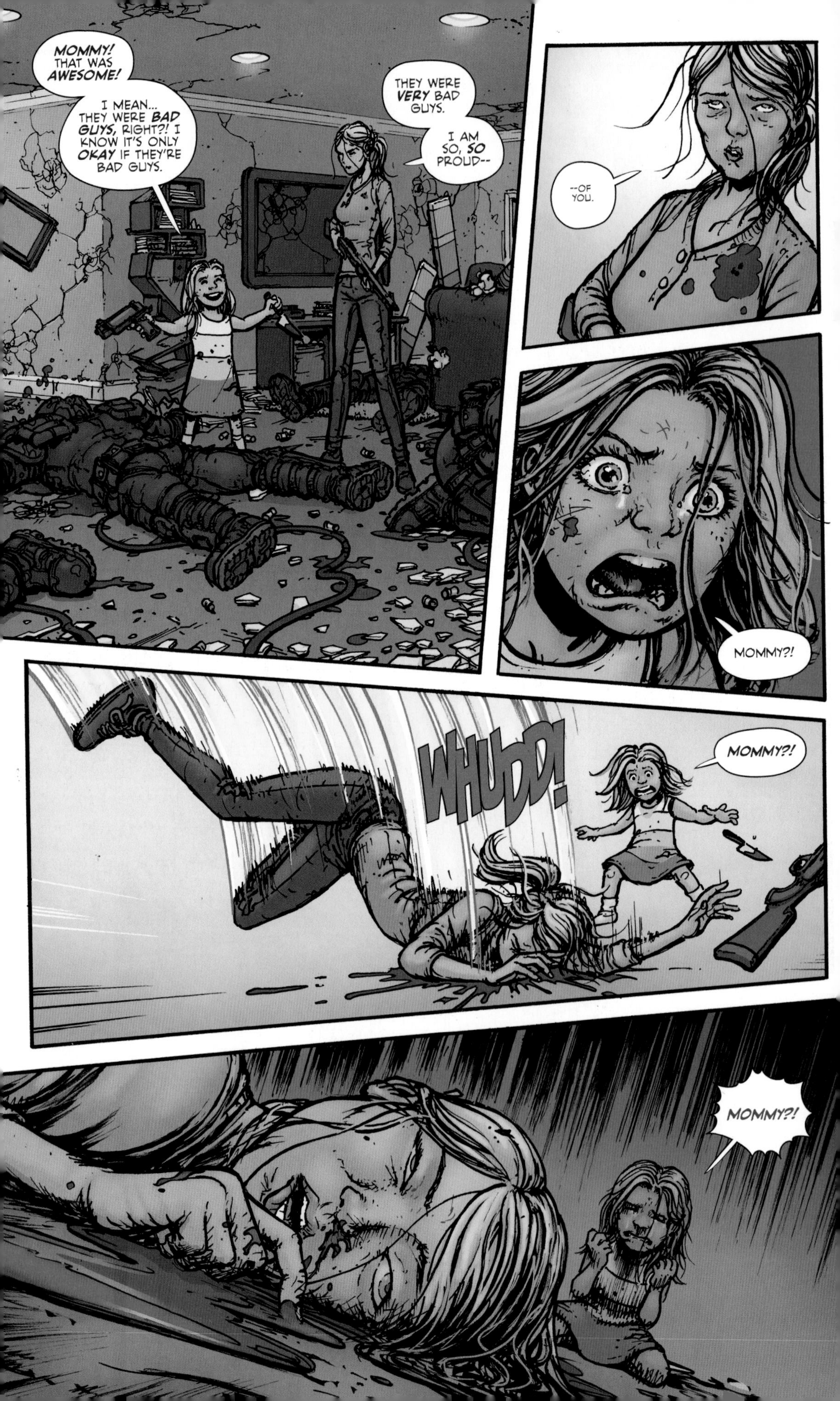

MOMMY! THAT WAS AWESOME!
I MEAN... THEY WERE BAD GUYS, RIGHT?! I KNOW IT'S ONLY OKAY IF THEY'RE BAD GUYS.
THEY WERE VERY BAD GUYS.
I AM SO, SO PROUD--
--OF YOU.
MOMMY?!
WHUDD!
MOMMY?!
MOMMY?!

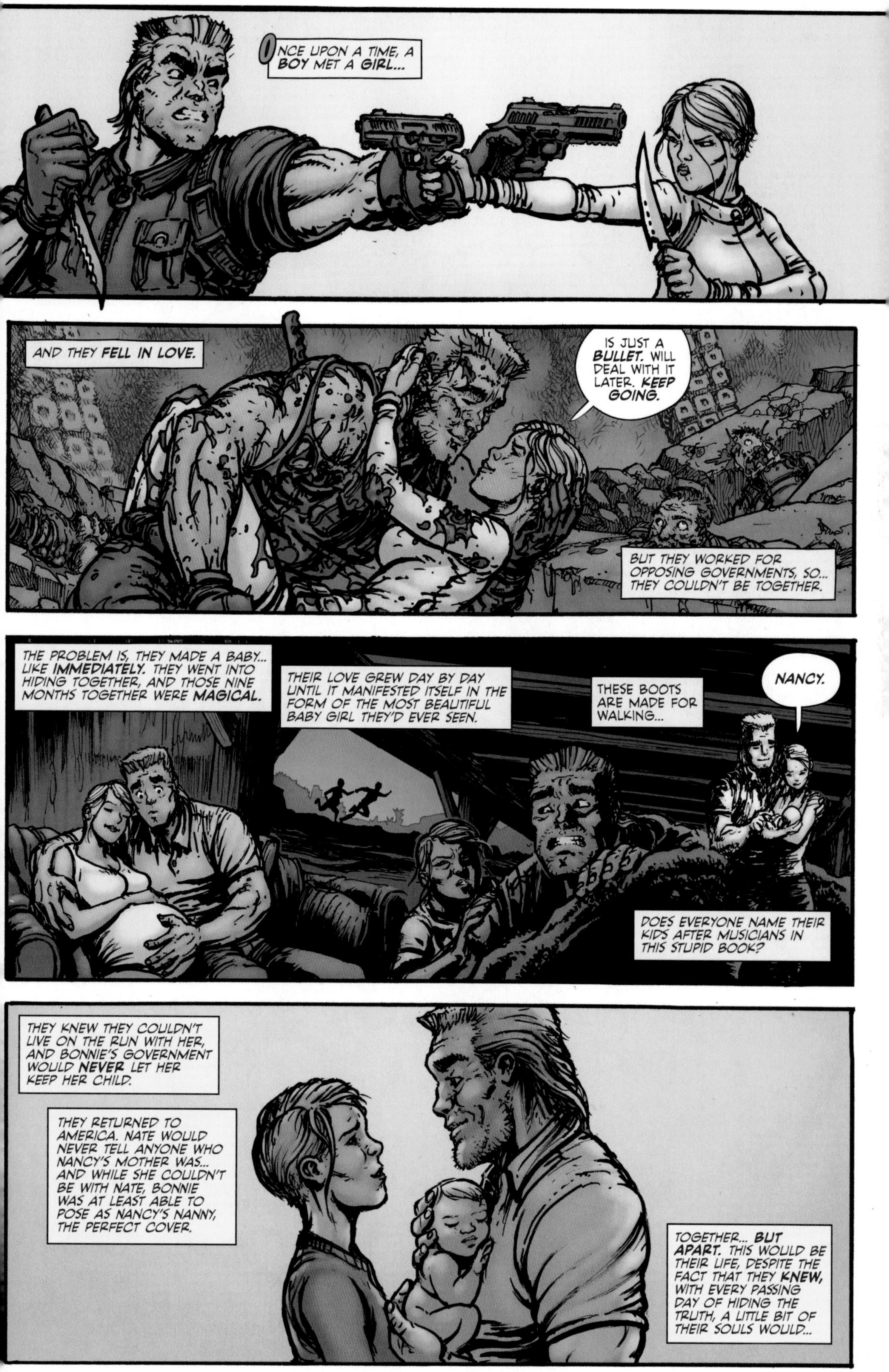
ONCE UPON A TIME, A BOY MET A GIRL...
AND THEY FELL IN LOVE.
IS JUST A BULLET. WILL DEAL WITH IT LATER. KEEP GOING.
BUT THEY WORKED FOR OPPOSING GOVERNMENTS, SO... THEY COULDN'T BE TOGETHER.
THE PROBLEM IS, THEY MADE A BABY... LIKE IMMEDIATELY. THEY WENT INTO HIDING TOGETHER, AND THOSE NINE MONTHS TOGETHER WERE MAGICAL.
THEIR LOVE GREW DAY BY DAY UNTIL IT MANIFESTED ITSELF IN THE FORM OF THE MOST BEAUTIFUL BABY GIRL THEY'D EVER SEEN.
THESE BOOTS ARE MADE FOR WALKING...
NANCY.
DOES EVERYONE NAME THEIR KIDS AFTER MUSICIANS IN THIS STUPID BOOK?
THEY KNEW THEY COULDN'T LIVE ON THE RUN WITH HER, AND BONNIE'S GOVERNMENT WOULD NEVER LET HER KEEP HER CHILD.
THEY RETURNED TO AMERICA. NATE WOULD NEVER TELL ANYONE WHO NANCY'S MOTHER WAS... AND WHILE SHE COULDN'T BE WITH NATE, BONNIE WAS AT LEAST ABLE TO POSE AS NANCY'S NANNY, THE PERFECT COVER.
TOGETHER... BUT APART. THIS WOULD BE THEIR LIFE, DESPITE THE FACT THAT THEY KNEW, WITH EVERY PASSING DAY OF HIDING THE TRUTH, A LITTLE BIT OF THEIR SOULS WOULD...

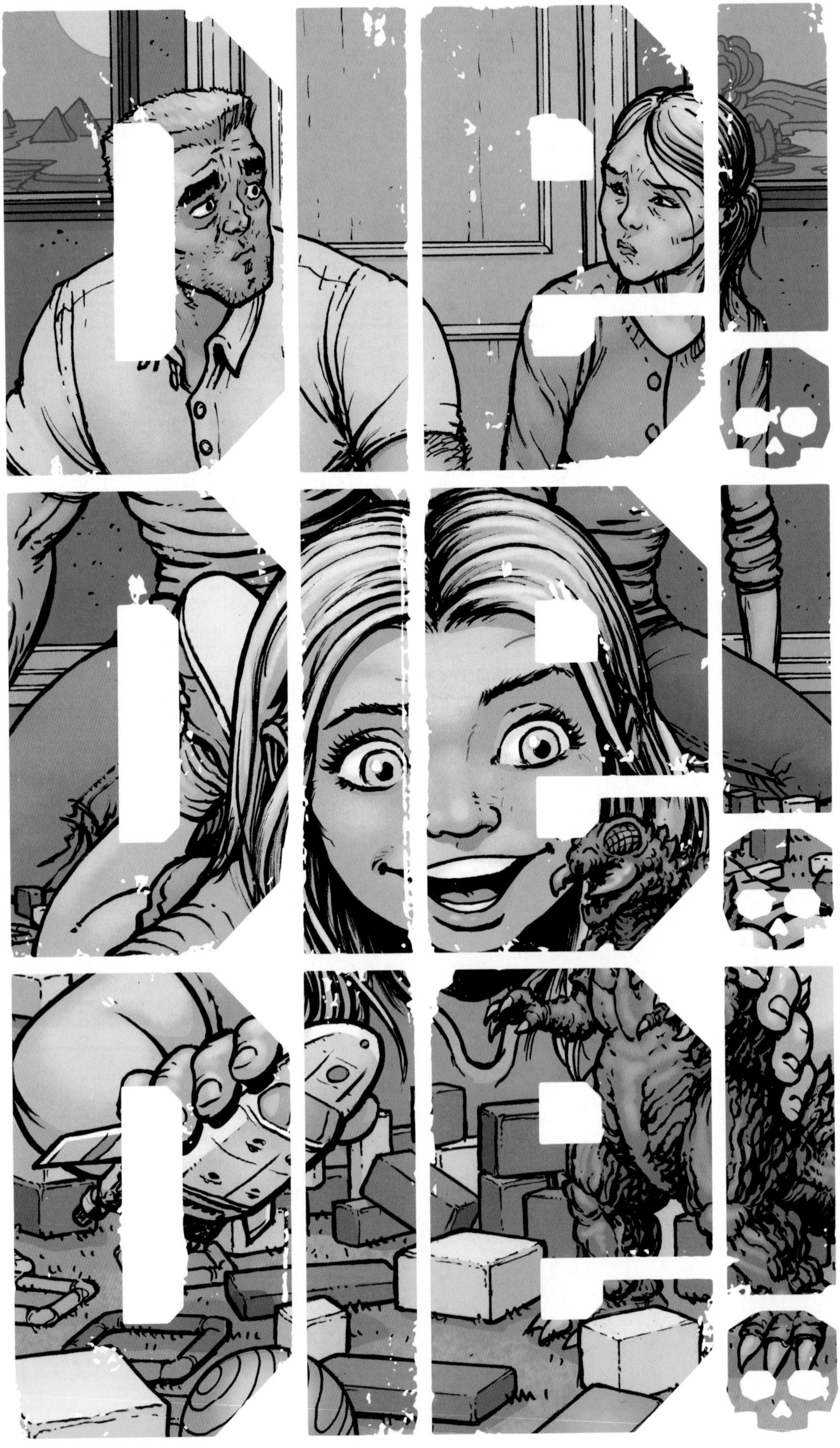
DIE!
DIE!
DIE!

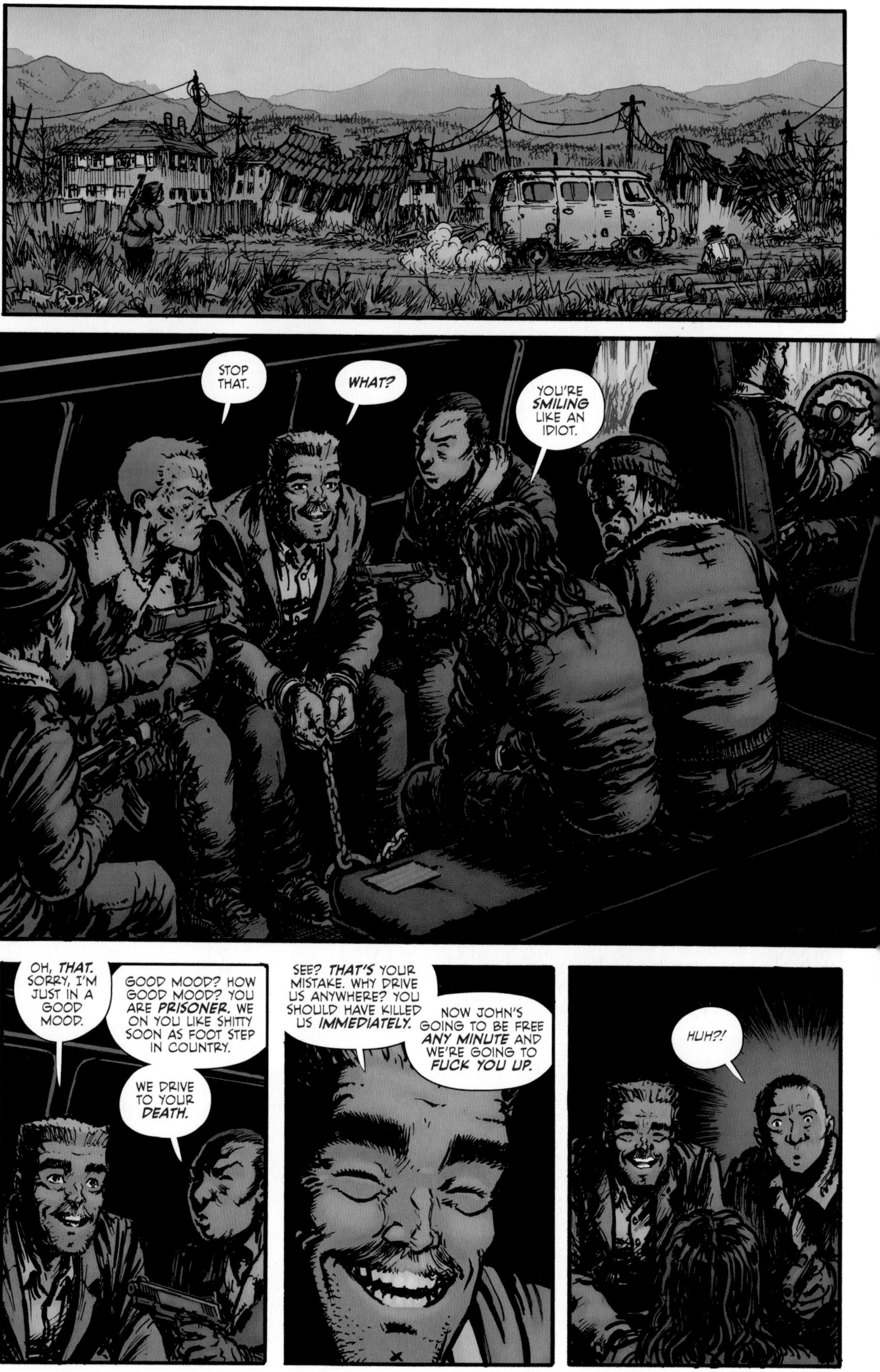
STOP THAT.
WHAT?
YOU'RE SMILING LIKE AN IDIOT.
OH, THAT. SORRY, I'M JUST IN A GOOD MOOD.
GOOD MOOD? HOW GOOD MOOD? YOU ARE PRISONER. WE ON YOU LIKE SHITTY SOON AS FOOT STEP IN COUNTRY.
WE DRIVE TO YOUR DEATH.
SEE? THAT'S YOUR MISTAKE. WHY DRIVE US ANYWHERE? YOU SHOULD HAVE KILLED US IMMEDIATELY.
NOW JOHN'S GOING TO BE FREE ANY MINUTE AND WE'RE GOING TO FUCK YOU UP.
HUH?!

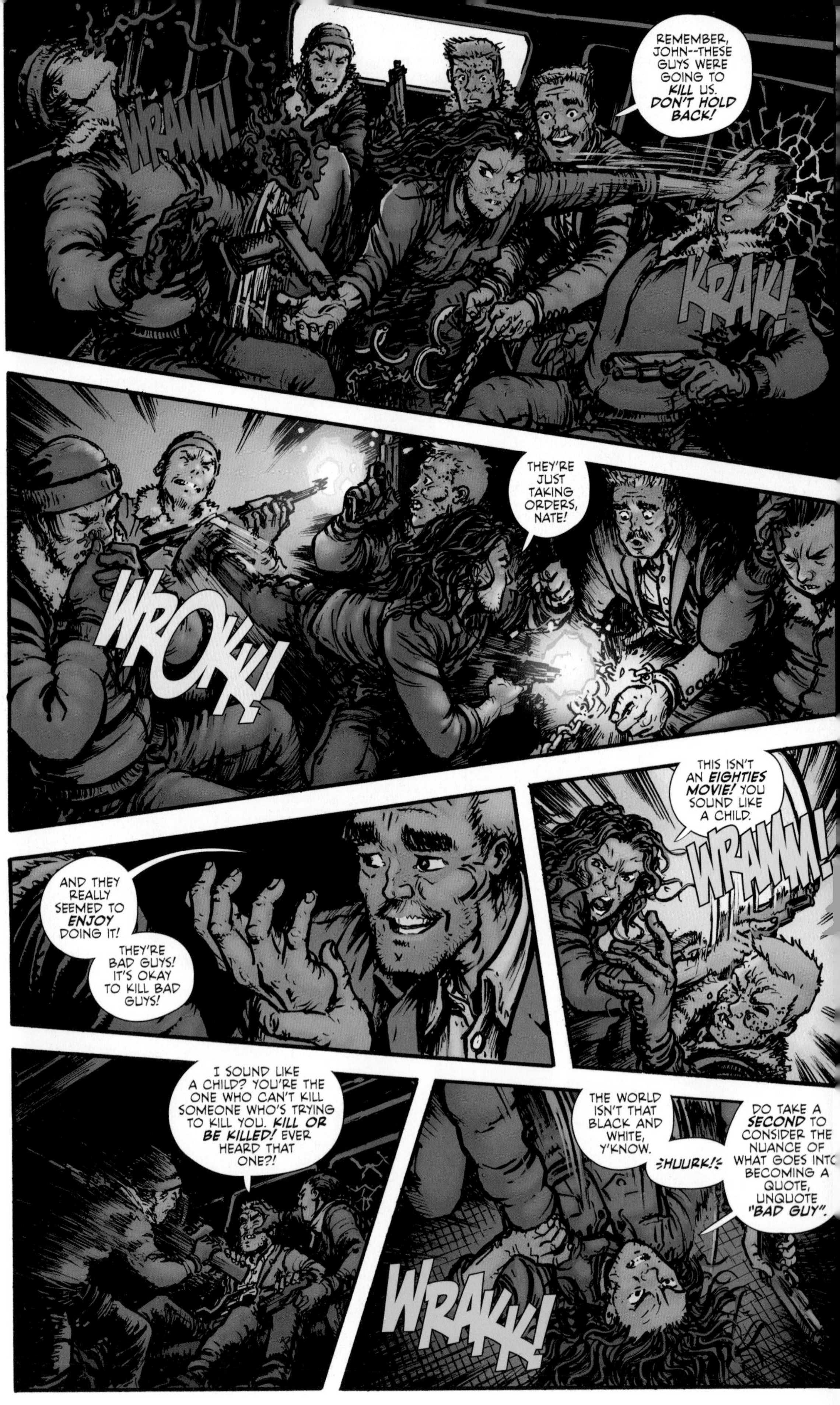
WRAMM!
REMEMBER, JOHN--THESE GUYS WERE GOING TO KILL US. DON'T HOLD BACK!
KRAK!
THEY'RE JUST TAKING ORDERS, NATE!
WROKK!
AND THEY REALLY SEEMED TO ENJOY DOING IT!
THEY'RE BAD GUYS! IT'S OKAY TO KILL BAD GUYS!
THIS ISN'T AN EIGHTIES MOVIE! YOU SOUND LIKE A CHILD.
WRAMM!
I SOUND LIKE A CHILD? YOU'RE THE ONE WHO CAN'T KILL SOMEONE WHO'S TRYING TO KILL YOU. KILL OR BE KILLED! EVER HEARD THAT ONE?!
WRAKK!
THE WORLD ISN'T THAT BLACK AND WHITE, Y'KNOW.
HUURK!
DO TAKE A SECOND TO CONSIDER THE NUANCE OF WHAT GOES INTO BECOMING A QUOTE, UNQUOTE "BAD GUY".

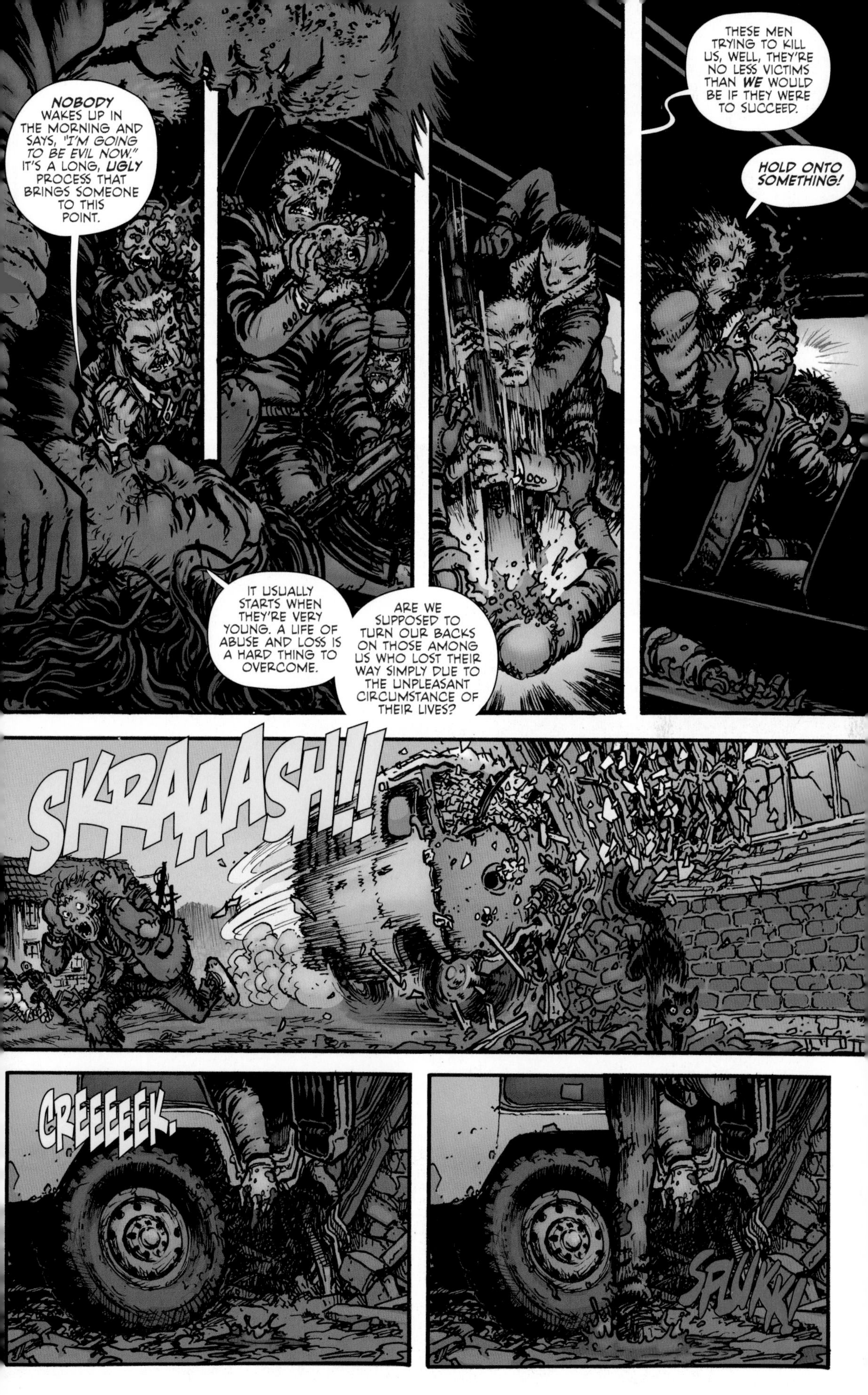
NOBODY WAKES UP IN THE MORNING AND SAYS, "I'M GOING TO BE EVIL NOW." IT'S A LONG, UGLY PROCESS THAT BRINGS SOMEONE TO THIS POINT.
IT USUALLY STARTS WHEN THEY'RE VERY YOUNG. A LIFE OF ABUSE AND LOSS IS A HARD THING TO OVERCOME.
ARE WE SUPPOSED TO TURN OUR BACKS ON THOSE AMONG US WHO LOST THEIR WAY SIMPLY DUE TO THE UNPLEASANT CIRCUMSTANCE OF THEIR LIVES?
THESE MEN TRYING TO KILL US, WELL, THEY'RE NO LESS VICTIMS THAN WE WOULD BE IF THEY WERE TO SUCCEED.
HOLD ONTO SOMETHING!
SKRAAASH!!
CREEEEEK.
SPLUKK!

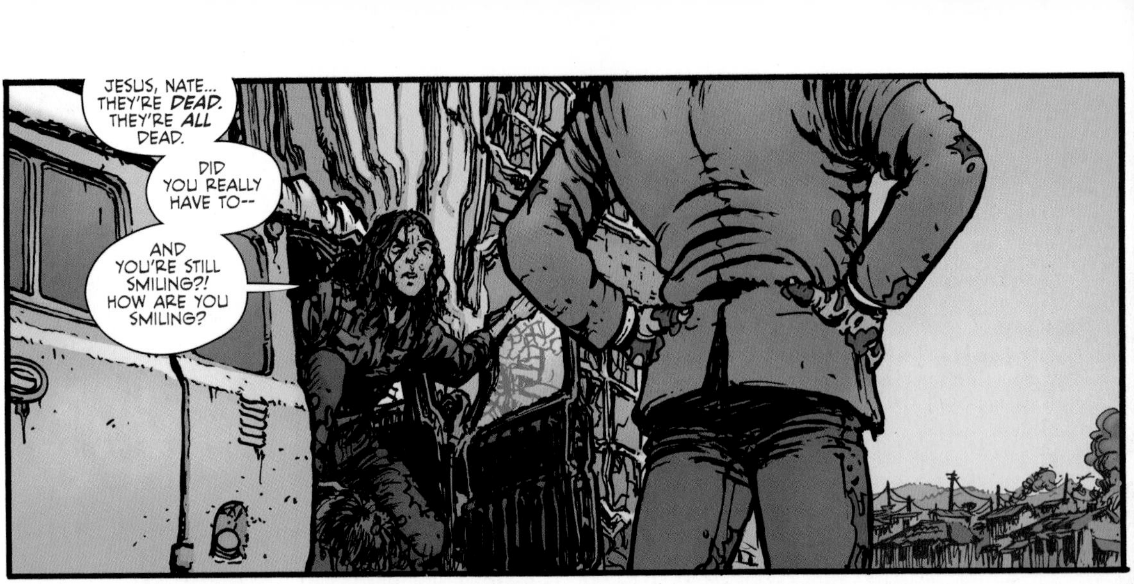
JESUS, NATE... THEY'RE DEAD. THEY'RE ALL DEAD.
DID YOU REALLY HAVE TO--
AND YOU'RE STILL SMILING?! HOW ARE YOU SMILING?

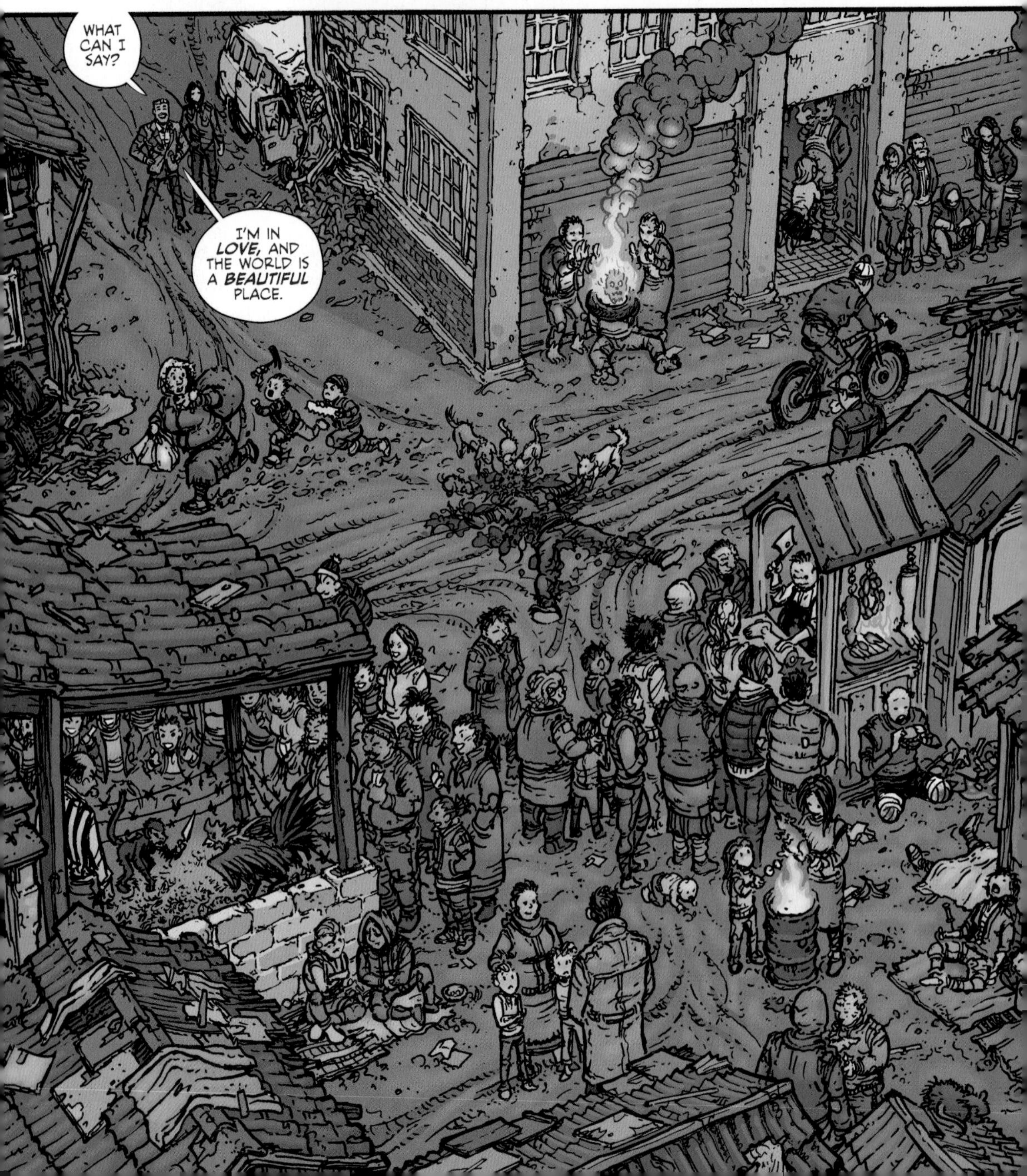
WHAT CAN I SAY?
I'M IN LOVE, AND THE WORLD IS A BEAUTIFUL PLACE.

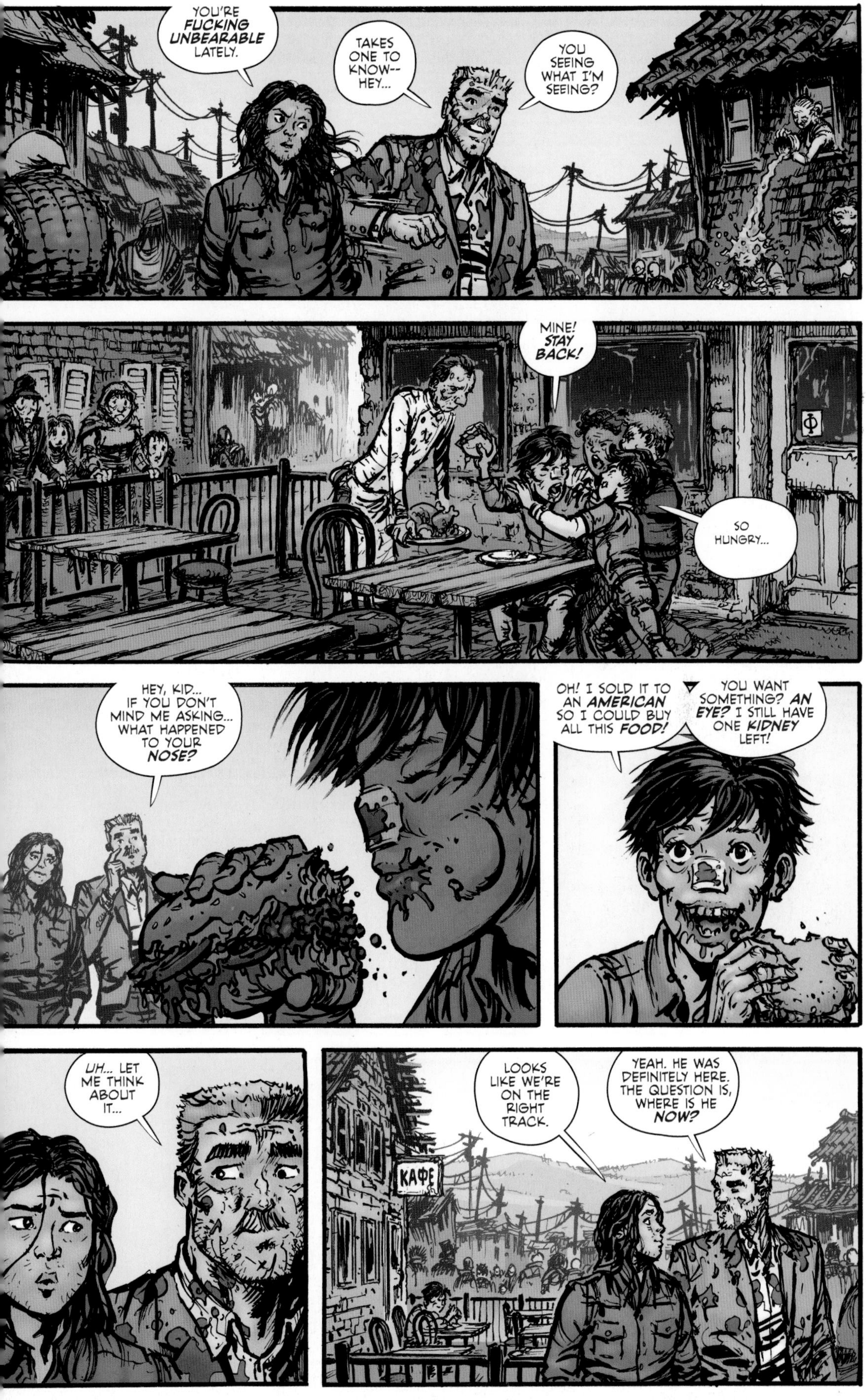

YOU'RE FUCKING UNBEARABLE LATELY.
TAKES ONE TO KNOW-- HEY...
YOU SEEING WHAT I'M SEEING?
MINE! STAY BACK!
SO HUNGRY...
HEY, KID... IF YOU DON'T MIND ME ASKING... WHAT HAPPENED TO YOUR NOSE?
OH! I SOLD IT TO AN AMERICAN SO I COULD BUY ALL THIS FOOD!
YOU WANT SOMETHING? AN EYE? I STILL HAVE ONE KIDNEY LEFT!
UH... LET ME THINK ABOUT IT...
LOOKS LIKE WE'RE ON THE RIGHT TRACK.
YEAH. HE WAS DEFINITELY HERE. THE QUESTION IS, WHERE IS HE NOW?
ΚΑΦΕ

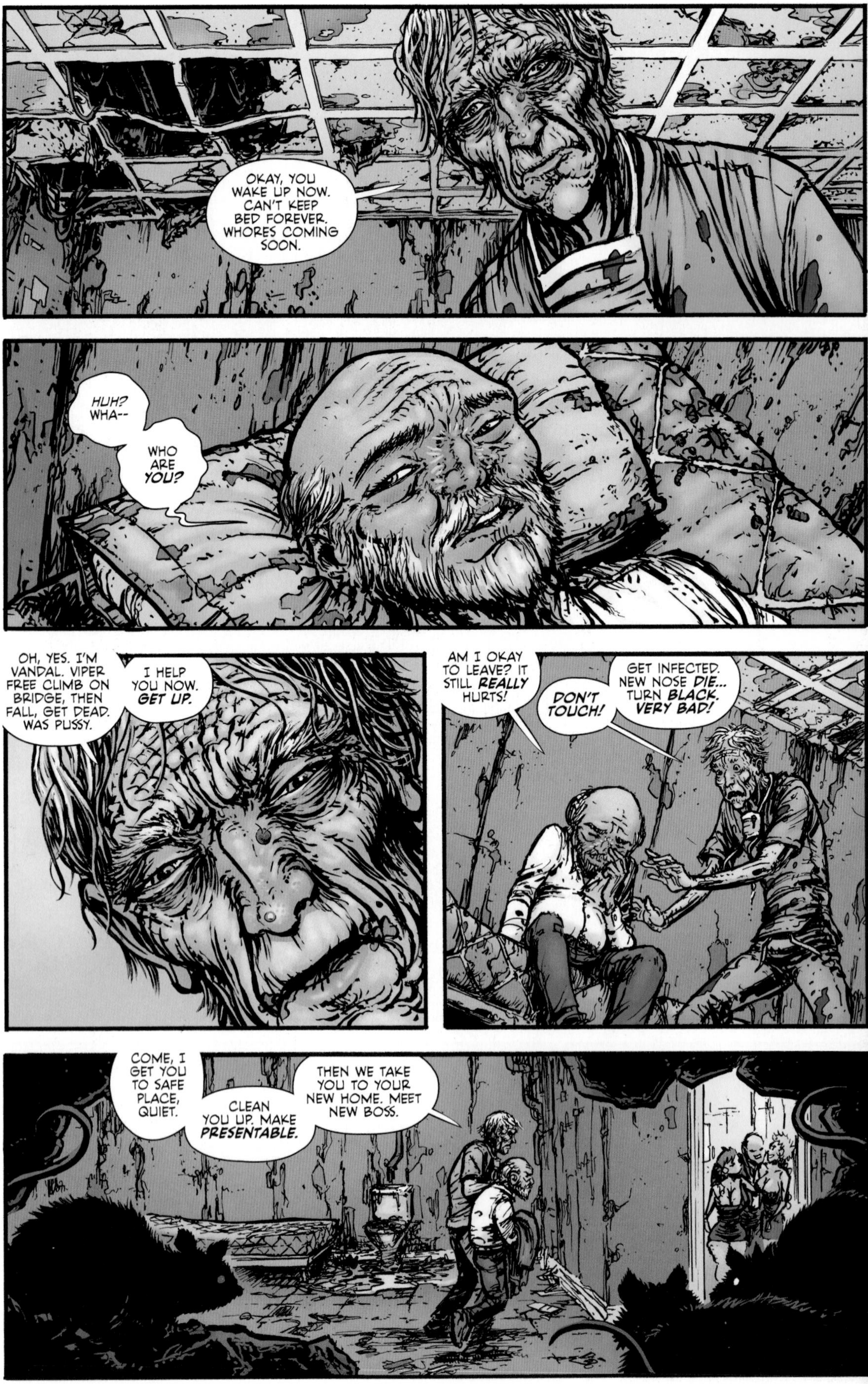
OKAY, YOU WAKE UP NOW. CAN'T KEEP BED FOREVER. WHORES COMING SOON.
HUH? WHA--
WHO ARE *YOU?*
OH, YES. I'M VANDAL. VIPER FREE CLIMB ON BRIDGE, THEN FALL, GET DEAD. WAS PUSSY.
I HELP YOU NOW. *GET UP.*
AM I OKAY TO LEAVE? IT STILL *REALLY* HURTS!
DON'T TOUCH!
GET INFECTED. NEW NOSE *DIE...* TURN *BLACK. VERY BAD!*
COME, I GET YOU TO SAFE PLACE, QUIET.
CLEAN YOU UP. MAKE *PRESENTABLE.*
THEN WE TAKE YOU TO YOUR NEW HOME. MEET NEW BOSS.

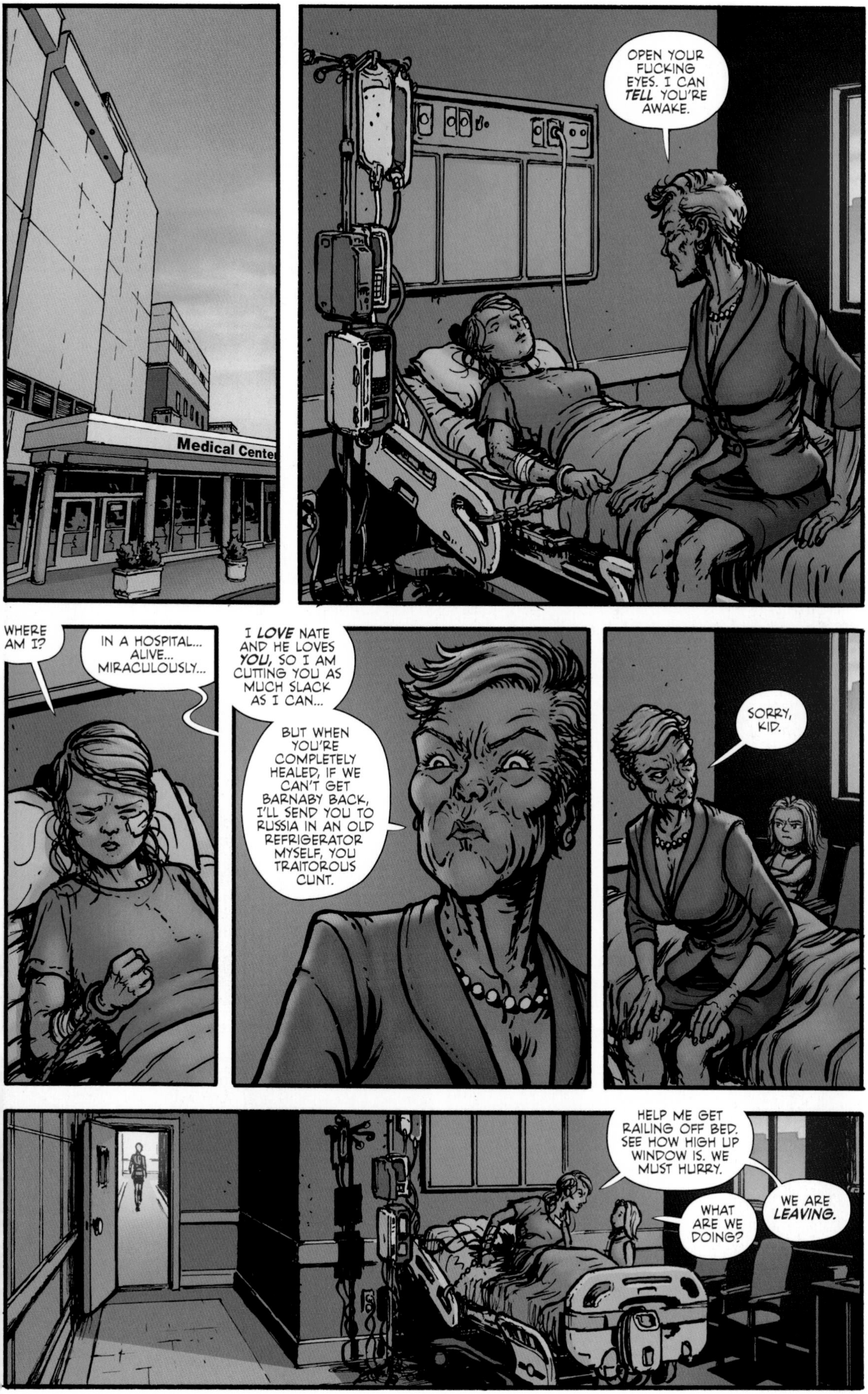
Medical Center
OPEN YOUR FUCKING EYES. I CAN *TELL* YOU'RE AWAKE.
WHERE AM I?
IN A HOSPITAL... ALIVE... MIRACULOUSLY...
I *LOVE* NATE AND HE LOVES *YOU,* SO I AM CUTTING YOU AS MUCH SLACK AS I CAN...
BUT WHEN YOU'RE COMPLETELY HEALED, IF WE CAN'T GET BARNABY BACK, I'LL SEND YOU TO RUSSIA IN AN OLD REFRIGERATOR MYSELF, YOU TRAITOROUS CUNT.
SORRY, KID.
HELP ME GET RAILING OFF BED. SEE HOW HIGH UP WINDOW IS. WE MUST HURRY.
WHAT ARE WE DOING?
WE ARE *LEAVING.*

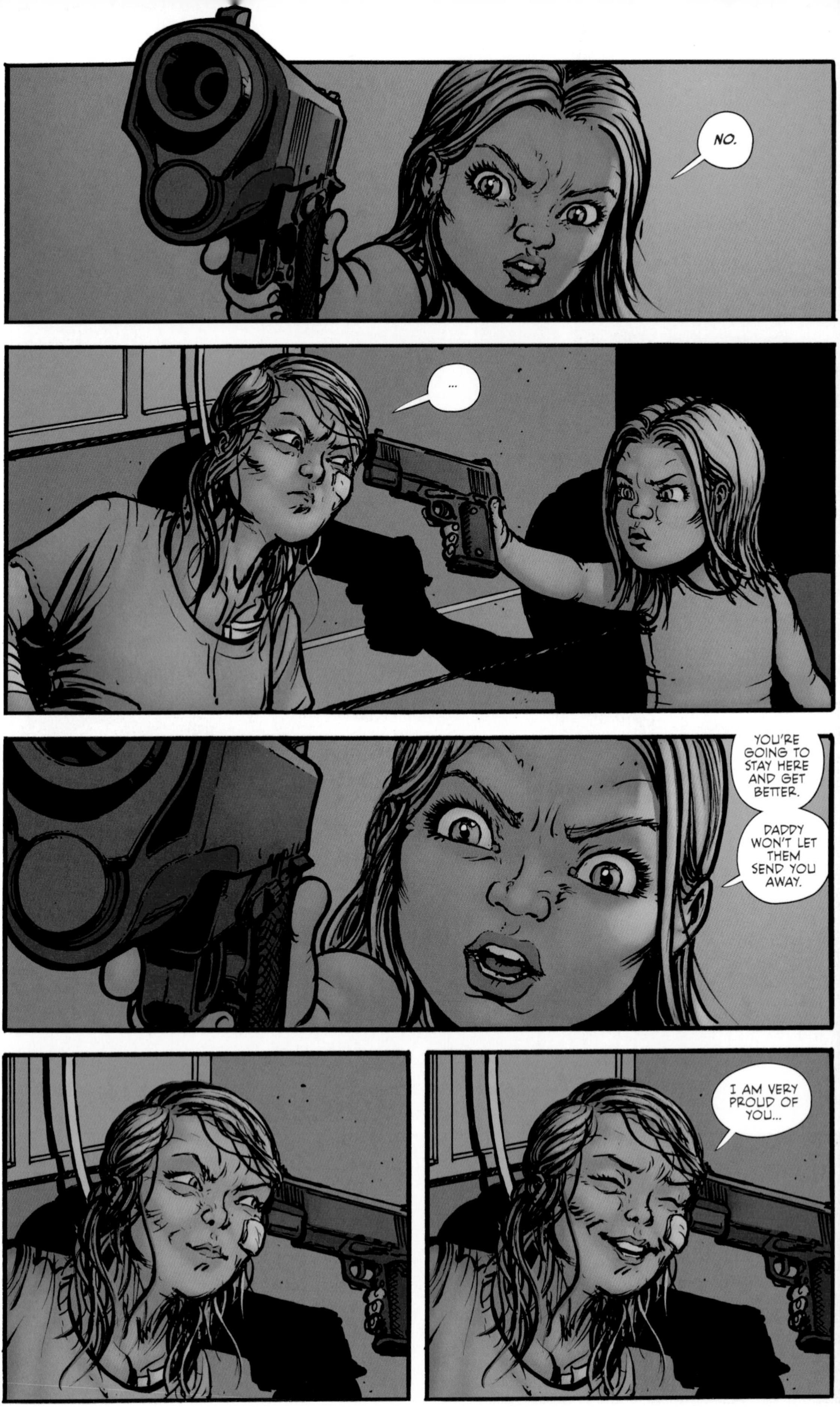
NO.
...
YOU'RE GOING TO STAY HERE AND GET BETTER.
DADDY WON'T LET THEM SEND YOU AWAY.
I AM VERY PROUD OF YOU...

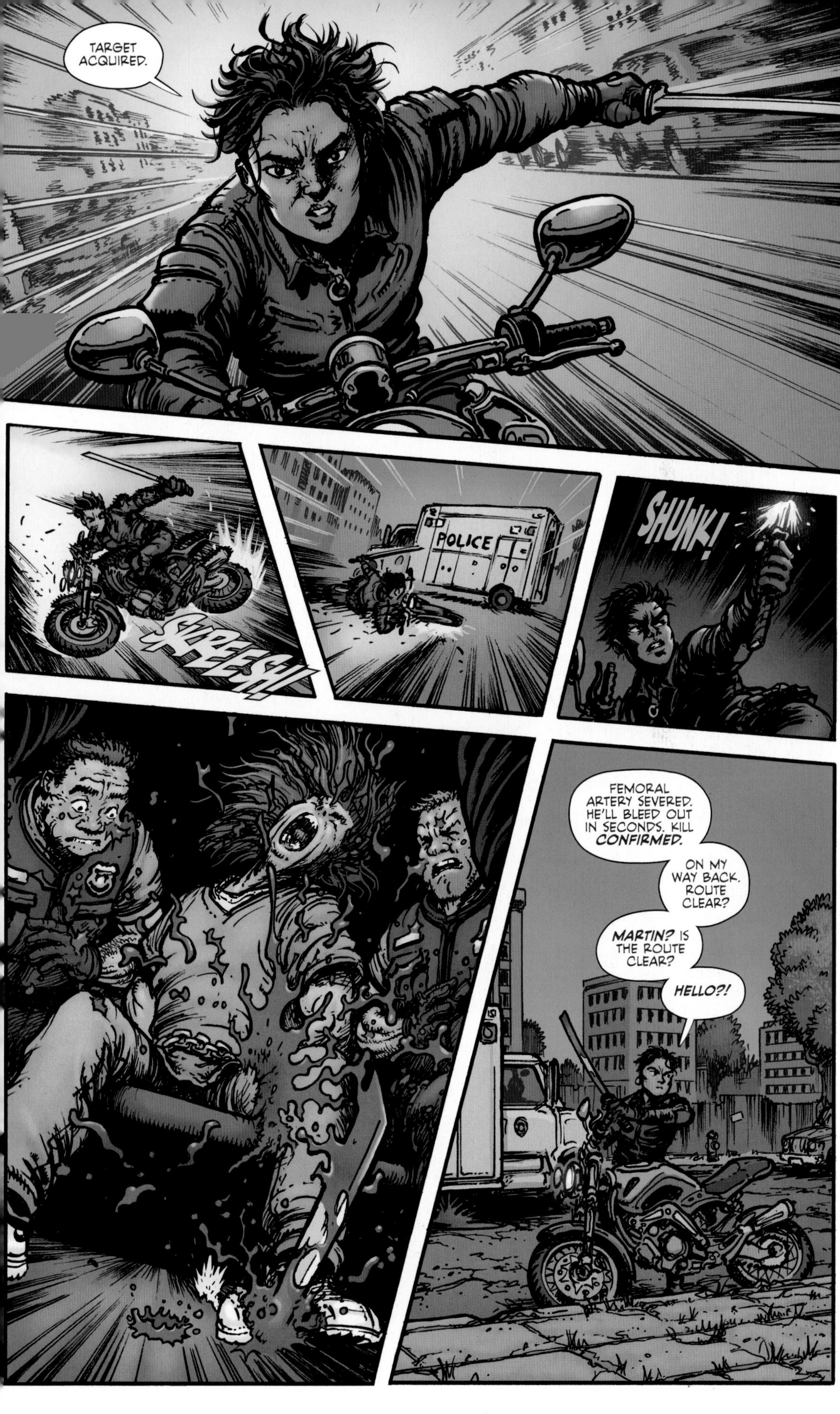
TARGET ACQUIRED.
SKREESH!
POLICE
SHUNK!
FEMORAL ARTERY SEVERED. HE'LL BLEED OUT IN SECONDS. KILL CONFIRMED.
ON MY WAY BACK. ROUTE CLEAR?
MARTIN? IS THE ROUTE CLEAR?
HELLO?!

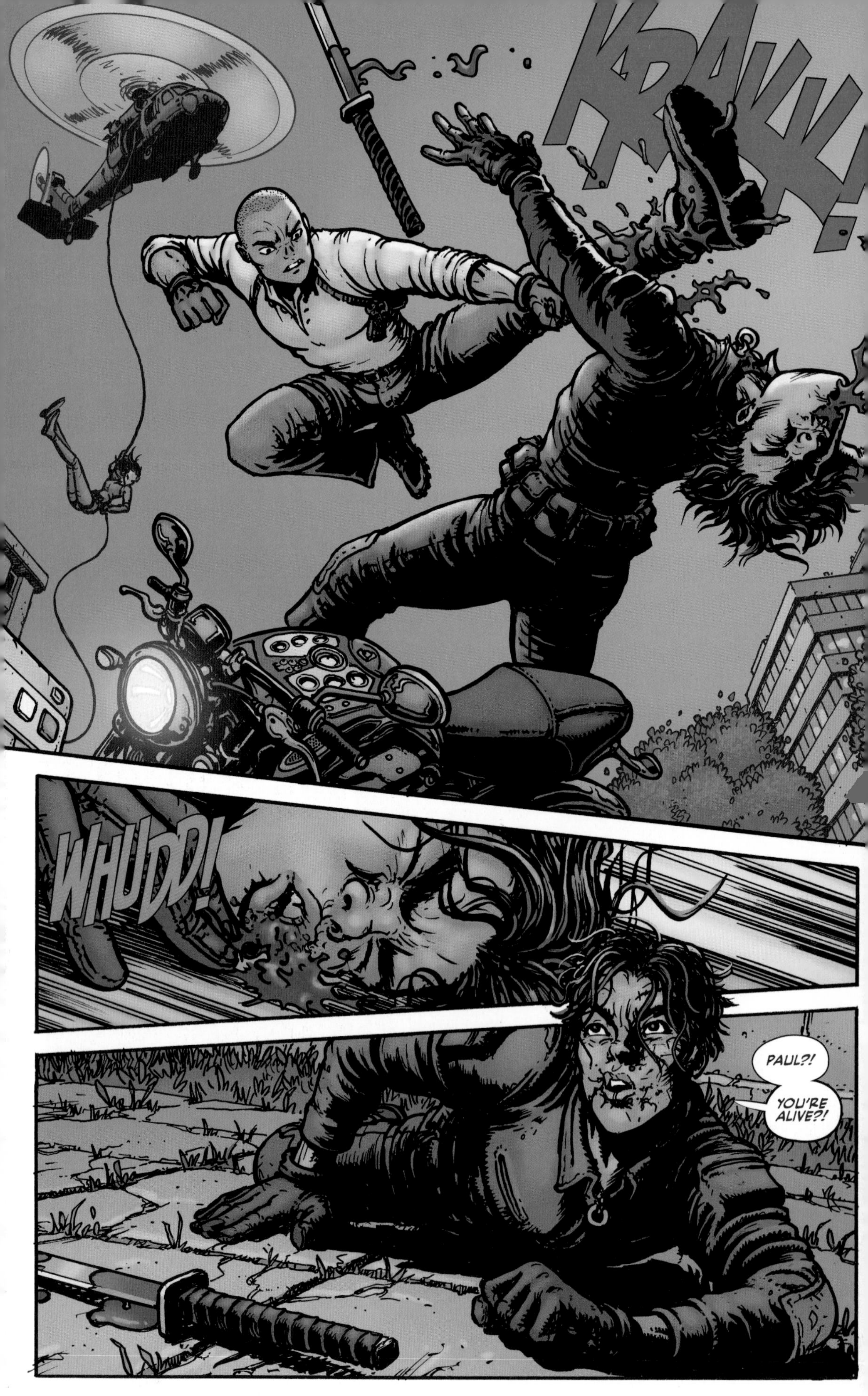
KRAKK!
WHUDD!
PAUL?!
YOU'RE ALIVE?!

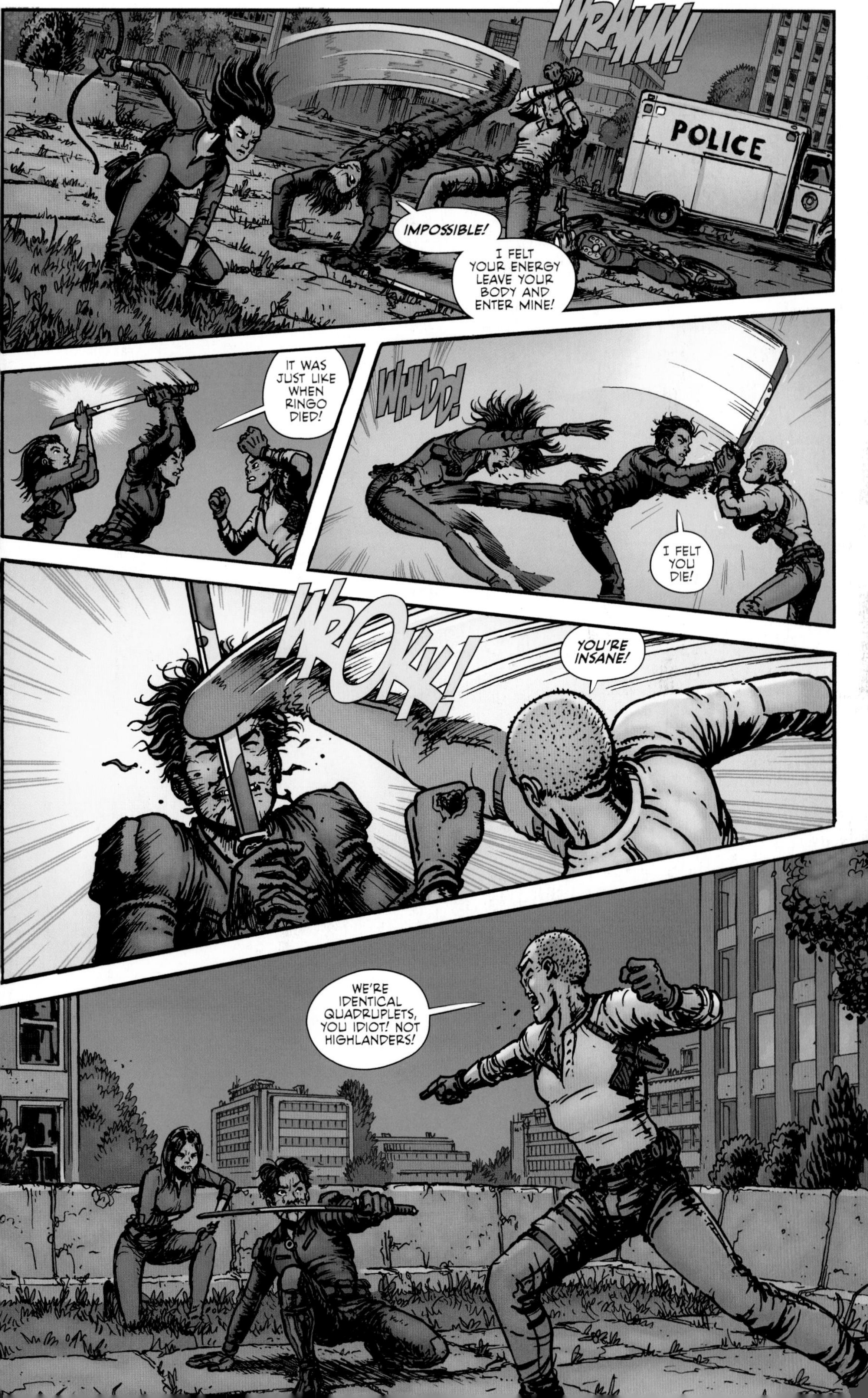
WRAMM!
POLICE
IMPOSSIBLE!
I FELT YOUR ENERGY LEAVE YOUR BODY AND ENTER MINE!
IT WAS JUST LIKE WHEN RINGO DIED!
WHUDD!
I FELT YOU DIE!
WROKK!
YOU'RE INSANE!
WE'RE IDENTICAL QUADRUPLETS, YOU IDIOT! NOT HIGHLANDERS!

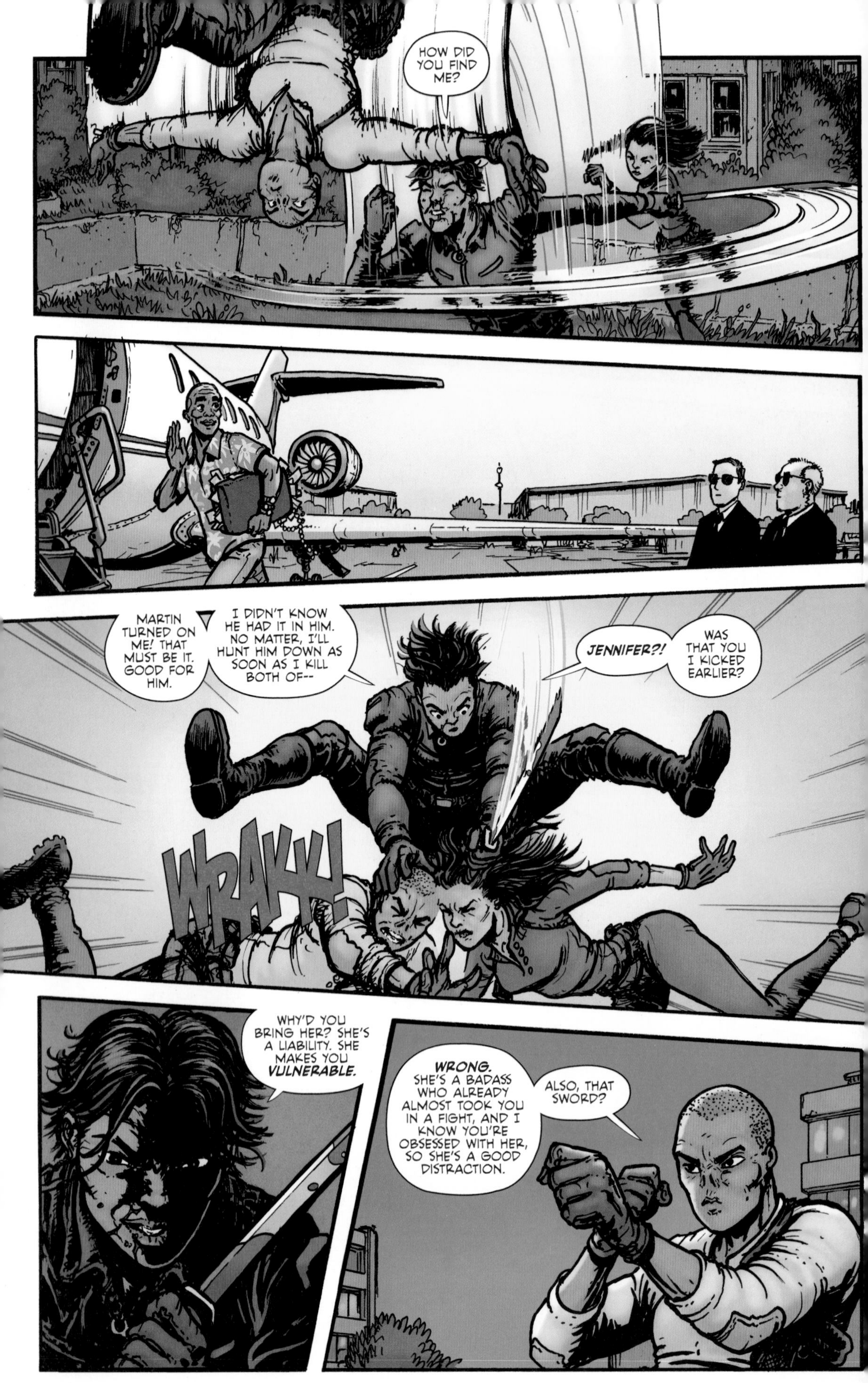
HOW DID YOU FIND ME?
MARTIN TURNED ON ME! THAT MUST BE IT. GOOD FOR HIM.
I DIDN'T KNOW HE HAD IT IN HIM. NO MATTER, I'LL HUNT HIM DOWN AS SOON AS I KILL BOTH OF--
JENNIFER?!
WAS THAT YOU I KICKED EARLIER?
WRAKK!
WHY'D YOU BRING HER? SHE'S A LIABILITY. SHE MAKES YOU VULNERABLE.
WRONG. SHE'S A BADASS WHO ALREADY ALMOST TOOK YOU IN A FIGHT, AND I KNOW YOU'RE OBSESSED WITH HER, SO SHE'S A GOOD DISTRACTION.
ALSO, THAT SWORD?

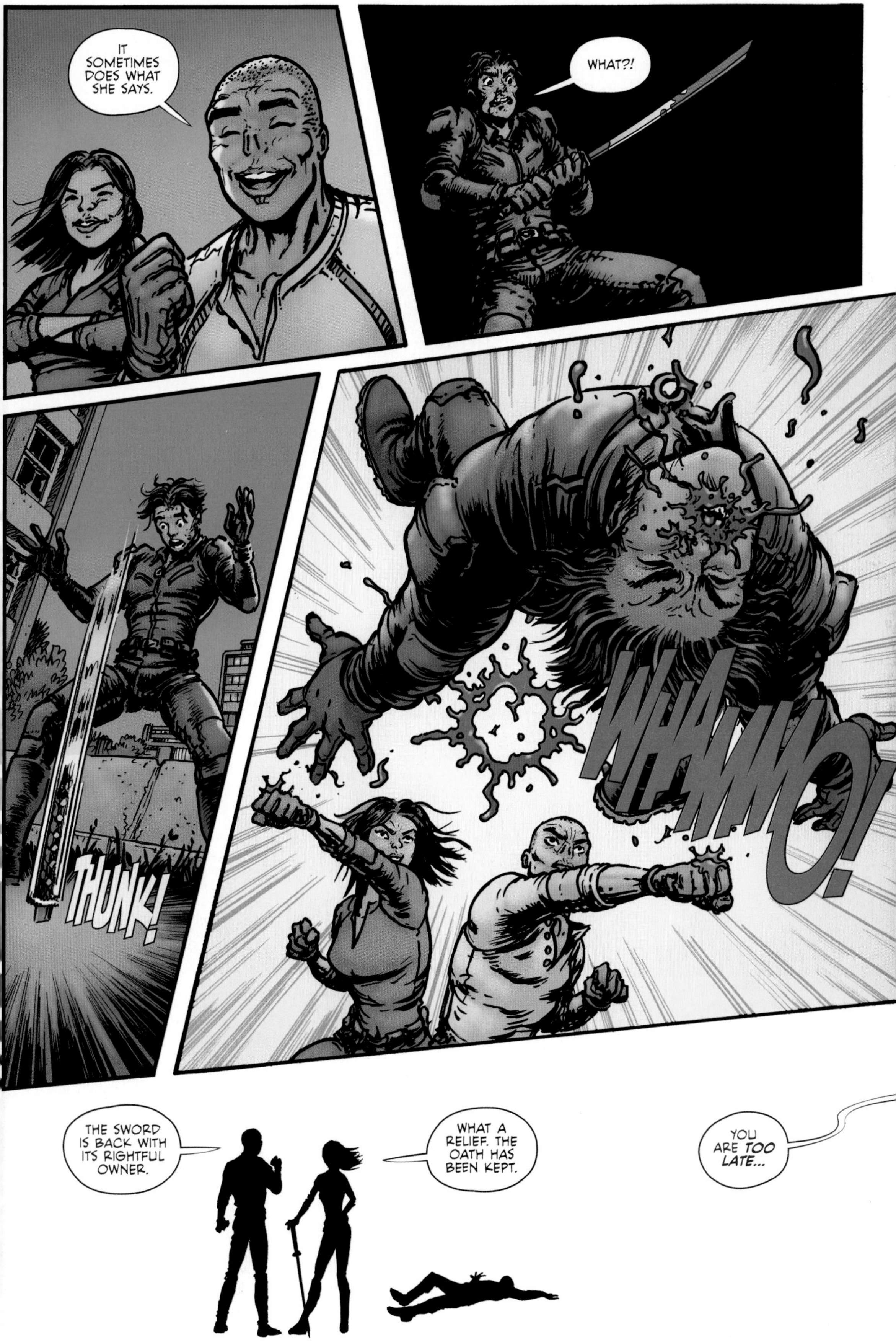

IT SOMETIMES DOES WHAT SHE SAYS.
WHAT?!
THUNK!
WHAMMO!
THE SWORD IS BACK WITH ITS RIGHTFUL OWNER.
WHAT A RELIEF. THE OATH HAS BEEN KEPT.
YOU ARE *TOO LATE...*

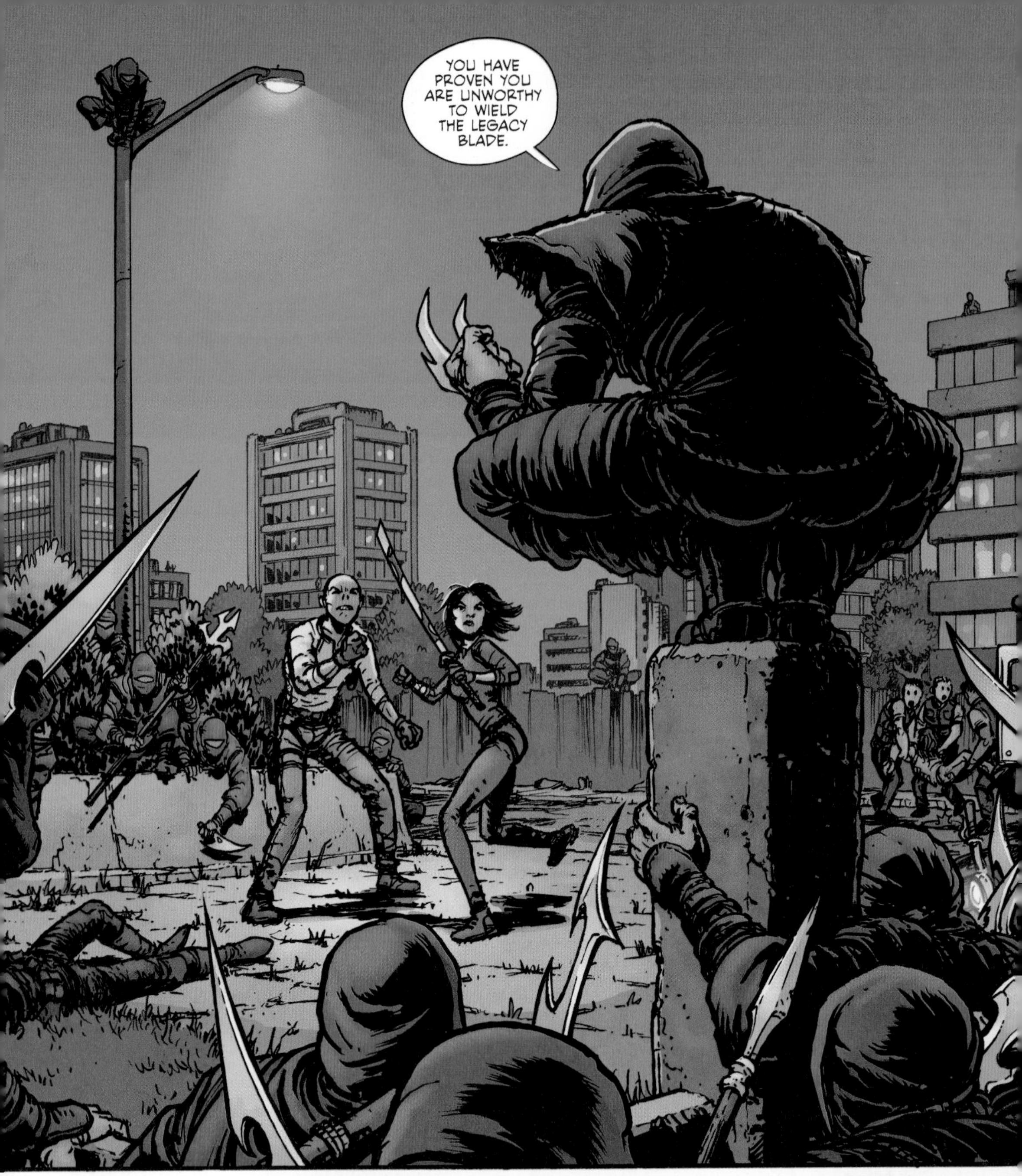
YOU HAVE PROVEN YOU ARE UNWORTHY TO WIELD THE LEGACY BLADE.

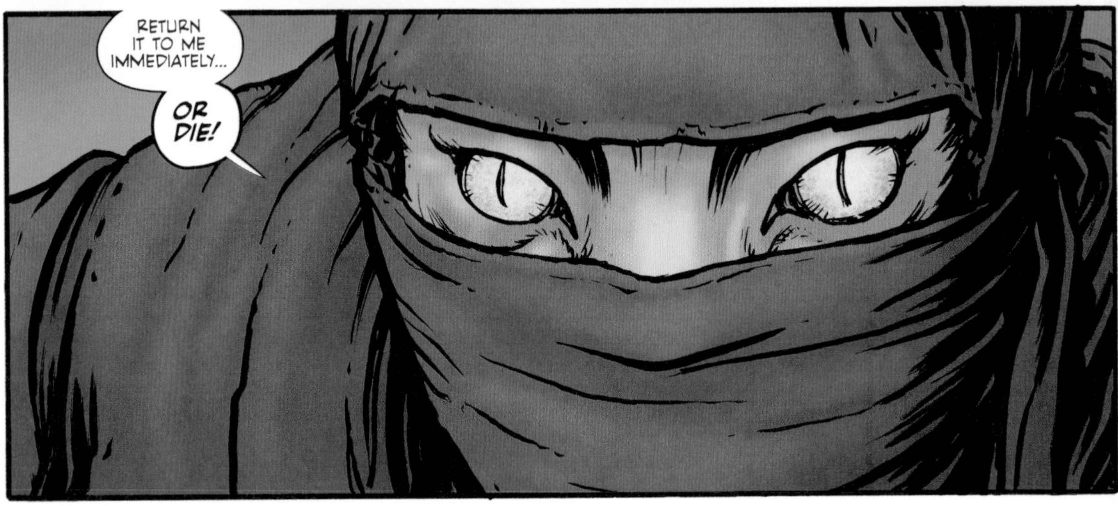
RETURN IT TO ME IMMEDIATELY...
OR DIE!

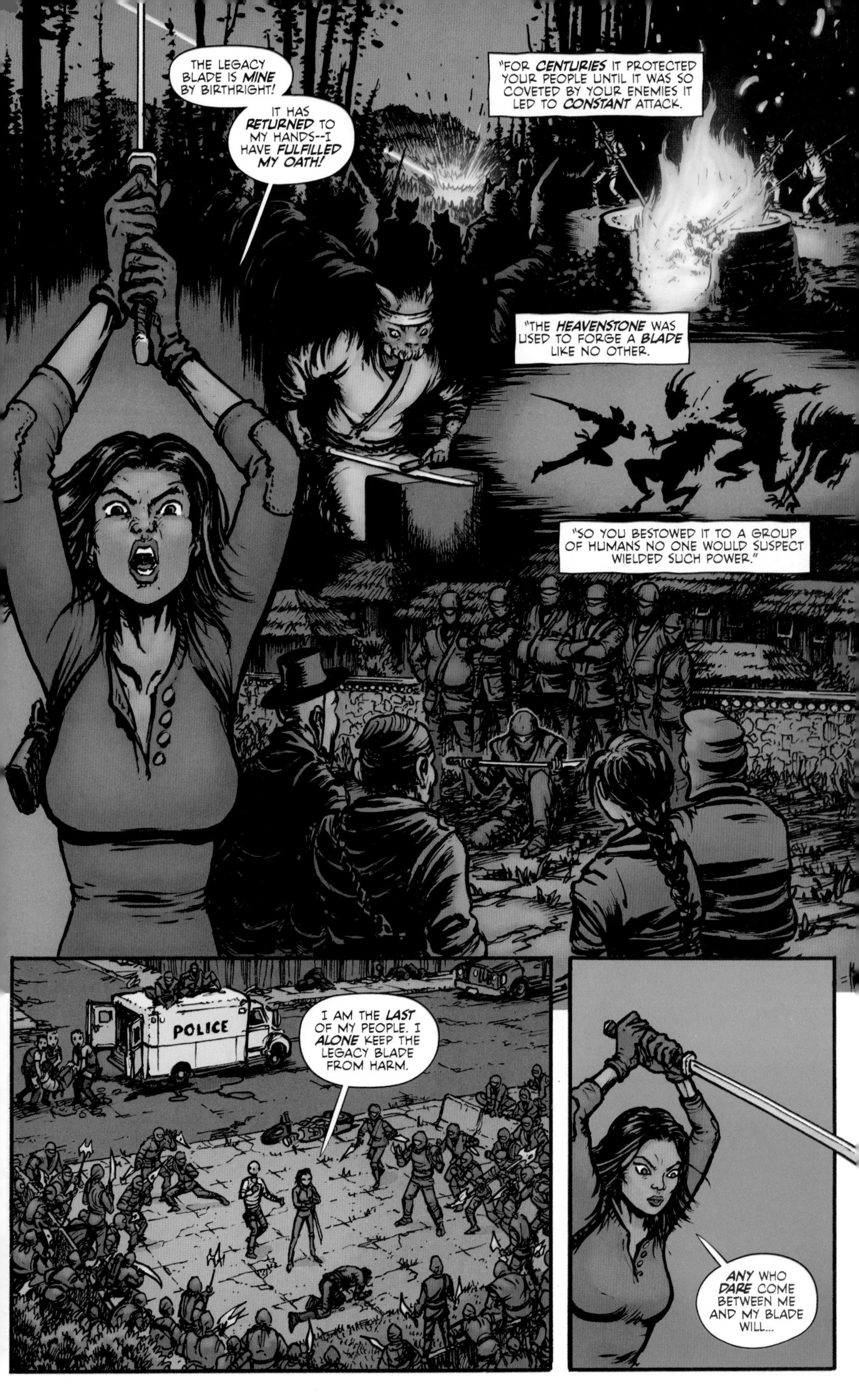
THE LEGACY BLADE IS MINE BY BIRTHRIGHT!
IT HAS RETURNED TO MY HANDS--I HAVE FULFILLED MY OATH!
"FOR CENTURIES IT PROTECTED YOUR PEOPLE UNTIL IT WAS SO COVETED BY YOUR ENEMIES IT LED TO CONSTANT ATTACK.
"THE HEAVENSTONE WAS USED TO FORGE A BLADE LIKE NO OTHER.
"SO YOU BESTOWED IT TO A GROUP OF HUMANS NO ONE WOULD SUSPECT WIELDED SUCH POWER."
POLICE
I AM THE LAST OF MY PEOPLE. I ALONE KEEP THE LEGACY BLADE FROM HARM.
ANY WHO DARE COME BETWEEN ME AND MY BLADE WILL...

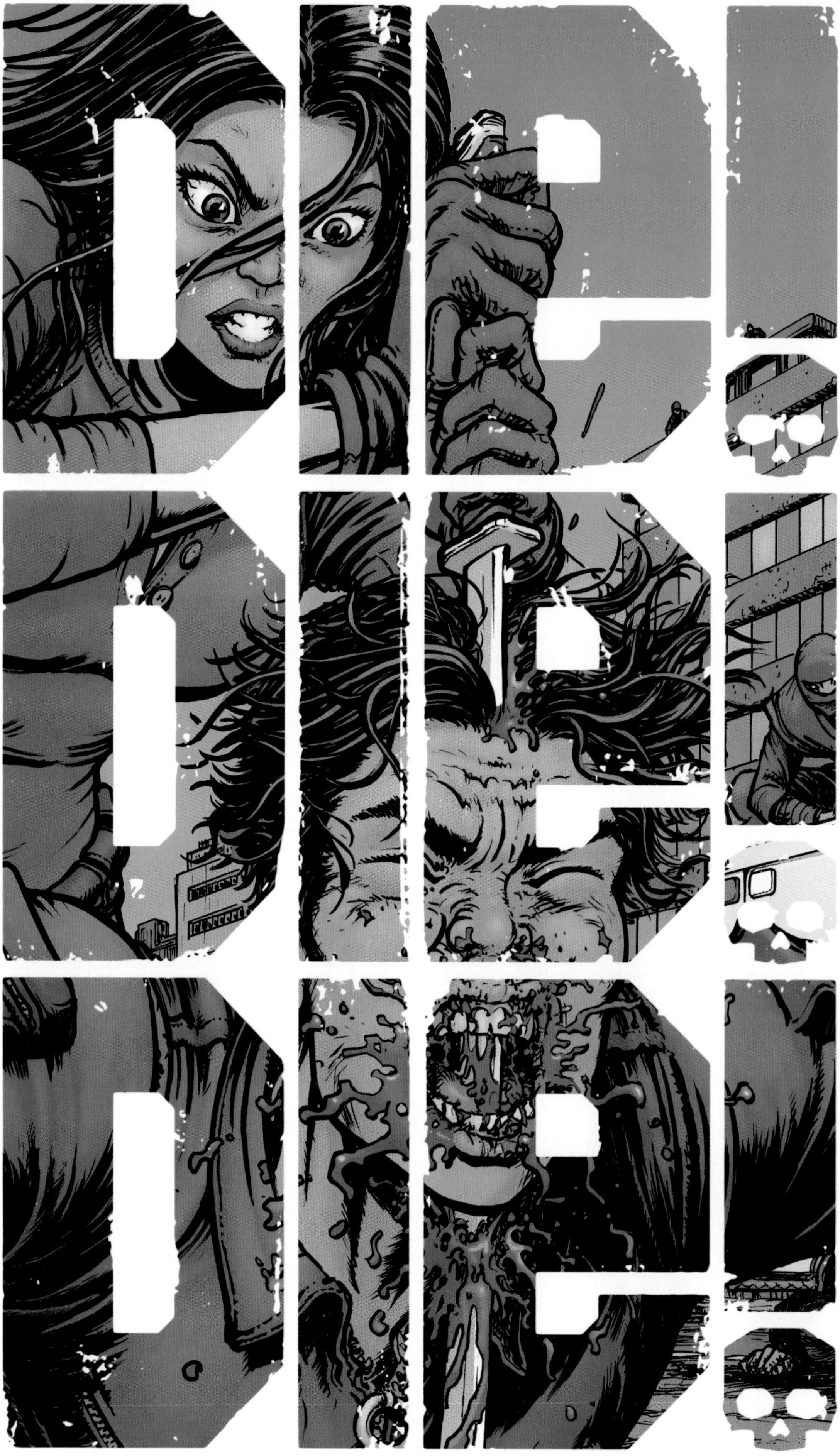
DIE!
DIE!
DIE!

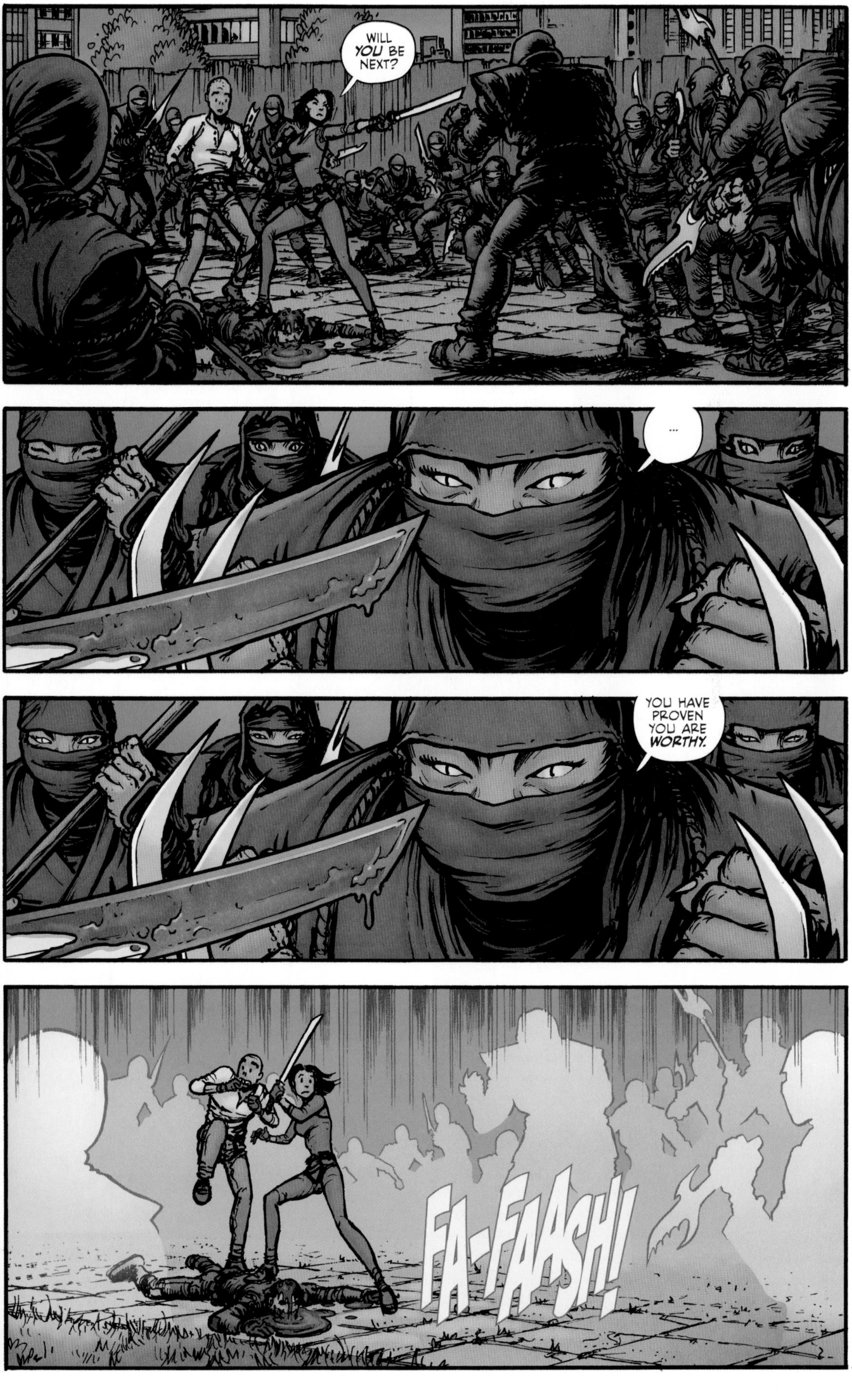
WILL YOU BE NEXT?
...
YOU HAVE PROVEN YOU ARE WORTHY.
FA-FAASH!

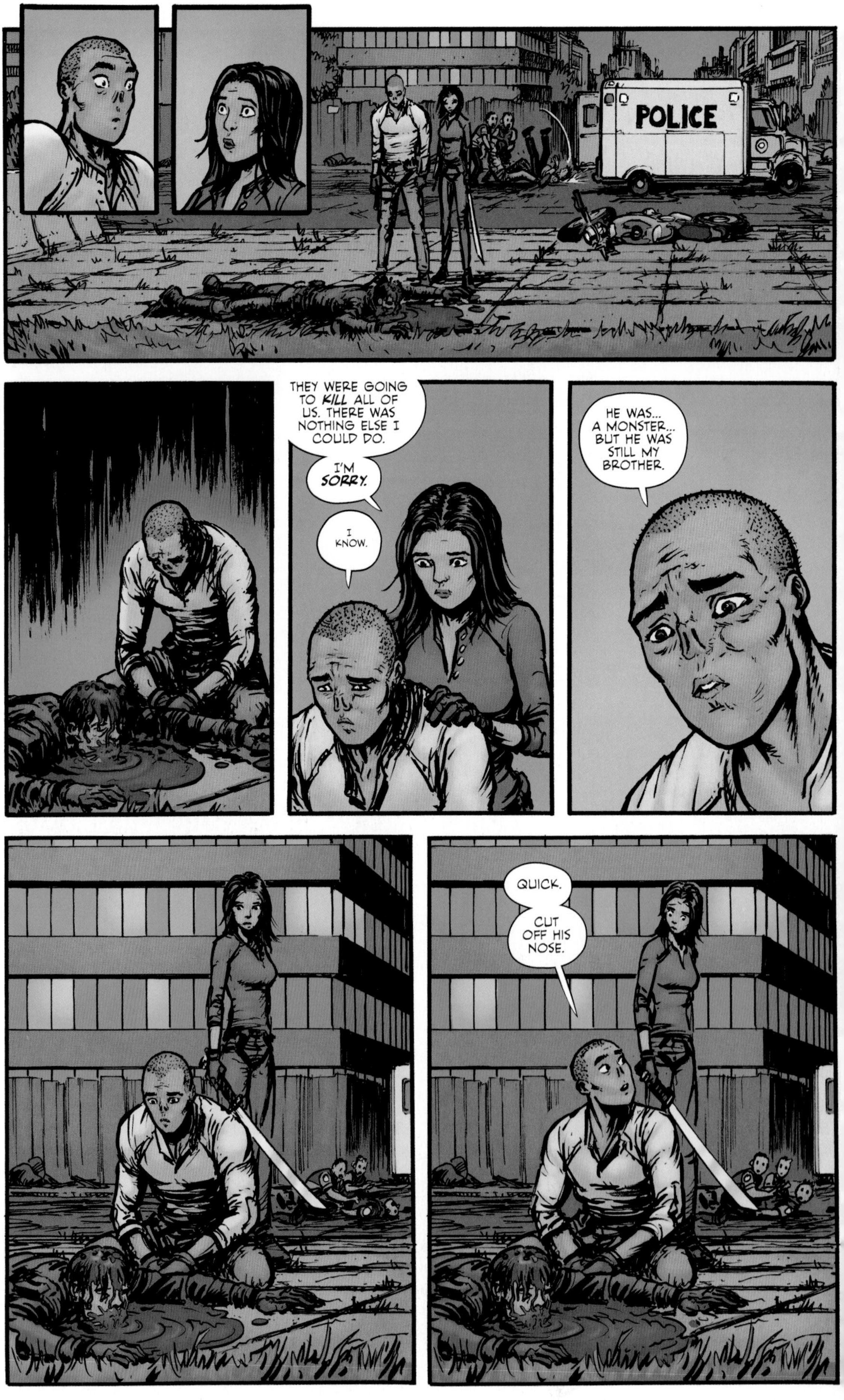
POLICE
THEY WERE GOING TO KILL ALL OF US. THERE WAS NOTHING ELSE I COULD DO.
I'M SORRY.
I KNOW.
HE WAS... A MONSTER... BUT HE WAS STILL MY BROTHER.
QUICK.
CUT OFF HIS NOSE.

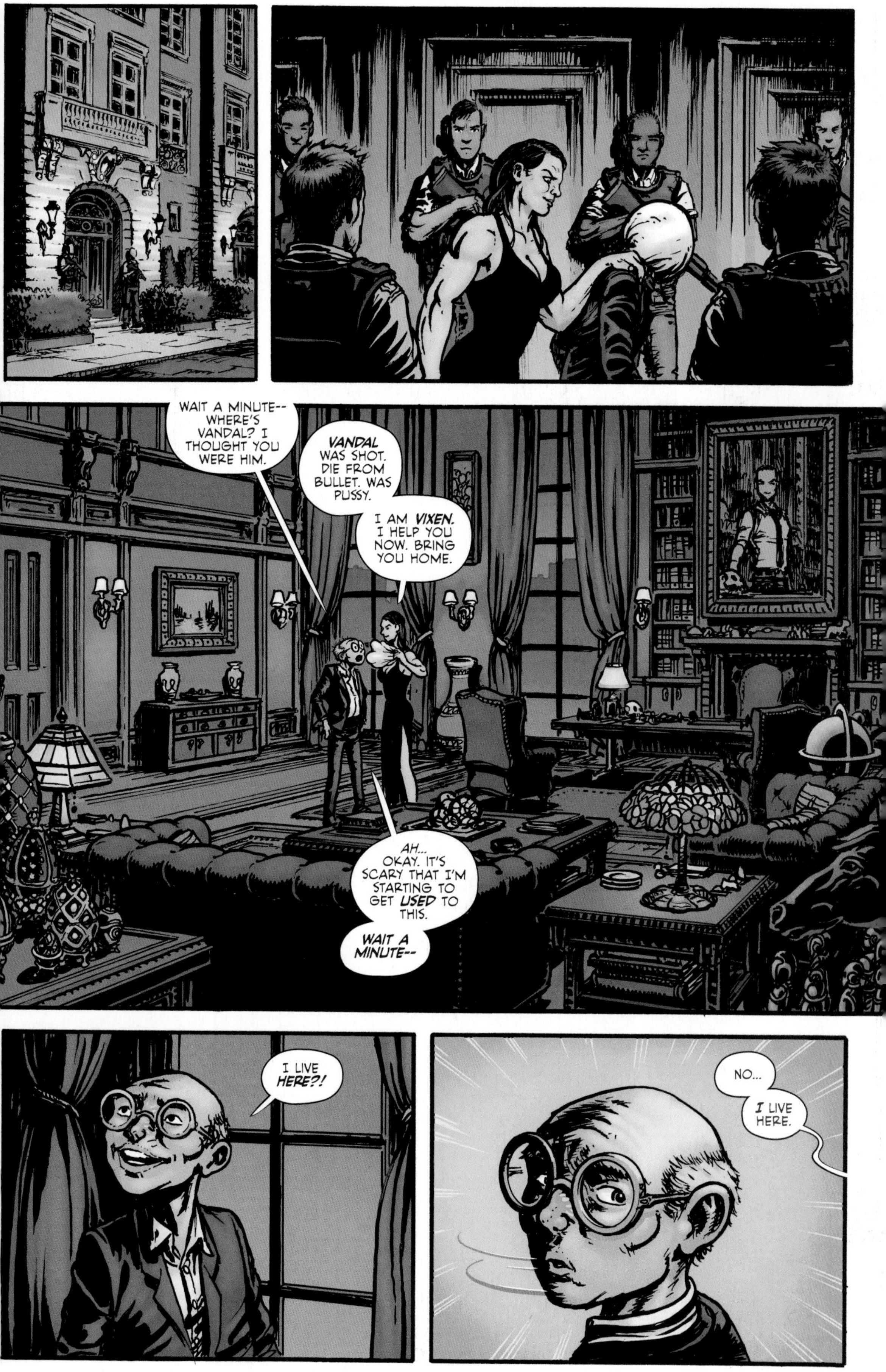
WAIT A MINUTE-- WHERE'S VANDAL? I THOUGHT YOU WERE HIM.
VANDAL WAS SHOT. DIE FROM BULLET. WAS PUSSY.
I AM VIXEN. I HELP YOU NOW. BRING YOU HOME.
AH... OKAY. IT'S SCARY THAT I'M STARTING TO GET USED TO THIS.
WAIT A MINUTE--
I LIVE HERE?!
NO...
I LIVE HERE.

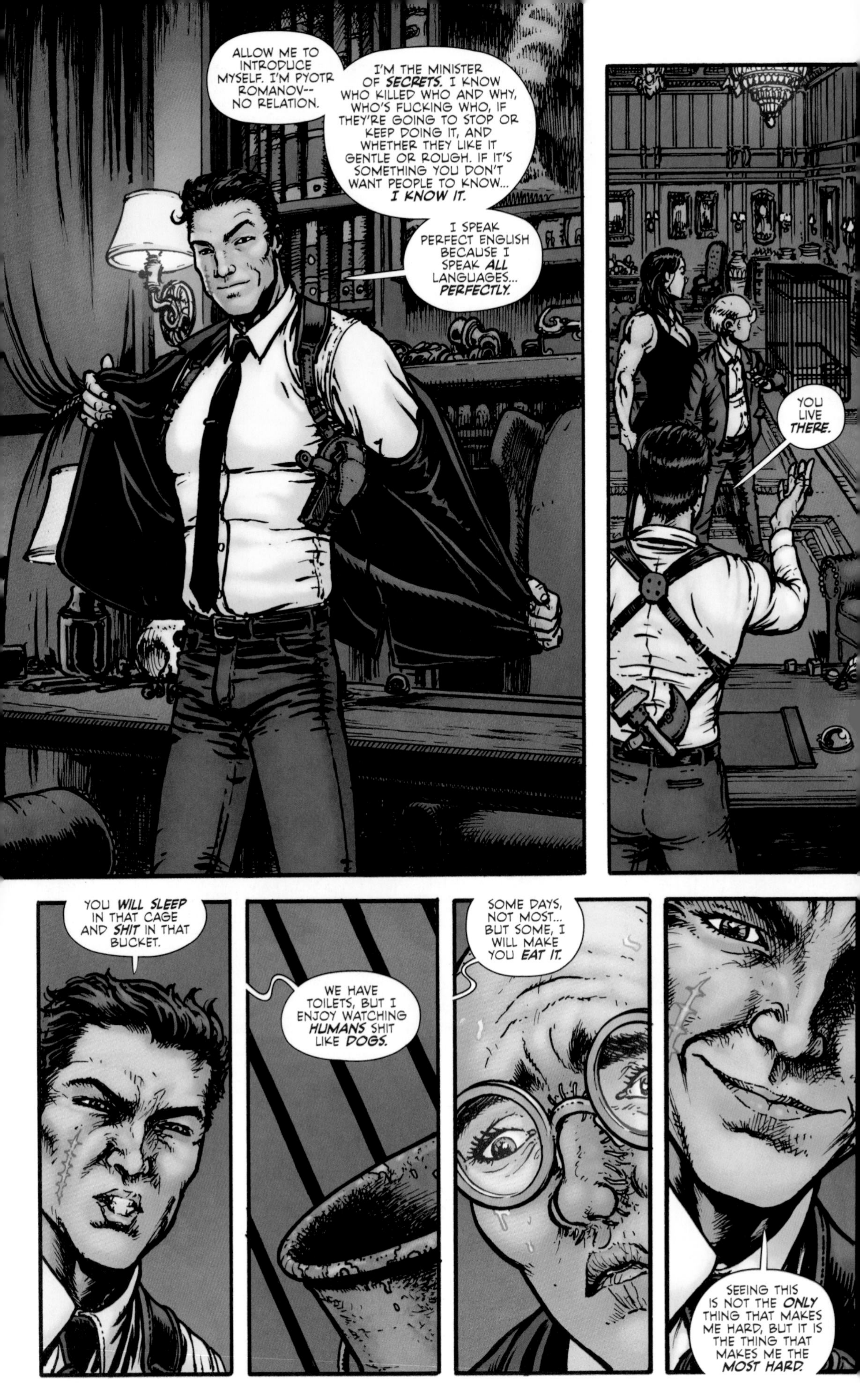
ALLOW ME TO INTRODUCE MYSELF. I'M PYOTR ROMANOV-- NO RELATION.
I'M THE MINISTER OF SECRETS. I KNOW WHO KILLED WHO AND WHY, WHO'S FUCKING WHO, IF THEY'RE GOING TO STOP OR KEEP DOING IT, AND WHETHER THEY LIKE IT GENTLE OR ROUGH. IF IT'S SOMETHING YOU DON'T WANT PEOPLE TO KNOW... I KNOW IT.
I SPEAK PERFECT ENGLISH BECAUSE I SPEAK ALL LANGUAGES... PERFECTLY.
YOU LIVE THERE.
YOU WILL SLEEP IN THAT CAGE AND SHIT IN THAT BUCKET.
WE HAVE TOILETS, BUT I ENJOY WATCHING HUMANS SHIT LIKE DOGS.
SOME DAYS, NOT MOST... BUT SOME, I WILL MAKE YOU EAT IT.
SEEING THIS IS NOT THE ONLY THING THAT MAKES ME HARD, BUT IT IS THE THING THAT MAKES ME THE MOST HARD.

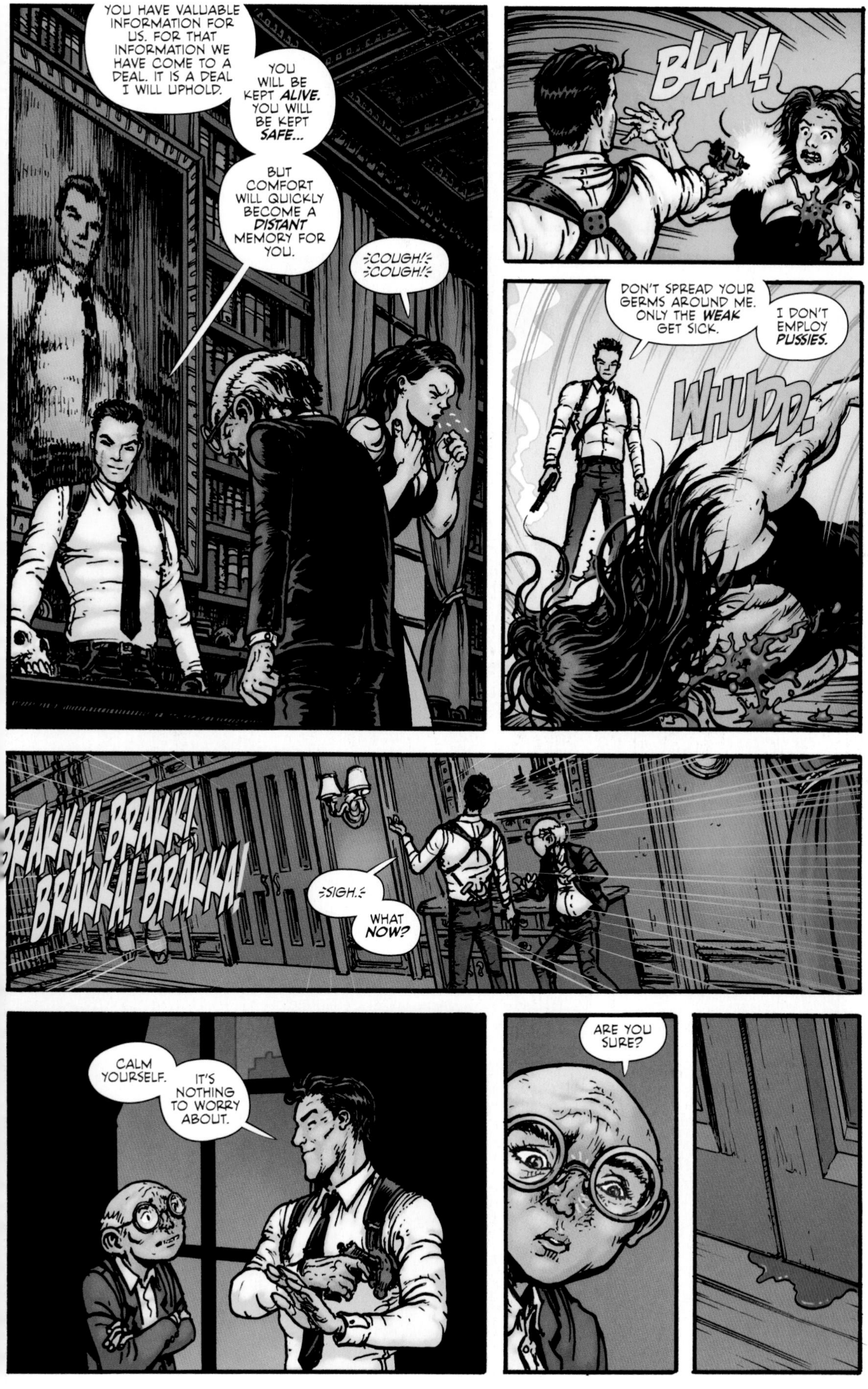
YOU HAVE VALUABLE INFORMATION FOR US. FOR THAT INFORMATION WE HAVE COME TO A DEAL. IT IS A DEAL I WILL UPHOLD.
YOU WILL BE KEPT ALIVE. YOU WILL BE KEPT SAFE...
BUT COMFORT WILL QUICKLY BECOME A DISTANT MEMORY FOR YOU.
COUGH! COUGH!
BLAM!
DON'T SPREAD YOUR GERMS AROUND ME. ONLY THE WEAK GET SICK.
I DON'T EMPLOY PUSSIES.
WHUDD.
BRAKKA! BRAKKA! BRAKKA! BRAKKA!
SIGH.
WHAT NOW?
CALM YOURSELF.
IT'S NOTHING TO WORRY ABOUT.
ARE YOU SURE?

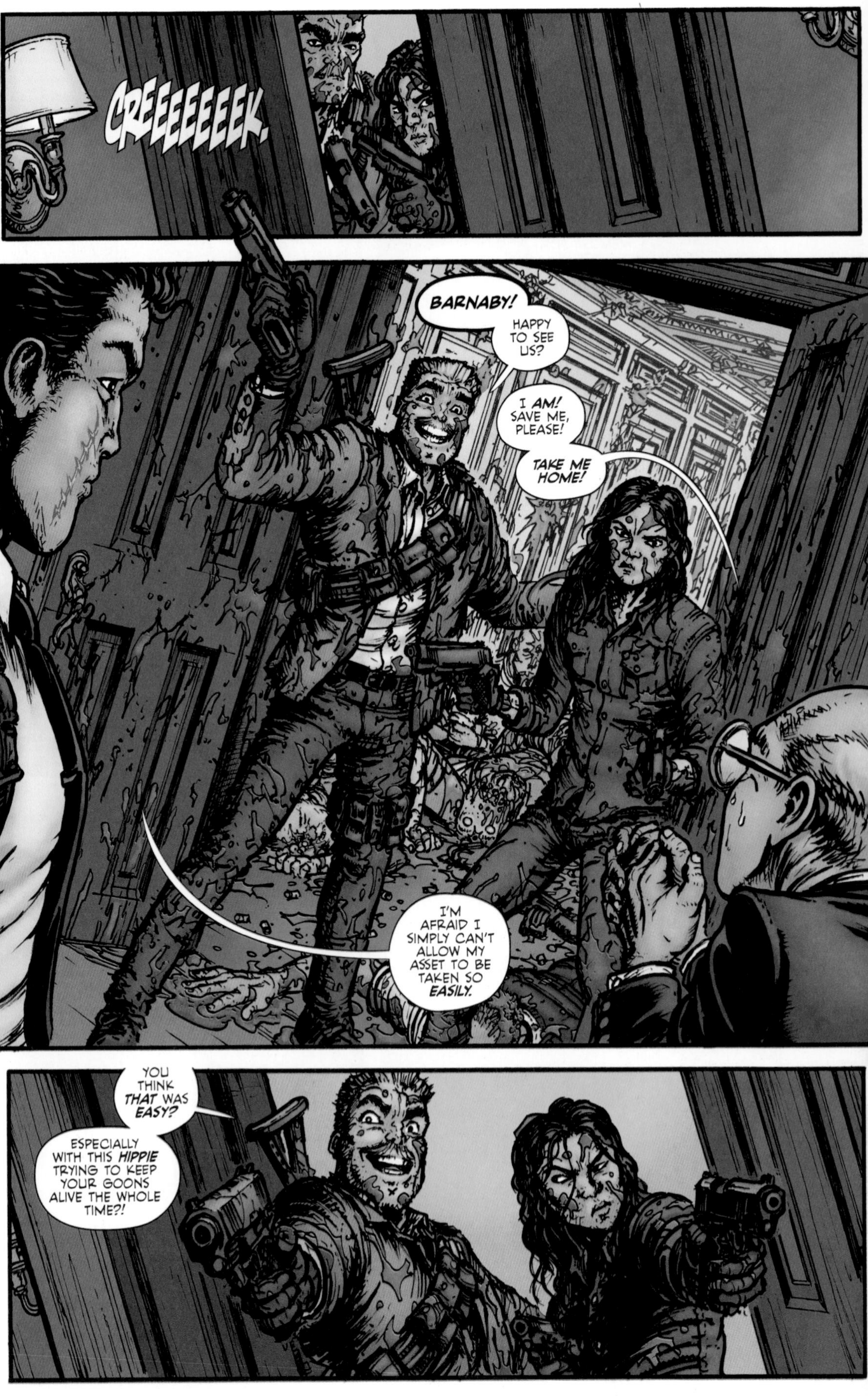
CREEEEEEEK.
BARNABY!
HAPPY TO SEE US?
I AM! SAVE ME, PLEASE!
TAKE ME HOME!
I'M AFRAID I SIMPLY CAN'T ALLOW MY ASSET TO BE TAKEN SO EASILY.
YOU THINK THAT WAS EASY?
ESPECIALLY WITH THIS HIPPIE TRYING TO KEEP YOUR GOONS ALIVE THE WHOLE TIME?!

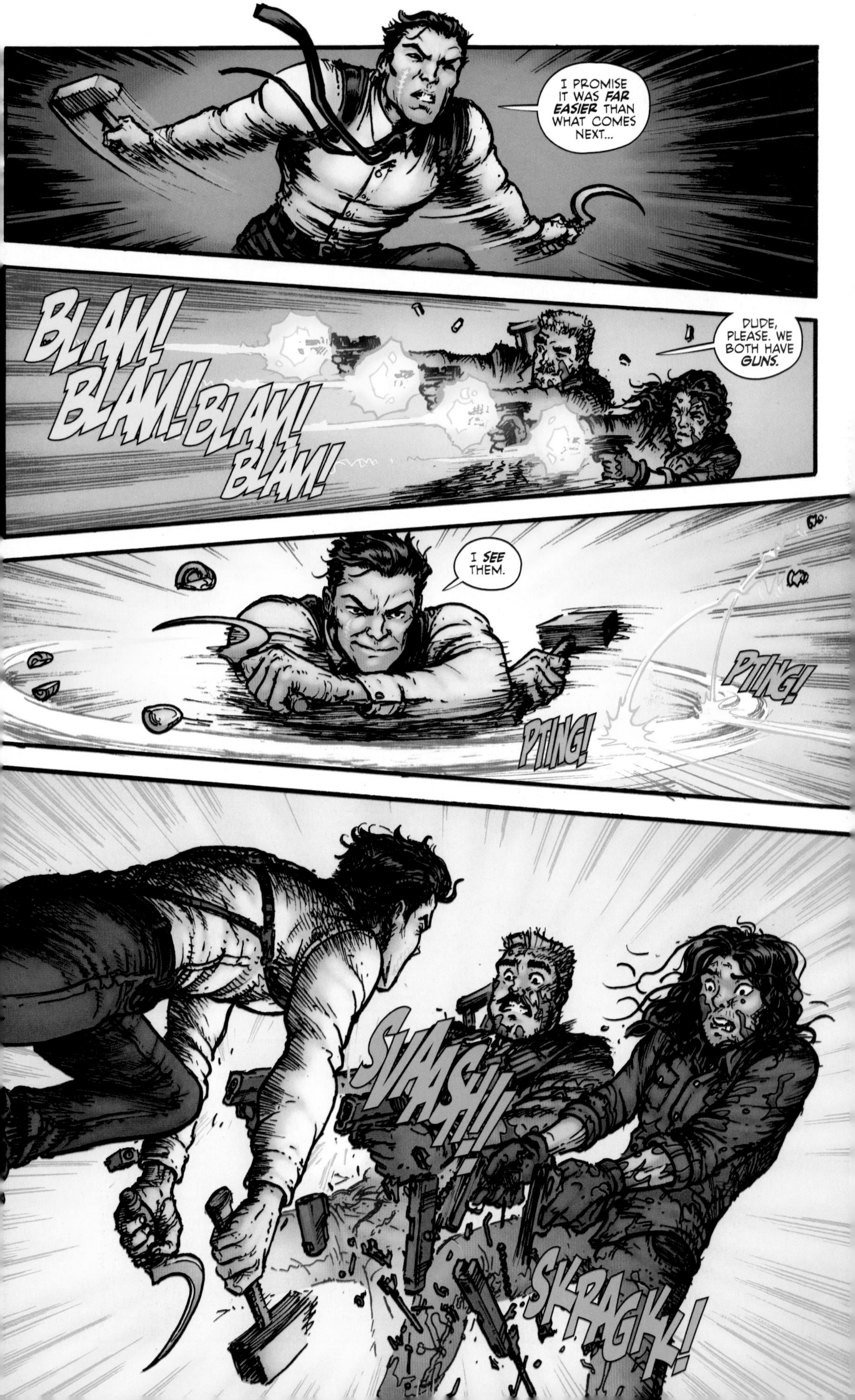

I PROMISE IT WAS FAR EASIER THAN WHAT COMES NEXT...
BLAM! BLAM! BLAM! BLAM!
DUDE, PLEASE. WE BOTH HAVE GUNS.
I SEE THEM.
PTING!
PTING!
SWASH!!
SKRAGK!

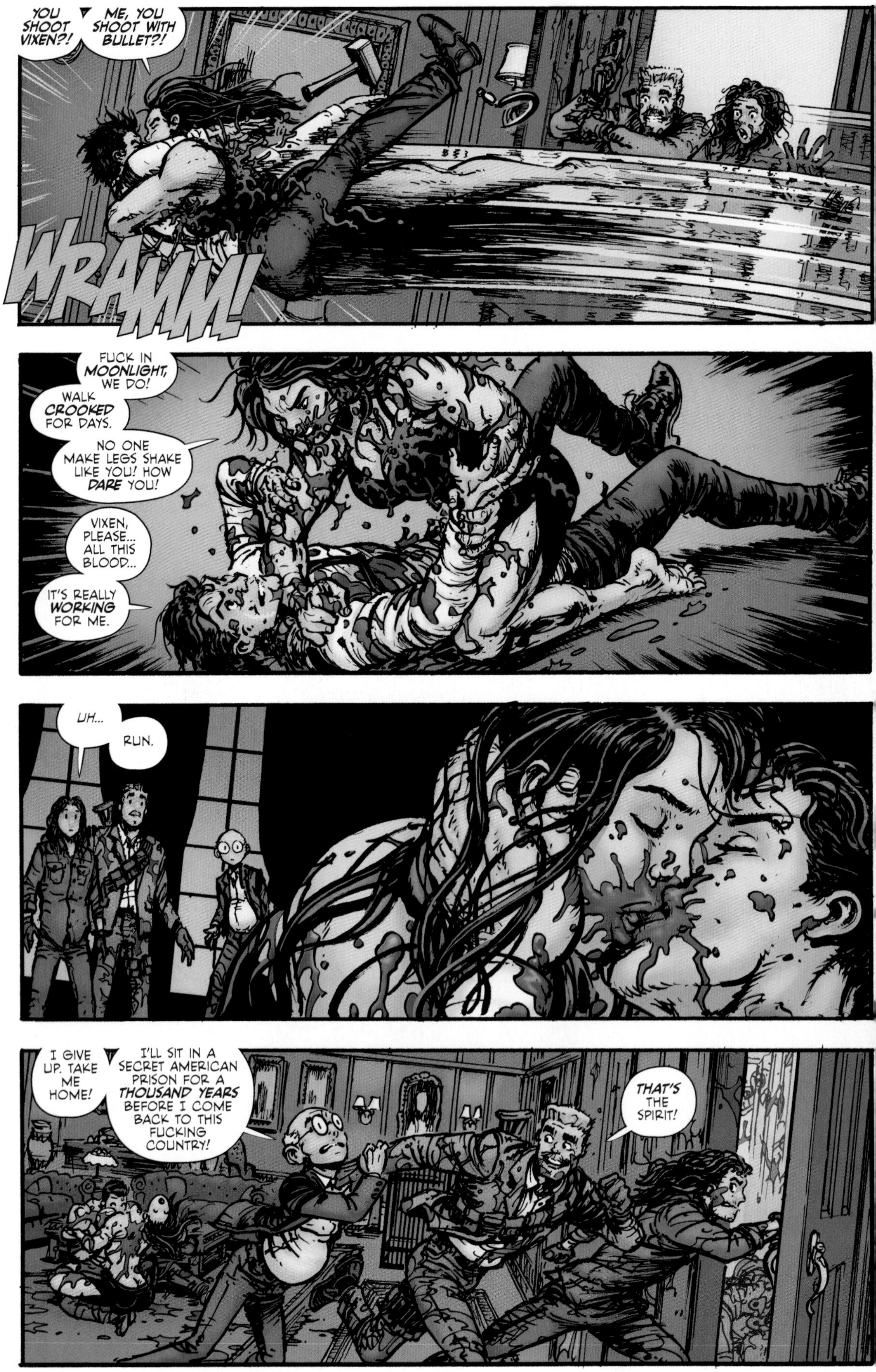
YOU SHOOT VIXEN?!
ME, YOU SHOOT WITH BULLET?!
WRAMM!
FUCK IN MOONLIGHT, WE DO!
WALK CROOKED FOR DAYS.
NO ONE MAKE LEGS SHAKE LIKE YOU! HOW DARE YOU!
VIXEN, PLEASE... ALL THIS BLOOD...
IT'S REALLY WORKING FOR ME.
UH...
RUN.
I GIVE UP. TAKE ME HOME!
I'LL SIT IN A SECRET AMERICAN PRISON FOR A THOUSAND YEARS BEFORE I COME BACK TO THIS FUCKING COUNTRY!
THAT'S THE SPIRIT!

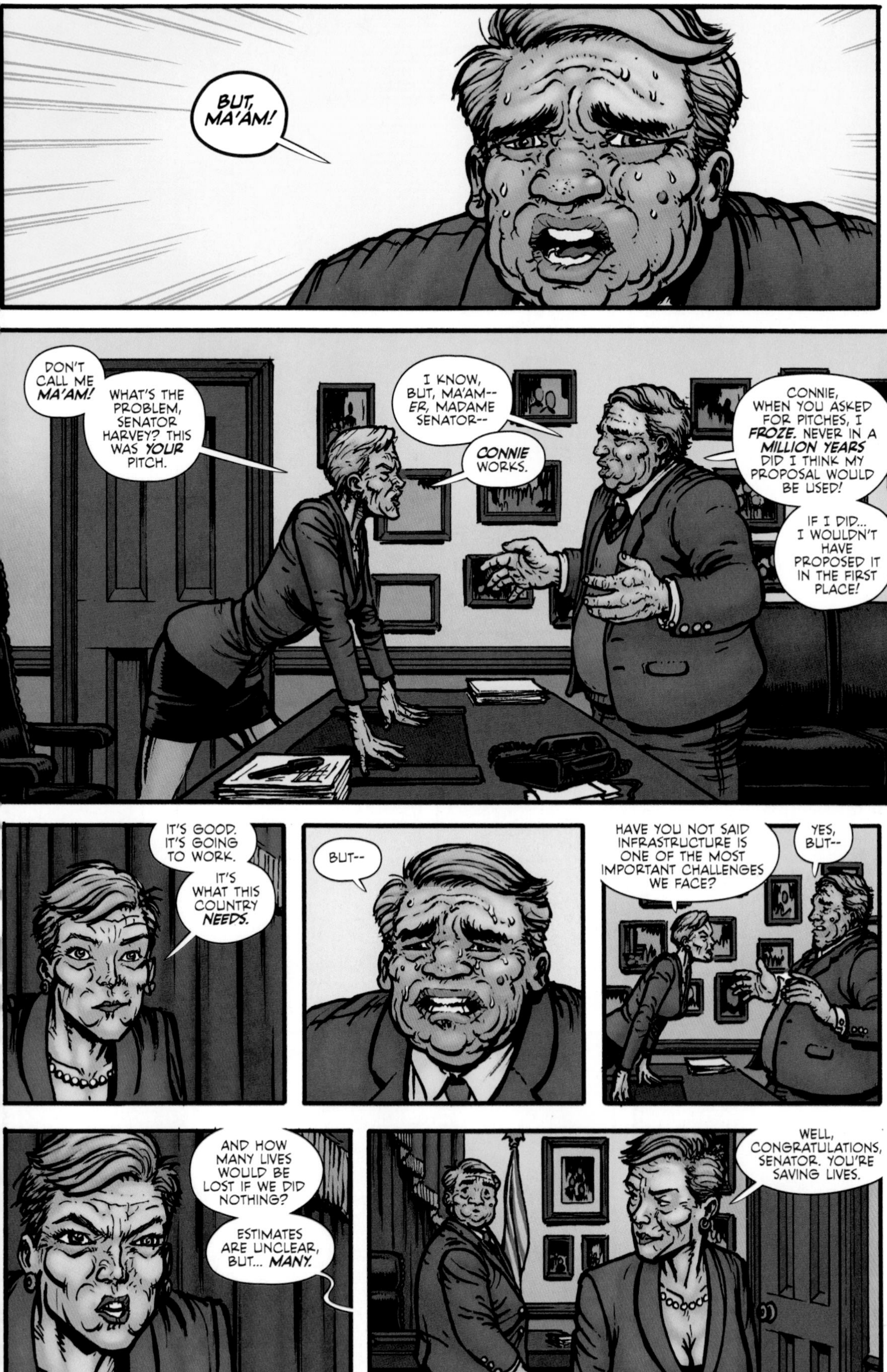
BUT, MA'AM!
DON'T CALL ME *MA'AM!*
WHAT'S THE PROBLEM, SENATOR HARVEY? THIS WAS *YOUR* PITCH.
I KNOW, BUT, MA'AM-- *ER*, MADAME SENATOR--
CONNIE WORKS.
CONNIE, WHEN YOU ASKED FOR PITCHES, I *FROZE.* NEVER IN A *MILLION YEARS* DID I THINK MY PROPOSAL WOULD BE USED!
IF I DID... I WOULDN'T HAVE PROPOSED IT IN THE FIRST PLACE!
IT'S GOOD. IT'S GOING TO WORK.
IT'S WHAT THIS COUNTRY *NEEDS.*
BUT--
HAVE YOU NOT SAID INFRASTRUCTURE IS ONE OF THE MOST IMPORTANT CHALLENGES WE FACE?
YES, BUT--
AND HOW MANY LIVES WOULD BE LOST IF WE DID NOTHING?
ESTIMATES ARE UNCLEAR, BUT... *MANY.*
WELL, CONGRATULATIONS, SENATOR. YOU'RE SAVING LIVES.

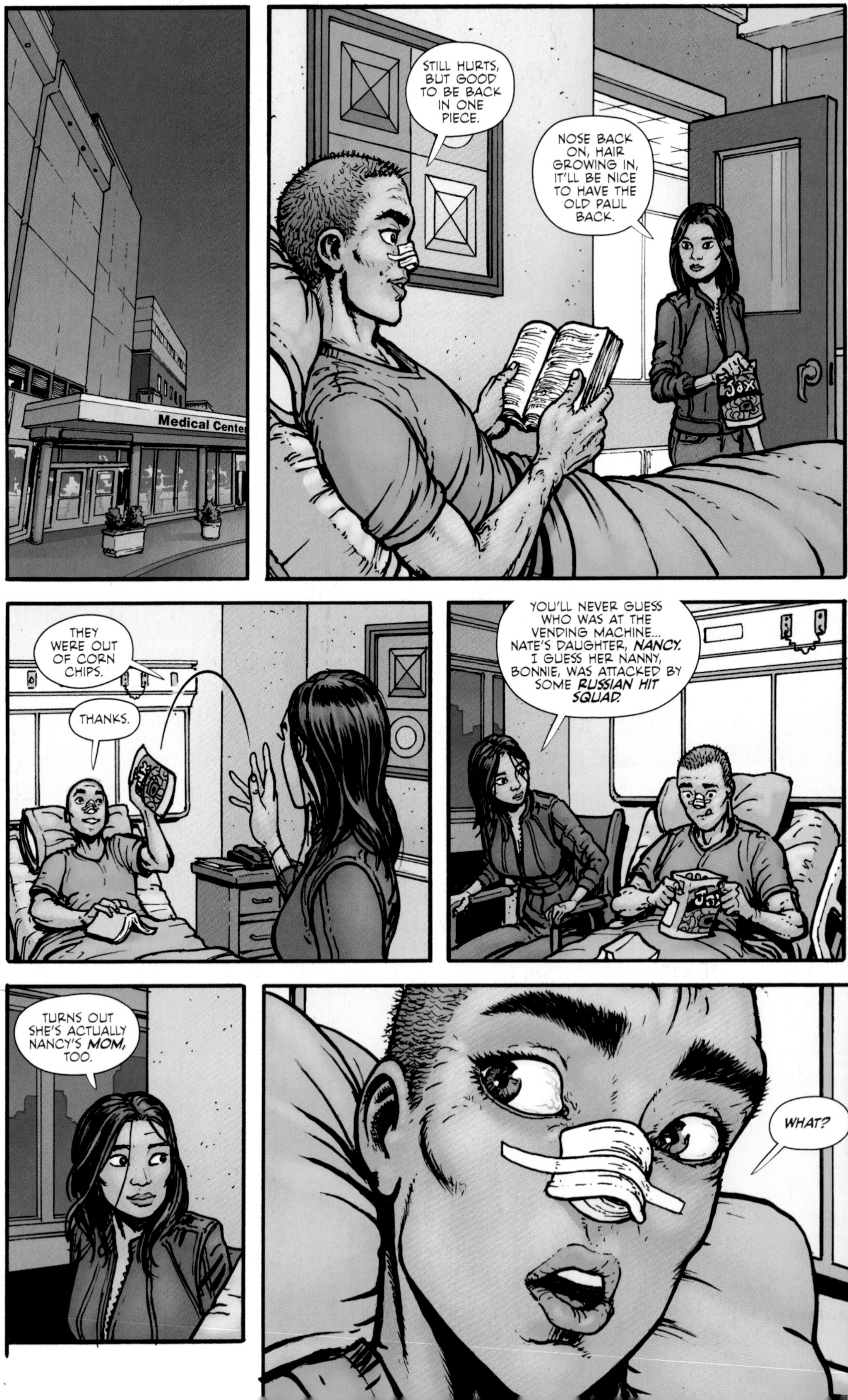
Medical Center
STILL HURTS, BUT GOOD TO BE BACK IN ONE PIECE.
NOSE BACK ON, HAIR GROWING IN, IT'LL BE NICE TO HAVE THE OLD PAUL BACK.
THEY WERE OUT OF CORN CHIPS.
THANKS.
YOU'LL NEVER GUESS WHO WAS AT THE VENDING MACHINE... NATE'S DAUGHTER, NANCY. I GUESS HER NANNY, BONNIE, WAS ATTACKED BY SOME RUSSIAN HIT SQUAD.
TURNS OUT SHE'S ACTUALLY NANCY'S MOM, TOO.
WHAT?

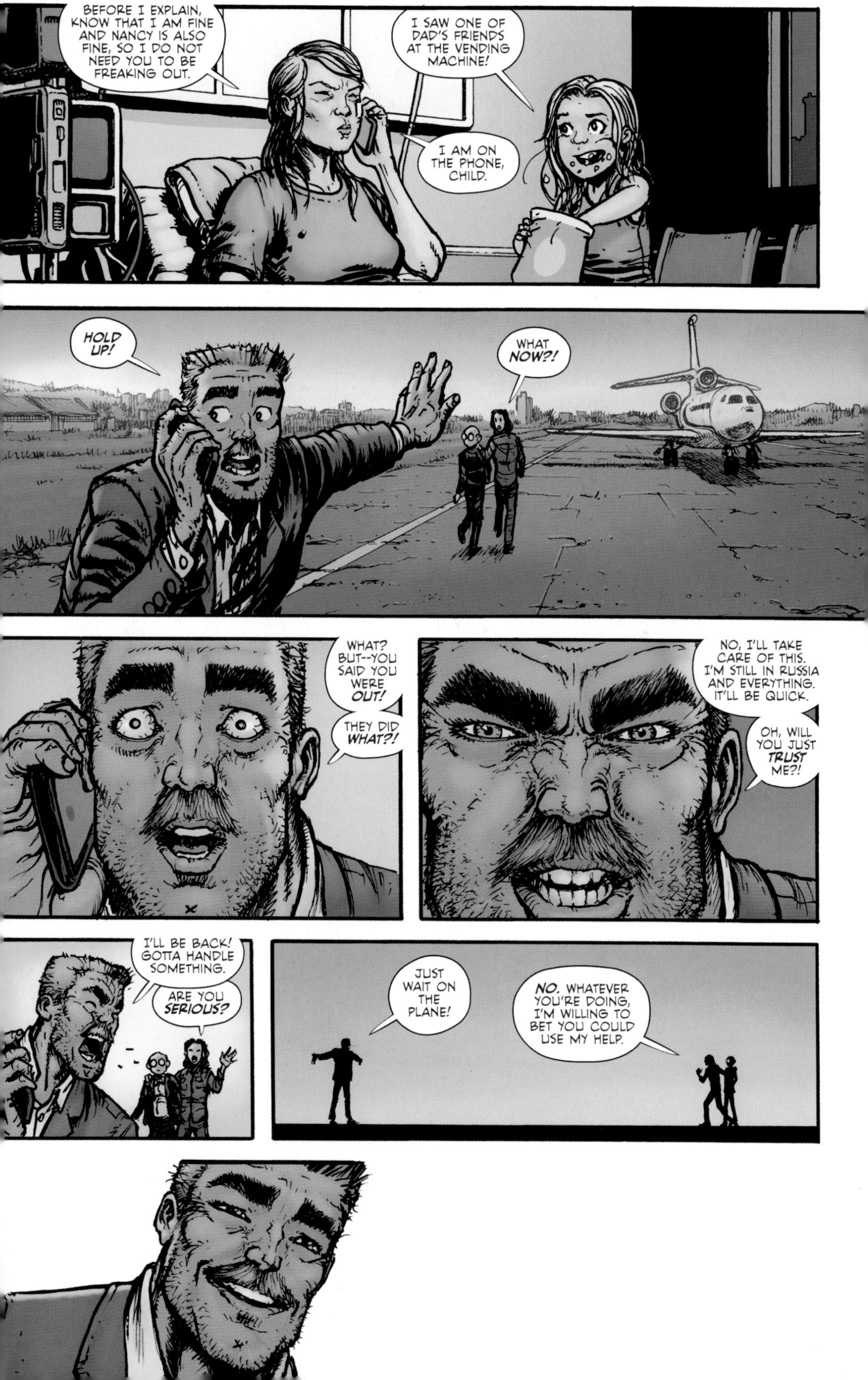
BEFORE I EXPLAIN, KNOW THAT I AM FINE AND NANCY IS ALSO FINE, SO I DO NOT NEED YOU TO BE FREAKING OUT.
I SAW ONE OF DAD'S FRIENDS AT THE VENDING MACHINE!
I AM ON THE PHONE, CHILD.
HOLD UP!
WHAT NOW?!
WHAT? BUT--YOU SAID YOU WERE OUT!
THEY DID WHAT?!
NO, I'LL TAKE CARE OF THIS. I'M STILL IN RUSSIA AND EVERYTHING. IT'LL BE QUICK.
OH, WILL YOU JUST TRUST ME?!
I'LL BE BACK! GOTTA HANDLE SOMETHING.
ARE YOU SERIOUS?
JUST WAIT ON THE PLANE!
NO. WHATEVER YOU'RE DOING, I'M WILLING TO BET YOU COULD USE MY HELP.

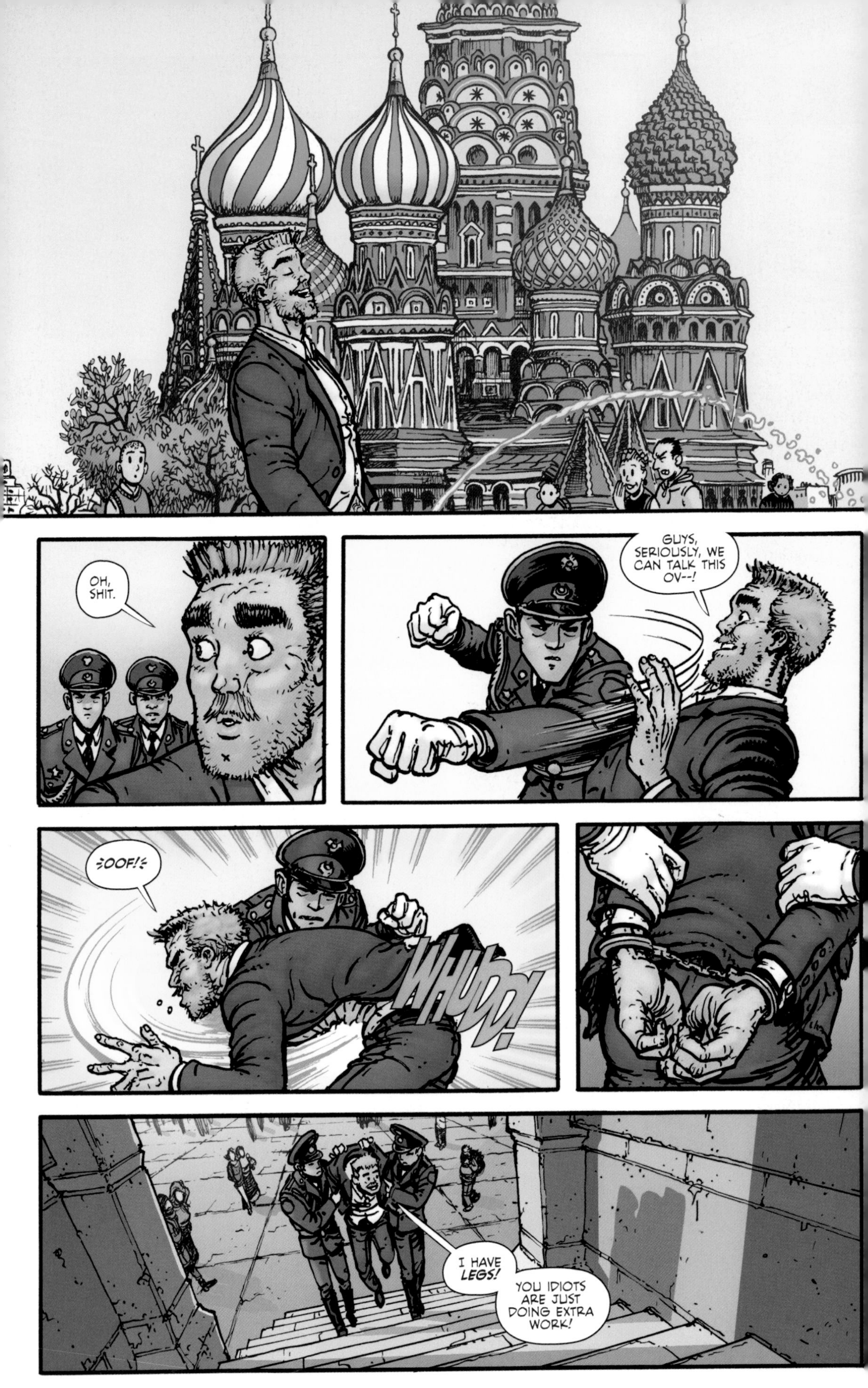
OH, SHIT.
GUYS, SERIOUSLY, WE CAN TALK THIS OV--!
OOF!
WHUDD!
I HAVE LEGS!
YOU IDIOTS ARE JUST DOING EXTRA WORK!

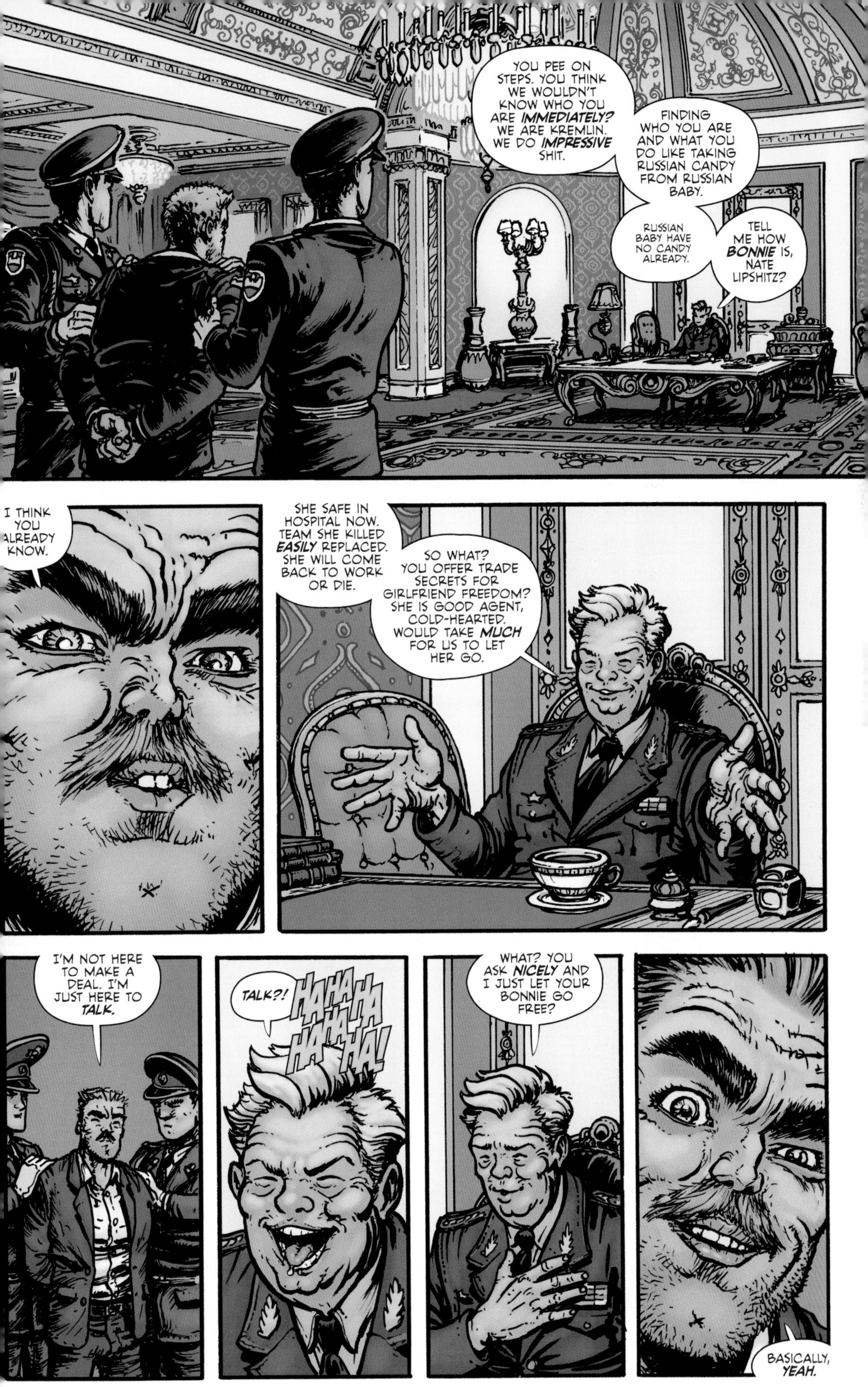
YOU PEE ON STEPS. YOU THINK WE WOULDN'T KNOW WHO YOU ARE IMMEDIATELY? WE ARE KREMLIN. WE DO IMPRESSIVE SHIT.
FINDING WHO YOU ARE AND WHAT YOU DO LIKE TAKING RUSSIAN CANDY FROM RUSSIAN BABY.
RUSSIAN BABY HAVE NO CANDY ALREADY.
TELL ME HOW BONNIE IS, NATE LIPSHITZ?
I THINK YOU ALREADY KNOW.
SHE SAFE IN HOSPITAL NOW. TEAM SHE KILLED EASILY REPLACED. SHE WILL COME BACK TO WORK OR DIE.
SO WHAT? YOU OFFER TRADE SECRETS FOR GIRLFRIEND FREEDOM? SHE IS GOOD AGENT, COLD-HEARTED. WOULD TAKE MUCH FOR US TO LET HER GO.
I'M NOT HERE TO MAKE A DEAL. I'M JUST HERE TO TALK.
TALK?!
HAHAHA HAHAHA HAHA!
WHAT? YOU ASK NICELY AND I JUST LET YOUR BONNIE GO FREE?
BASICALLY, YEAH.

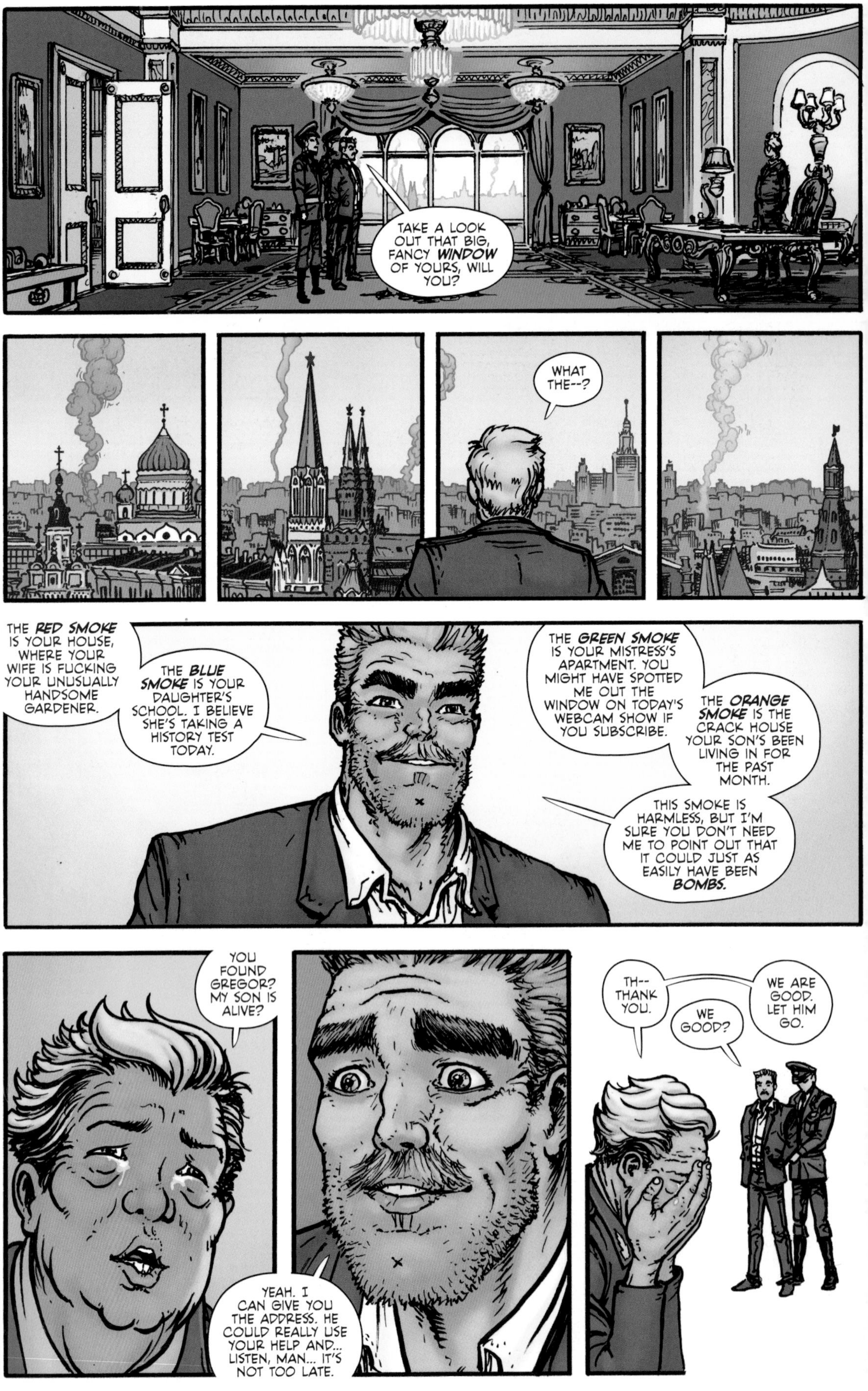
TAKE A LOOK OUT THAT BIG, FANCY WINDOW OF YOURS, WILL YOU?
WHAT THE--?
THE RED SMOKE IS YOUR HOUSE, WHERE YOUR WIFE IS FUCKING YOUR UNUSUALLY HANDSOME GARDENER.
THE BLUE SMOKE IS YOUR DAUGHTER'S SCHOOL. I BELIEVE SHE'S TAKING A HISTORY TEST TODAY.
THE GREEN SMOKE IS YOUR MISTRESS'S APARTMENT. YOU MIGHT HAVE SPOTTED ME OUT THE WINDOW ON TODAY'S WEBCAM SHOW IF YOU SUBSCRIBE.
THE ORANGE SMOKE IS THE CRACK HOUSE YOUR SON'S BEEN LIVING IN FOR THE PAST MONTH.
THIS SMOKE IS HARMLESS, BUT I'M SURE YOU DON'T NEED ME TO POINT OUT THAT IT COULD JUST AS EASILY HAVE BEEN BOMBS.
YOU FOUND GREGOR? MY SON IS ALIVE?
YEAH. I CAN GIVE YOU THE ADDRESS. HE COULD REALLY USE YOUR HELP AND... LISTEN, MAN... IT'S NOT TOO LATE.
TH-- THANK YOU.
WE GOOD?
WE ARE GOOD. LET HIM GO.

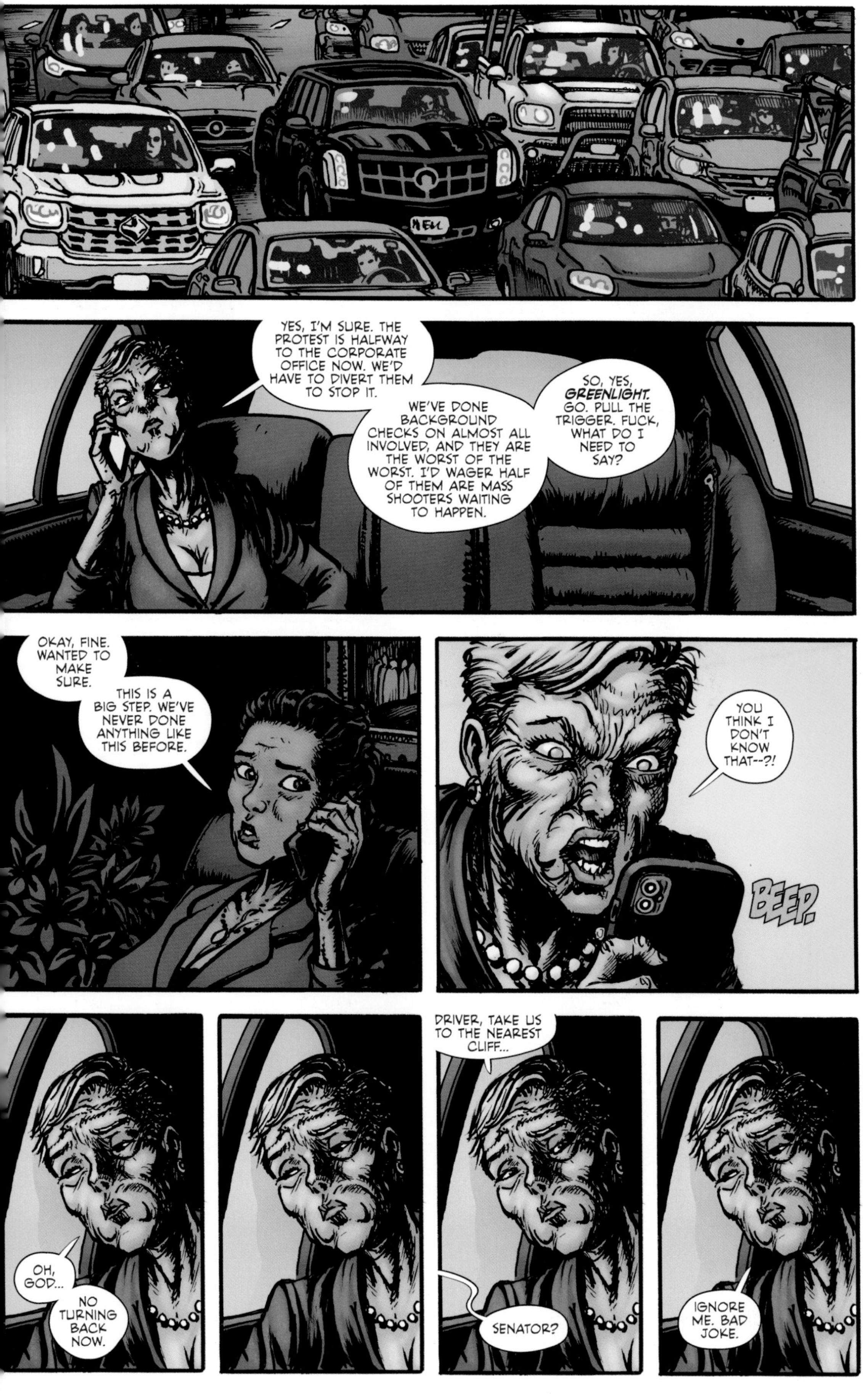
YES, I'M SURE. THE PROTEST IS HALFWAY TO THE CORPORATE OFFICE NOW. WE'D HAVE TO DIVERT THEM TO STOP IT.
WE'VE DONE BACKGROUND CHECKS ON ALMOST ALL INVOLVED, AND THEY ARE THE WORST OF THE WORST. I'D WAGER HALF OF THEM ARE MASS SHOOTERS WAITING TO HAPPEN.
SO, YES, *GREENLIGHT.* GO. PULL THE TRIGGER. FUCK, WHAT DO I NEED TO SAY?
OKAY, FINE. WANTED TO MAKE SURE.
THIS IS A BIG STEP. WE'VE NEVER DONE ANYTHING LIKE THIS BEFORE.
YOU THINK I DON'T KNOW THAT--?!
BEEP.
OH, GOD...
NO TURNING BACK NOW.
DRIVER, TAKE US TO THE NEAREST CLIFF...
SENATOR?
IGNORE ME. BAD JOKE.

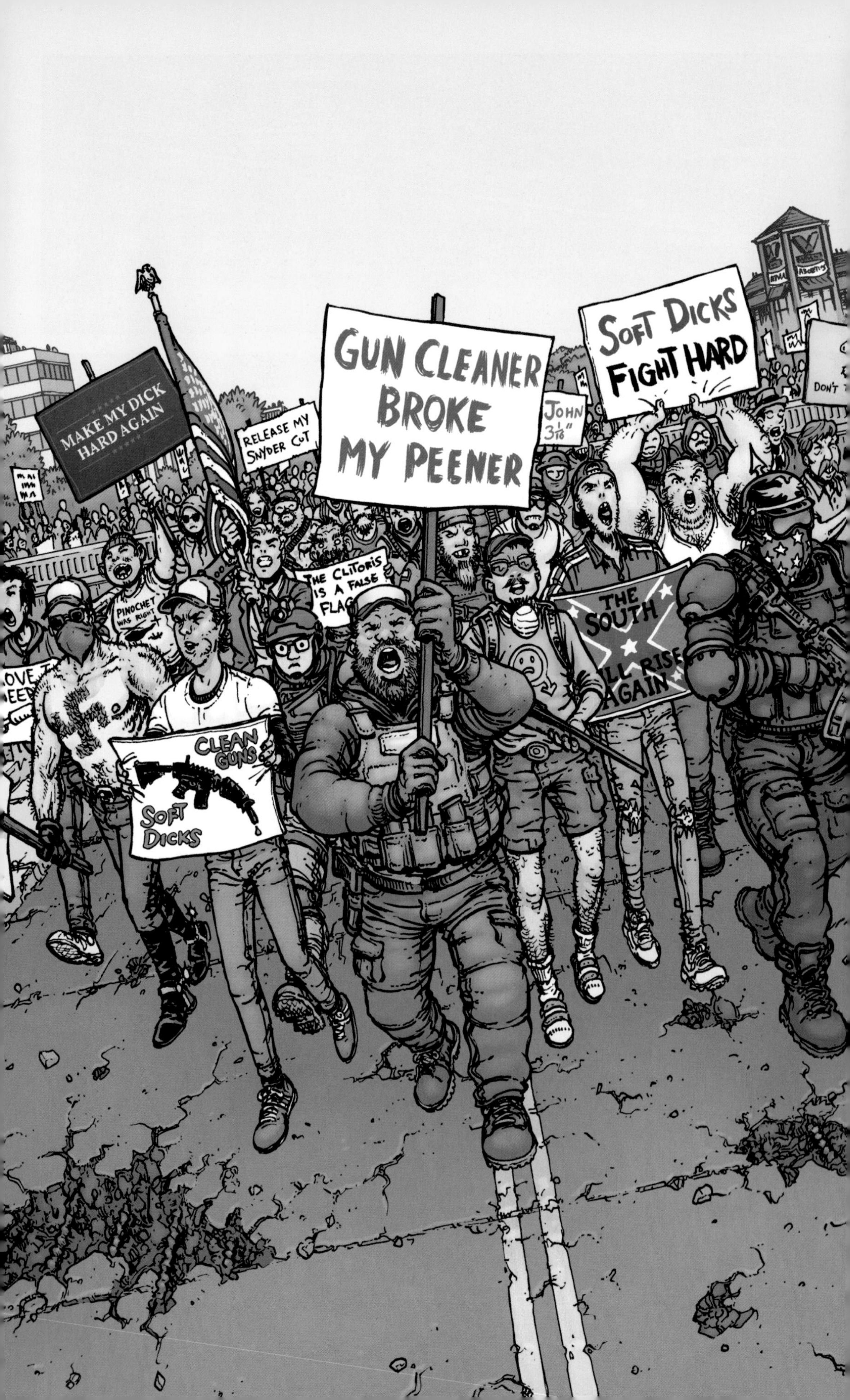
MAKE MY DICK HARD AGAIN
RELEASE MY SNYDER CUT
GUN CLEANER BROKE MY PEENER
JOHN 3 1/16"
SOFT DICKS FIGHT HARD
DON'T
PINOCHET WAS RIGHT
THE CLITORIS IS A FALSE FLA
THE SOUTH
AGAIN
CLEAN GUNS
SOFT DICKS

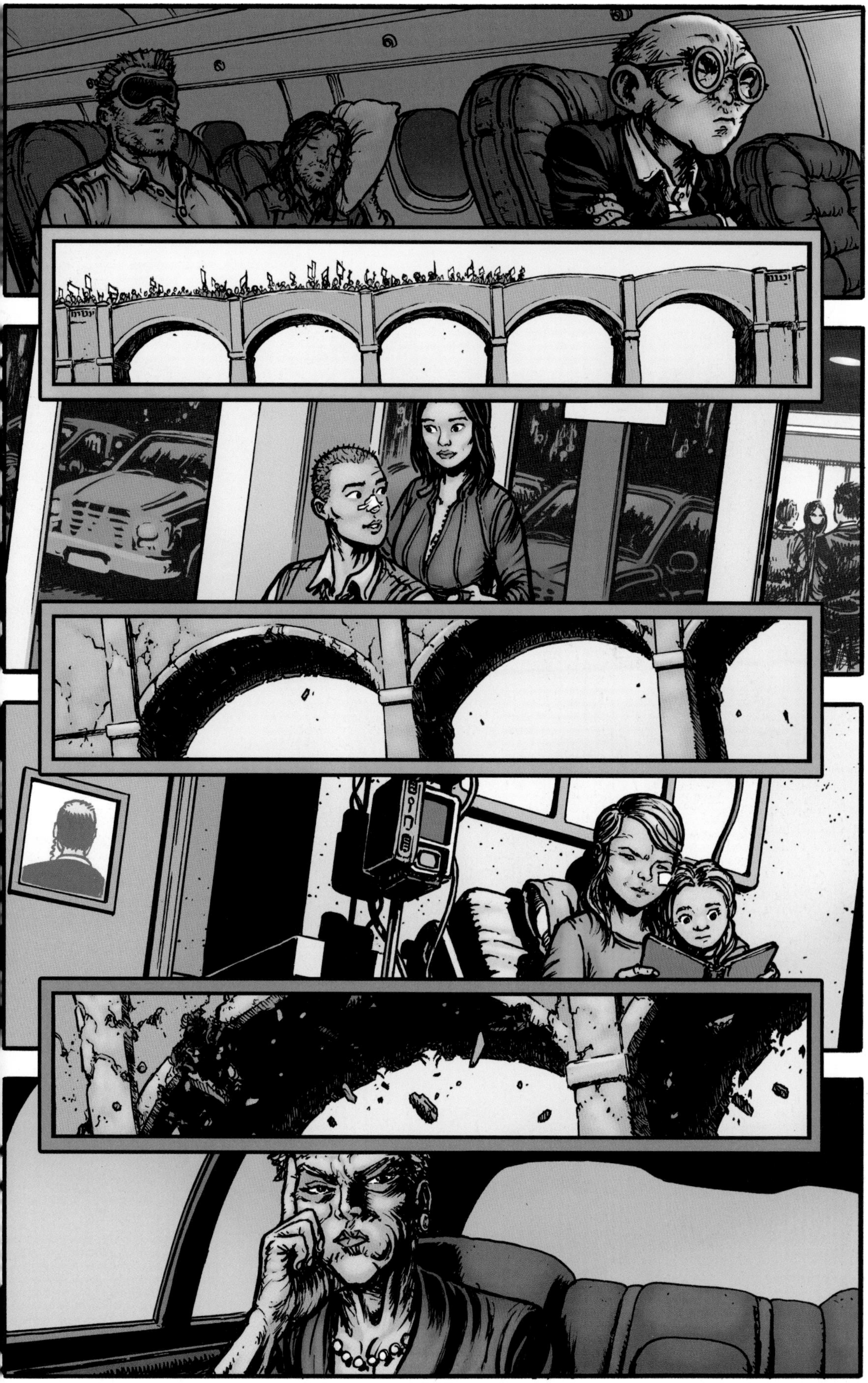

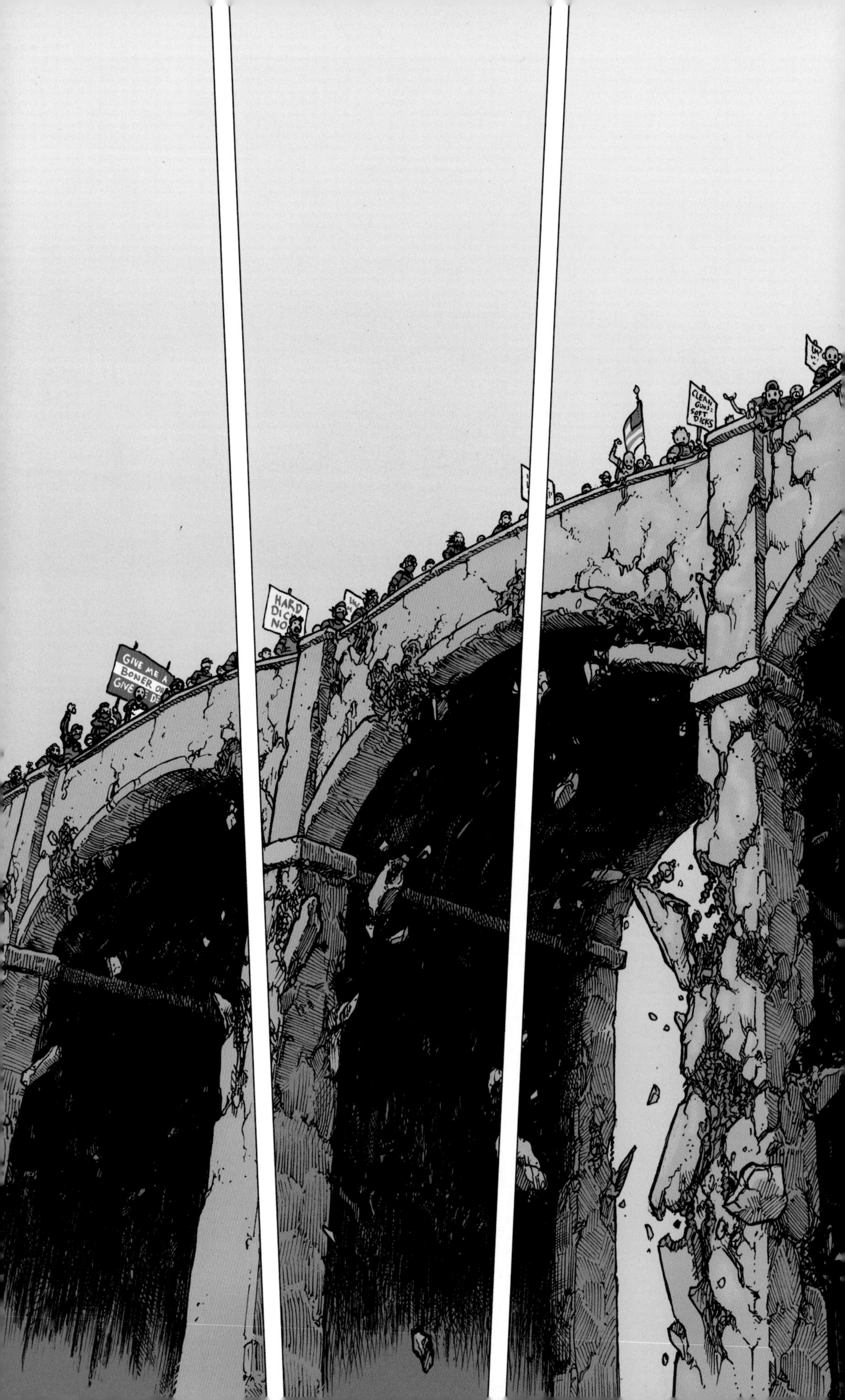
GIVE ME A
BONER OR
HARD
DICK
CLEAN GUNS = SOFT DICKS

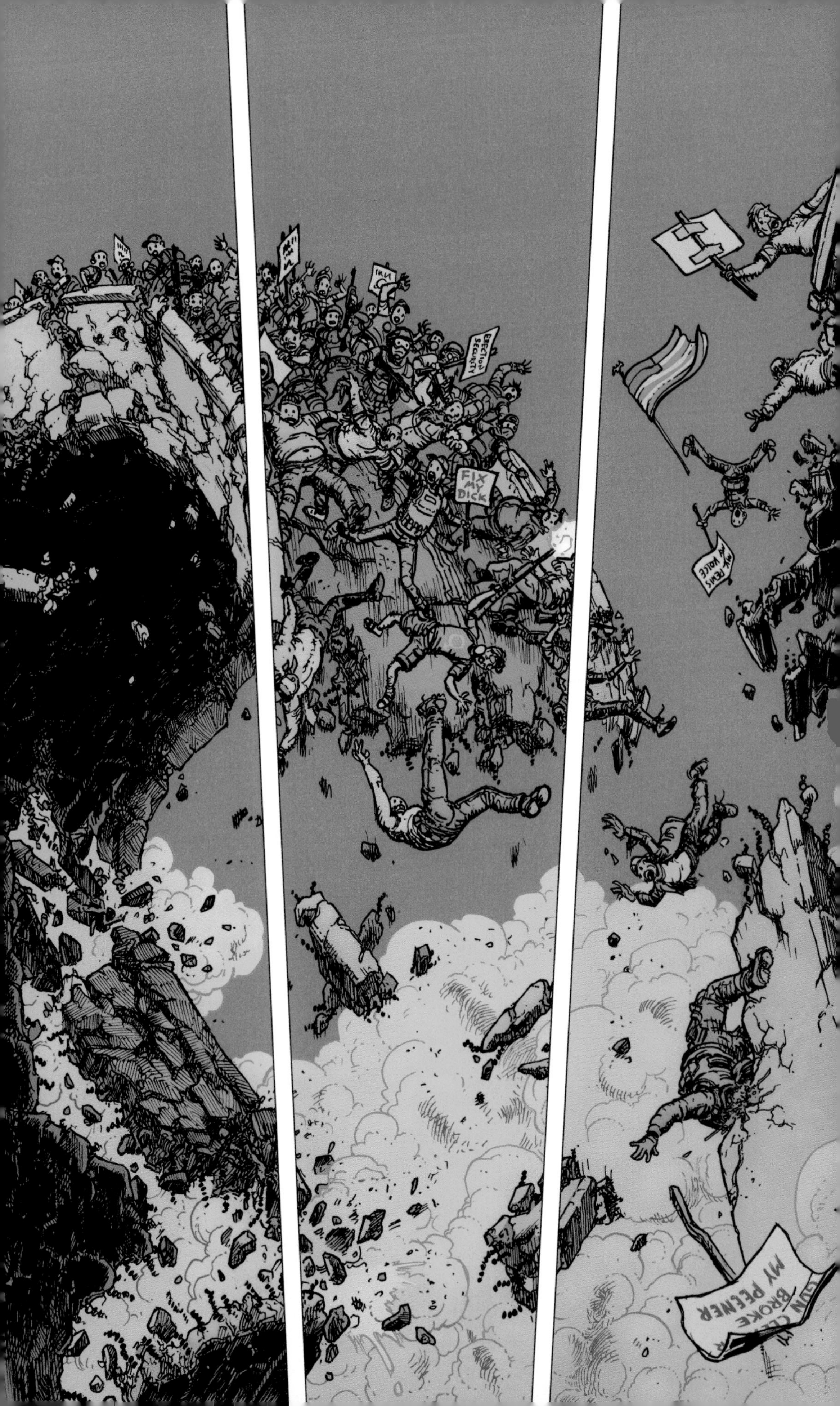
ELECTION SECURITY
FIX MY DICK
MY PENIS MY VOICE
BROKE MY PEENER

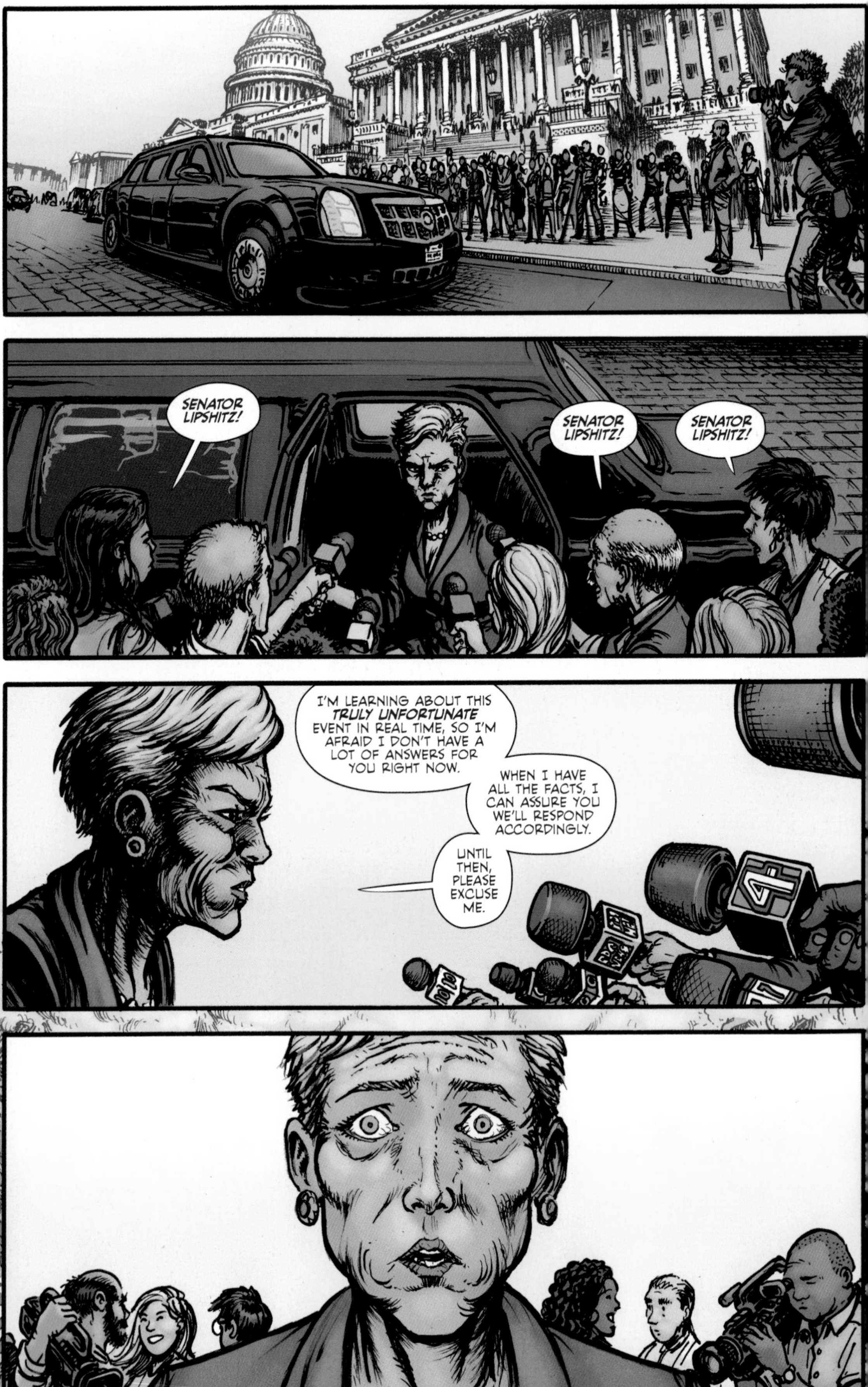
SENATOR LIPSHITZ!
SENATOR LIPSHITZ!
SENATOR LIPSHITZ!
I'M LEARNING ABOUT THIS *TRULY UNFORTUNATE* EVENT IN REAL TIME, SO I'M AFRAID I DON'T HAVE A LOT OF ANSWERS FOR YOU RIGHT NOW.
WHEN I HAVE ALL THE FACTS, I CAN ASSURE YOU WE'LL RESPOND ACCORDINGLY.
UNTIL THEN, PLEASE EXCUSE ME.

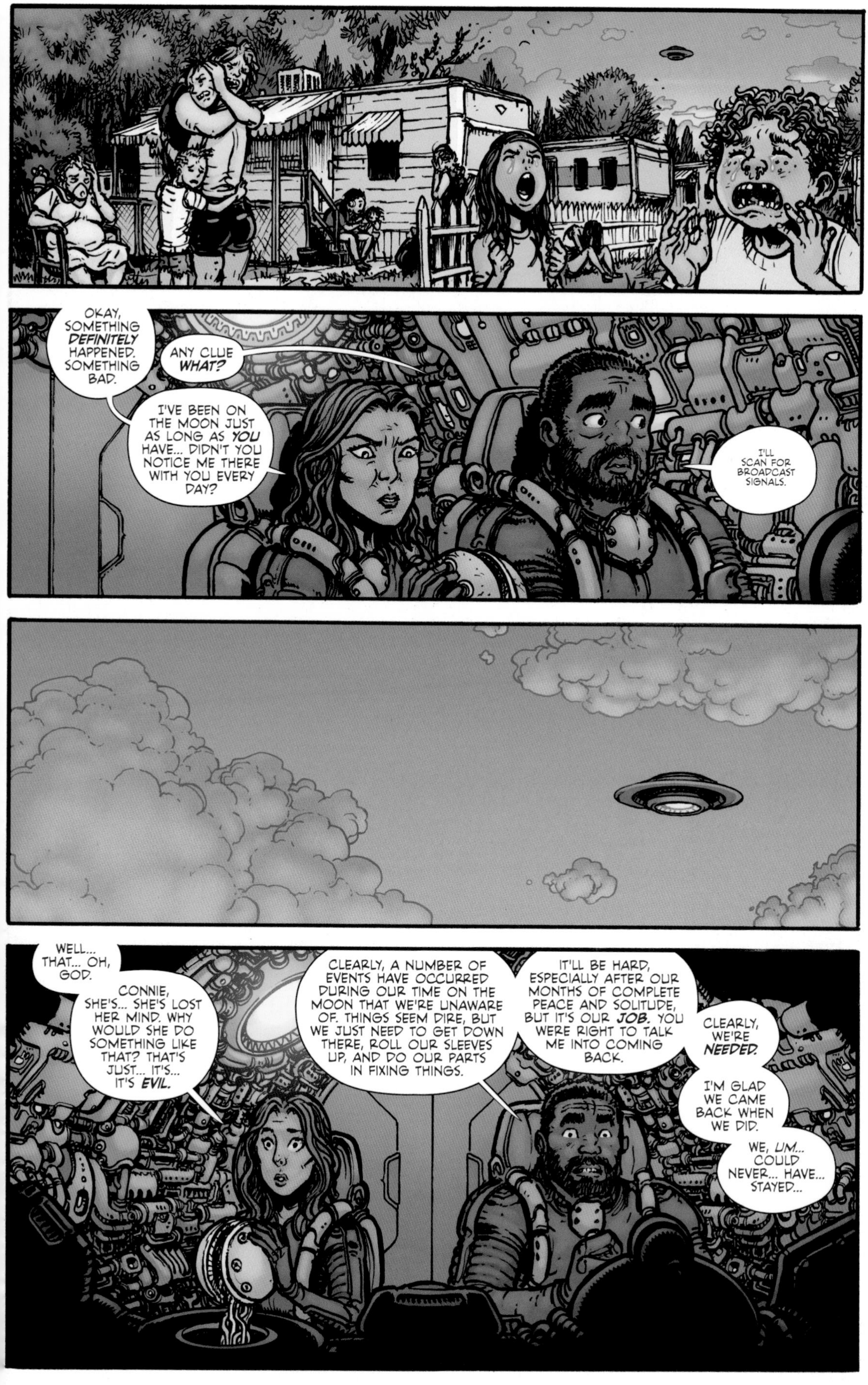
OKAY, SOMETHING DEFINITELY HAPPENED. SOMETHING BAD.
ANY CLUE WHAT?
I'VE BEEN ON THE MOON JUST AS LONG AS YOU HAVE... DIDN'T YOU NOTICE ME THERE WITH YOU EVERY DAY?
I'LL SCAN FOR BROADCAST SIGNALS.
WELL... THAT... OH, GOD.
CONNIE, SHE'S... SHE'S LOST HER MIND. WHY WOULD SHE DO SOMETHING LIKE THAT? THAT'S JUST... IT'S... IT'S EVIL.
CLEARLY, A NUMBER OF EVENTS HAVE OCCURRED DURING OUR TIME ON THE MOON THAT WE'RE UNAWARE OF. THINGS SEEM DIRE, BUT WE JUST NEED TO GET DOWN THERE, ROLL OUR SLEEVES UP, AND DO OUR PARTS IN FIXING THINGS.
IT'LL BE HARD, ESPECIALLY AFTER OUR MONTHS OF COMPLETE PEACE AND SOLITUDE, BUT IT'S OUR JOB. YOU WERE RIGHT TO TALK ME INTO COMING BACK.
CLEARLY, WE'RE NEEDED.
I'M GLAD WE CAME BACK WHEN WE DID.
WE, UM... COULD NEVER... HAVE... STAYED...

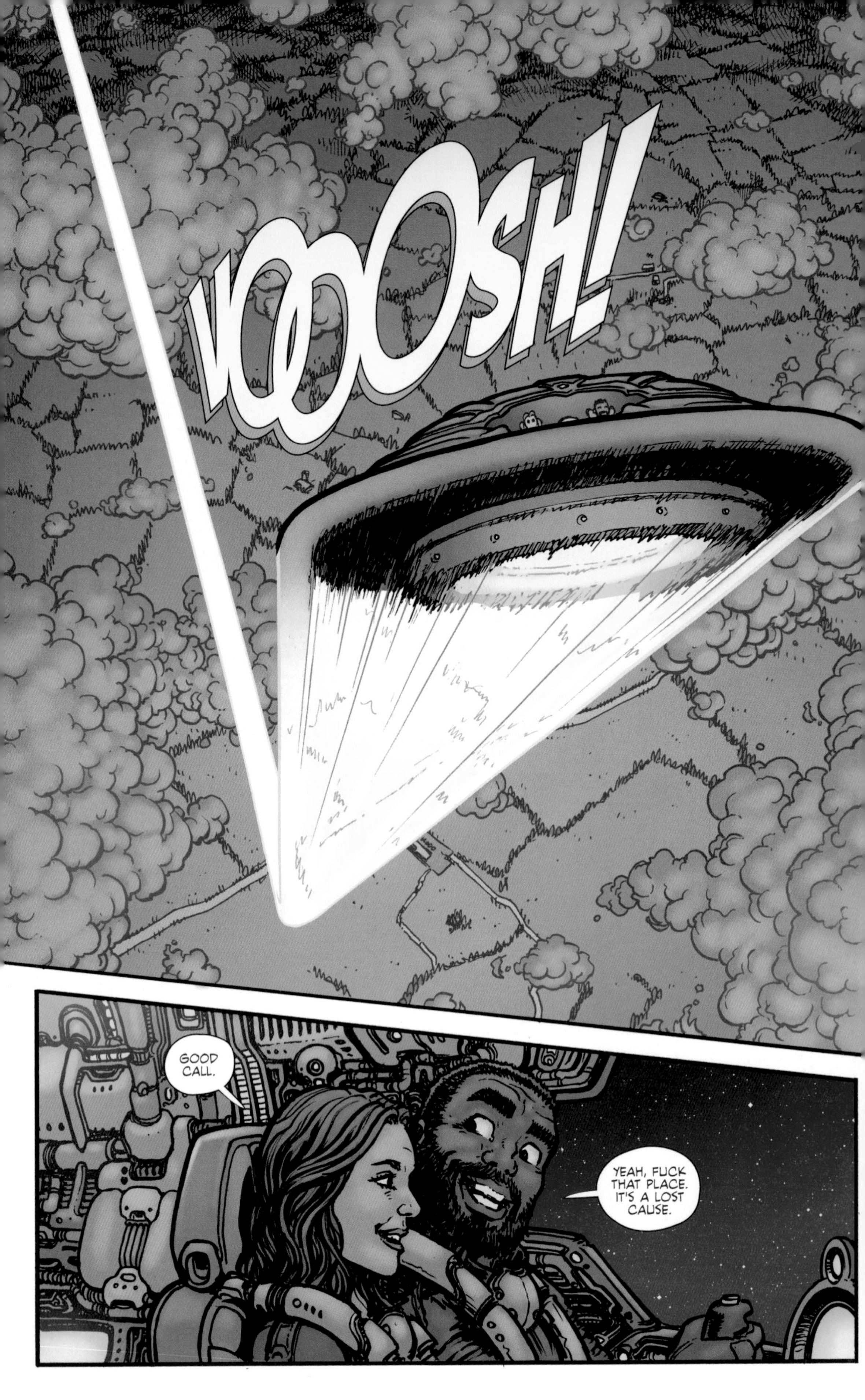
VOOOSH!!
GOOD CALL.
YEAH, FUCK THAT PLACE. IT'S A LOST CAUSE.

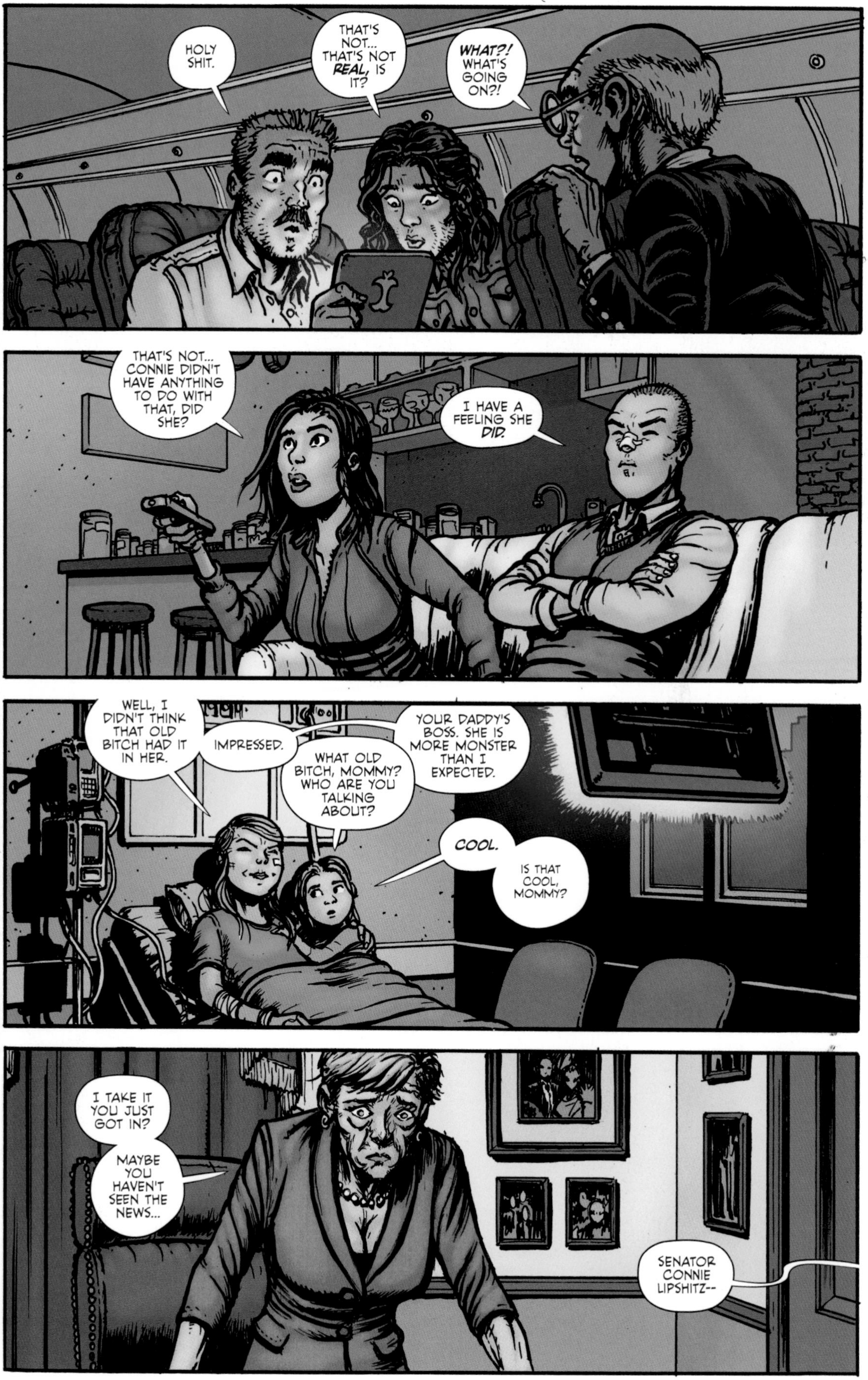
HOLY SHIT.
THAT'S NOT... THAT'S NOT REAL, IS IT?
WHAT?! WHAT'S GOING ON?!
THAT'S NOT... CONNIE DIDN'T HAVE ANYTHING TO DO WITH THAT, DID SHE?
I HAVE A FEELING SHE DID.
WELL, I DIDN'T THINK THAT OLD BITCH HAD IT IN HER.
IMPRESSED.
YOUR DADDY'S BOSS. SHE IS MORE MONSTER THAN I EXPECTED.
WHAT OLD BITCH, MOMMY? WHO ARE YOU TALKING ABOUT?
COOL.
IS THAT COOL, MOMMY?
I TAKE IT YOU JUST GOT IN?
MAYBE YOU HAVEN'T SEEN THE NEWS...
SENATOR CONNIE LIPSHITZ--

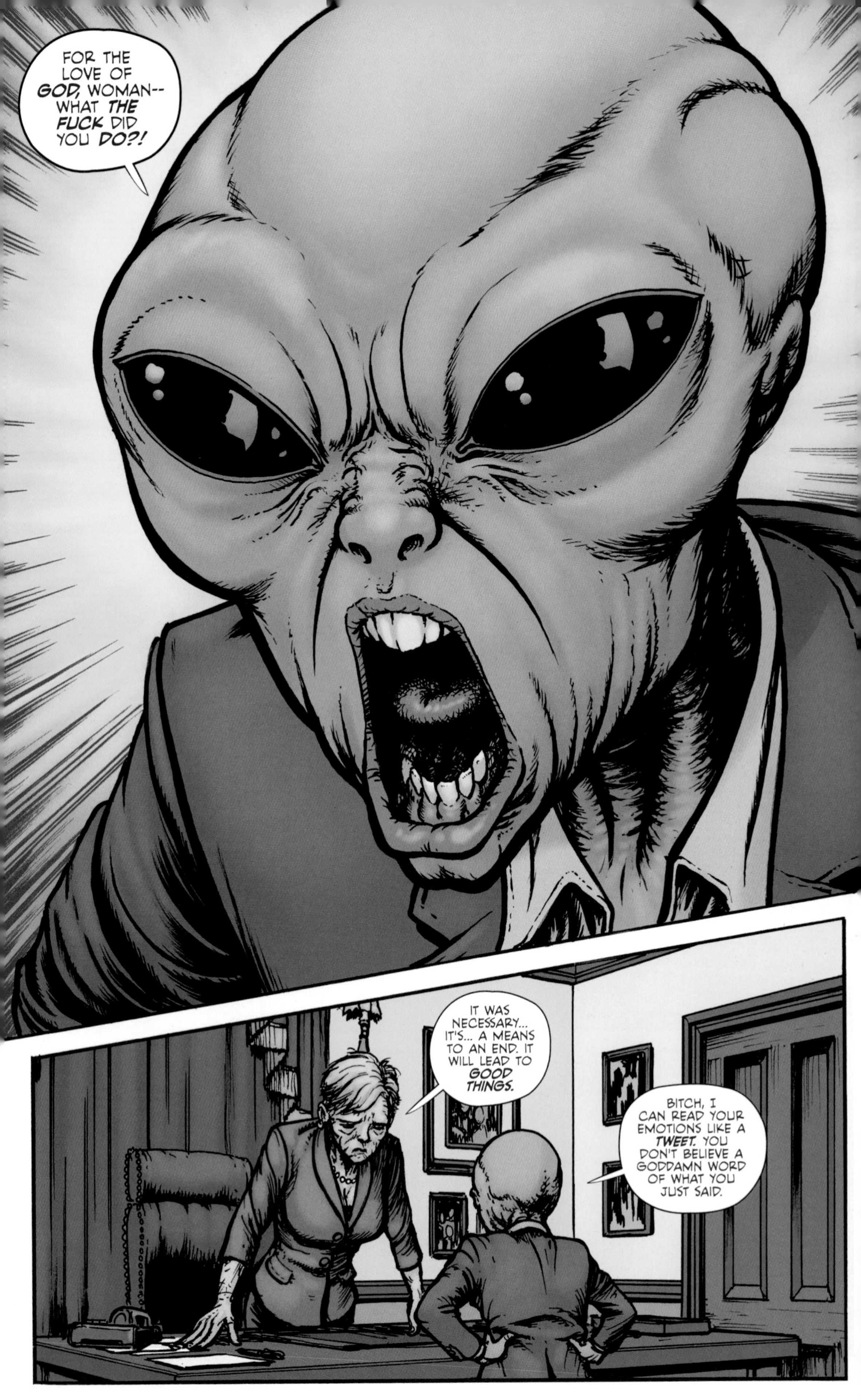
FOR THE LOVE OF GOD, WOMAN-- WHAT THE FUCK DID YOU DO?!
IT WAS NECESSARY... IT'S... A MEANS TO AN END. IT WILL LEAD TO GOOD THINGS.
BITCH, I CAN READ YOUR EMOTIONS LIKE A TWEET. YOU DON'T BELIEVE A GODDAMN WORD OF WHAT YOU JUST SAID.

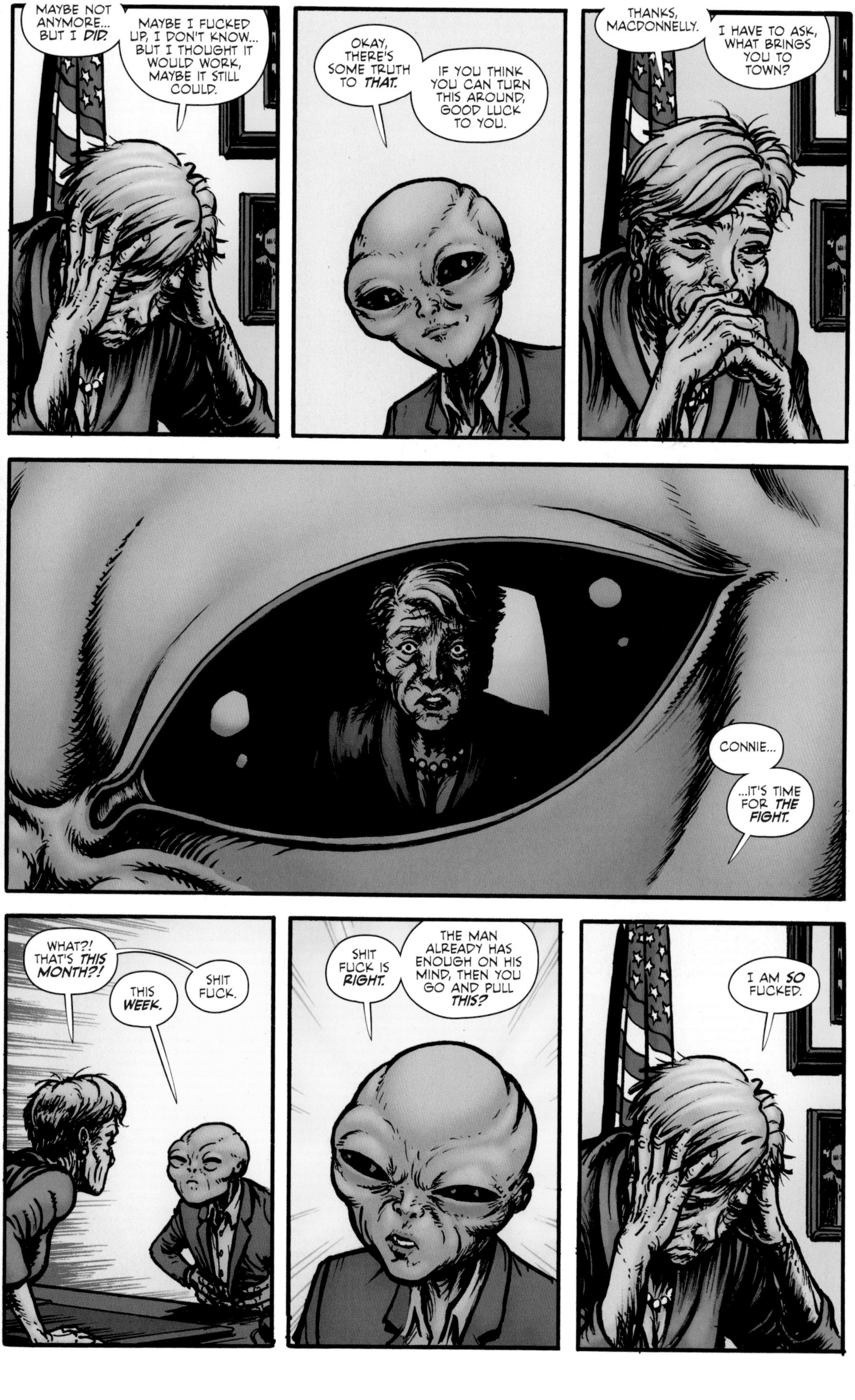
MAYBE NOT ANYMORE... BUT I DID.
MAYBE I FUCKED UP, I DON'T KNOW... BUT I THOUGHT IT WOULD WORK, MAYBE IT STILL COULD.
OKAY, THERE'S SOME TRUTH TO THAT.
IF YOU THINK YOU CAN TURN THIS AROUND, GOOD LUCK TO YOU.
THANKS, MACDONNELLY.
I HAVE TO ASK, WHAT BRINGS YOU TO TOWN?
CONNIE...
...IT'S TIME FOR THE FIGHT.
WHAT?! THAT'S THIS MONTH?!
THIS WEEK.
SHIT FUCK.
SHIT FUCK IS RIGHT.
THE MAN ALREADY HAS ENOUGH ON HIS MIND, THEN YOU GO AND PULL THIS?
I AM SO FUCKED.

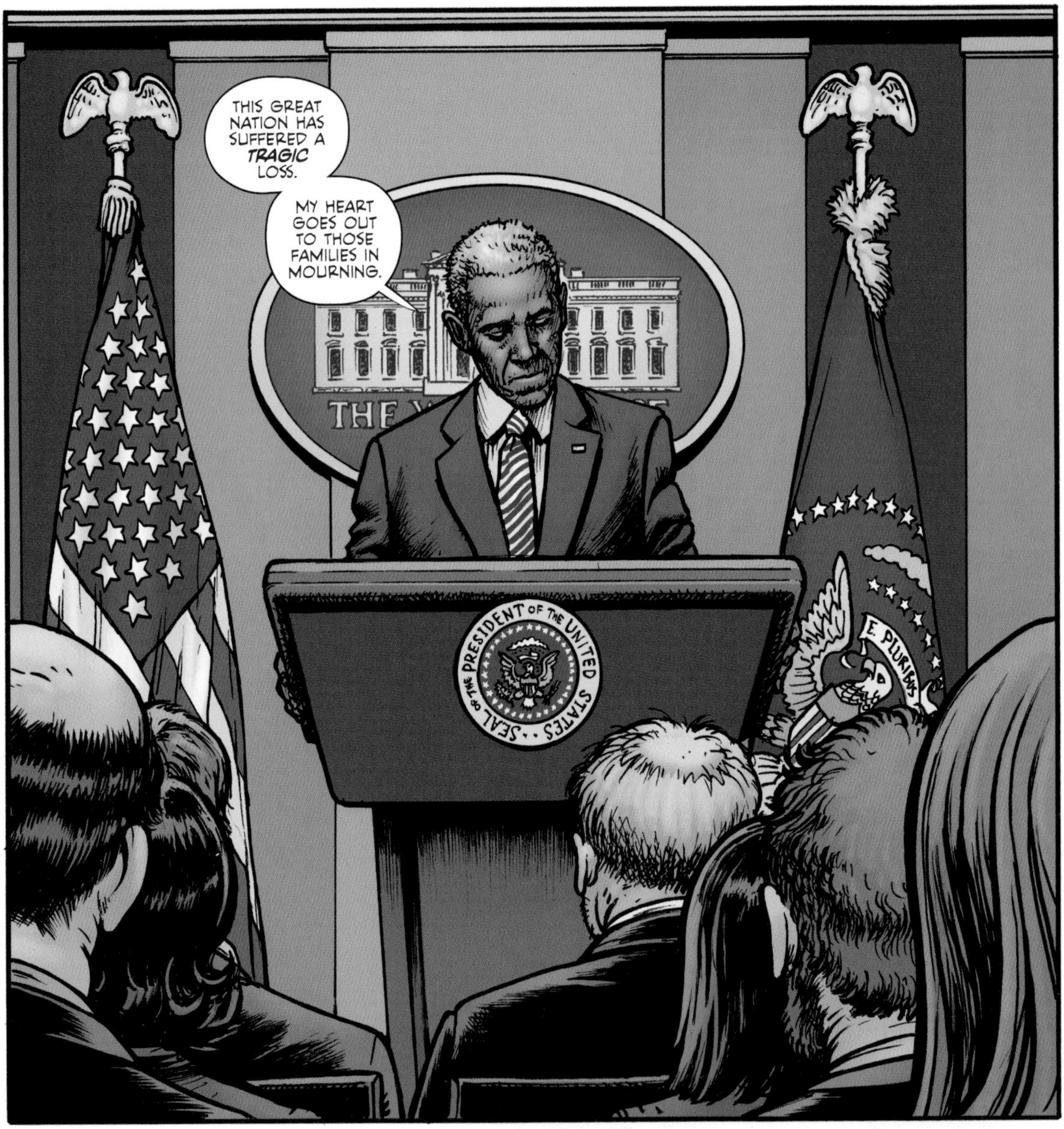
THIS GREAT NATION HAS SUFFERED A *TRAGIC* LOSS.
MY HEART GOES OUT TO THOSE FAMILIES IN MOURNING.
SEAL OF THE PRESIDENT OF THE UNITED STATES
E PLURIBUS

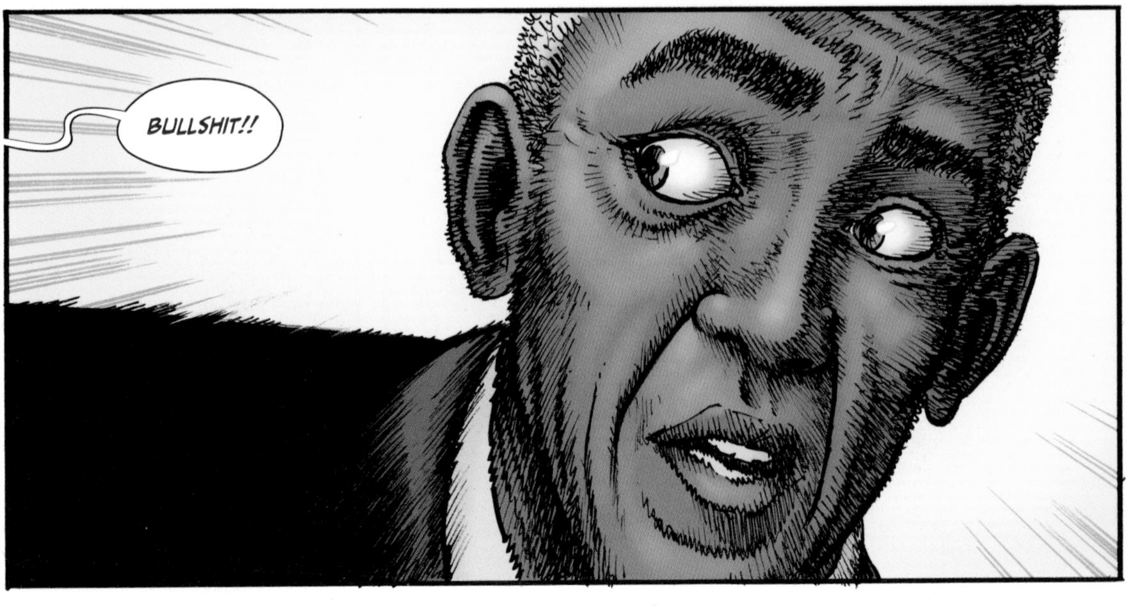
BULLSHIT!!

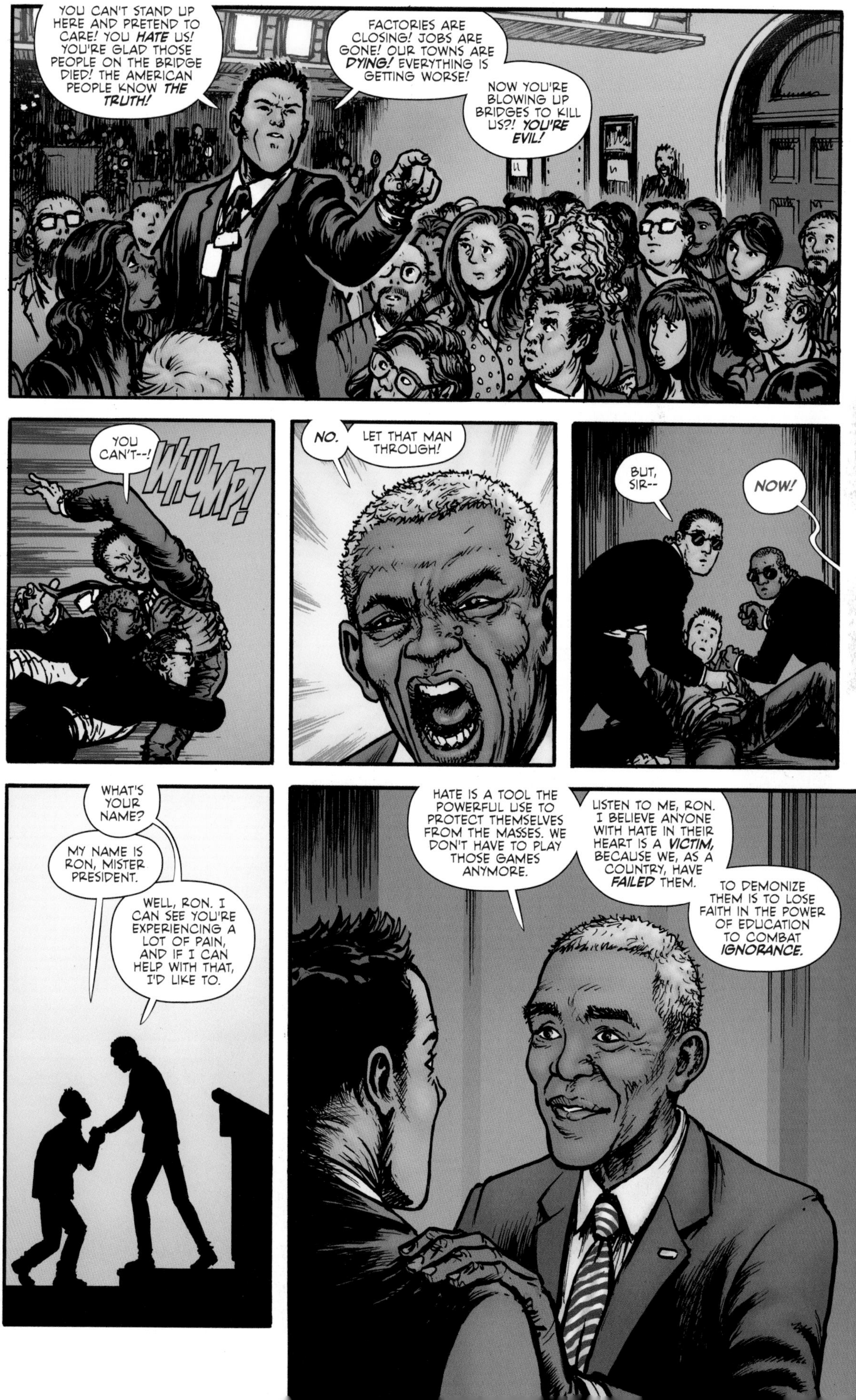
YOU CAN'T STAND UP HERE AND PRETEND TO CARE! YOU HATE US! YOU'RE GLAD THOSE PEOPLE ON THE BRIDGE DIED! THE AMERICAN PEOPLE KNOW THE TRUTH!
FACTORIES ARE CLOSING! JOBS ARE GONE! OUR TOWNS ARE DYING! EVERYTHING IS GETTING WORSE!
NOW YOU'RE BLOWING UP BRIDGES TO KILL US?! YOU'RE EVIL!
YOU CAN'T--!
WHUMP!
NO.
LET THAT MAN THROUGH!
BUT, SIR--
NOW!
WHAT'S YOUR NAME?
MY NAME IS RON, MISTER PRESIDENT.
WELL, RON. I CAN SEE YOU'RE EXPERIENCING A LOT OF PAIN, AND IF I CAN HELP WITH THAT, I'D LIKE TO.
HATE IS A TOOL THE POWERFUL USE TO PROTECT THEMSELVES FROM THE MASSES. WE DON'T HAVE TO PLAY THOSE GAMES ANYMORE.
LISTEN TO ME, RON. I BELIEVE ANYONE WITH HATE IN THEIR HEART IS A VICTIM, BECAUSE WE, AS A COUNTRY, HAVE FAILED THEM.
TO DEMONIZE THEM IS TO LOSE FAITH IN THE POWER OF EDUCATION TO COMBAT IGNORANCE.

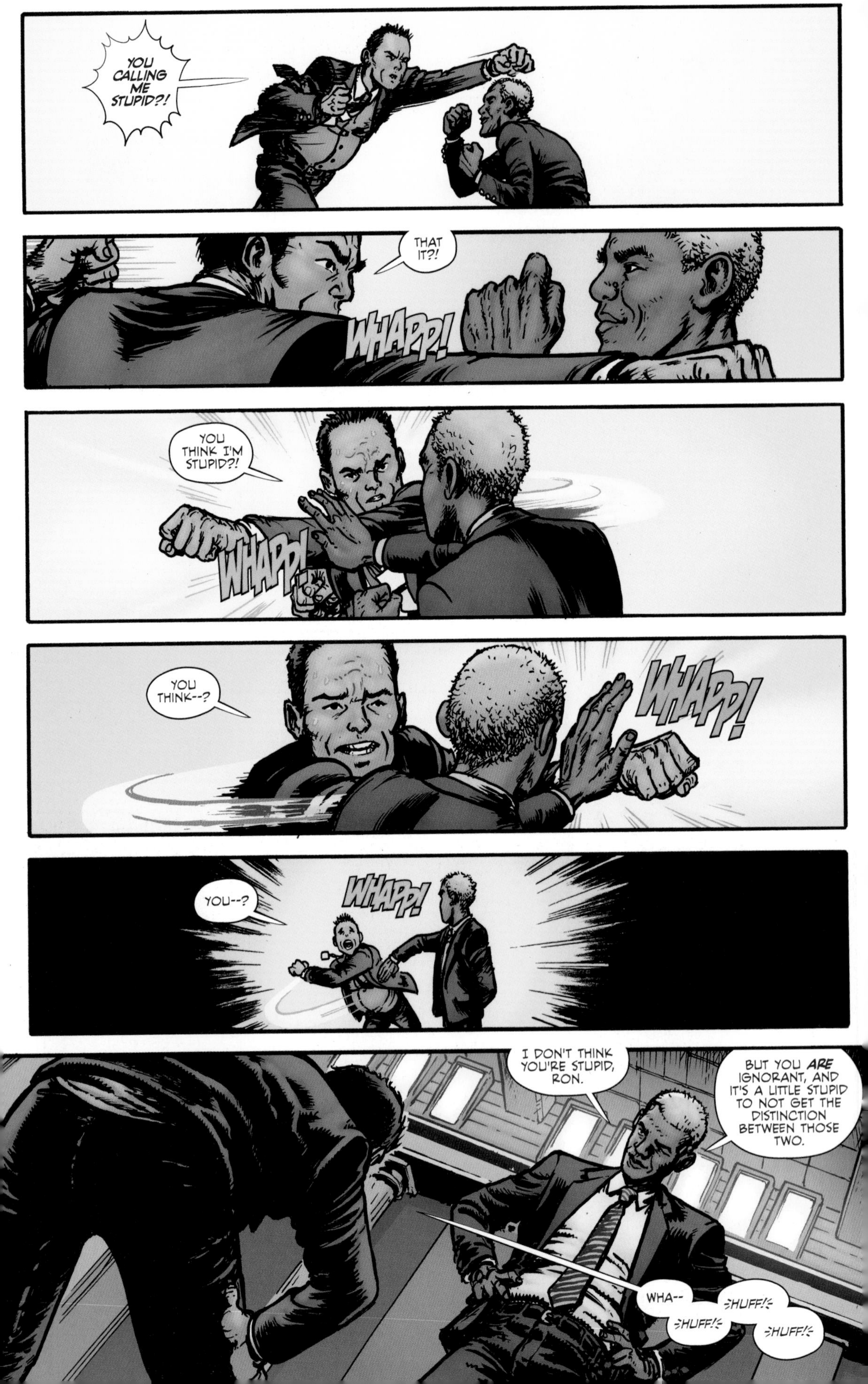
YOU CALLING ME STUPID?!
THAT IT?!
WHAPP!
YOU THINK I'M STUPID?!
WHAPP!
YOU THINK--?
WHAPP!
YOU--?
WHAPP!
I DON'T THINK YOU'RE STUPID, RON.
BUT YOU ARE IGNORANT, AND IT'S A LITTLE STUPID TO NOT GET THE DISTINCTION BETWEEN THOSE TWO.
WHA--
HUFF!
HUFF!
HUFF!

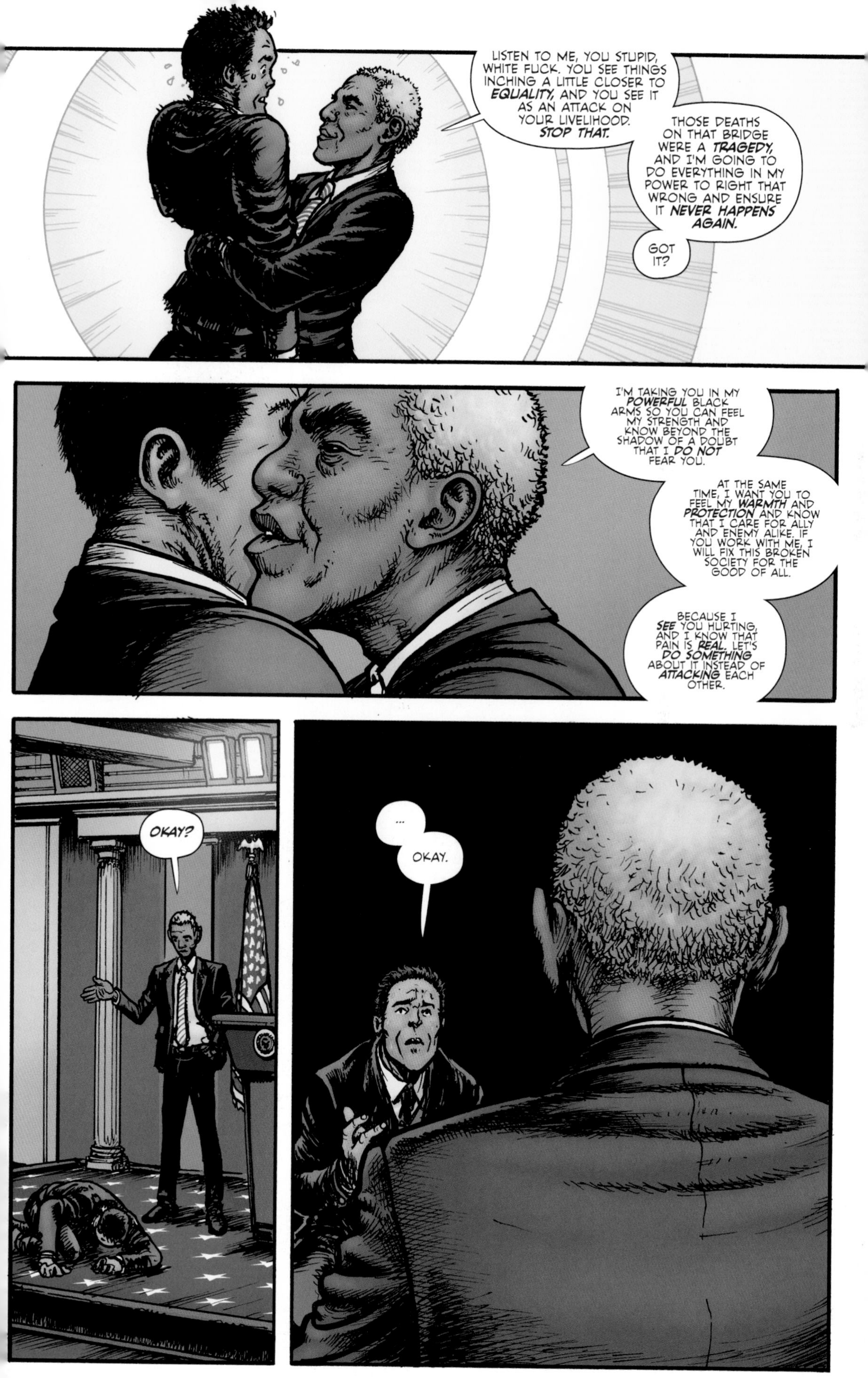
LISTEN TO ME, YOU STUPID, WHITE FUCK. YOU SEE THINGS INCHING A LITTLE CLOSER TO EQUALITY, AND YOU SEE IT AS AN ATTACK ON YOUR LIVELIHOOD. STOP THAT.
THOSE DEATHS ON THAT BRIDGE WERE A TRAGEDY, AND I'M GOING TO DO EVERYTHING IN MY POWER TO RIGHT THAT WRONG AND ENSURE IT NEVER HAPPENS AGAIN.
GOT IT?
I'M TAKING YOU IN MY POWERFUL BLACK ARMS SO YOU CAN FEEL MY STRENGTH AND KNOW BEYOND THE SHADOW OF A DOUBT THAT I DO NOT FEAR YOU.
AT THE SAME TIME, I WANT YOU TO FEEL MY WARMTH AND PROTECTION AND KNOW THAT I CARE FOR ALLY AND ENEMY ALIKE. IF YOU WORK WITH ME, I WILL FIX THIS BROKEN SOCIETY FOR THE GOOD OF ALL.
BECAUSE I SEE YOU HURTING, AND I KNOW THAT PAIN IS REAL. LET'S DO SOMETHING ABOUT IT INSTEAD OF ATTACKING EACH OTHER.
OKAY?
...
OKAY.

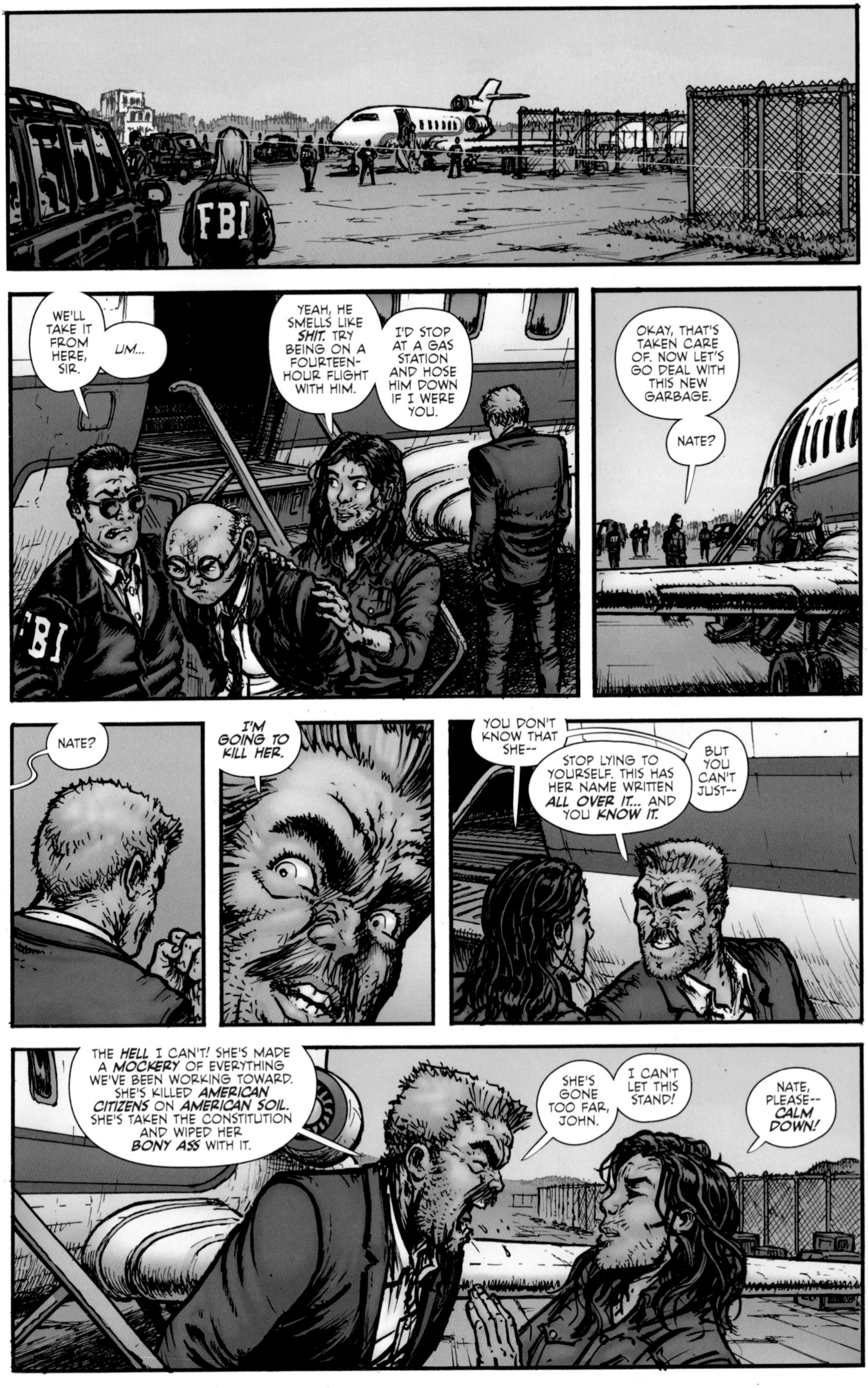
FBI
WE'LL TAKE IT FROM HERE, SIR.
UM...
YEAH, HE SMELLS LIKE SHIT. TRY BEING ON A FOURTEEN-HOUR FLIGHT WITH HIM.
I'D STOP AT A GAS STATION AND HOSE HIM DOWN IF I WERE YOU.
FBI
OKAY, THAT'S TAKEN CARE OF. NOW LET'S GO DEAL WITH THIS NEW GARBAGE.
NATE?
NATE?
I'M GOING TO KILL HER.
YOU DON'T KNOW THAT SHE--
STOP LYING TO YOURSELF. THIS HAS HER NAME WRITTEN ALL OVER IT... AND YOU KNOW IT.
BUT YOU CAN'T JUST--
THE HELL I CAN'T! SHE'S MADE A MOCKERY OF EVERYTHING WE'VE BEEN WORKING TOWARD. SHE'S KILLED AMERICAN CITIZENS ON AMERICAN SOIL. SHE'S TAKEN THE CONSTITUTION AND WIPED HER BONY ASS WITH IT.
SHE'S GONE TOO FAR, JOHN.
I CAN'T LET THIS STAND!
NATE, PLEASE-- CALM DOWN!

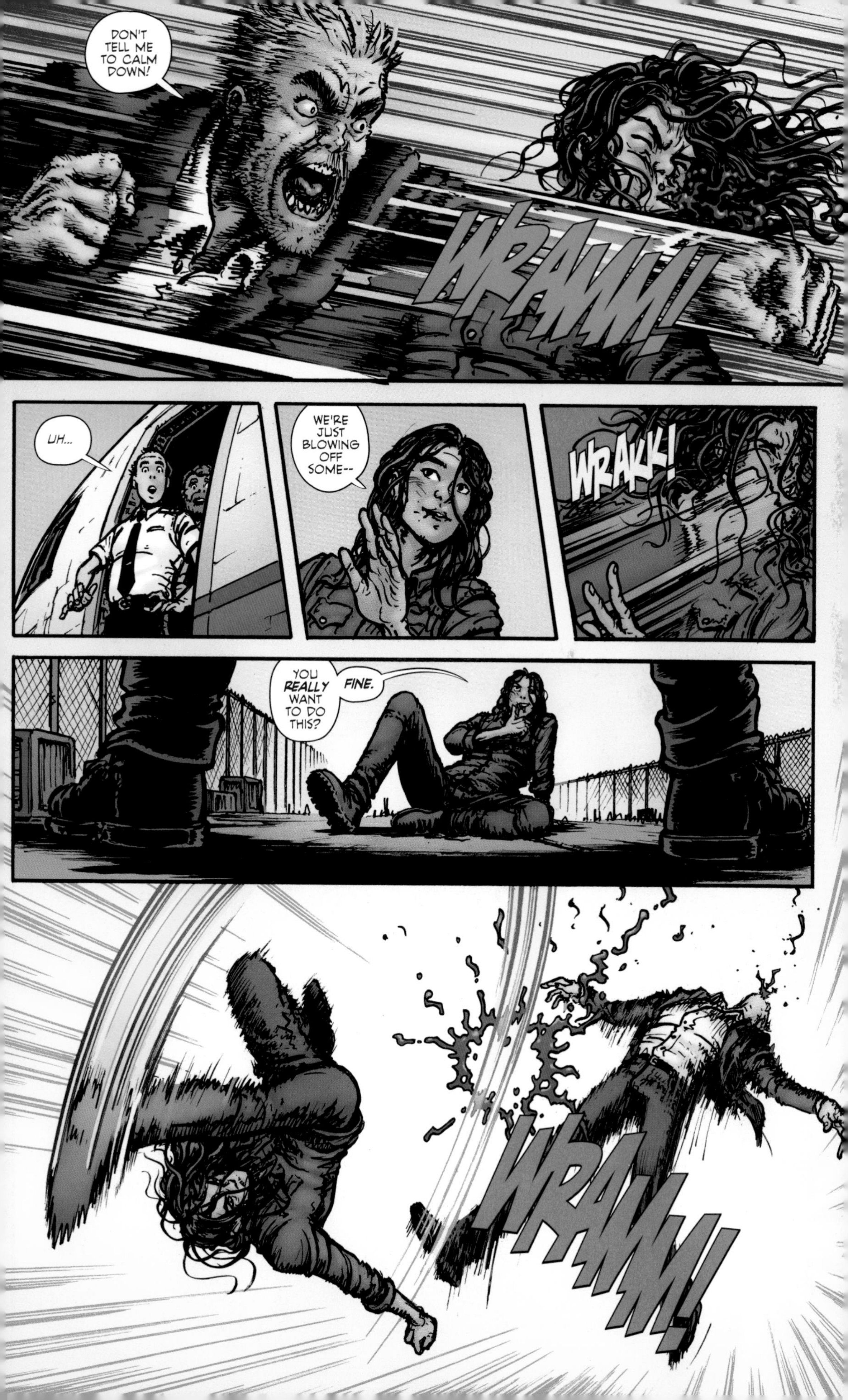
DON'T TELL ME TO CALM DOWN!
WRAMM!
UH...
WE'RE JUST BLOWING OFF SOME--
WRAKK!
FINE.
YOU REALLY WANT TO DO THIS?
WRAMM!

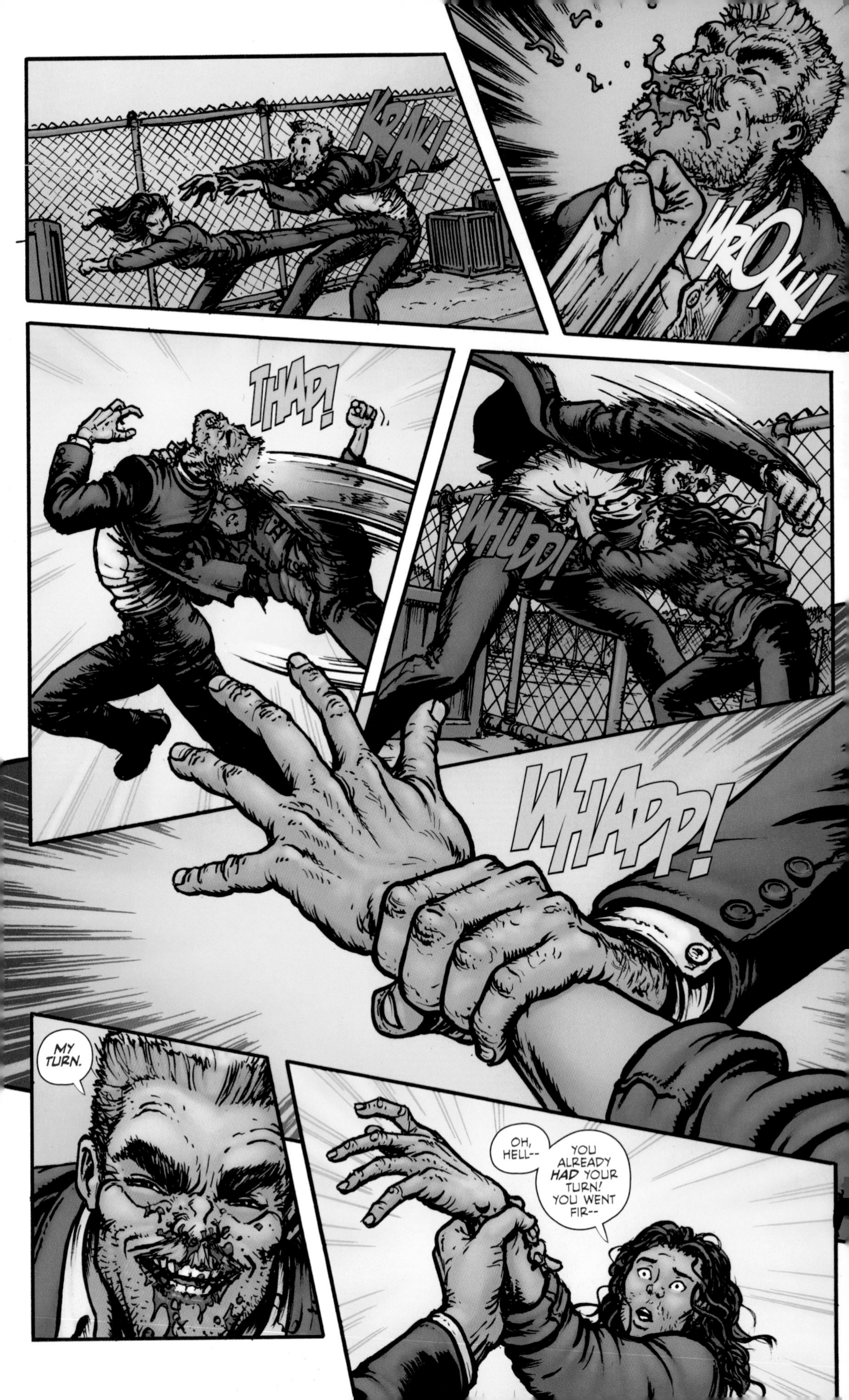
KRAK!
WROKK!
THAP!
WHUDD!
WHAPP!
MY TURN.
OH, HELL--
YOU ALREADY HAD YOUR TURN! YOU WENT FIR--

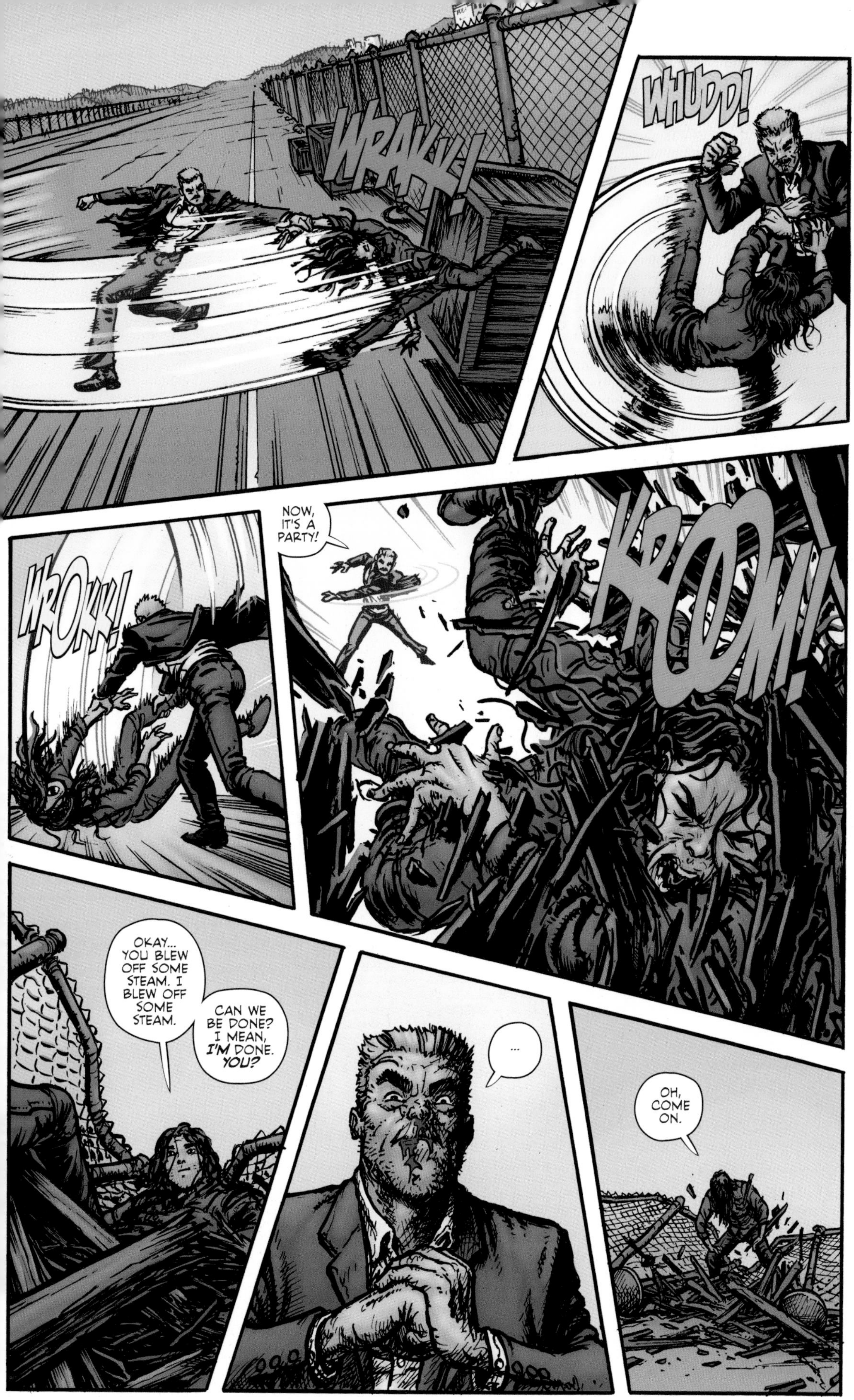
WRAKK!
WHUDD!
WROKK!
NOW, IT'S A PARTY!
KROOM!
OKAY... YOU BLEW OFF SOME STEAM. I BLEW OFF SOME STEAM.
CAN WE BE DONE? I MEAN, *I'M* DONE. *YOU?*
...
OH, COME ON.

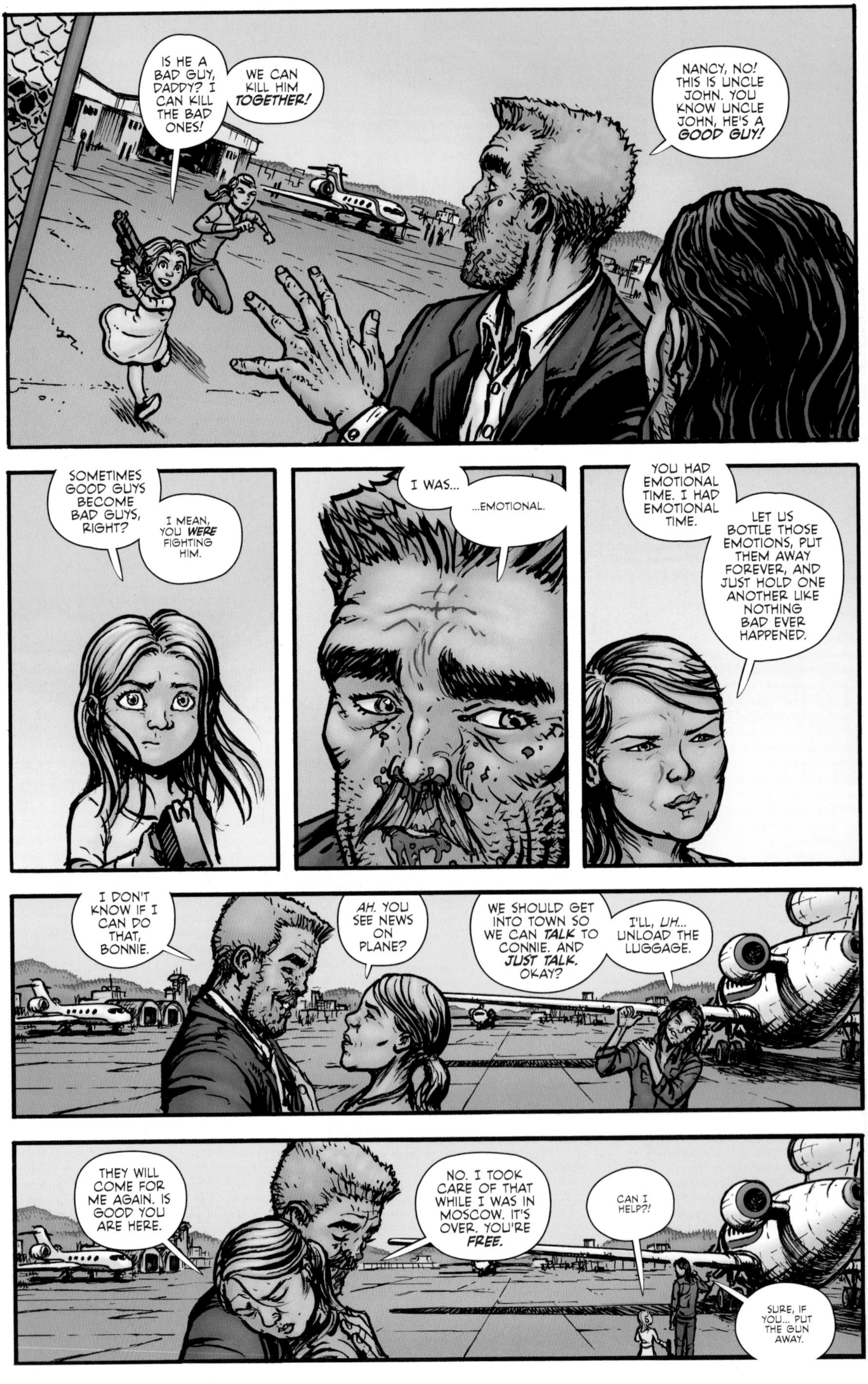
IS HE A BAD GUY, DADDY? I CAN KILL THE BAD ONES!
WE CAN KILL HIM TOGETHER!
NANCY, NO! THIS IS UNCLE JOHN. YOU KNOW UNCLE JOHN, HE'S A GOOD GUY!
SOMETIMES GOOD GUYS BECOME BAD GUYS, RIGHT?
I MEAN, YOU WERE FIGHTING HIM.
I WAS...
...EMOTIONAL.
YOU HAD EMOTIONAL TIME. I HAD EMOTIONAL TIME.
LET US BOTTLE THOSE EMOTIONS, PUT THEM AWAY FOREVER, AND JUST HOLD ONE ANOTHER LIKE NOTHING BAD EVER HAPPENED.
I DON'T KNOW IF I CAN DO THAT, BONNIE.
AH. YOU SEE NEWS ON PLANE?
WE SHOULD GET INTO TOWN SO WE CAN TALK TO CONNIE. AND JUST TALK. OKAY?
I'LL, UH... UNLOAD THE LUGGAGE.
THEY WILL COME FOR ME AGAIN. IS GOOD YOU ARE HERE.
NO. I TOOK CARE OF THAT WHILE I WAS IN MOSCOW. IT'S OVER. YOU'RE FREE.
CAN I HELP?!
SURE, IF YOU... PUT THE GUN AWAY.

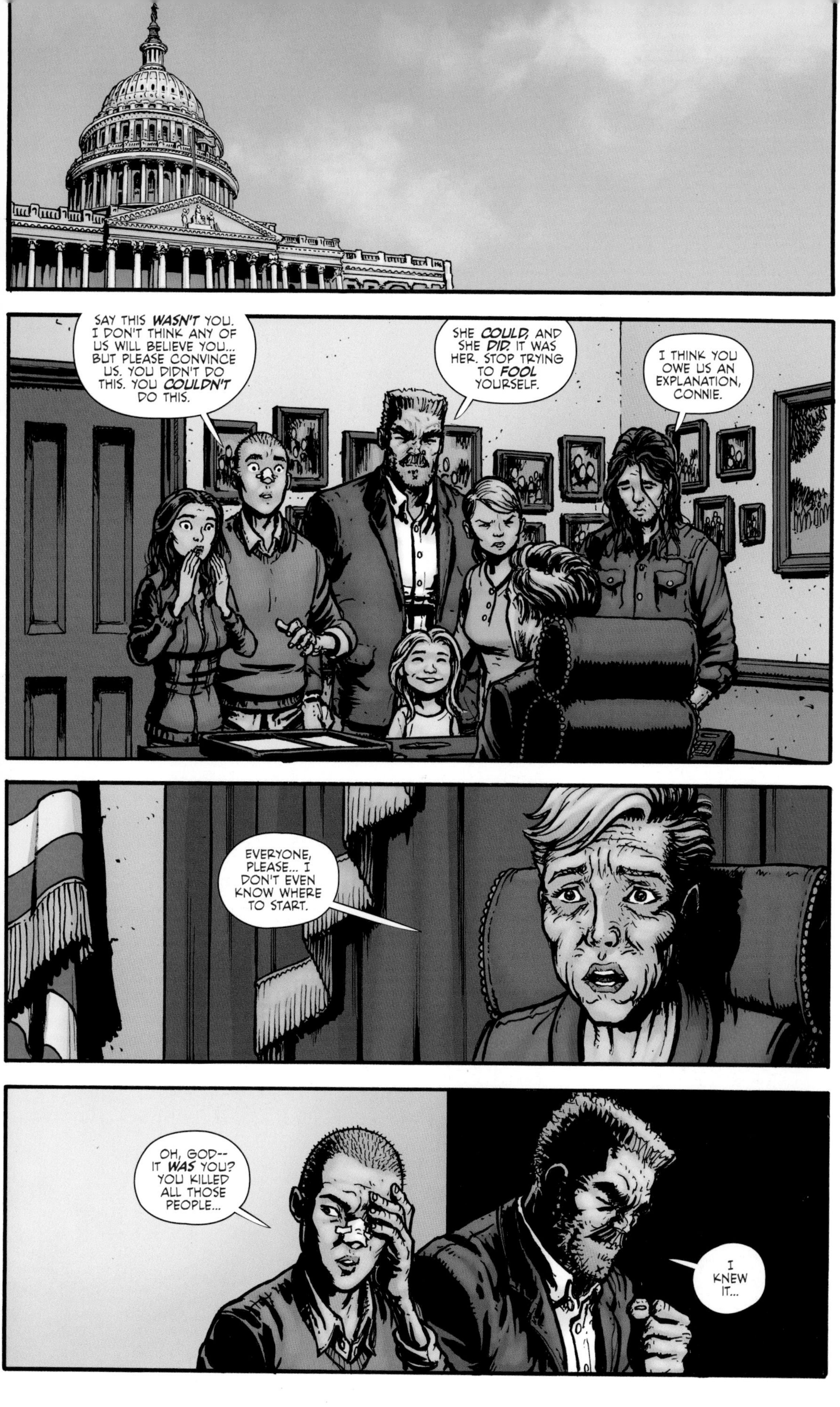
SAY THIS WASN'T YOU. I DON'T THINK ANY OF US WILL BELIEVE YOU... BUT PLEASE CONVINCE US. YOU DIDN'T DO THIS. YOU COULDN'T DO THIS.
SHE COULD, AND SHE DID. IT WAS HER. STOP TRYING TO FOOL YOURSELF.
I THINK YOU OWE US AN EXPLANATION, CONNIE.
EVERYONE, PLEASE... I DON'T EVEN KNOW WHERE TO START.
OH, GOD-- IT WAS YOU? YOU KILLED ALL THOSE PEOPLE...
I KNEW IT...

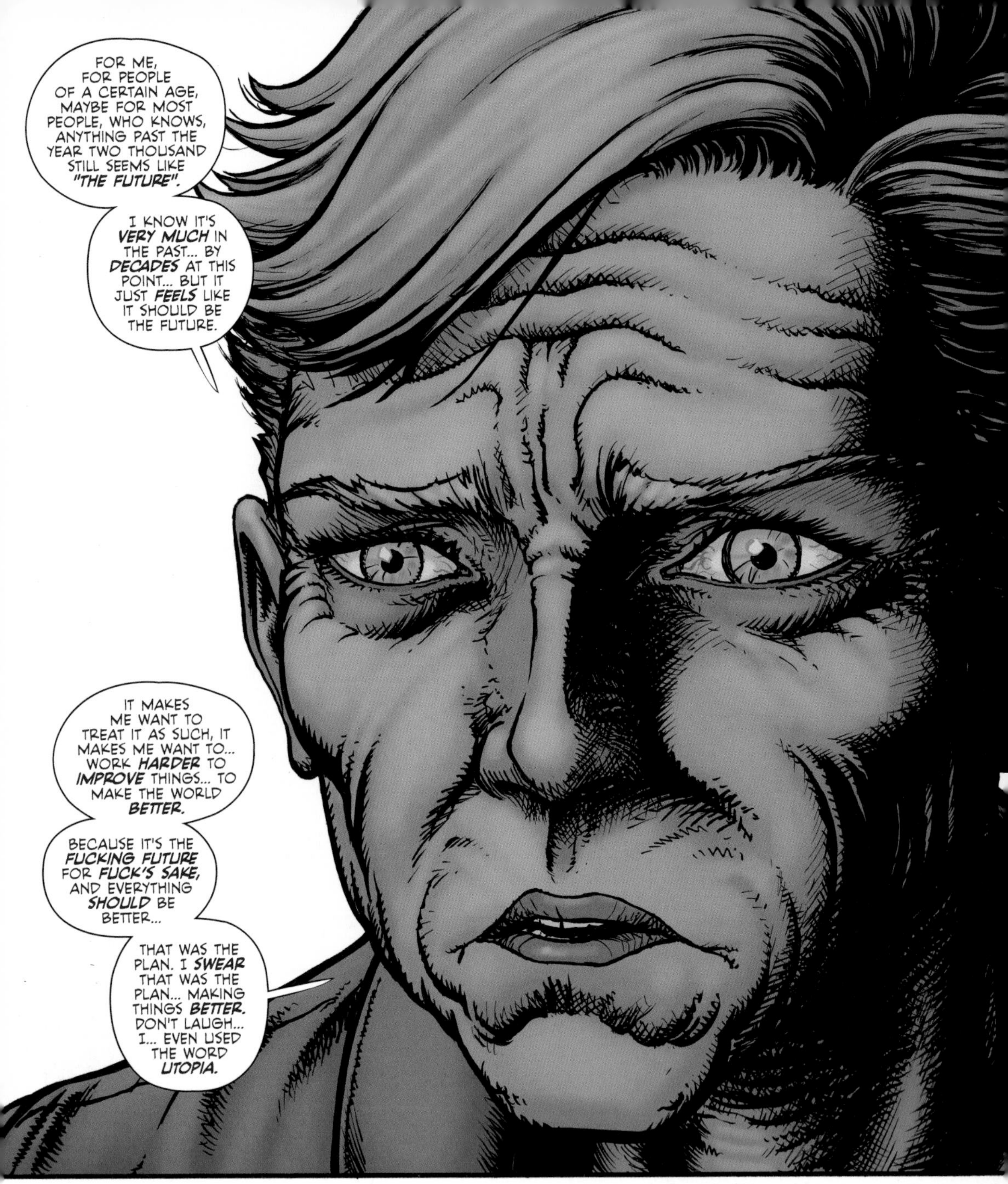
FOR ME, FOR PEOPLE OF A CERTAIN AGE, MAYBE FOR MOST PEOPLE, WHO KNOWS, ANYTHING PAST THE YEAR TWO THOUSAND STILL SEEMS LIKE ***"THE FUTURE".***
I KNOW IT'S ***VERY MUCH*** IN THE PAST... BY ***DECADES*** AT THIS POINT... BUT IT JUST ***FEELS*** LIKE IT SHOULD BE THE FUTURE.
IT MAKES ME WANT TO TREAT IT AS SUCH, IT MAKES ME WANT TO... WORK ***HARDER*** TO ***IMPROVE*** THINGS... TO MAKE THE WORLD ***BETTER.***
BECAUSE IT'S THE ***FUCKING FUTURE*** FOR ***FUCK'S SAKE,*** AND EVERYTHING ***SHOULD*** BE BETTER...
THAT WAS THE PLAN. I ***SWEAR*** THAT WAS THE PLAN... MAKING THINGS ***BETTER.*** DON'T LAUGH... I... EVEN USED THE WORD ***UTOPIA.***

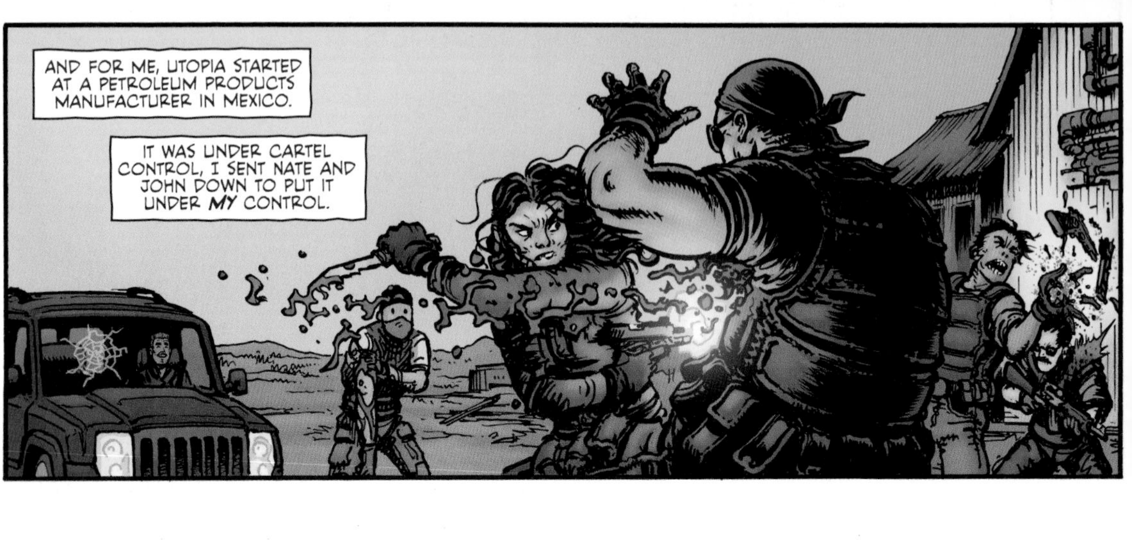
AND FOR ME, UTOPIA STARTED AT A PETROLEUM PRODUCTS MANUFACTURER IN MEXICO.
IT WAS UNDER CARTEL CONTROL, I SENT NATE AND JOHN DOWN TO PUT IT UNDER ***MY*** CONTROL.

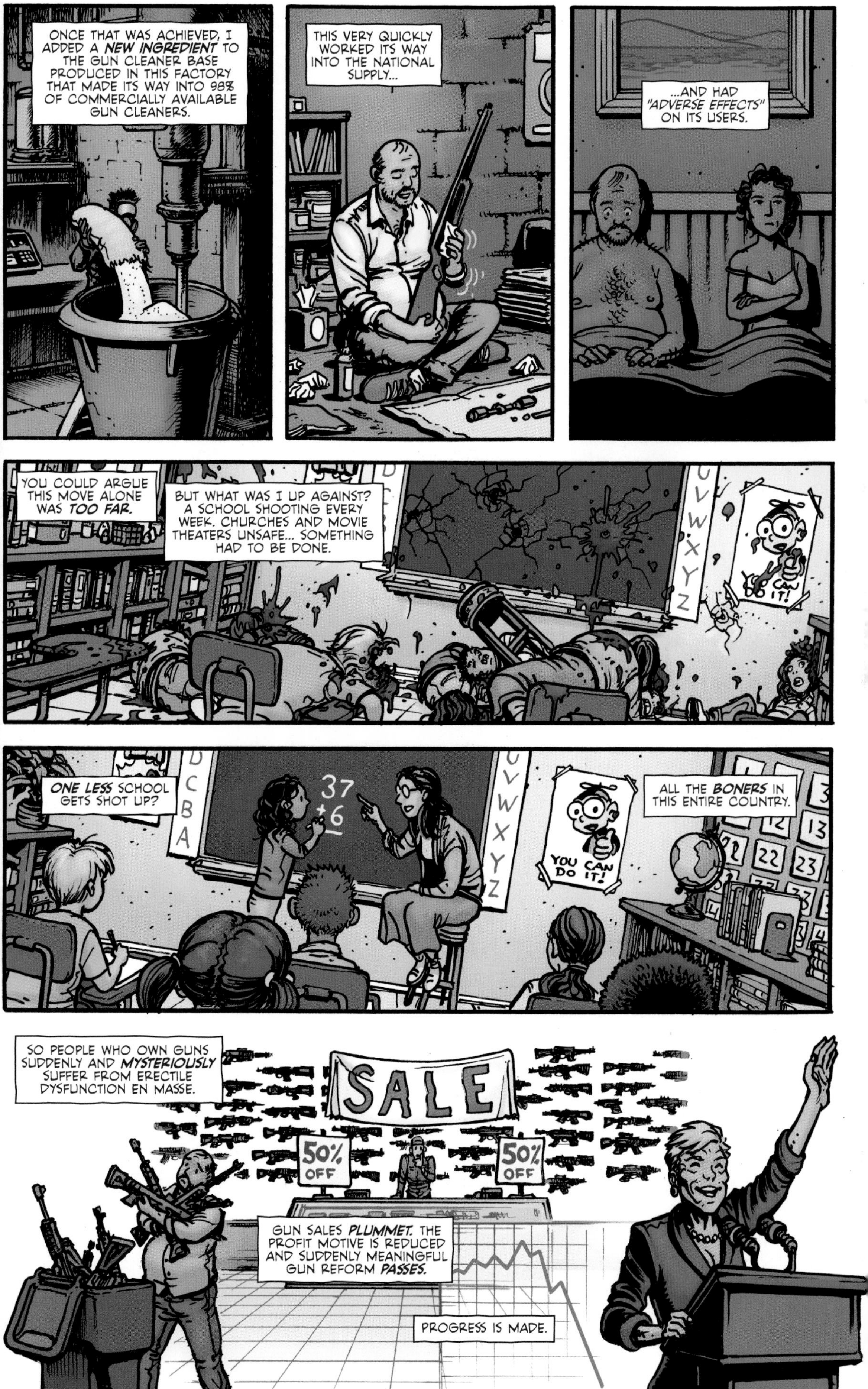
ONCE THAT WAS ACHIEVED, I ADDED A NEW INGREDIENT TO THE GUN CLEANER BASE PRODUCED IN THIS FACTORY THAT MADE ITS WAY INTO 98% OF COMMERCIALLY AVAILABLE GUN CLEANERS.
THIS VERY QUICKLY WORKED ITS WAY INTO THE NATIONAL SUPPLY...
...AND HAD "ADVERSE EFFECTS" ON ITS USERS.
YOU COULD ARGUE THIS MOVE ALONE WAS TOO FAR.
BUT WHAT WAS I UP AGAINST? A SCHOOL SHOOTING EVERY WEEK. CHURCHES AND MOVIE THEATERS UNSAFE... SOMETHING HAD TO BE DONE.
YOU CAN DO IT!
ONE LESS SCHOOL GETS SHOT UP?
37
+6
YOU CAN DO IT!
ALL THE BONERS IN THIS ENTIRE COUNTRY.
SO PEOPLE WHO OWN GUNS SUDDENLY AND MYSTERIOUSLY SUFFER FROM ERECTILE DYSFUNCTION EN MASSE.
SALE
50% OFF
50% OFF
GUN SALES PLUMMET. THE PROFIT MOTIVE IS REDUCED AND SUDDENLY MEANINGFUL GUN REFORM PASSES.
PROGRESS IS MADE.

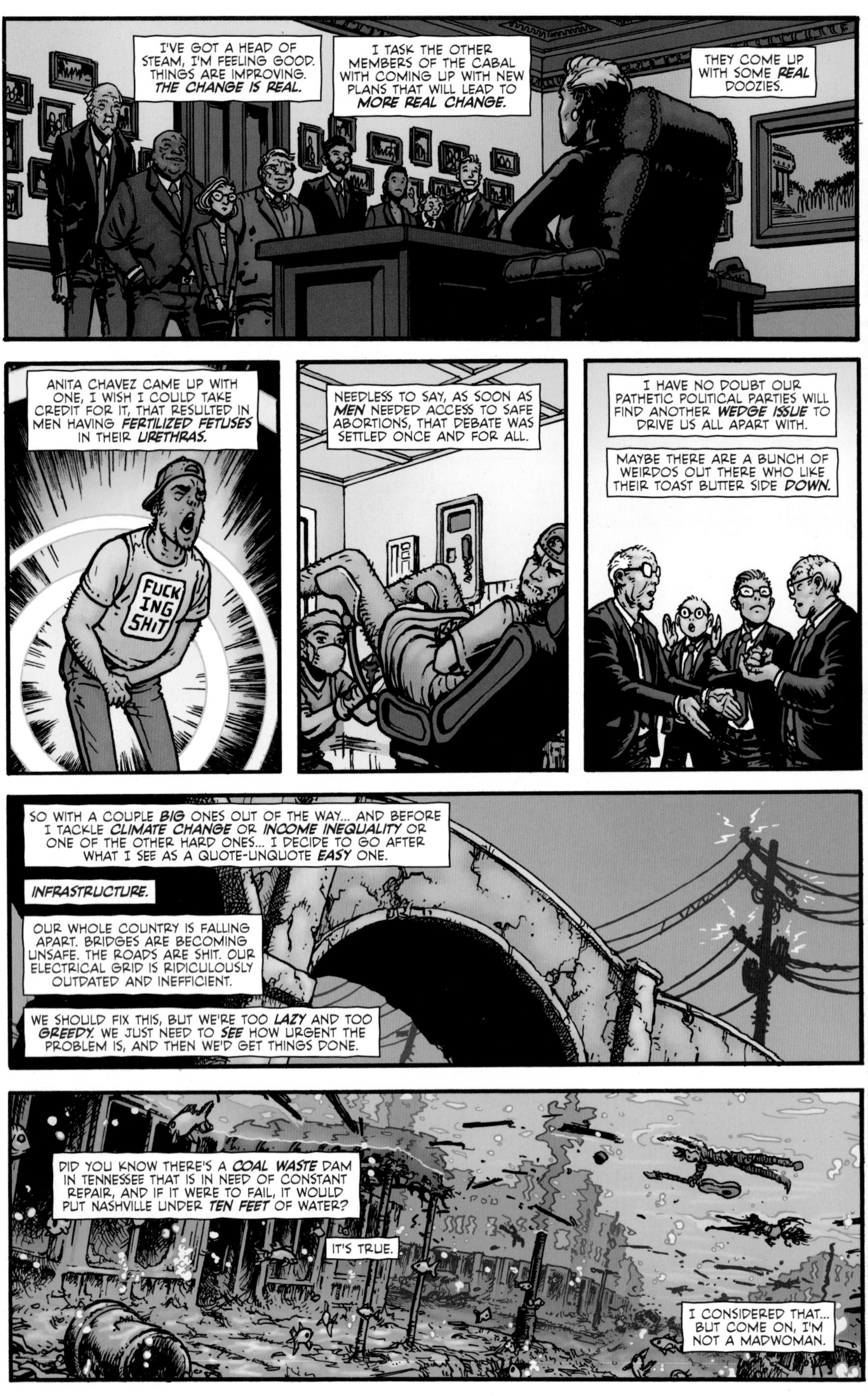

I'VE GOT A HEAD OF STEAM, I'M FEELING GOOD. THINGS ARE IMPROVING. *THE CHANGE IS REAL.*
I TASK THE OTHER MEMBERS OF THE CABAL WITH COMING UP WITH NEW PLANS THAT WILL LEAD TO *MORE REAL CHANGE.*
THEY COME UP WITH SOME *REAL* DOOZIES.
ANITA CHAVEZ CAME UP WITH ONE, I WISH I COULD TAKE CREDIT FOR IT, THAT RESULTED IN MEN HAVING *FERTILIZED FETUSES* IN THEIR *URETHRAS.*
FUCK ING SHIT
NEEDLESS TO SAY, AS SOON AS *MEN* NEEDED ACCESS TO SAFE ABORTIONS, THAT DEBATE WAS SETTLED ONCE AND FOR ALL.
I HAVE NO DOUBT OUR PATHETIC POLITICAL PARTIES WILL FIND ANOTHER *WEDGE ISSUE* TO DRIVE US ALL APART WITH.
MAYBE THERE ARE A BUNCH OF WEIRDOS OUT THERE WHO LIKE THEIR TOAST BUTTER SIDE *DOWN.*
SO WITH A COUPLE *BIG* ONES OUT OF THE WAY... AND BEFORE I TACKLE *CLIMATE CHANGE* OR *INCOME INEQUALITY* OR ONE OF THE OTHER HARD ONES... I DECIDE TO GO AFTER WHAT I SEE AS A QUOTE-UNQUOTE *EASY* ONE.
INFRASTRUCTURE.
OUR WHOLE COUNTRY IS FALLING APART. BRIDGES ARE BECOMING UNSAFE. THE ROADS ARE SHIT. OUR ELECTRICAL GRID IS RIDICULOUSLY OUTDATED AND INEFFICIENT.
WE SHOULD FIX THIS, BUT WE'RE TOO *LAZY* AND TOO *GREEDY.* WE JUST NEED TO *SEE* HOW URGENT THE PROBLEM IS, AND THEN WE'D GET THINGS DONE.
DID YOU KNOW THERE'S A *COAL WASTE* DAM IN TENNESSEE THAT IS IN NEED OF CONSTANT REPAIR, AND IF IT WERE TO FAIL, IT WOULD PUT NASHVILLE UNDER *TEN FEET* OF WATER?
IT'S TRUE.
I CONSIDERED THAT... BUT COME ON, I'M NOT A MADWOMAN.

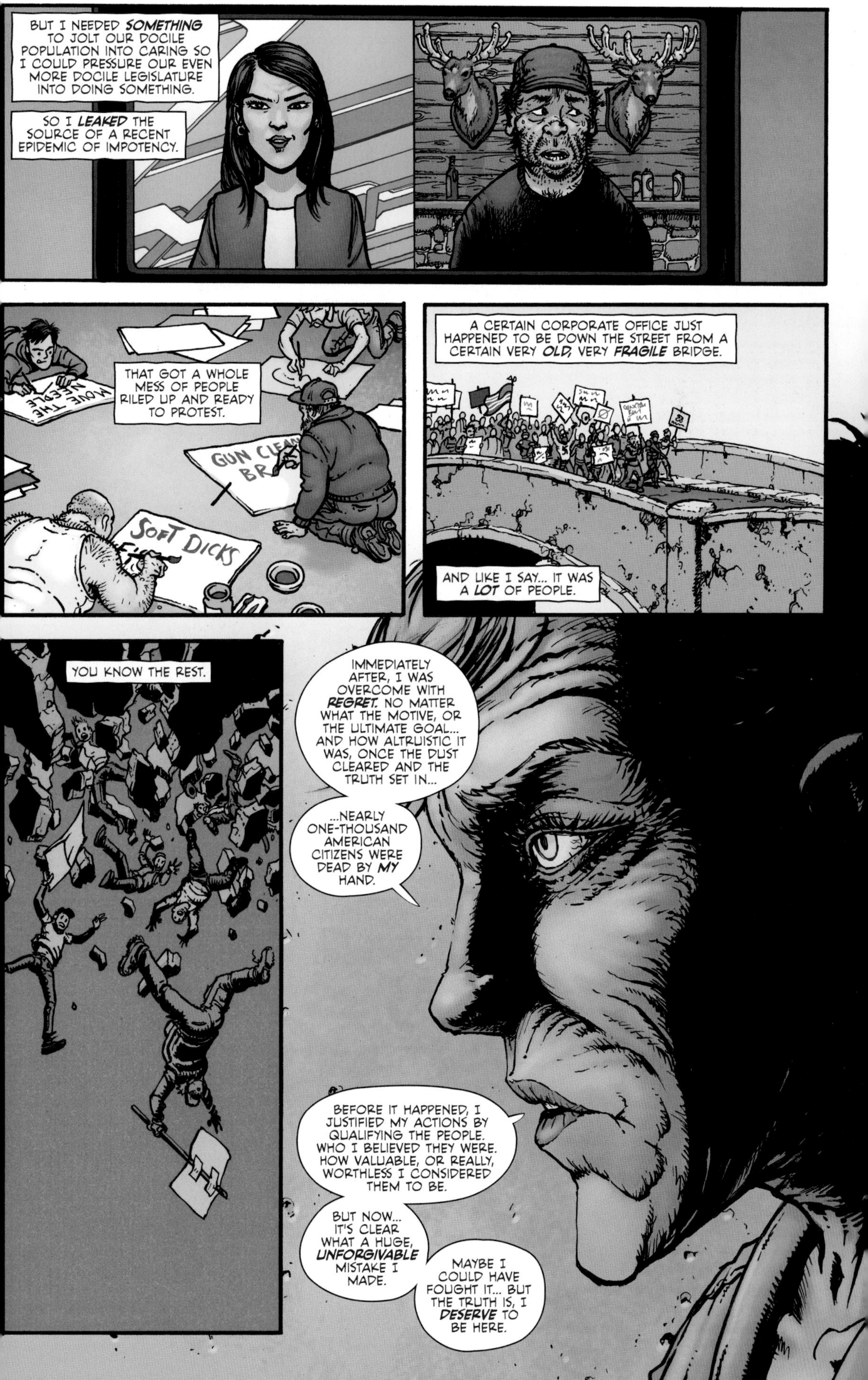
BUT I NEEDED SOMETHING TO JOLT OUR DOCILE POPULATION INTO CARING SO I COULD PRESSURE OUR EVEN MORE DOCILE LEGISLATURE INTO DOING SOMETHING.
SO I LEAKED THE SOURCE OF A RECENT EPIDEMIC OF IMPOTENCY.
THAT GOT A WHOLE MESS OF PEOPLE RILED UP AND READY TO PROTEST.
MOVE THE NEEDLE
SOFT DICKS
A CERTAIN CORPORATE OFFICE JUST HAPPENED TO BE DOWN THE STREET FROM A CERTAIN VERY OLD, VERY FRAGILE BRIDGE.
AND LIKE I SAY... IT WAS A LOT OF PEOPLE.
YOU KNOW THE REST.
IMMEDIATELY AFTER, I WAS OVERCOME WITH REGRET. NO MATTER WHAT THE MOTIVE, OR THE ULTIMATE GOAL... AND HOW ALTRUISTIC IT WAS, ONCE THE DUST CLEARED AND THE TRUTH SET IN...
...NEARLY ONE-THOUSAND AMERICAN CITIZENS WERE DEAD BY MY HAND.
BEFORE IT HAPPENED, I JUSTIFIED MY ACTIONS BY QUALIFYING THE PEOPLE. WHO I BELIEVED THEY WERE. HOW VALUABLE, OR REALLY, WORTHLESS I CONSIDERED THEM TO BE.
BUT NOW... IT'S CLEAR WHAT A HUGE, UNFORGIVABLE MISTAKE I MADE.
MAYBE I COULD HAVE FOUGHT IT... BUT THE TRUTH IS, I DESERVE TO BE HERE.

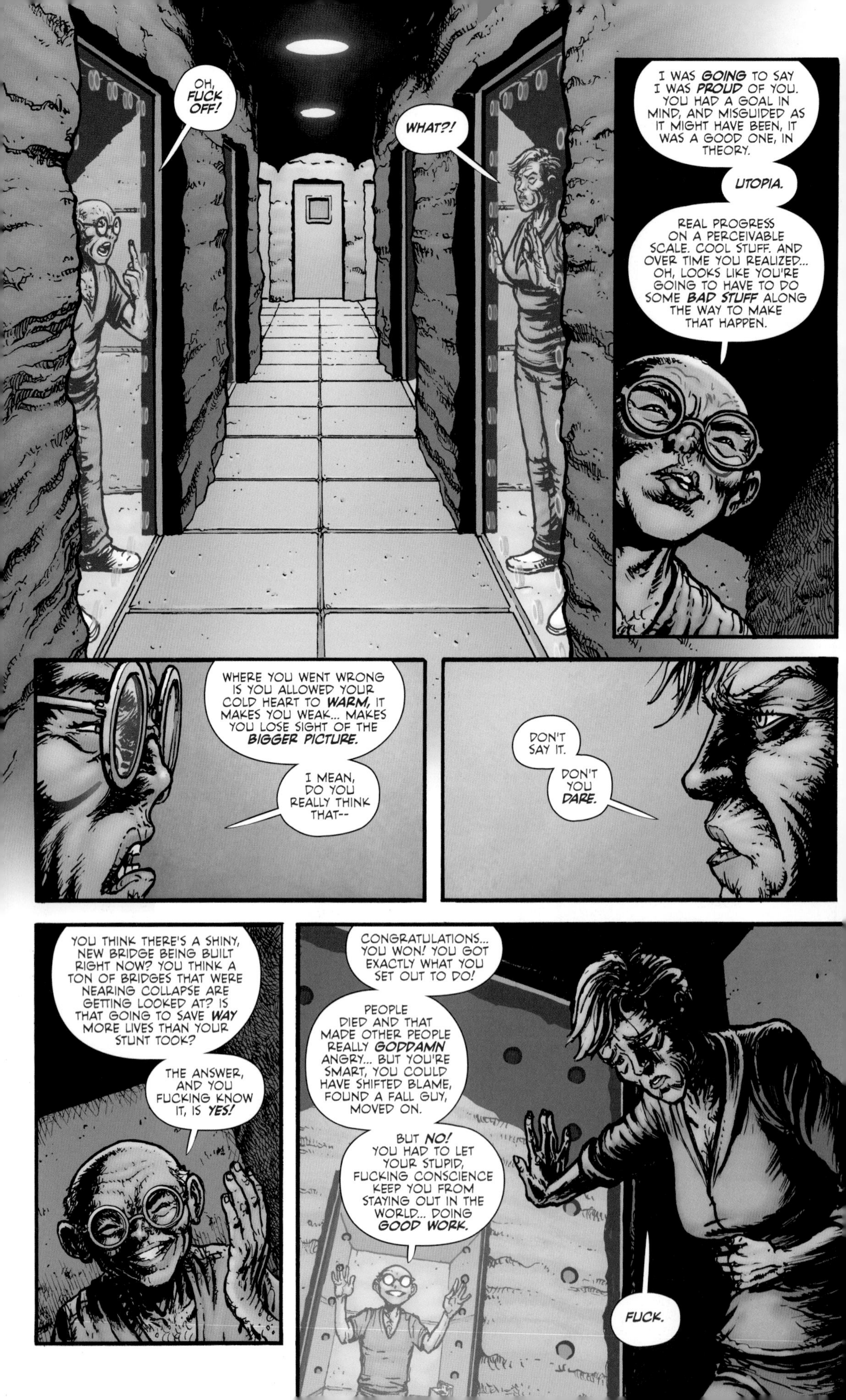
OH, FUCK OFF!
WHAT?!
I WAS GOING TO SAY I WAS PROUD OF YOU. YOU HAD A GOAL IN MIND, AND MISGUIDED AS IT MIGHT HAVE BEEN, IT WAS A GOOD ONE, IN THEORY.
UTOPIA.
REAL PROGRESS ON A PERCEIVABLE SCALE. COOL STUFF. AND OVER TIME YOU REALIZED... OH, LOOKS LIKE YOU'RE GOING TO HAVE TO DO SOME BAD STUFF ALONG THE WAY TO MAKE THAT HAPPEN.
WHERE YOU WENT WRONG IS YOU ALLOWED YOUR COLD HEART TO WARM, IT MAKES YOU WEAK... MAKES YOU LOSE SIGHT OF THE BIGGER PICTURE.
I MEAN, DO YOU REALLY THINK THAT--
DON'T SAY IT.
DON'T YOU DARE.
YOU THINK THERE'S A SHINY, NEW BRIDGE BEING BUILT RIGHT NOW? YOU THINK A TON OF BRIDGES THAT WERE NEARING COLLAPSE ARE GETTING LOOKED AT? IS THAT GOING TO SAVE WAY MORE LIVES THAN YOUR STUNT TOOK?
THE ANSWER, AND YOU FUCKING KNOW IT, IS YES!
CONGRATULATIONS... YOU WON! YOU GOT EXACTLY WHAT YOU SET OUT TO DO!
PEOPLE DIED AND THAT MADE OTHER PEOPLE REALLY GODDAMN ANGRY... BUT YOU'RE SMART, YOU COULD HAVE SHIFTED BLAME, FOUND A FALL GUY, MOVED ON.
BUT NO! YOU HAD TO LET YOUR STUPID, FUCKING CONSCIENCE KEEP YOU FROM STAYING OUT IN THE WORLD... DOING GOOD WORK.
FUCK.

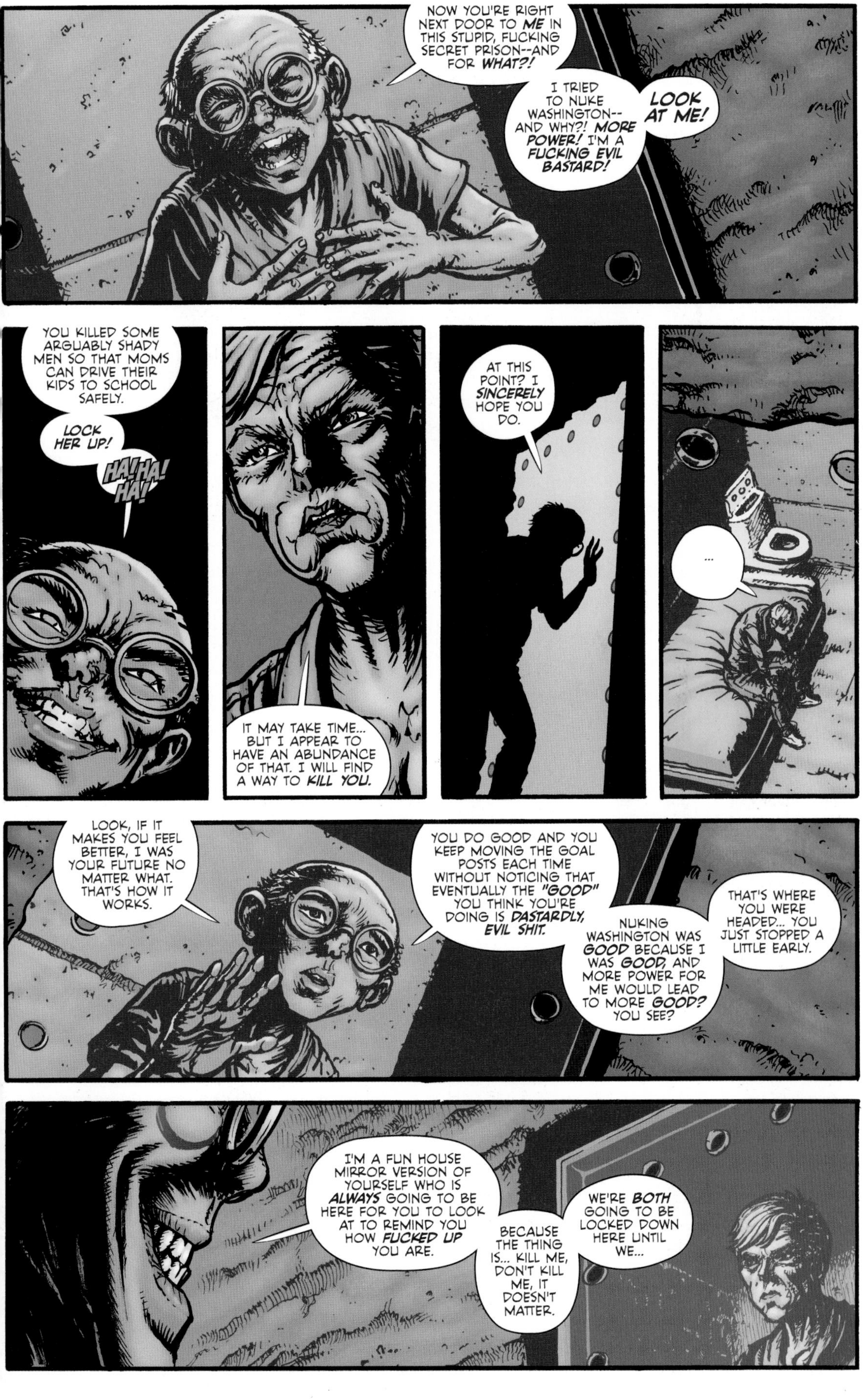
NOW YOU'RE RIGHT NEXT DOOR TO ME IN THIS STUPID, FUCKING SECRET PRISON--AND FOR WHAT?!
I TRIED TO NUKE WASHINGTON--AND WHY?! MORE POWER! I'M A FUCKING EVIL BASTARD!
LOOK AT ME!
YOU KILLED SOME ARGUABLY SHADY MEN SO THAT MOMS CAN DRIVE THEIR KIDS TO SCHOOL SAFELY.
LOCK HER UP!
HA! HA! HA!
IT MAY TAKE TIME... BUT I APPEAR TO HAVE AN ABUNDANCE OF THAT. I WILL FIND A WAY TO KILL YOU.
AT THIS POINT? I SINCERELY HOPE YOU DO.
...
LOOK, IF IT MAKES YOU FEEL BETTER, I WAS YOUR FUTURE NO MATTER WHAT. THAT'S HOW IT WORKS.
YOU DO GOOD AND YOU KEEP MOVING THE GOAL POSTS EACH TIME WITHOUT NOTICING THAT EVENTUALLY THE "GOOD" YOU THINK YOU'RE DOING IS DASTARDLY, EVIL SHIT.
NUKING WASHINGTON WAS GOOD BECAUSE I WAS GOOD, AND MORE POWER FOR ME WOULD LEAD TO MORE GOOD? YOU SEE?
THAT'S WHERE YOU WERE HEADED... YOU JUST STOPPED A LITTLE EARLY.
I'M A FUN HOUSE MIRROR VERSION OF YOURSELF WHO IS ALWAYS GOING TO BE HERE FOR YOU TO LOOK AT TO REMIND YOU HOW FUCKED UP YOU ARE.
BECAUSE THE THING IS... KILL ME, DON'T KILL ME, IT DOESN'T MATTER.
WE'RE BOTH GOING TO BE LOCKED DOWN HERE UNTIL WE...

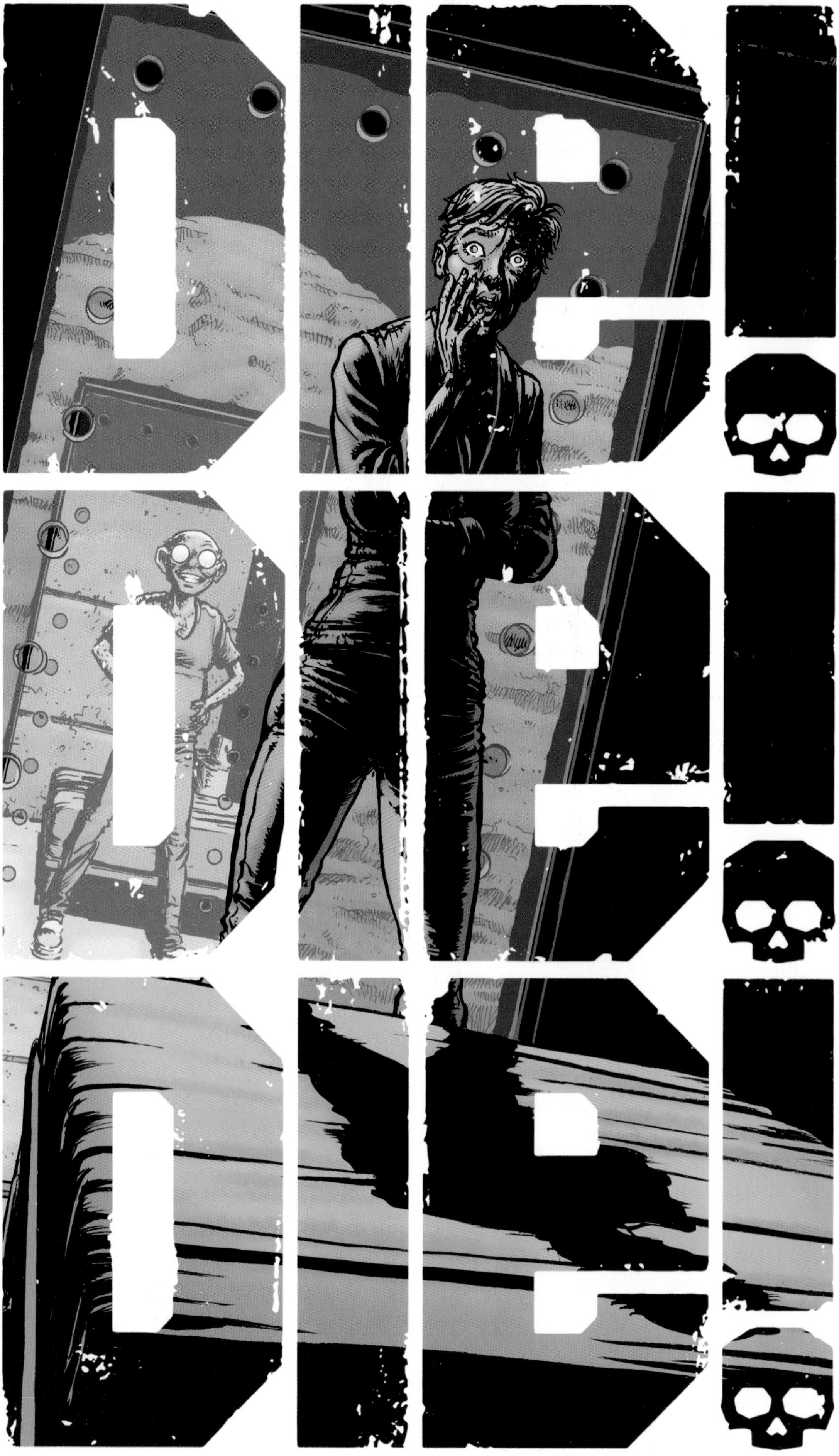
DIE!
DIE!
DIE!

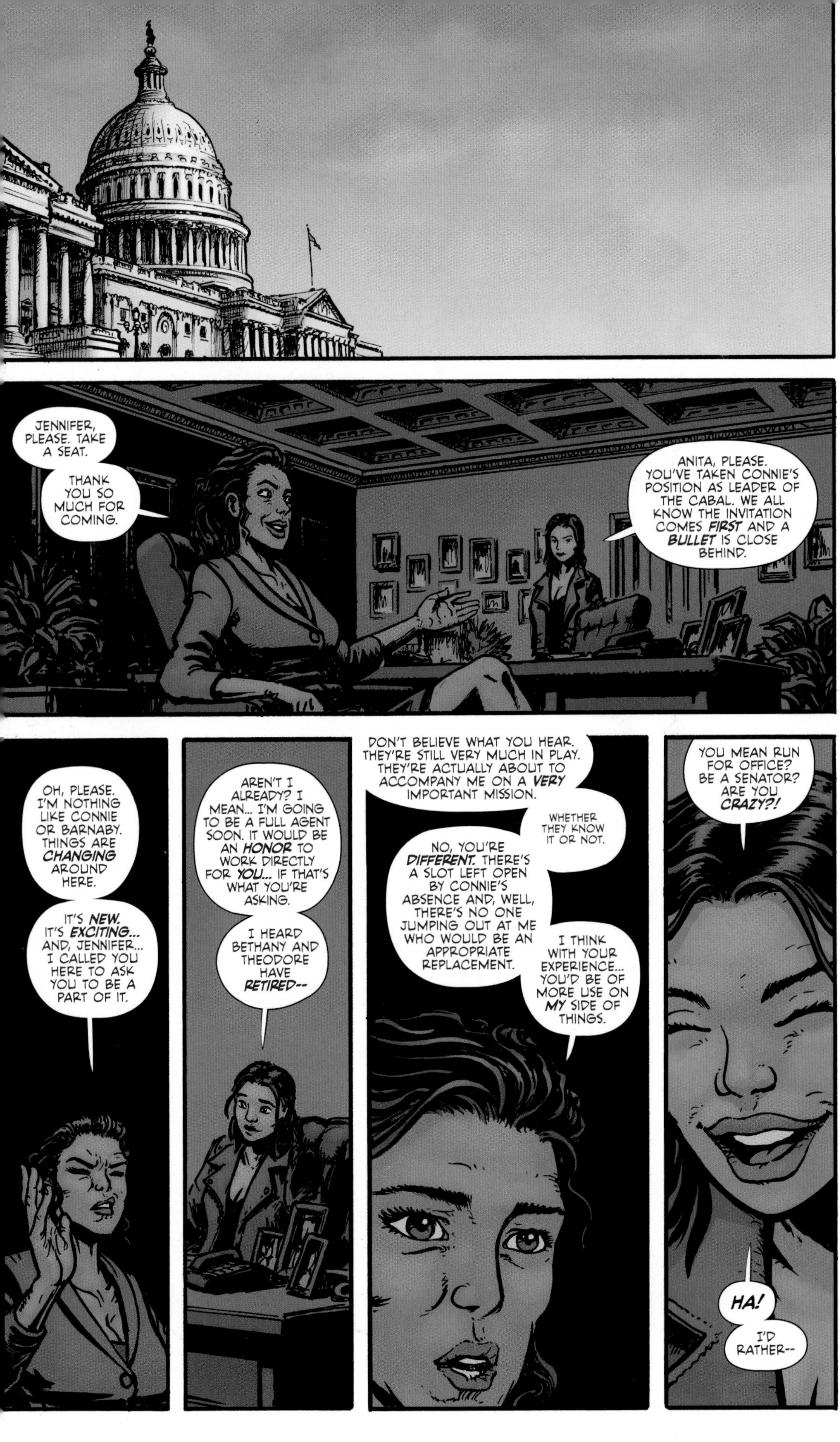

JENNIFER, PLEASE. TAKE A SEAT.
THANK YOU SO MUCH FOR COMING.
ANITA, PLEASE. YOU'VE TAKEN CONNIE'S POSITION AS LEADER OF THE CABAL. WE ALL KNOW THE INVITATION COMES FIRST AND A BULLET IS CLOSE BEHIND.
OH, PLEASE. I'M NOTHING LIKE CONNIE OR BARNABY. THINGS ARE CHANGING AROUND HERE.
IT'S NEW. IT'S EXCITING... AND, JENNIFER... I CALLED YOU HERE TO ASK YOU TO BE A PART OF IT.
AREN'T I ALREADY? I MEAN... I'M GOING TO BE A FULL AGENT SOON. IT WOULD BE AN HONOR TO WORK DIRECTLY FOR YOU... IF THAT'S WHAT YOU'RE ASKING.
I HEARD BETHANY AND THEODORE HAVE RETIRED--
DON'T BELIEVE WHAT YOU HEAR. THEY'RE STILL VERY MUCH IN PLAY. THEY'RE ACTUALLY ABOUT TO ACCOMPANY ME ON A VERY IMPORTANT MISSION.
WHETHER THEY KNOW IT OR NOT.
NO, YOU'RE DIFFERENT. THERE'S A SLOT LEFT OPEN BY CONNIE'S ABSENCE AND, WELL, THERE'S NO ONE JUMPING OUT AT ME WHO WOULD BE AN APPROPRIATE REPLACEMENT.
I THINK WITH YOUR EXPERIENCE... YOU'D BE OF MORE USE ON MY SIDE OF THINGS.
YOU MEAN RUN FOR OFFICE? BE A SENATOR? ARE YOU CRAZY?!
HA!
I'D RATHER--

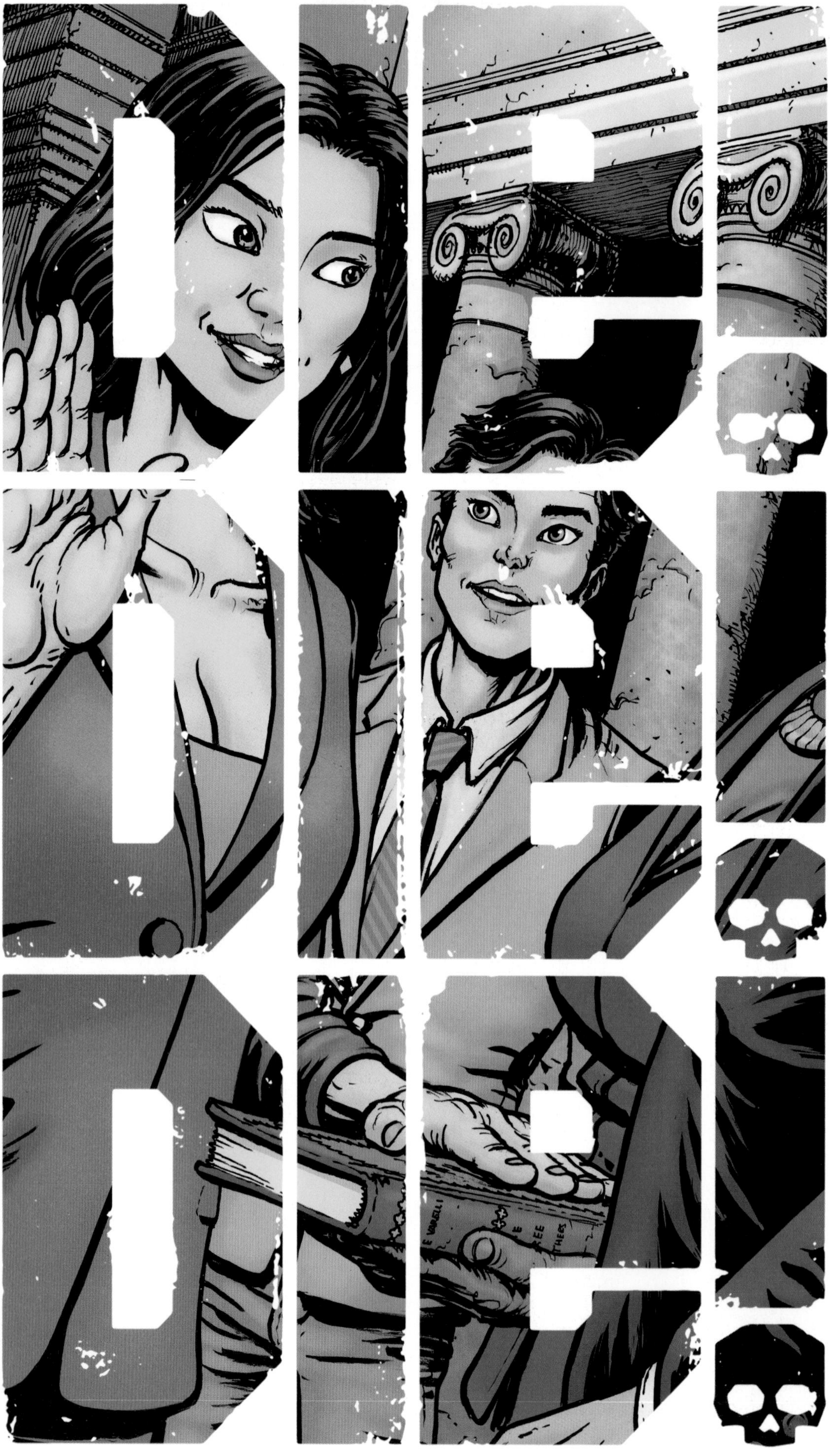
DIE!
DIE!
DIE!

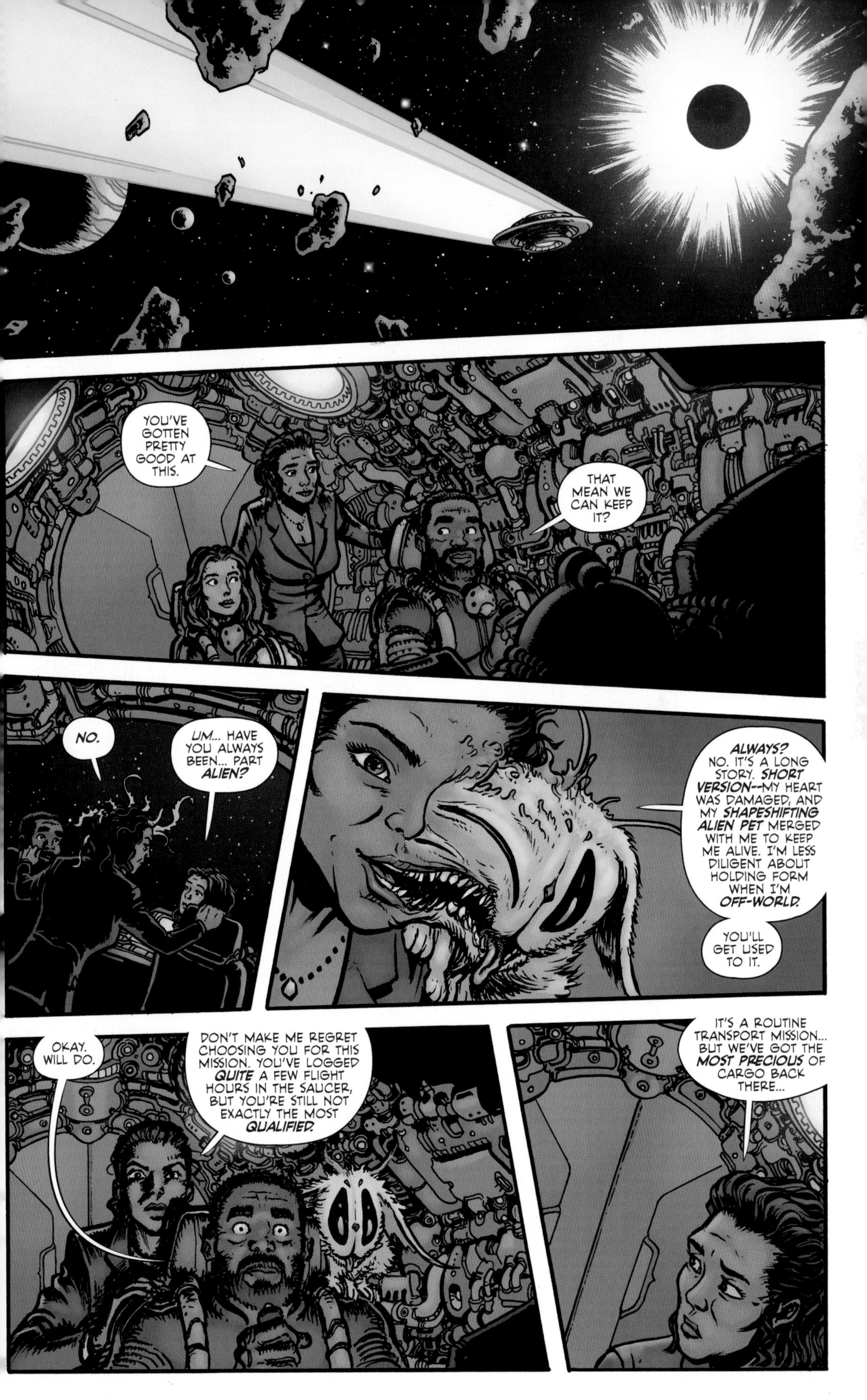
YOU'VE GOTTEN PRETTY GOOD AT THIS.
THAT MEAN WE CAN KEEP IT?
NO.
UM... HAVE YOU ALWAYS BEEN... PART ALIEN?
ALWAYS? NO. IT'S A LONG STORY. SHORT VERSION--MY HEART WAS DAMAGED, AND MY SHAPESHIFTING ALIEN PET MERGED WITH ME TO KEEP ME ALIVE. I'M LESS DILIGENT ABOUT HOLDING FORM WHEN I'M OFF-WORLD.
YOU'LL GET USED TO IT.
DON'T MAKE ME REGRET CHOOSING YOU FOR THIS MISSION. YOU'VE LOGGED QUITE A FEW FLIGHT HOURS IN THE SAUCER, BUT YOU'RE STILL NOT EXACTLY THE MOST QUALIFIED.
OKAY. WILL DO.
IT'S A ROUTINE TRANSPORT MISSION... BUT WE'VE GOT THE MOST PRECIOUS OF CARGO BACK THERE...

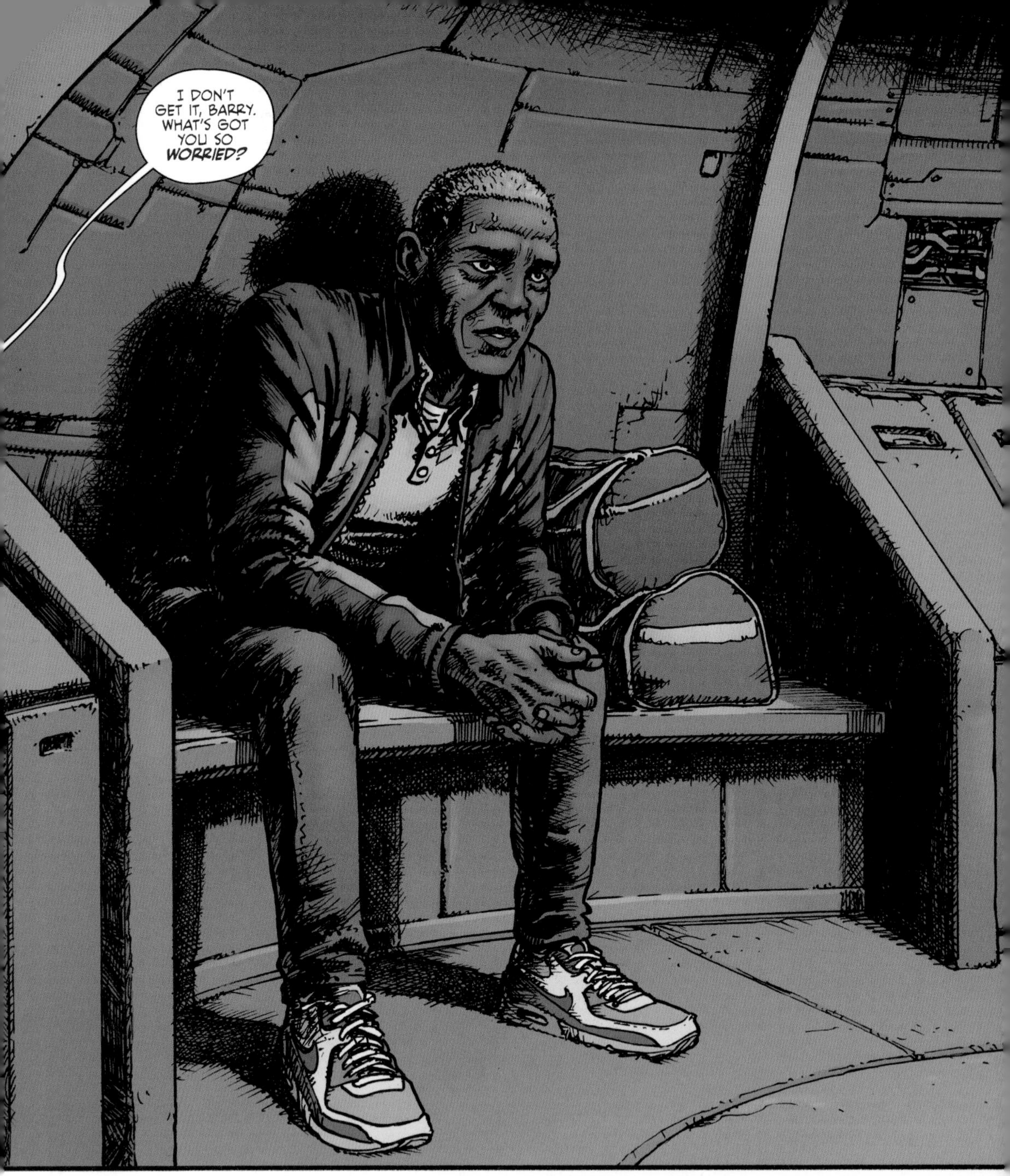
I DON'T GET IT, BARRY. WHAT'S GOT YOU SO WORRIED?

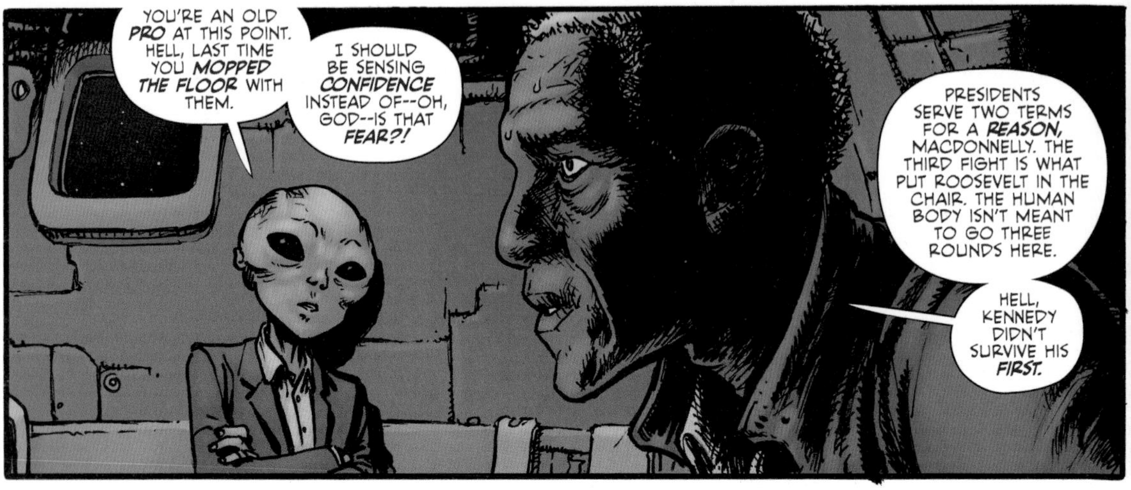
YOU'RE AN OLD PRO AT THIS POINT. HELL, LAST TIME YOU MOPPED THE FLOOR WITH THEM.
I SHOULD BE SENSING CONFIDENCE INSTEAD OF--OH, GOD--IS THAT FEAR?!
PRESIDENTS SERVE TWO TERMS FOR A REASON, MACDONNELLY. THE THIRD FIGHT IS WHAT PUT ROOSEVELT IN THE CHAIR. THE HUMAN BODY ISN'T MEANT TO GO THREE ROUNDS HERE.
HELL, KENNEDY DIDN'T SURVIVE HIS FIRST.

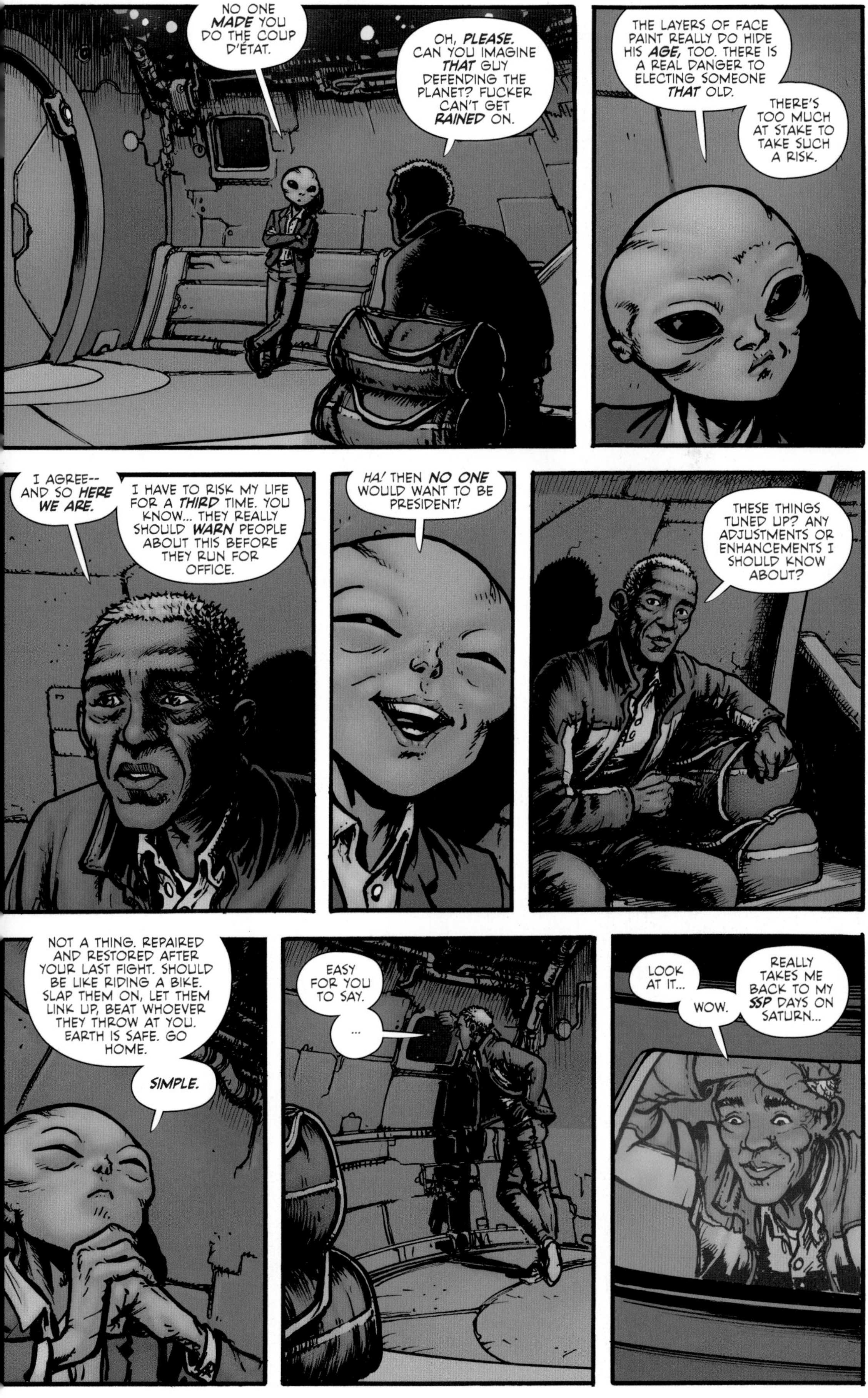
NO ONE MADE YOU DO THE COUP D'ÉTAT.
OH, PLEASE. CAN YOU IMAGINE THAT GUY DEFENDING THE PLANET? FUCKER CAN'T GET RAINED ON.
THE LAYERS OF FACE PAINT REALLY DO HIDE HIS AGE, TOO. THERE IS A REAL DANGER TO ELECTING SOMEONE THAT OLD.
THERE'S TOO MUCH AT STAKE TO TAKE SUCH A RISK.
I AGREE-- AND SO HERE WE ARE.
I HAVE TO RISK MY LIFE FOR A THIRD TIME. YOU KNOW... THEY REALLY SHOULD WARN PEOPLE ABOUT THIS BEFORE THEY RUN FOR OFFICE.
HA! THEN NO ONE WOULD WANT TO BE PRESIDENT!
THESE THINGS TUNED UP? ANY ADJUSTMENTS OR ENHANCEMENTS I SHOULD KNOW ABOUT?
NOT A THING. REPAIRED AND RESTORED AFTER YOUR LAST FIGHT. SHOULD BE LIKE RIDING A BIKE. SLAP THEM ON, LET THEM LINK UP, BEAT WHOEVER THEY THROW AT YOU. EARTH IS SAFE. GO HOME.
SIMPLE.
EASY FOR YOU TO SAY.
...
LOOK AT IT...
WOW.
REALLY TAKES ME BACK TO MY SSP DAYS ON SATURN...

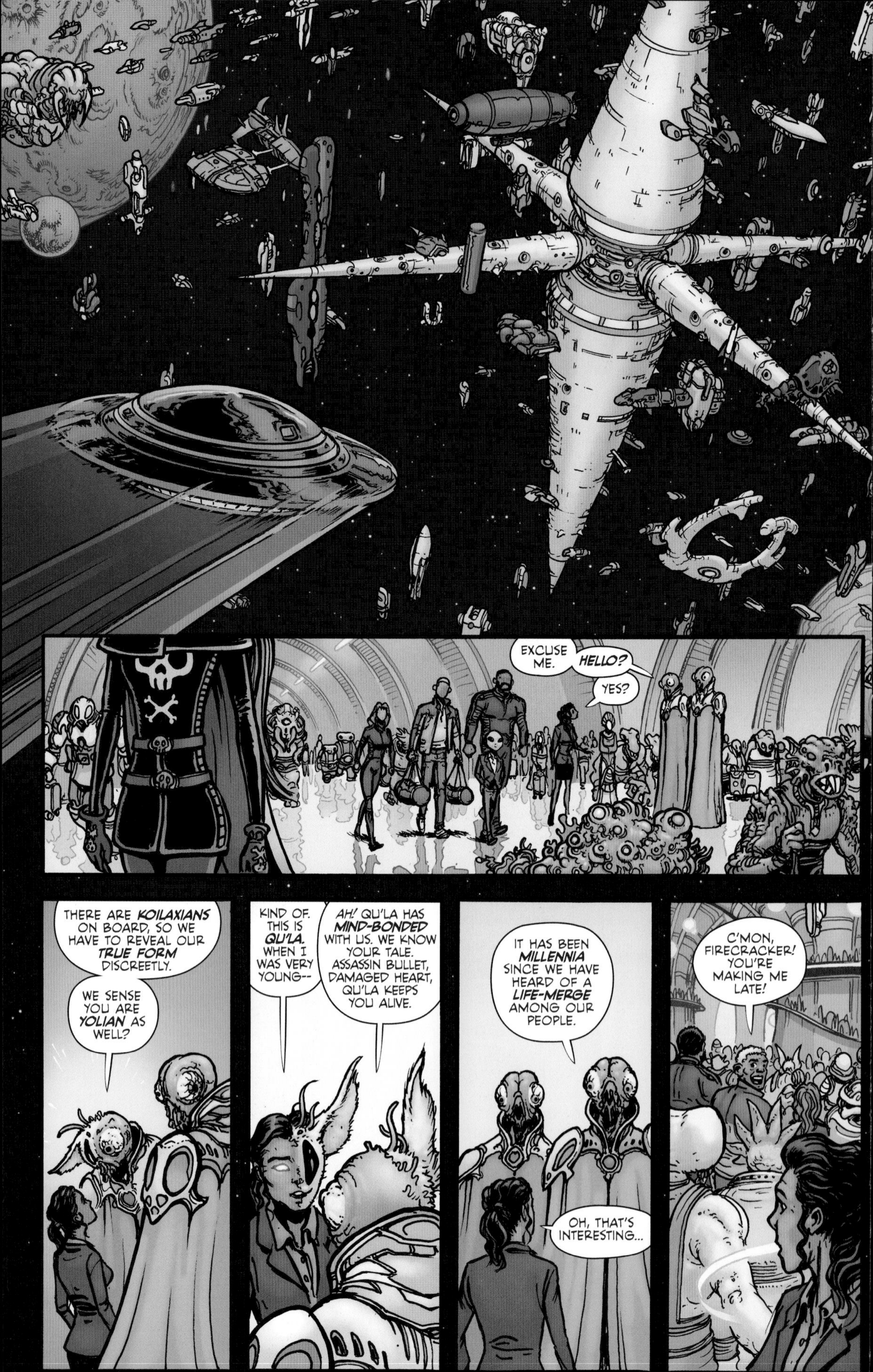
EXCUSE ME.
HELLO?
YES?
THERE ARE KOILAXIANS ON BOARD, SO WE HAVE TO REVEAL OUR TRUE FORM DISCREETLY.
WE SENSE YOU ARE YOLIAN AS WELL?
KIND OF. THIS IS QU'LA. WHEN I WAS VERY YOUNG--
AH! QU'LA HAS MIND-BONDED WITH US. WE KNOW YOUR TALE. ASSASSIN BULLET, DAMAGED HEART, QU'LA KEEPS YOU ALIVE.
IT HAS BEEN MILLENNIA SINCE WE HAVE HEARD OF A LIFE-MERGE AMONG OUR PEOPLE.
OH, THAT'S INTERESTING...
C'MON, FIRECRACKER! YOU'RE MAKING ME LATE!

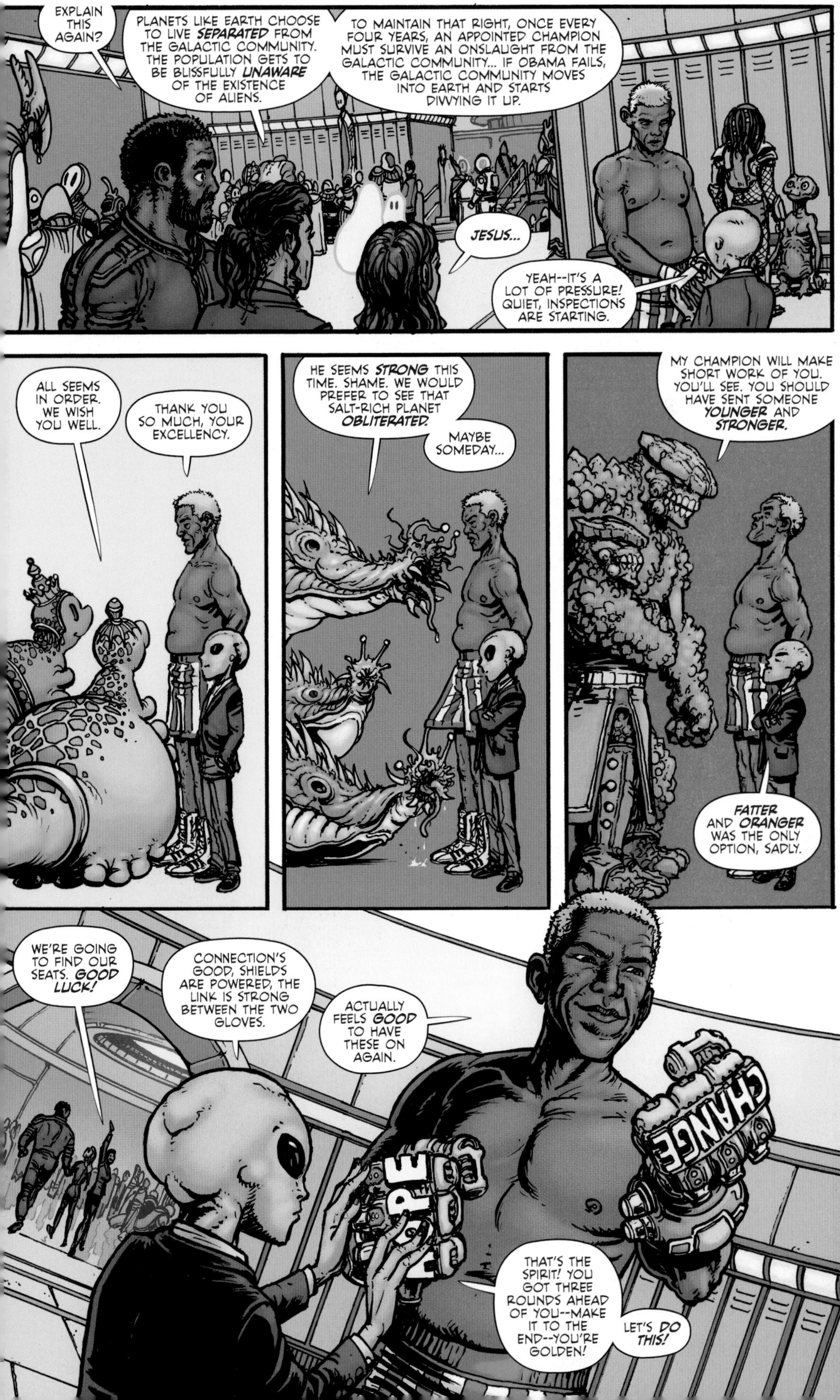
EXPLAIN THIS AGAIN?
PLANETS LIKE EARTH CHOOSE TO LIVE SEPARATED FROM THE GALACTIC COMMUNITY. THE POPULATION GETS TO BE BLISSFULLY UNAWARE OF THE EXISTENCE OF ALIENS.
TO MAINTAIN THAT RIGHT, ONCE EVERY FOUR YEARS, AN APPOINTED CHAMPION MUST SURVIVE AN ONSLAUGHT FROM THE GALACTIC COMMUNITY... IF OBAMA FAILS, THE GALACTIC COMMUNITY MOVES INTO EARTH AND STARTS DIVVYING IT UP.
JESUS...
YEAH--IT'S A LOT OF PRESSURE! QUIET, INSPECTIONS ARE STARTING.
ALL SEEMS IN ORDER. WE WISH YOU WELL.
THANK YOU SO MUCH, YOUR EXCELLENCY.
HE SEEMS STRONG THIS TIME. SHAME. WE WOULD PREFER TO SEE THAT SALT-RICH PLANET OBLITERATED.
MAYBE SOMEDAY...
MY CHAMPION WILL MAKE SHORT WORK OF YOU. YOU'LL SEE. YOU SHOULD HAVE SENT SOMEONE YOUNGER AND STRONGER.
FATTER AND ORANGER WAS THE ONLY OPTION, SADLY.
WE'RE GOING TO FIND OUR SEATS. GOOD LUCK!
CONNECTION'S GOOD, SHIELDS ARE POWERED, THE LINK IS STRONG BETWEEN THE TWO GLOVES.
ACTUALLY FEELS GOOD TO HAVE THESE ON AGAIN.
CHANGE
THAT'S THE SPIRIT! YOU GOT THREE ROUNDS AHEAD OF YOU--MAKE IT TO THE END--YOU'RE GOLDEN!
LET'S DO THIS!

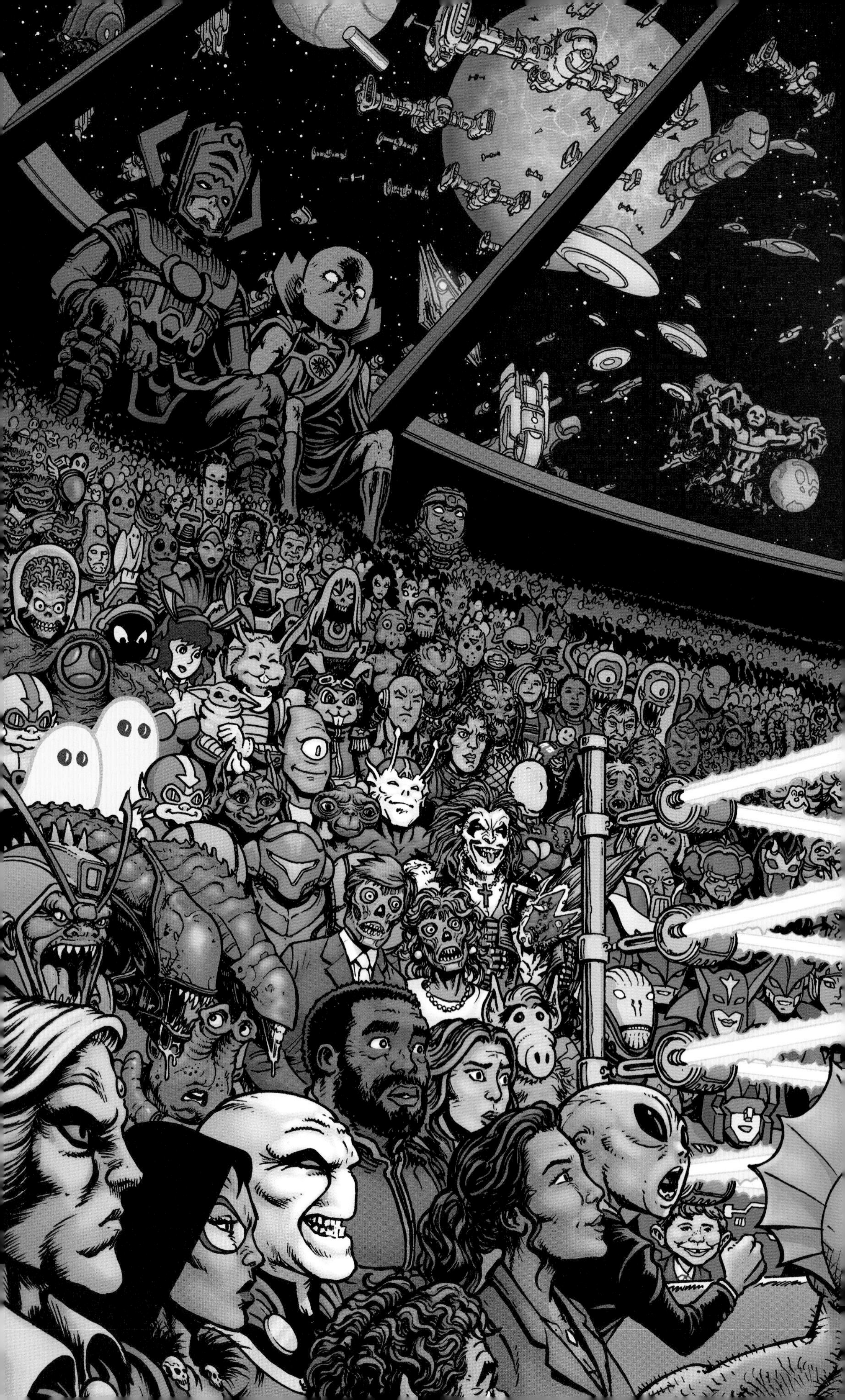

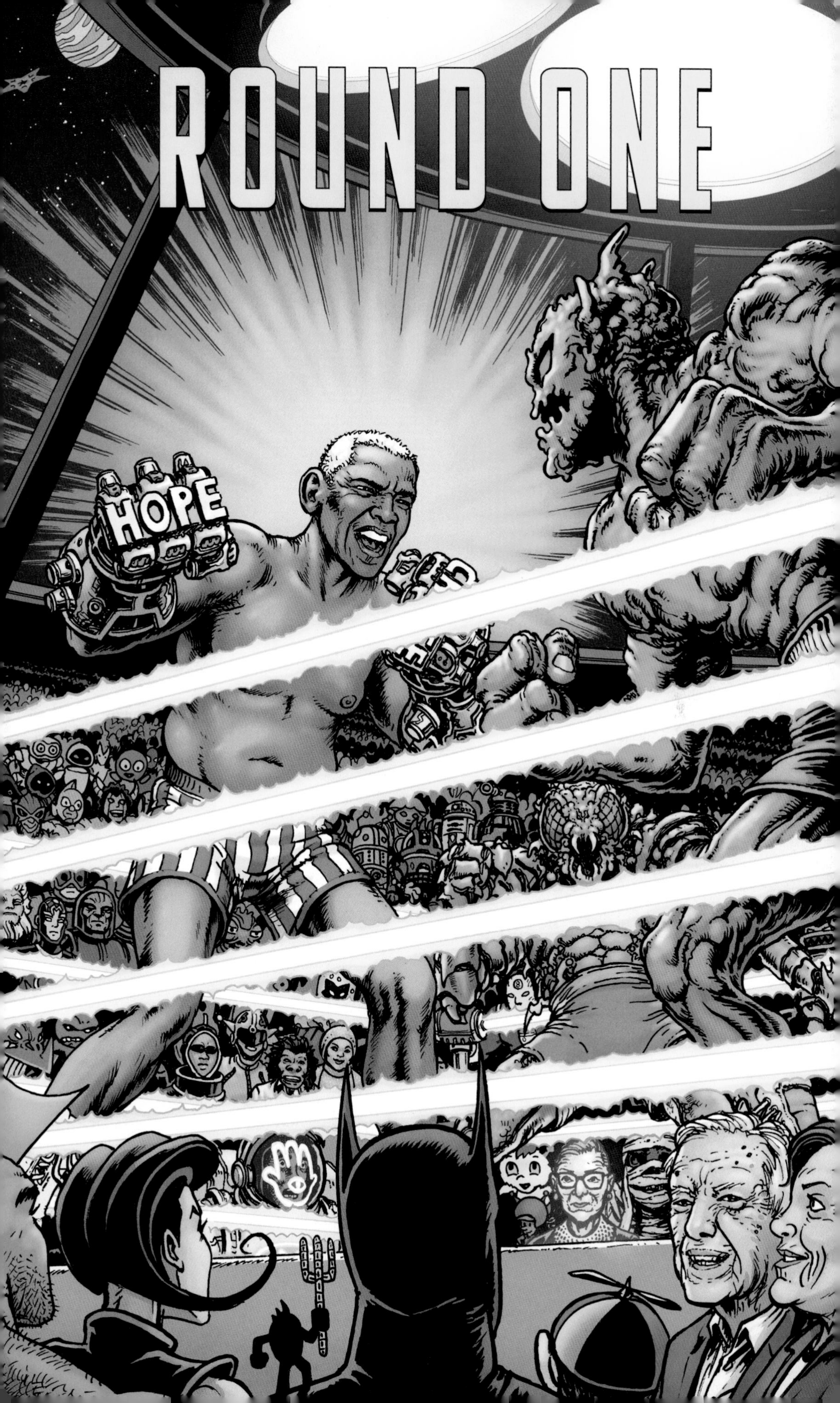
ROUND ONE
HOPE

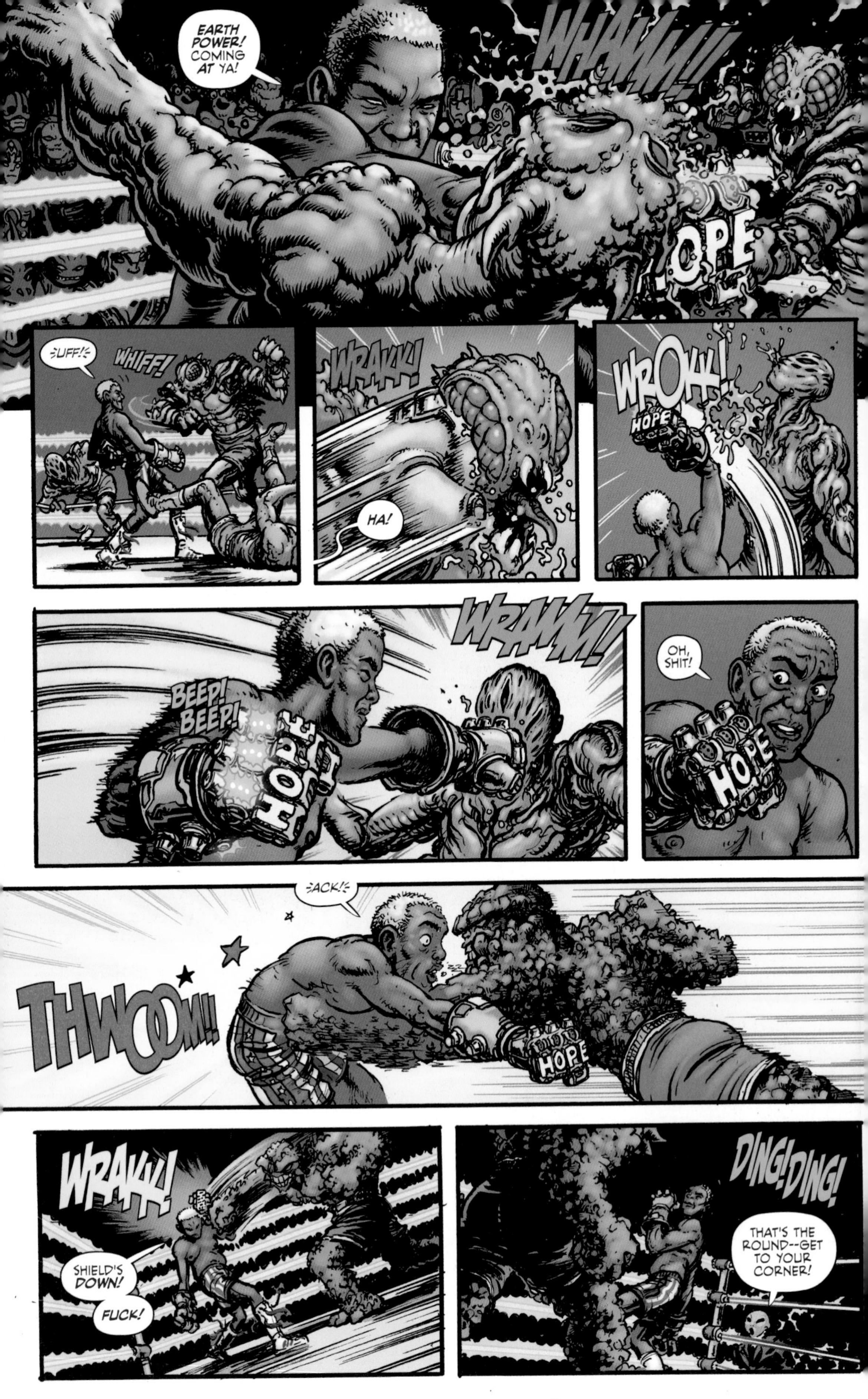
EARTH POWER! COMING AT YA!
WHAMM!!
HOPE
-UFF!-
WHIFF!
WRAKK!
HA!
WROKK!
HOPE
WRAMM!!
BEEP! BEEP!
HOPE
OH, SHIT!
HOPE
-ACK!-
THWOOM!!
HOPE
WRAKK!
SHIELD'S DOWN!
FUCK!
DING! DING!
THAT'S THE ROUND--GET TO YOUR CORNER!

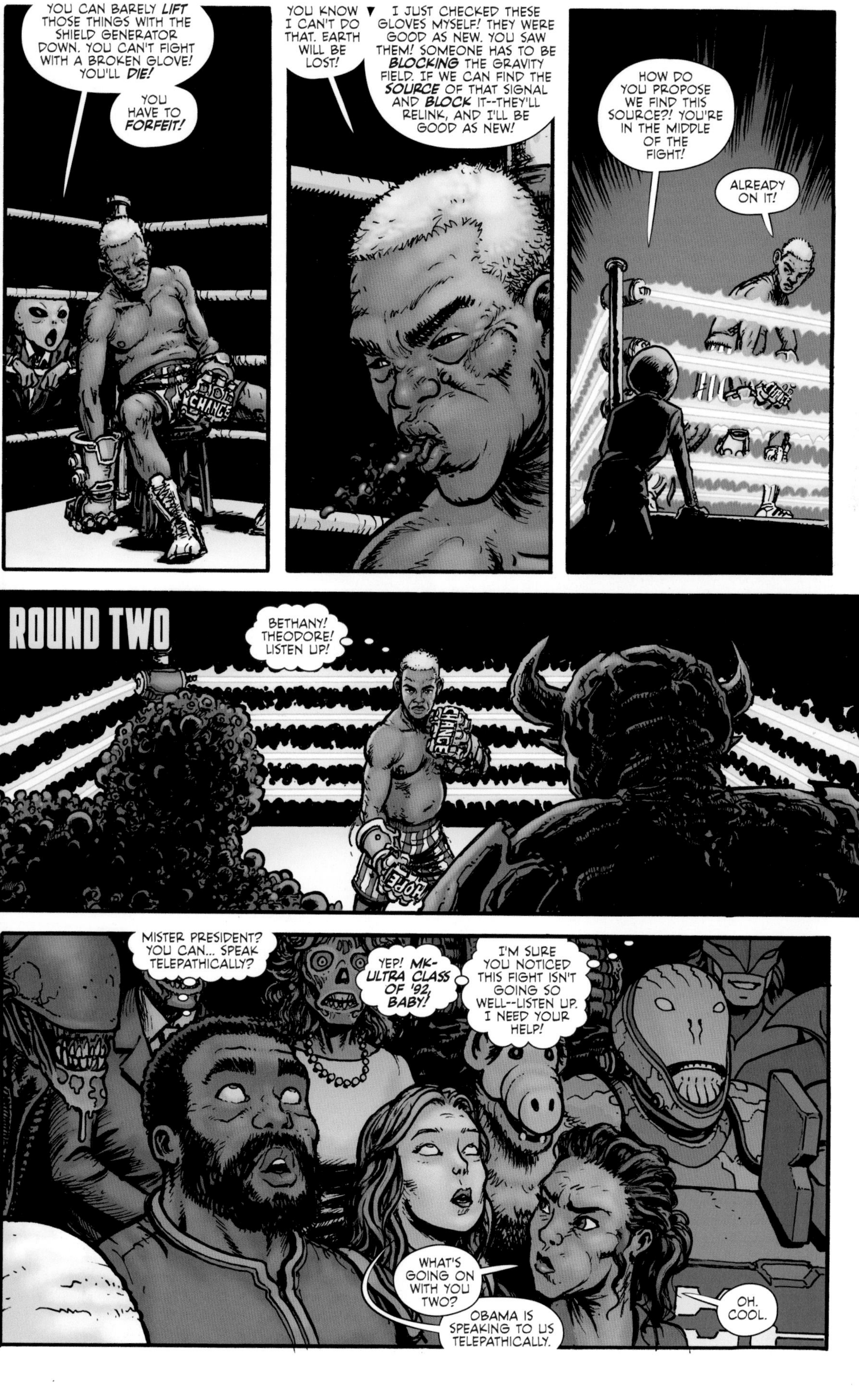
YOU CAN BARELY *LIFT* THOSE THINGS WITH THE SHIELD GENERATOR DOWN. YOU CAN'T FIGHT WITH A BROKEN GLOVE! YOU'LL *DIE!*
YOU HAVE TO *FORFEIT!*
YOU KNOW I CAN'T DO THAT. EARTH WILL BE LOST!
I JUST CHECKED THESE GLOVES MYSELF! THEY WERE GOOD AS NEW. YOU SAW THEM! SOMEONE HAS TO BE *BLOCKING* THE GRAVITY FIELD. IF WE CAN FIND THE *SOURCE* OF THAT SIGNAL AND *BLOCK* IT--THEY'LL RELINK, AND I'LL BE GOOD AS NEW!
HOW DO YOU PROPOSE WE FIND THIS SOURCE?! YOU'RE IN THE MIDDLE OF THE FIGHT!
ALREADY ON IT!
ROUND TWO
BETHANY! THEODORE! LISTEN UP!
MISTER PRESIDENT? YOU CAN... SPEAK TELEPATHICALLY?
YEP! *MK-ULTRA CLASS OF '92, BABY!*
I'M SURE YOU NOTICED THIS FIGHT ISN'T GOING SO WELL--LISTEN UP. I NEED YOUR HELP!
WHAT'S GOING ON WITH YOU TWO?
OBAMA IS SPEAKING TO US TELEPATHICALLY.
OH. COOL.

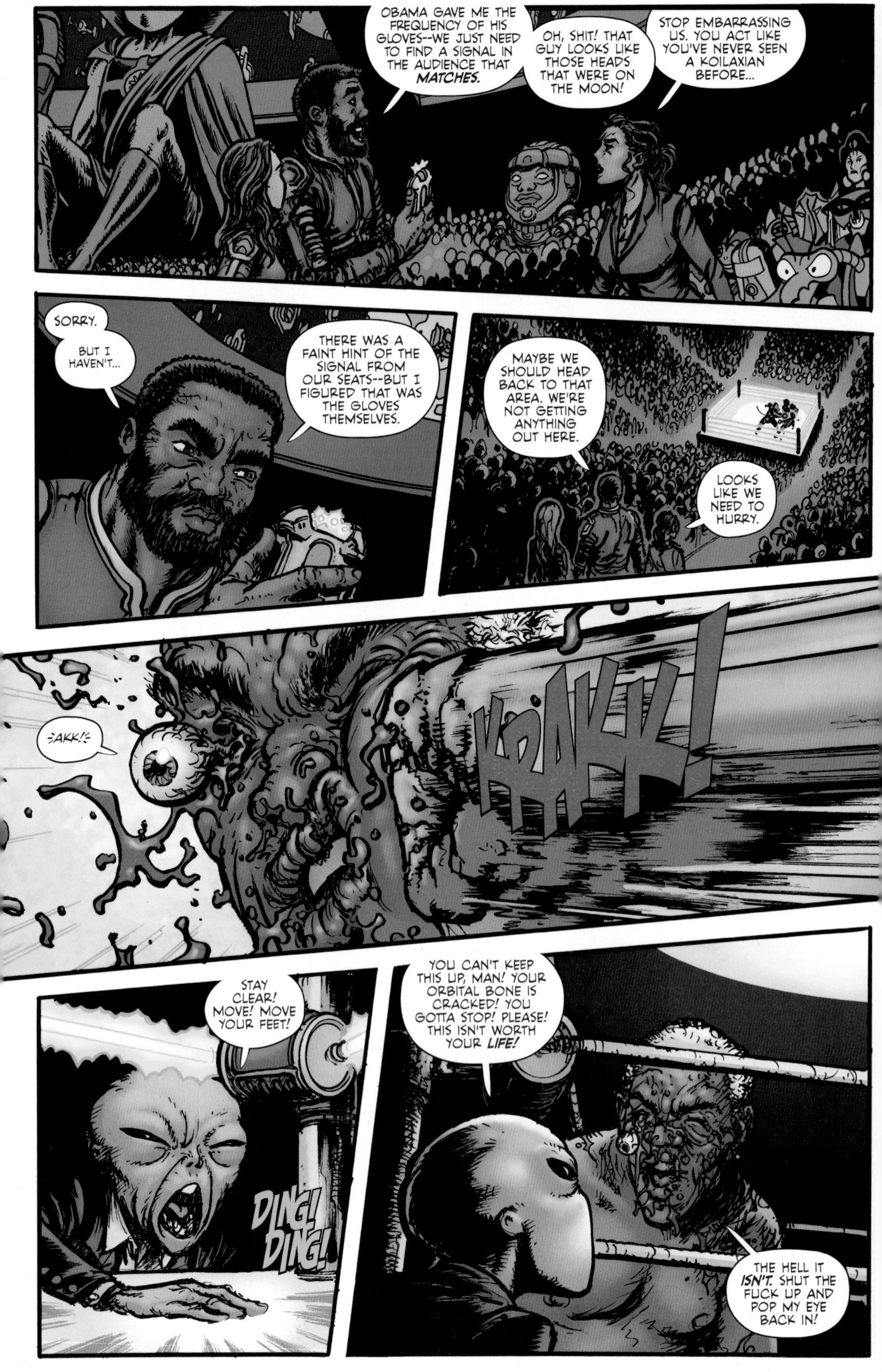
OBAMA GAVE ME THE FREQUENCY OF HIS GLOVES--WE JUST NEED TO FIND A SIGNAL IN THE AUDIENCE THAT *MATCHES.*
OH, SHIT! THAT GUY LOOKS LIKE THOSE HEADS THAT WERE ON THE MOON!
STOP EMBARRASSING US. YOU ACT LIKE YOU'VE NEVER SEEN A KOILAXIAN BEFORE...
SORRY.
BUT I HAVEN'T...
THERE WAS A FAINT HINT OF THE SIGNAL FROM OUR SEATS--BUT I FIGURED THAT WAS THE GLOVES THEMSELVES.
MAYBE WE SHOULD HEAD BACK TO THAT AREA. WE'RE NOT GETTING ANYTHING OUT HERE.
LOOKS LIKE WE NEED TO HURRY.
KRAKK!
AKK!
STAY CLEAR! MOVE! MOVE YOUR FEET!
DING! DING!
YOU CAN'T KEEP THIS UP, MAN! YOUR ORBITAL BONE IS CRACKED! YOU GOTTA STOP! PLEASE! THIS ISN'T WORTH YOUR *LIFE!*
THE HELL IT *ISN'T.* SHUT THE FUCK UP AND POP MY EYE BACK IN!

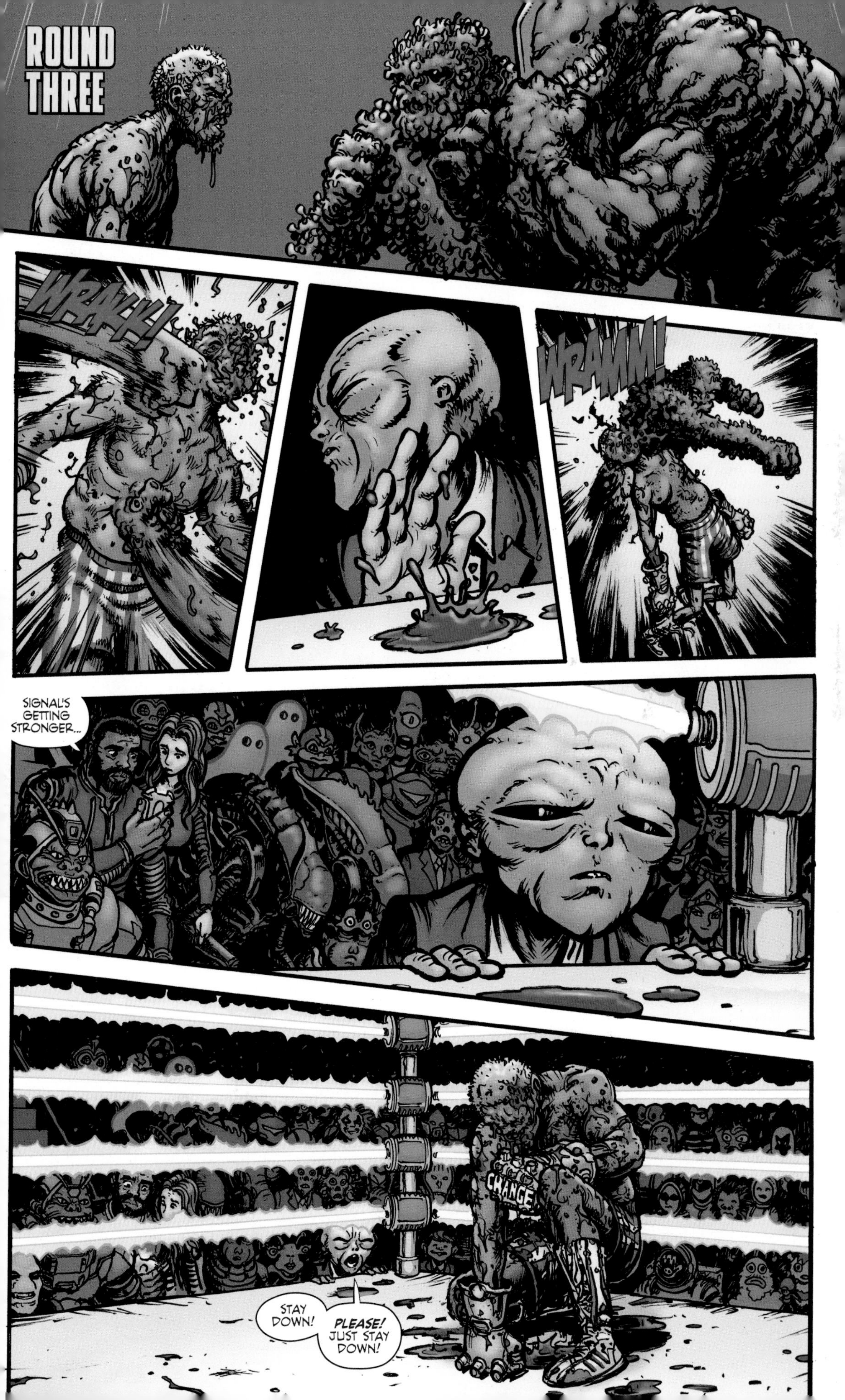
ROUND THREE
WRAKK!
WRAMM!
SIGNAL'S GETTING STRONGER...
CHANGE
STAY DOWN!
PLEASE! JUST STAY DOWN!

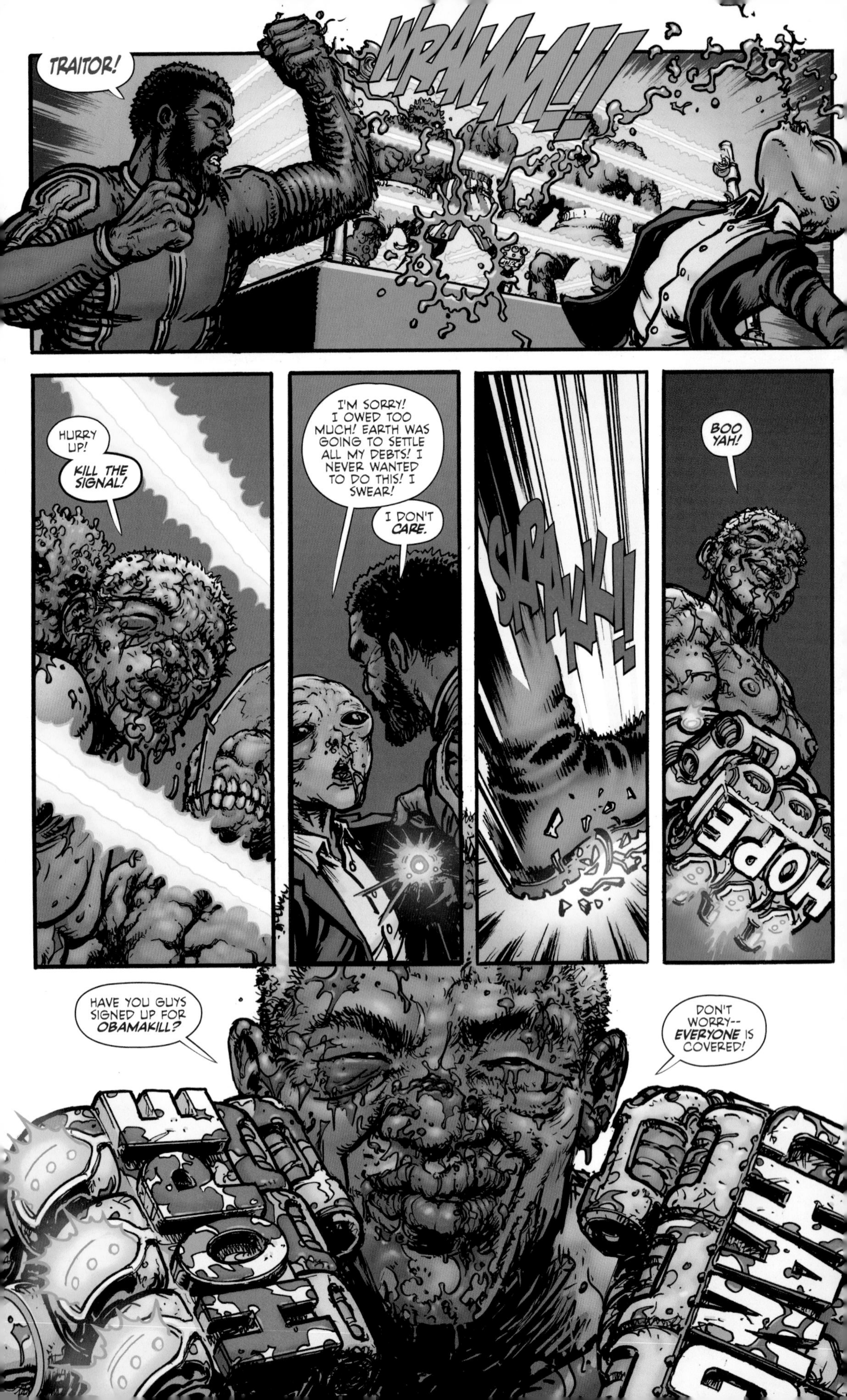
TRAITOR!
WRAAAAM!!
HURRY UP!
KILL THE SIGNAL!
I'M SORRY! I OWED TOO MUCH! EARTH WAS GOING TO SETTLE ALL MY DEBTS! I NEVER WANTED TO DO THIS! I SWEAR!
I DON'T CARE.
SKRAKK!!
BOO YAH!
HOPE
HAVE YOU GUYS SIGNED UP FOR OBAMAKILL?
DON'T WORRY-- EVERYONE IS COVERED!

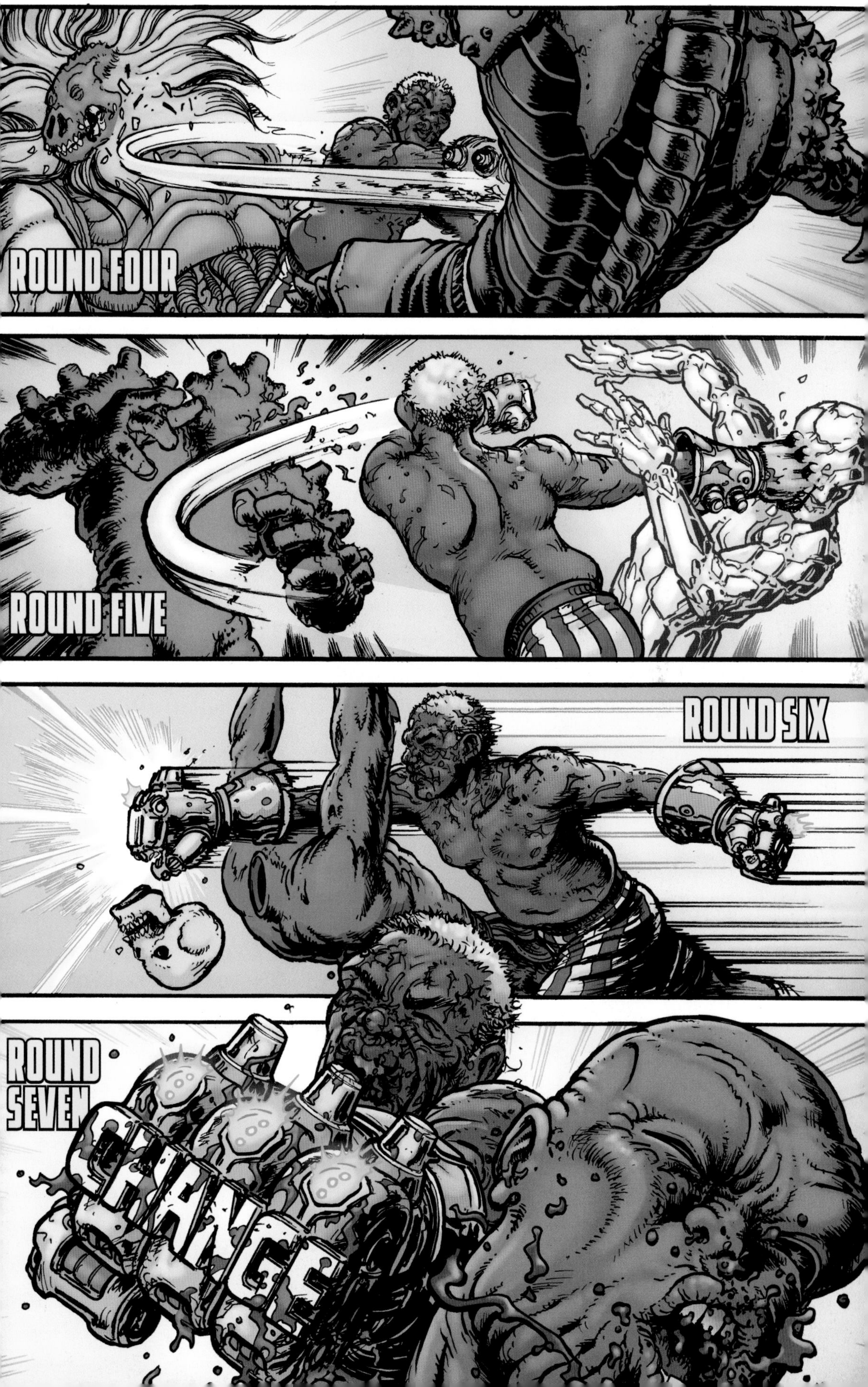
ROUND FOUR
ROUND FIVE
ROUND SIX
ROUND SEVEN
CHANGE

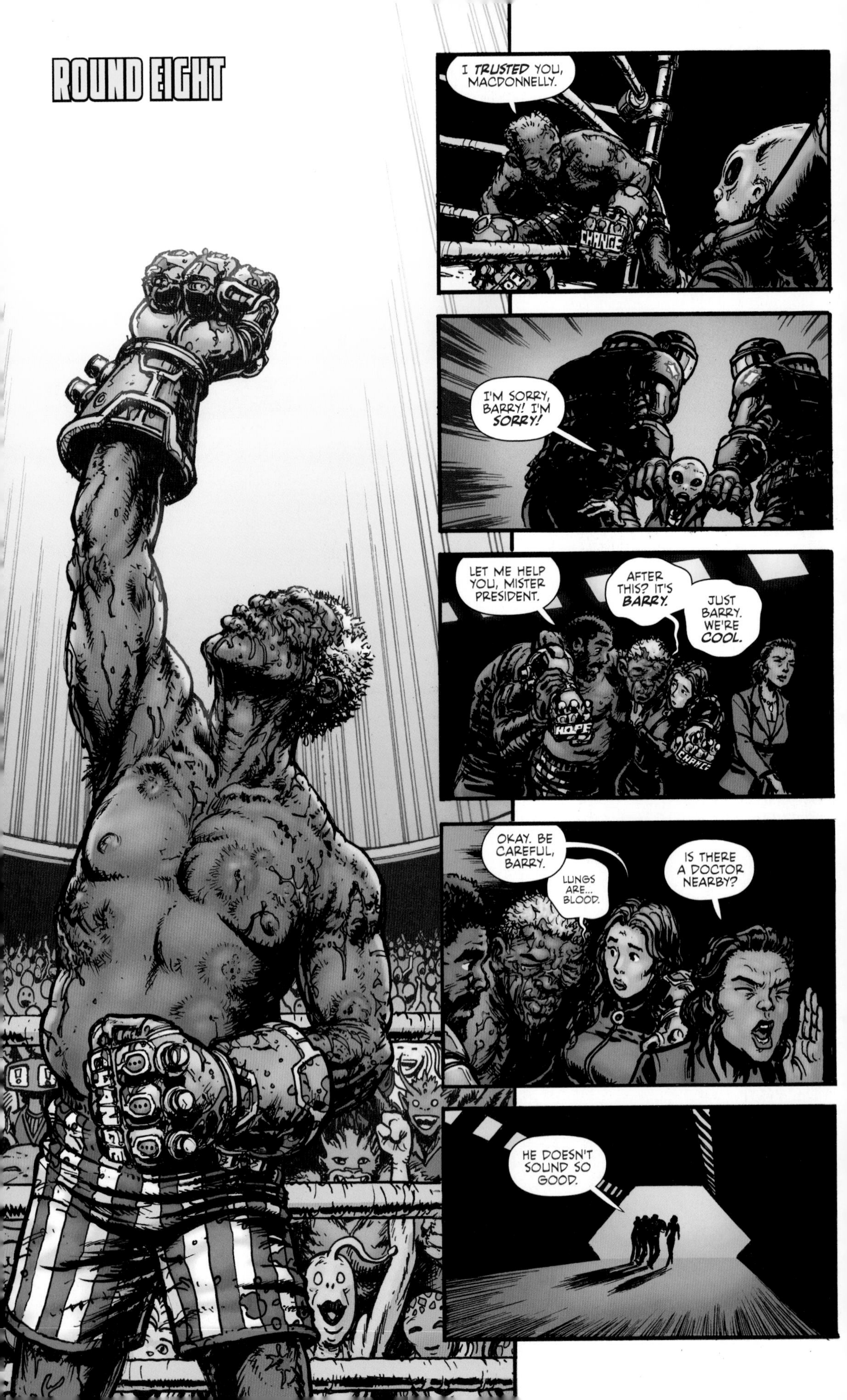
ROUND EIGHT
I TRUSTED YOU, MACDONNELLY.
CHANGE
I'M SORRY, BARRY! I'M SORRY!
LET ME HELP YOU, MISTER PRESIDENT.
AFTER THIS? IT'S BARRY.
JUST BARRY. WE'RE COOL.
HOPE
CHANGE
OKAY. BE CAREFUL, BARRY.
LUNGS ARE... BLOOD.
IS THERE A DOCTOR NEARBY?
HE DOESN'T SOUND SO GOOD.

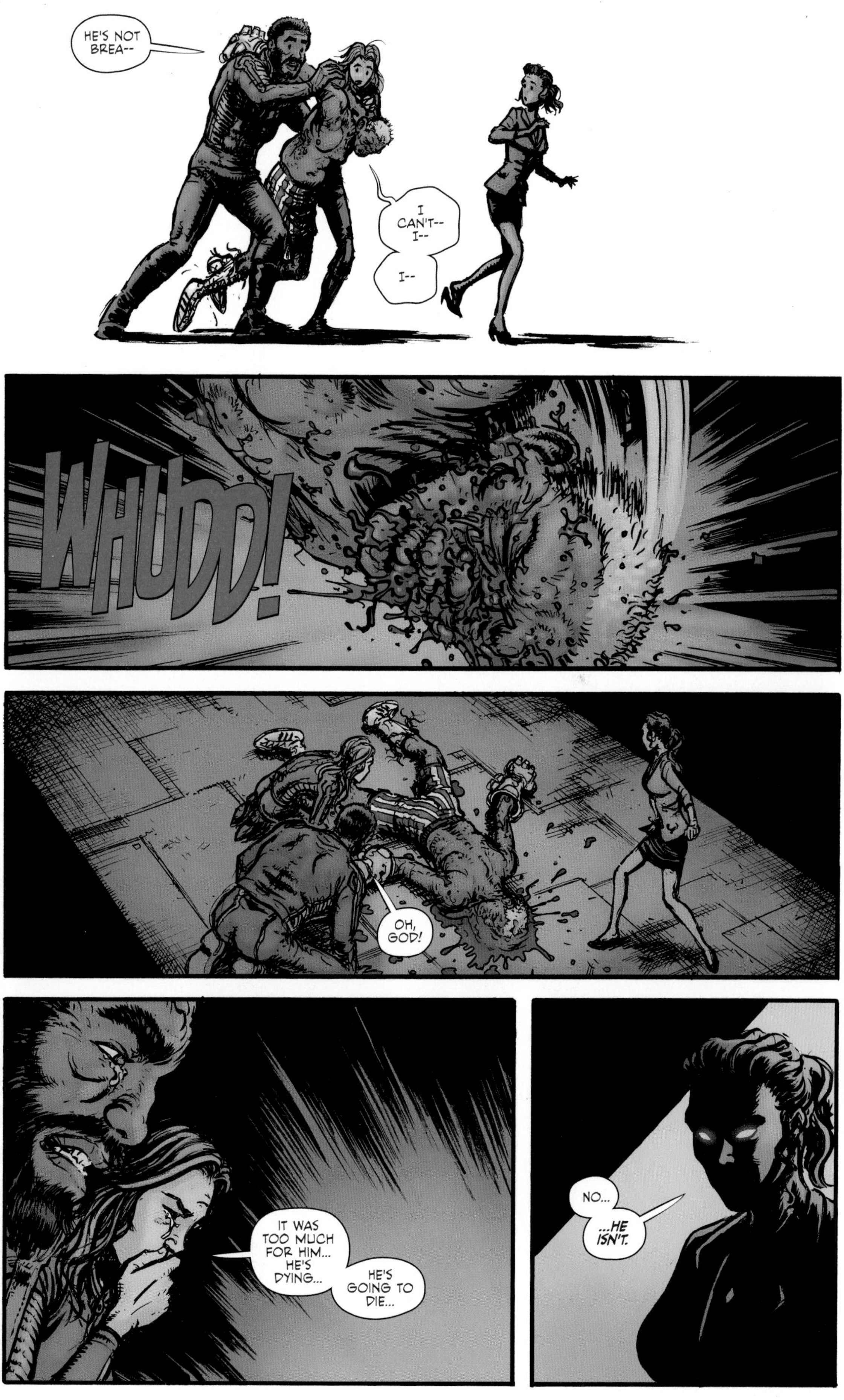
HE'S NOT BREA--
I CAN'T-- I--
I--
WHUDD!
OH, GOD!
IT WAS TOO MUCH FOR HIM... HE'S DYING...
HE'S GOING TO DIE...
NO...
...HE ISN'T.

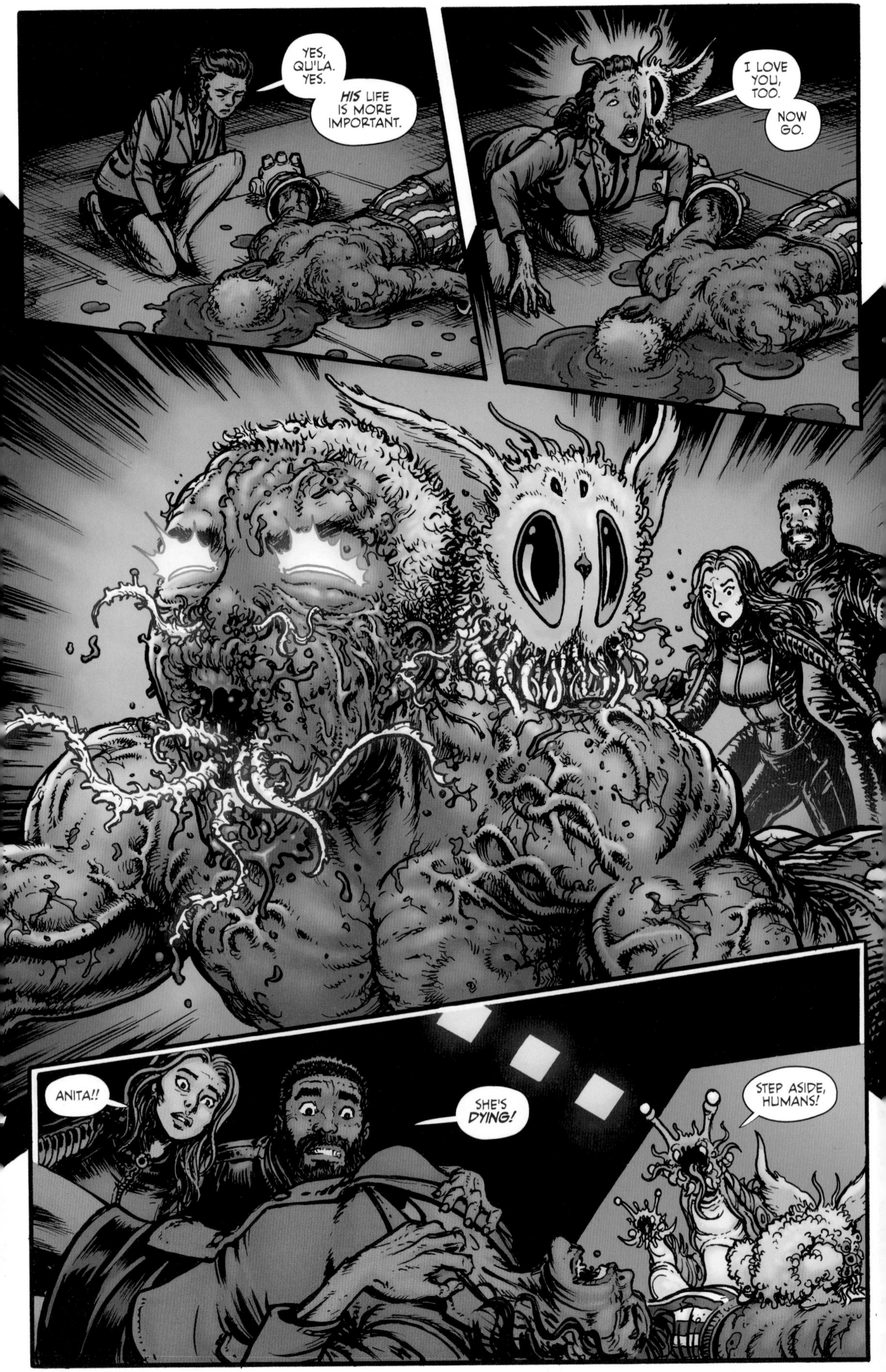
YES, QU'LA. YES.
HIS LIFE IS MORE IMPORTANT.
I LOVE YOU, TOO.
NOW GO.
ANITA!!
SHE'S *DYING!*
STEP ASIDE, HUMANS!

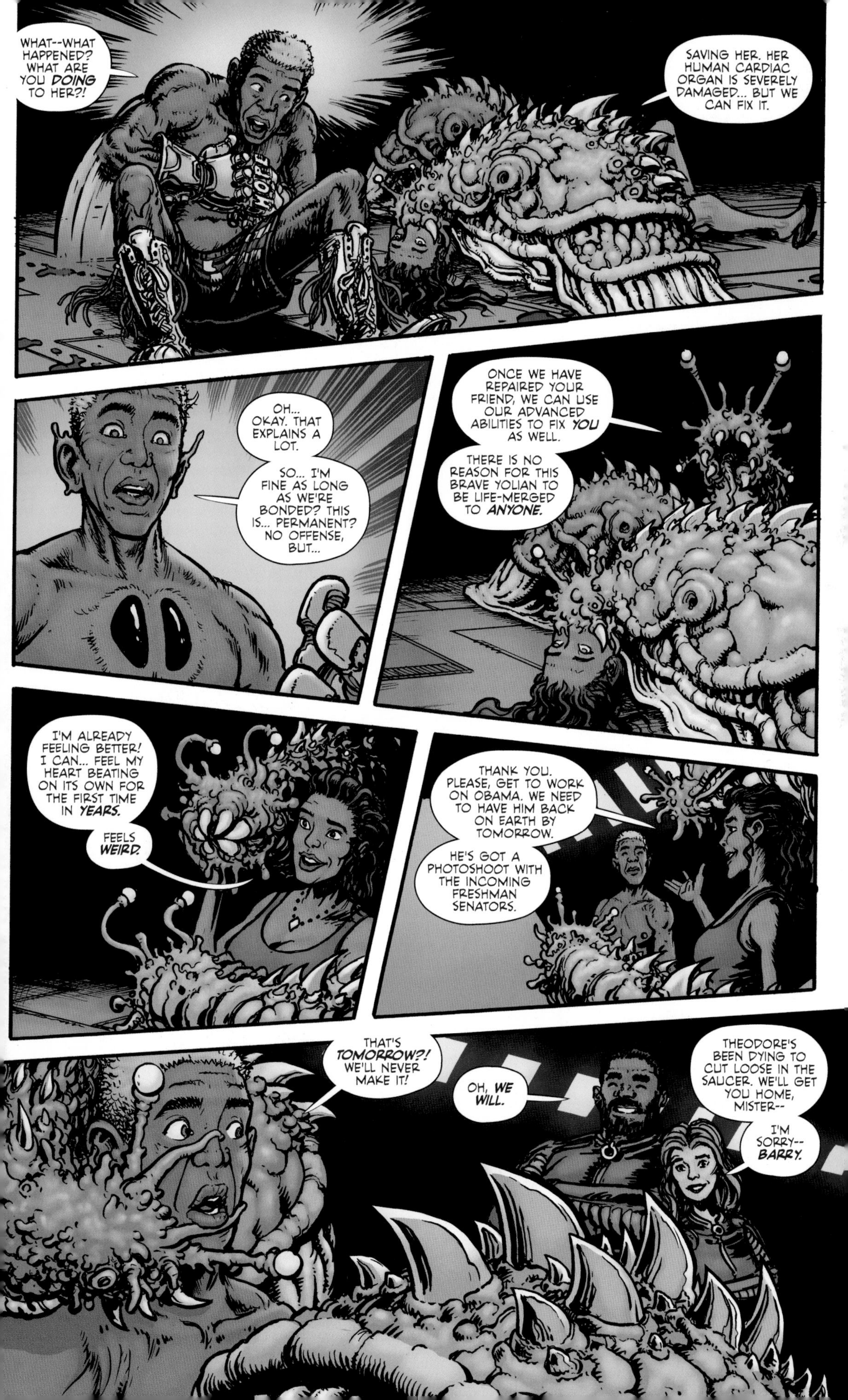
WHAT--WHAT HAPPENED? WHAT ARE YOU DOING TO HER?!
SAVING HER. HER HUMAN CARDIAC ORGAN IS SEVERELY DAMAGED... BUT WE CAN FIX IT.
OH... OKAY. THAT EXPLAINS A LOT.
SO... I'M FINE AS LONG AS WE'RE BONDED? THIS IS... PERMANENT? NO OFFENSE, BUT...
ONCE WE HAVE REPAIRED YOUR FRIEND, WE CAN USE OUR ADVANCED ABILITIES TO FIX YOU AS WELL.
THERE IS NO REASON FOR THIS BRAVE YOLIAN TO BE LIFE-MERGED TO ANYONE.
I'M ALREADY FEELING BETTER! I CAN... FEEL MY HEART BEATING ON ITS OWN FOR THE FIRST TIME IN YEARS.
FEELS WEIRD.
THANK YOU. PLEASE, GET TO WORK ON OBAMA. WE NEED TO HAVE HIM BACK ON EARTH BY TOMORROW.
HE'S GOT A PHOTOSHOOT WITH THE INCOMING FRESHMAN SENATORS.
THAT'S TOMORROW?! WE'LL NEVER MAKE IT!
OH, WE WILL.
THEODORE'S BEEN DYING TO CUT LOOSE IN THE SAUCER. WE'LL GET YOU HOME, MISTER--
I'M SORRY-- BARRY.

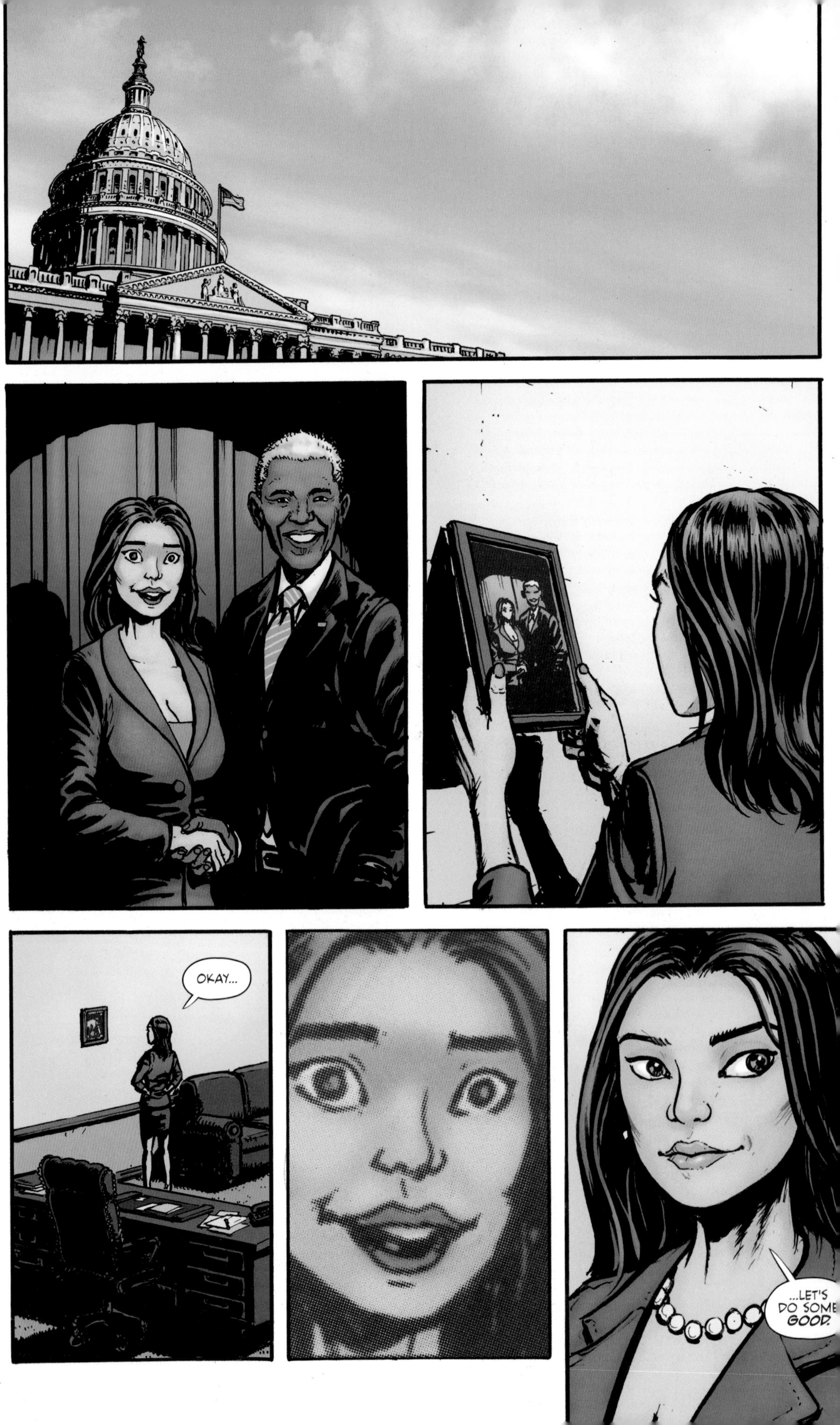
OKAY...
...LET'S DO SOME GOOD.

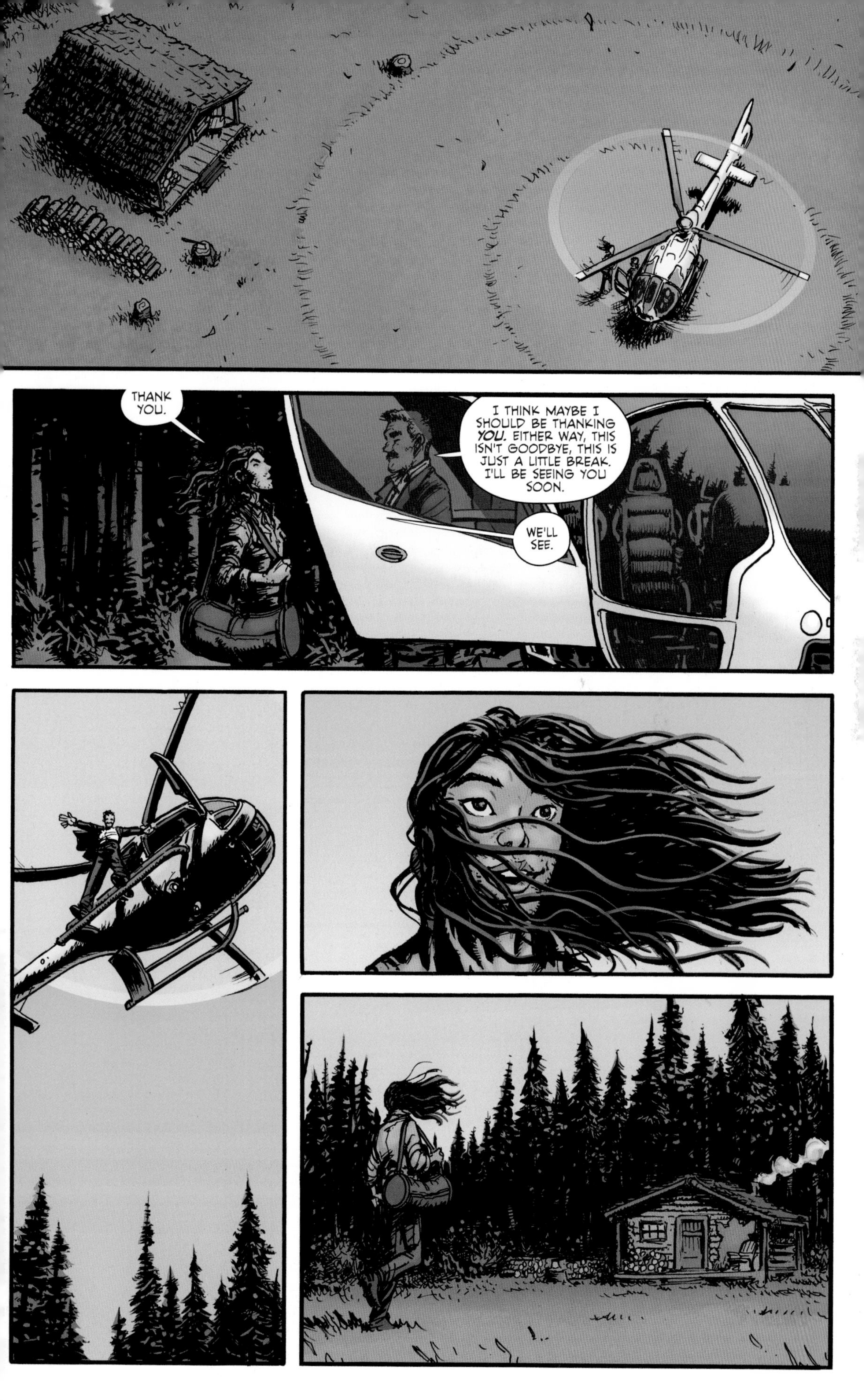
THANK YOU.
I THINK MAYBE I SHOULD BE THANKING *YOU.* EITHER WAY, THIS ISN'T GOODBYE, THIS IS JUST A LITTLE BREAK. I'LL BE SEEING YOU SOON.
WE'LL SEE.

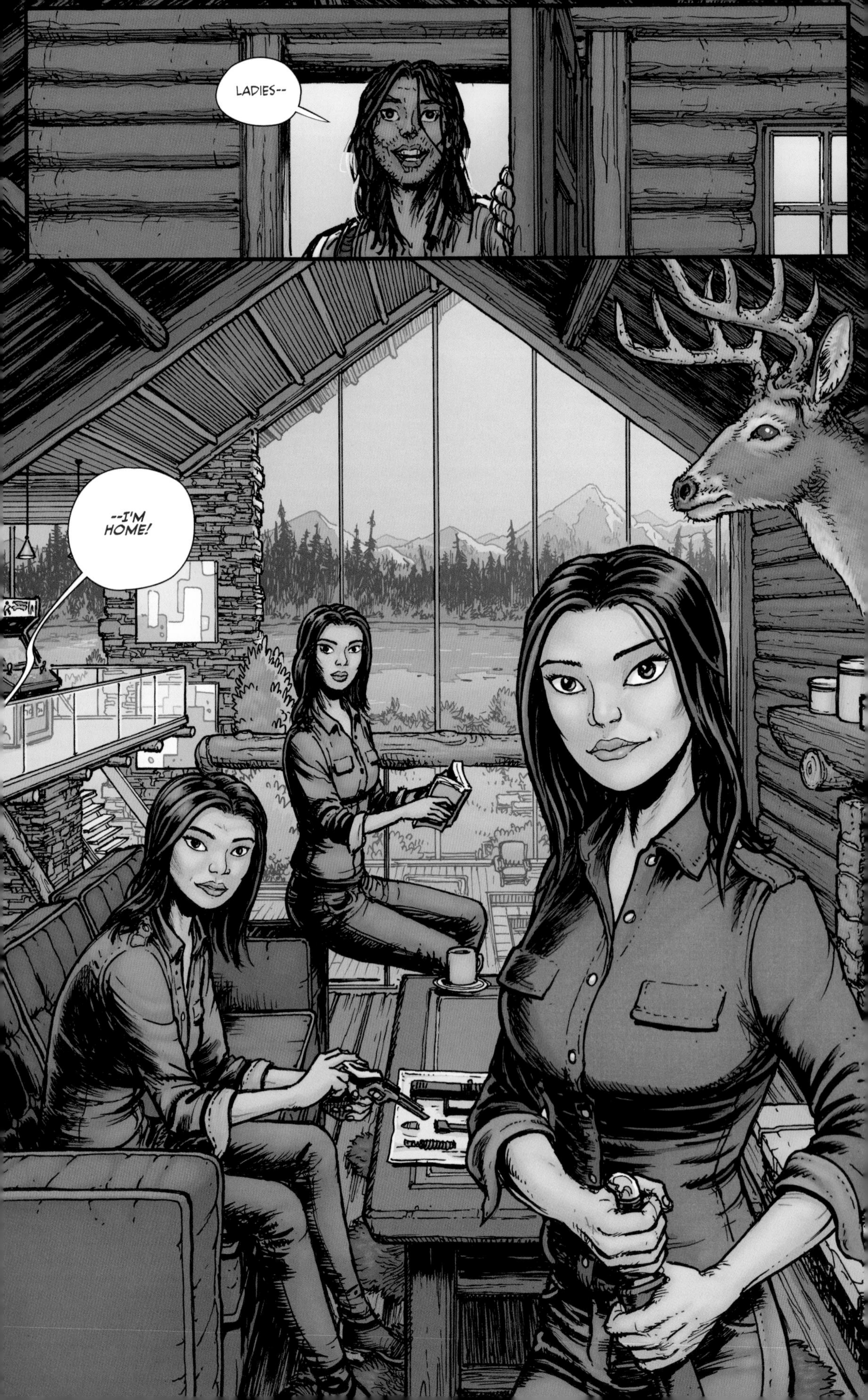
LADIES--
--I'M HOME!

TO BE
CONTINUED

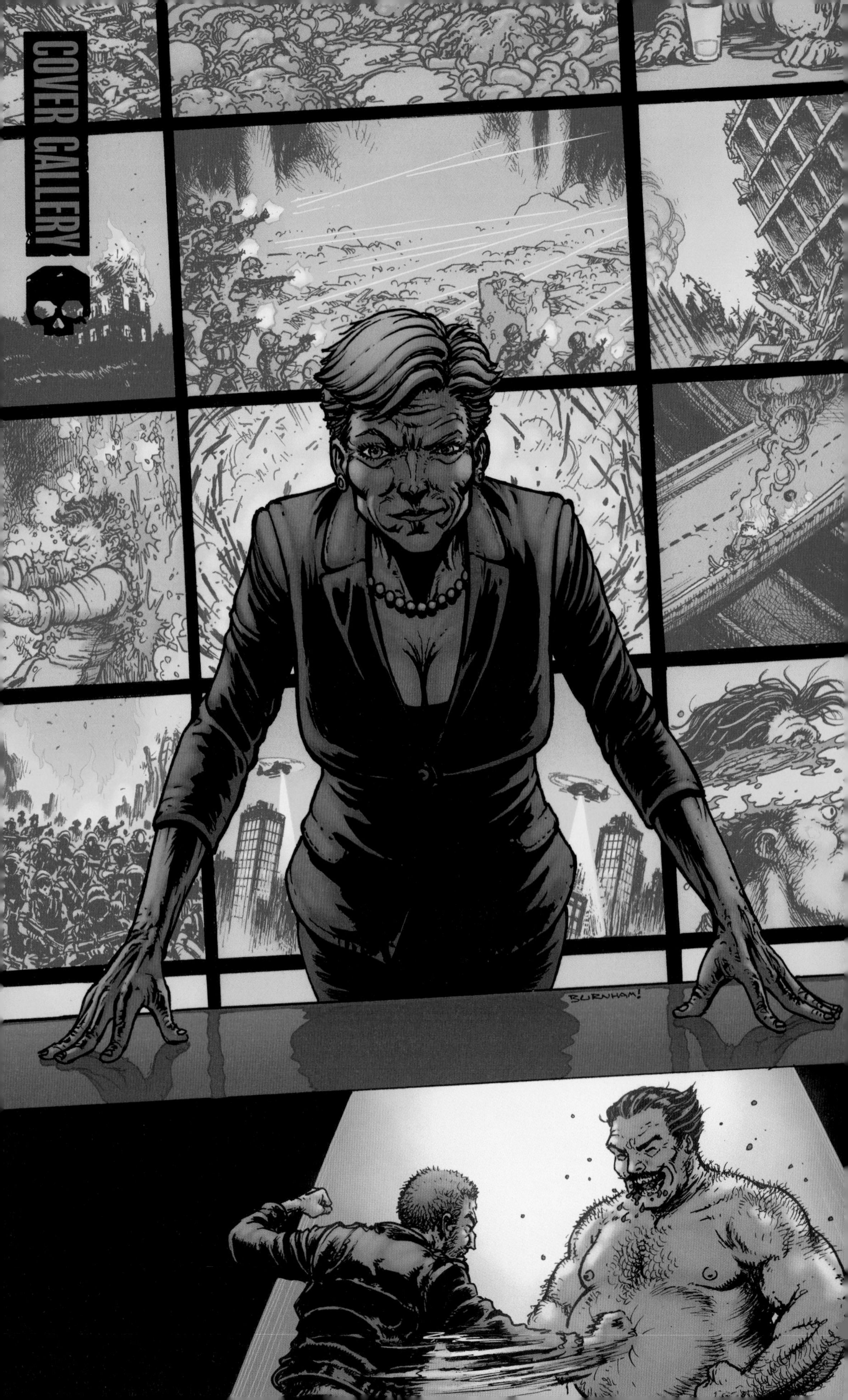
COVER GALLERY
BURNHAM!

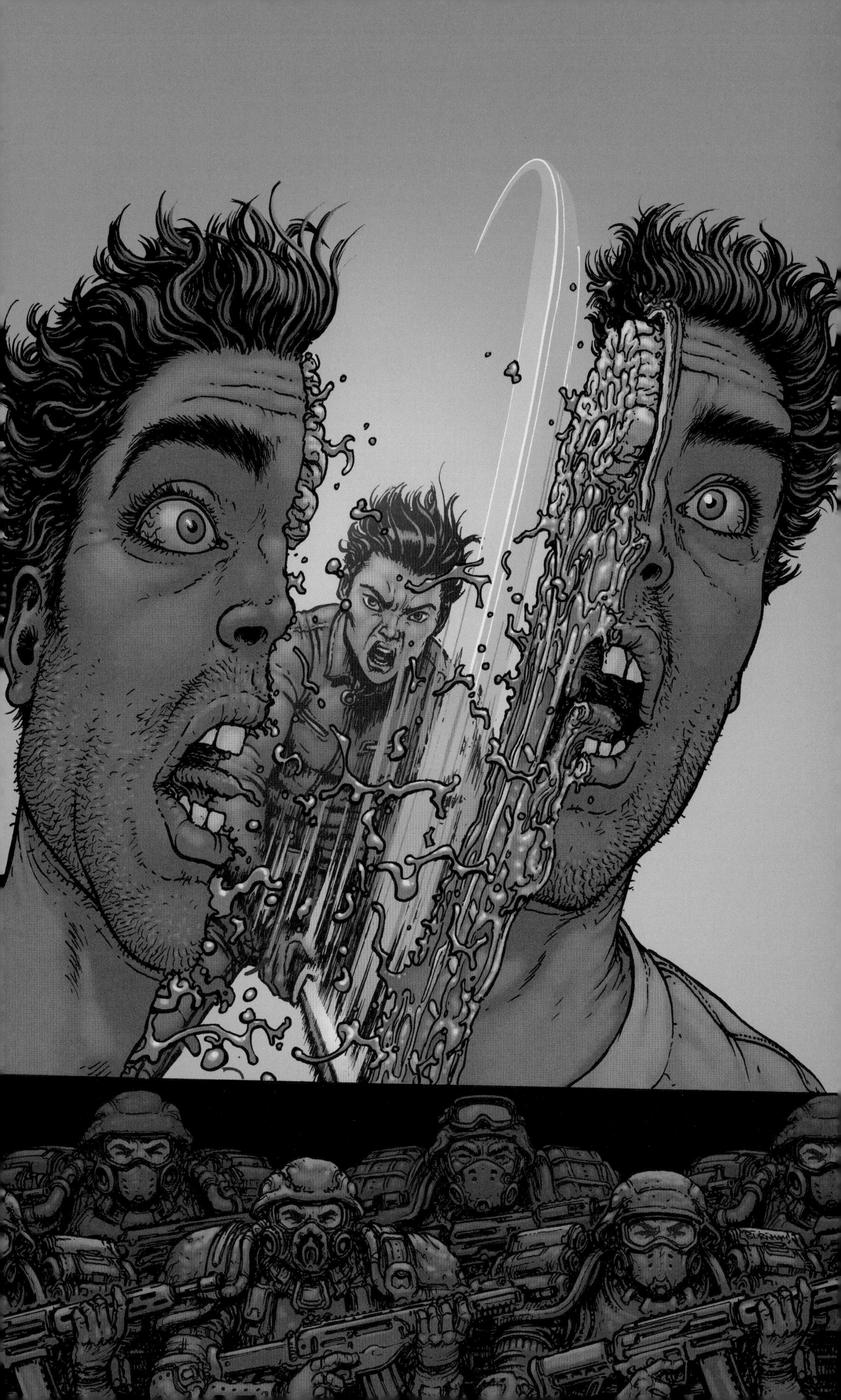

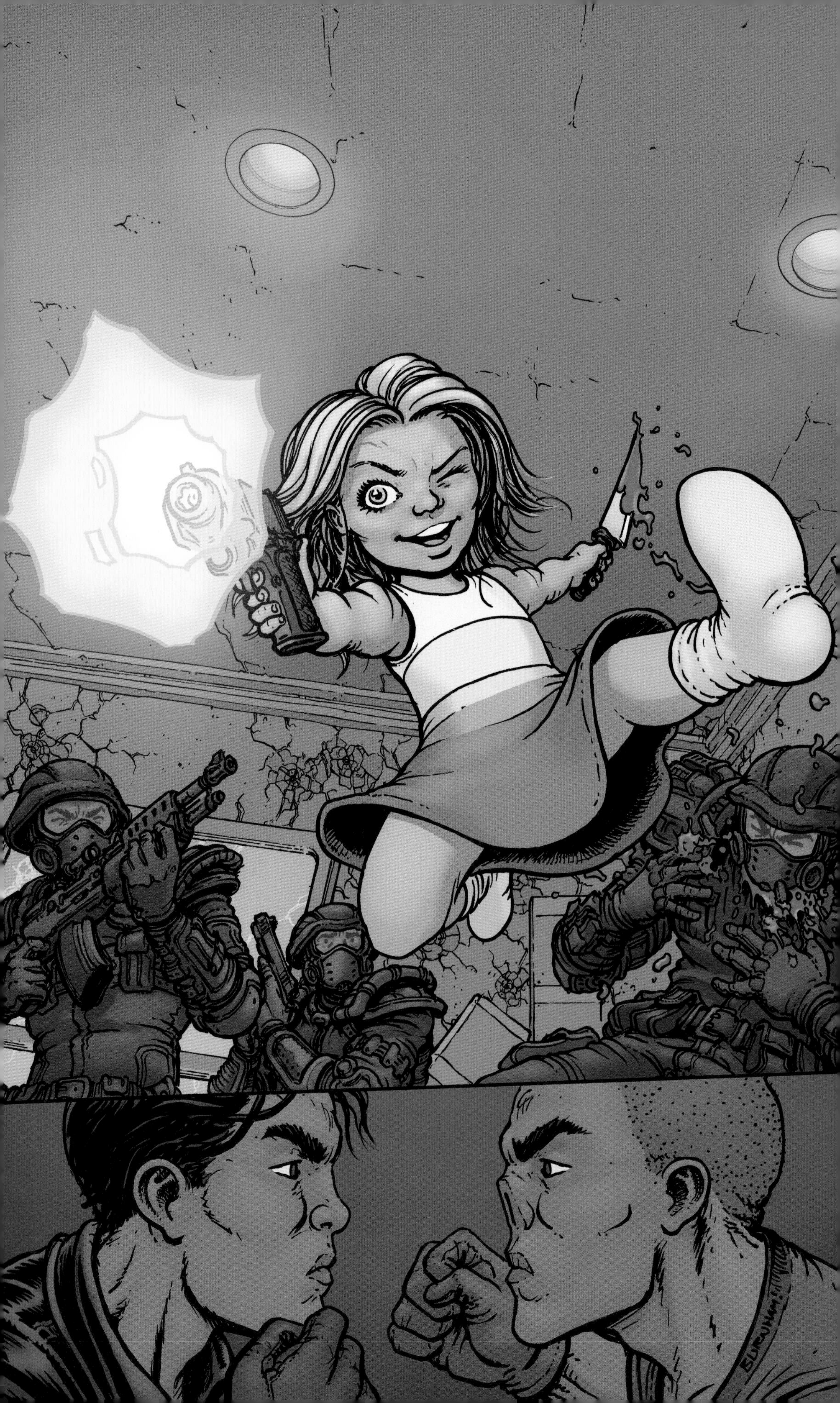

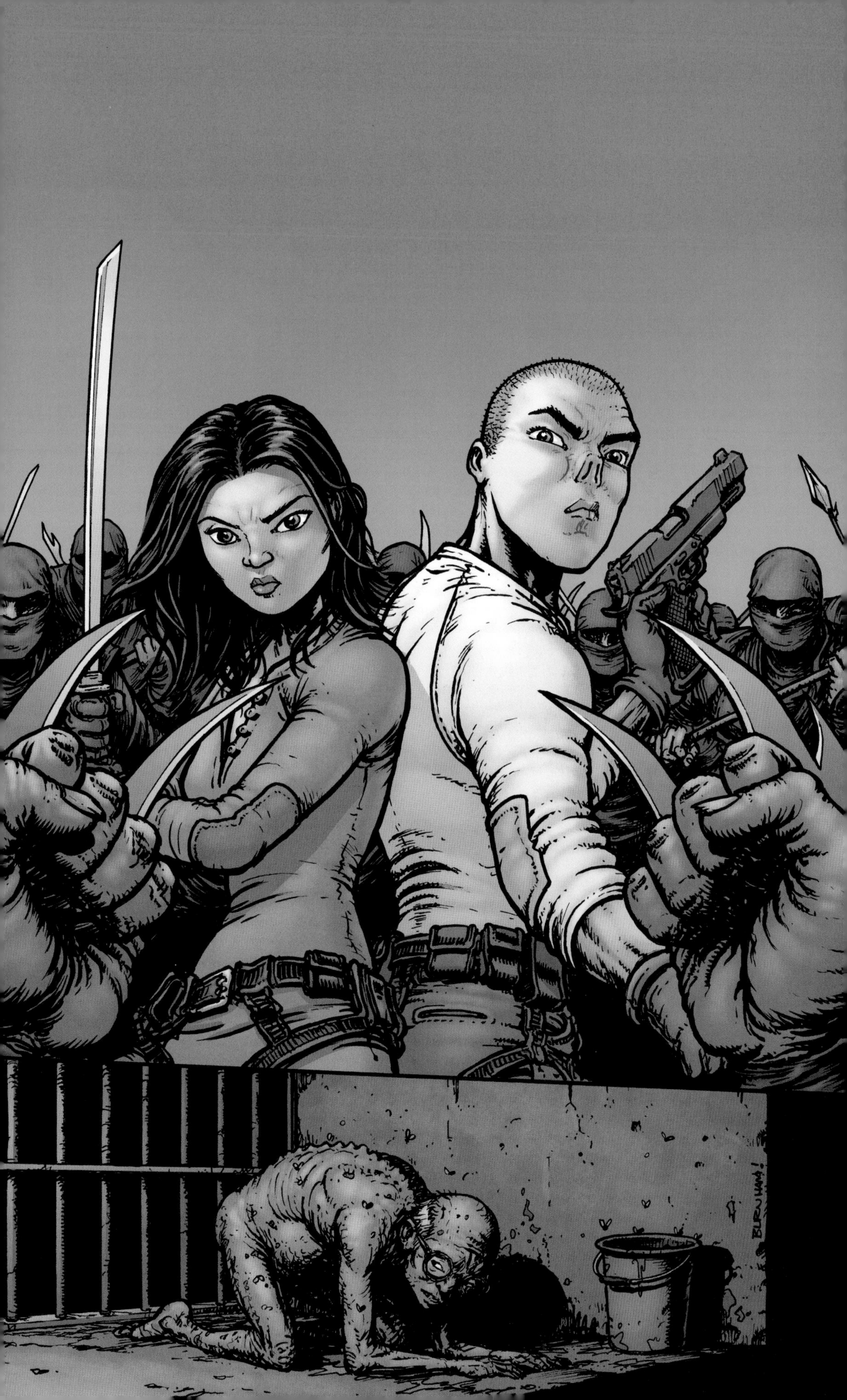

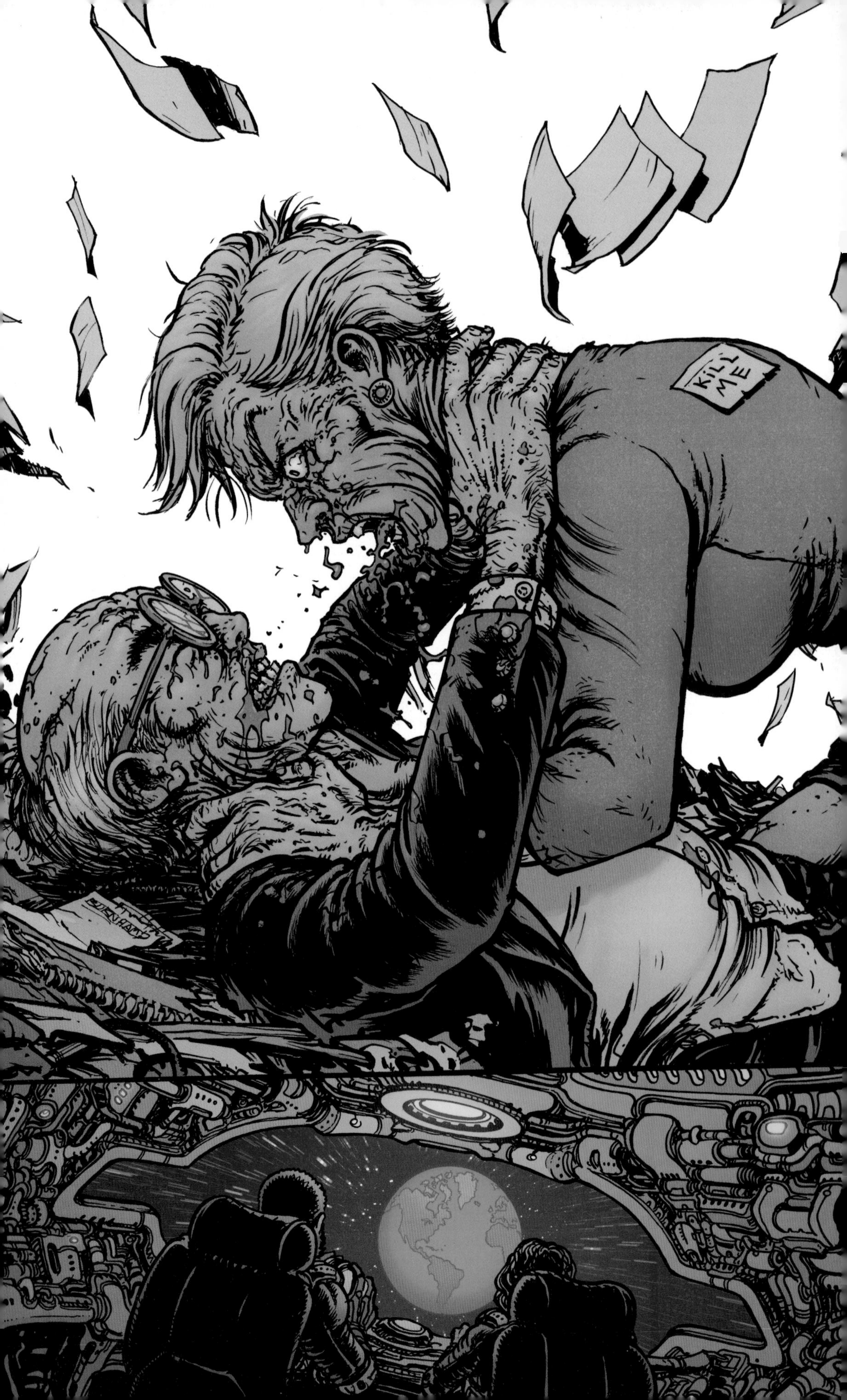
KILL
ME

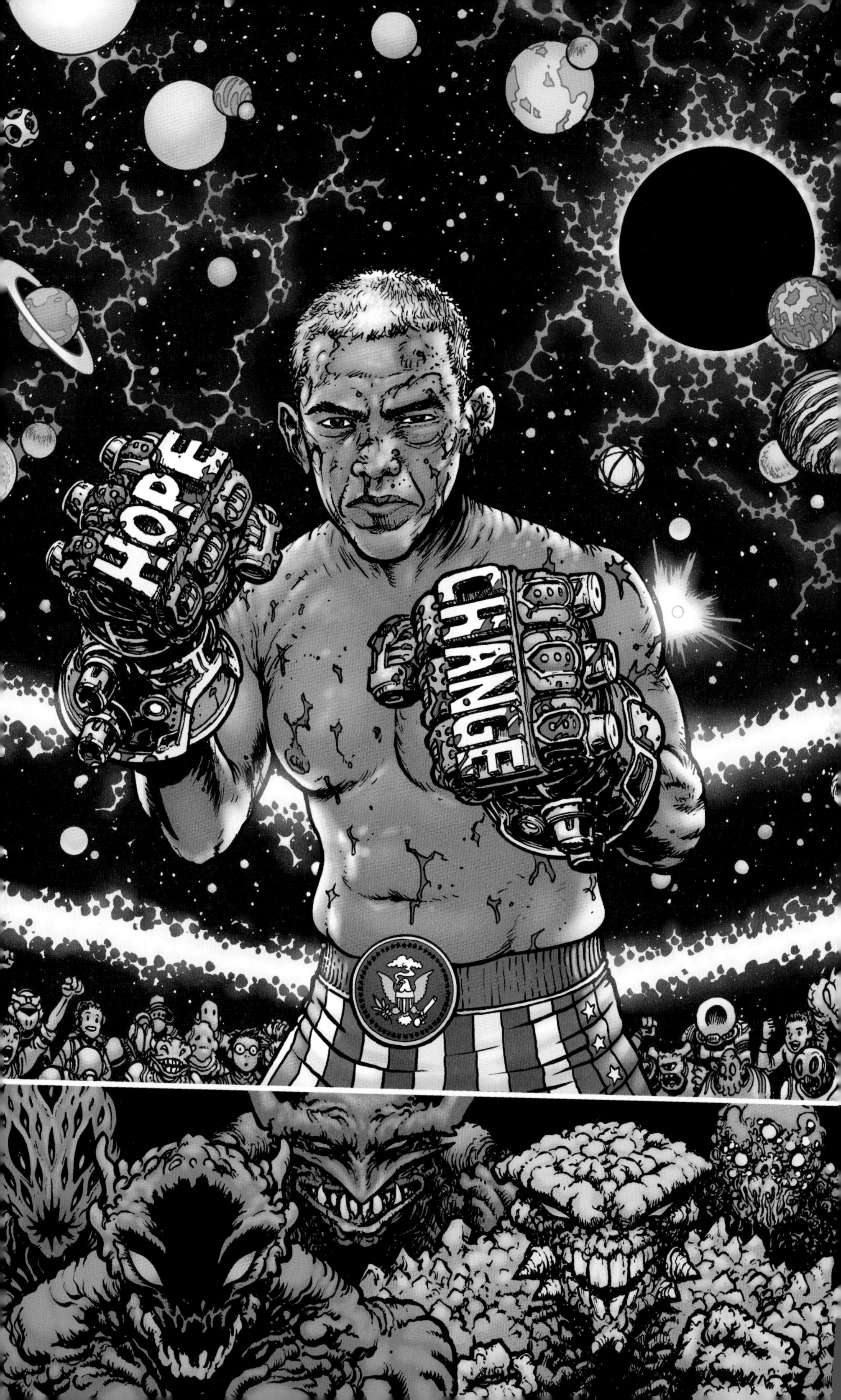
HOPE
CHANGE

FOR MORE TALES FROM ROBERT KIRKMAN AND SKYBOUND

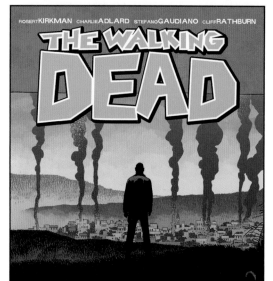

ROBERT KIRKMAN CHARLIE ADLARD STEFANO GAUDIANO CLIFF RATHBURN
THE WALKING DEAD
VOLUME 32
REST IN PEACE

VOL. 1: DAYS GONE BYE TP
ISBN: 978-1-58240-672-5
$14.99

VOL. 2: MILES BEHIND US TP
ISBN: 978-1-58240-775-3
$14.99

VOL. 3: SAFETY BEHIND BARS TP
ISBN: 978-1-58240-805-7
$14.99

VOL. 4: THE HEART'S DESIRE TP
ISBN: 978-1-58240-530-8
$14.99

VOL. 5: THE BEST DEFENSE TP
ISBN: 978-1-58240-612-1
$14.99

VOL. 6: THIS SORROWFUL LIFE TP
ISBN: 978-1-58240-684-8
$14.99

VOL. 7: THE CALM BEFORE TP
ISBN: 978-1-58240-828-6
$14.99

VOL. 8: MADE TO SUFFER TP
ISBN: 978-1-58240-883-5
$14.99

VOL. 9: HERE WE REMAIN TP
ISBN: 978-1-60706-022-2
$14.99

VOL. 10: WHAT WE BECOME TP
ISBN: 978-1-60706-075-8
$14.99

VOL. 11: FEAR THE HUNTERS TP
ISBN: 978-1-60706-181-6
$14.99

VOL. 12: LIFE AMONG THEM TP
ISBN: 978-1-60706-254-7
$14.99

VOL. 13: TOO FAR GONE TP
ISBN: 978-1-60706-329-2
$14.99

VOL. 14: NO WAY OUT TP
ISBN: 978-1-60706-392-6
$14.99

VOL. 15: WE FIND OURSELVES TP
ISBN: 978-1-60706-440-4
$14.99

VOL. 16: A LARGER WORLD TP
ISBN: 978-1-60706-559-3
$14.99

VOL. 17: SOMETHING TO FEAR TP
ISBN: 978-1-60706-615-6
$14.99

VOL. 18: WHAT COMES AFTER TP
ISBN: 978-1-60706-687-3
$14.99

VOL. 19: MARCH TO WAR TP
ISBN: 978-1-60706-818-1
$14.99

VOL. 20: ALL OUT WAR PART ONE TP
ISBN: 978-1-60706-882-2
$14.99

VOL. 21: ALL OUT WAR PART TWO TP
ISBN: 978-1-63215-030-1
$14.99

VOL. 22: A NEW BEGINNING TP
ISBN: 978-1-63215-041-7
$14.99

VOL. 23: WHISPERS INTO SCREAMS TP
ISBN: 978-1-63215-258-9
$14.99

VOL. 24: LIFE AND DEATH TP
ISBN: 978-1-63215-402-6
$14.99

VOL. 25: NO TURNING BACK TP
ISBN: 978-1-63215-659-4
$14.99

VOL. 26: CALL TO ARMS TP
ISBN: 978-1-63215-917-5
$14.99

VOL. 27: THE WHISPERER WAR TP
ISBN: 978-1-5343-0052-1
$14.99

VOL. 28: A CERTAIN DOOM TP
ISBN: 978-1-5343-0244-0
$14.99

VOL. 29: LINES WE CROSS TP
ISBN: 978-1-5343-0497-0
$16.99

VOL. 30: NEW WORLD ORDER TP
ISBN: 978-1-5343-0884-8
$16.99

VOL. 31: THE ROTTEN CORE TP
ISBN: 978-1-5343-1052-0
$16.99

VOL. 32: REST IN PEACE TP
ISBN: 978-1-5343-1241-8
$16.99

BOOK ONE HC
ISBN: 978-1-58240-619-0
$34.99

BOOK TWO HC
ISBN: 978-1-58240-698-5
$34.99

BOOK THREE HC
ISBN: 978-1-58240-825-5
$34.99

BOOK FOUR HC
ISBN: 978-1-60706-000-0
$34.99

BOOK FIVE HC
ISBN: 978-1-60706-171-7
$34.99

BOOK SIX HC
ISBN: 978-1-60706-327-8
$34.99

BOOK SEVEN HC
ISBN: 978-1-60706-439-8
$34.99

BOOK EIGHT HC
ISBN: 978-1-60706-593-7
$34.99

BOOK NINE HC
ISBN: 978-1-60706-798-6
$34.99

BOOK TEN HC
ISBN: 978-1-63215-034-9
$34.99

BOOK ELEVEN HC
ISBN: 978-1-63215-271-8
$34.99

BOOK TWELVE HC
ISBN: 978-1-63215-451-4
$34.99

BOOK THIRTEEN HC
ISBN: 978-1-63215-916-8
$34.99

BOOK FOURTEEN HC
ISBN: 978-1-5343-0329-4
$34.99

BOOK FIFTEEN HC
ISBN: 978-1-5343-0850-3
$34.99

BOOK SIXTEEN HC
ISBN: 978-1-5343-1325-5
$34.99

BIRTHRIGHT
WILLIAMSON BRESSAN LUCAS
VOLUME NINE
WAR OF THE WORLDS

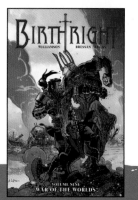

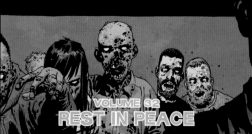

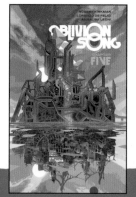

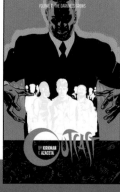

VOL. 1: HOMECOMING
ISBN: 978-1-63215-231-2 $9.99

VOL. 2: CALL TO ADVENTURE
ISBN: 978-1-63215-446-0 $12.99

VOL. 3: ALLIES AND ENEMIES
ISBN: 978-1-63215-683-9 $12.99

VOL. 4: FAMILY HISTORY
ISBN: 978-1-63215-871-0 $12.99

VOL. 5: BELLY OF THE BEAST
ISBN: 978-1-5343-0218-1 $12.99

VOL. 6: FATHERHOOD
ISBN: 978-1-53430-498-7 $14.99

VOL. 7: BLOOD BROTHERS
ISBN: 978-1-5343-1053-7 $14.99

VOL. 8: LIVE BY THE SWORD
ISBN: 978-1-5343-1368-2 $14.99

VOL. 9: WAR OF THE WORLDS
ISBN: 978-1-5343-1601-0 $14.99

ROBERT KIRKMAN
CHRIS SAMNEE
FIRE POWER
VOLUME 2 HOME FIRE

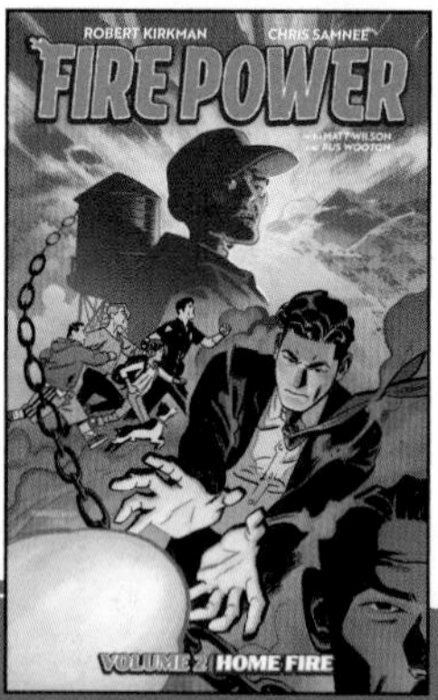

VOL. 1: PRELUDE
ISBN: 978-1-5343-1655-3
$9.99

VOL. 2: HOME FIRE
ISBN: 978-1-5343-1718-5
$16.99

ROBERT KIRKMAN
LORENZO DE FELICI
ANNALISA LEONI
OBLIVION SONG
CHAPTER FIVE

CHAPTER ONE
ISBN: 978-1-5343-0642-4
$9.99

CHAPTER TWO
ISBN: 978-1-5343-1057-5
$16.99

CHAPTER THREE
ISBN: 978-1-5343-1326-2
$16.99

CHAPTER FOUR
ISBN: 978-1-5343-1517-4
$16.99

CHAPTER FIVE
ISBN: 978-1-5343-1728-4
$16.99

VOLUME 7: THE DARKNESS GROWS
BY KIRKMAN & AZACETA
OUTCAST

VOL. 1: A DARKNESS SURROUNDS HIM
ISBN: 978-1-63215-053-0
$9.99

VOL. 2: A VAST AND UNENDING RUIN
ISBN: 978-1-63215-448-4
$14.99

VOL. 3: THIS LITTLE LIGHT
ISBN: 978-1-63215-693-8
$14.99

VOL. 4: UNDER DEVIL'S WING
ISBN: 978-1-5343-0050-7
$14.99

VOL. 5: THE NEW PATH
ISBN: 978-1-5343-0249-5
$16.99

VOL. 6: INVASION
ISBN: 978-1-5343-0751-3
$16.99

VOL. 7: THE DARKNESS GROWS
ISBN: 978-1-5343-1239-5
$16.99

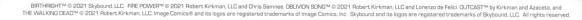